CW00447930

THE EX

A DS JENNA MORGAN INVESTIGATION

DIANE SAXON

I hope this gives you the shivers ...

Saxon

B
Boldwood

First published in Great Britain in 2021 by Boldwood Books Ltd.

Copyright © Diane Saxon, 2021

Cover Design by Head Design

Cover Photography: Shutterstock

A CIP catalogue record for this book is available from the British Library.

Paperback ISBN 978-1-80048-856-4

Large Print ISBN 978-1-83889-272-2

Hardback ISBN 978-1-80162-317-9

Ebook ISBN 978-1-83889-273-9

Kindle ISBN 978-1-83889-274-6

Audio CD ISBN 978-1-80048-854-0

MP3 CD ISBN 978-1-83889-270-8

Digital audio download ISBN 978-1-80048-855-7

Boldwood Books Ltd
23 Bowerdean Street
London SW6 3TN
www.boldwoodbooks.com

To my mum, Margaret Ann Saxon, without whom the art of exaggeration may well never have been gifted to me.

1

Emily Shenton punched open the door to the deserted ladies' room with the heel of her hand and stormed inside before it rebounded off the wall and slammed shut behind her.

The emptiness inside still failed to block out the rhythmic thud of music and only dimmed the laughter and conversation of over eighty people at the company's summer ball.

She hated them. Every single one of them. The gossipmongers who couldn't wait to spread their vileness under the guise of good wishes and happy vibes. When they knew. They all knew.

Temper spilled from her. A foetid pus spreading from the core of her in a boiling, seething mass.

She tipped her head back and drank straight from the full bottle of rosé she'd swiped from a deserted table on her way past. No one would notice, no one would care. She'd no idea why the company insisted on paying for so much wine – red, white and rosé – when most of the men wanted beer, for God's sake. The women preferred red or Prosecco and the rosé was left for the waiters to sweep away at the end of the night. Lucky bloody waiters.

She stepped into the oversized disabled cubicle and balled up the skirt of her black gown with one hand as she slapped her back against the chill of the wall and slid down until her backside met the floor. Sweat slicked the back of her knees as she pressed them flat to the floor tiles to absorb every bit of coolness. Heat pulsed through her chest and up her neck as she tore into the fine organza material of the overskirt, ripping weak nails until they were jagged. Tears burnt the back of her eyes as she ground her teeth and took another slug of wine.

She wished she'd never come. Wished she'd never overheard it. That's why she avoided these functions like the plague. She hated the gossip, preferred to keep to herself and block out the voices. But she'd felt good. Strong.

So strong, she'd decided not to take her medication.

Again.

Tears filled her eyes and washed over her vision.

It wasn't lack of medication that had her temper surging. It was the damned infernal gossip.

Bastards!

Why couldn't they keep their mouths shut?

They had to know she'd been stood on the edge of the circle when Chris Whittington raised his glass and hee-hawed like the ass he was as he brayed his drunken words. 'Here's to Zak Cheetham-Epstein and his new wife, Imelda.'

Nausea clawed the back of her throat.

How was it so many of them knew Zak, had evidently kept in contact?

Zak. The love of her life. The only man she'd truly loved.

There'd been others before him, of course there had, but they'd faded into insignificance in the heat of her adoration for Zak.

The bottle clinked as she placed it on the tiled floor at her side. She covered her face with her hands, a helpless moan slipped from her lips as the familiar hissing sound swirled around her head. 'For God's sake!' She tried to push it back, but it was insistent. The sound of a seashell shushing, filling her mind so she could no longer concentrate. She rolled her head from side to side, her hot, florid face couched in the palms of her sweaty hands.

She'd never forgive him for leaving. Leaving the company.

Leaving her.

But she knew. Knew he still loved her. He had to.

Memories nudged in with cruel disregard and she raised her head to stare through the open door of the cubicle at the row of white porcelain sinks in front of the glare of oversized mirrors.

She'd caught him flirting with the girl in accounts. The skinny emaciated little bitch with too much make-up and those tattooed eyebrows. The girl hadn't stayed at the firm long, not after it emerged she had a night job as a topless waitress servicing private parties.

It wasn't difficult to gather information on anyone. Facebook was the go-to stalking site. It was even easier to get that information into the public domain where assumptions were jumped to, judgements made.

Zak had taken umbrage. Said she was unreasonable. She'd lost her mind. Insisted she move out when she'd only just moved in.

He hadn't meant it, of course. His mother had influenced him. Emily knew the woman didn't like her. The feeling was mutual.

There was no denying Zak and Emily loved each other. He was her soulmate. Her destiny. Convinced of it, she'd told him enough times.

Begged.

Pleaded.

Even after he announced he'd found a new job and put his notice in, she'd continued to try and persuade him, right up until he left the company, claiming every holiday owed to him instead of taking them in lieu. Almost two years ago. She wanted to give him space back then, but he'd consumed her mind.

She'd checked the HR records under the pension scheme for his new address when he moved out of the flat they'd shared together. Started to set up home together. The one he'd already made her leave. Their little love nest he'd broken apart, with the help of his mother.

Emily had driven past the three-storey Victorian house he'd purchased since he'd left the company. Not something she'd have chosen for their lives together, but confident he'd change his mind, she waited. There would be time enough to persuade him to sell the place. Once they were together again. She just needed to give him some space. Space he needed to realise how much he missed her. How much he loved her.

She gave him the space. Resisted contacting him, but she couldn't let go altogether.

She couldn't help driving past his house again, and again. In the hope she'd catch a glimpse of him. So many times, until she made herself sick.

Wanda had made her better. Wanda Stilgoe. Her counsellor. Assigned to her when she had her meltdown a few months after Zak had gone, when the obsession had taken hold and wouldn't let go. Wanda, the only person who never treated her with disapproval or judgement. But Wanda had been gone for three weeks now and wouldn't be coming back.

Nor had Emily been assigned another counsellor yet. They were in no hurry, under pressure and short-staffed.

She was better, they said. They believed she was better, so she must be. They spoke once a week to her. Reassured her it wouldn't be long until they found someone suitable to talk to.

Emily ground her teeth as she dug her fingers deep into her scalp and wrenched at the perfect coiffure of teased curls tumbling from where they'd been piled on top of her head by Teresa at A-Head. She'd spent good money and time on the hairstyle to make certain it looked the very best of casual elegance. Teresa had accomplished that.

With a pained yowl, Emily yanked the pins out and hurled them across the stained floor of the ladies' room of the top-notch hotel the company had held their summer ball at for the past five years.

No originality or thought around the whole concept of the idea of the ball. A reward. An acknowledgement of the tough work, blood, sweat and tears that went into every day of hard slog. And it was a slog.

She hated her job, she hated the people.

Except for Zak. She loved him with her entire being. But he'd been gone for so long and nothing had been the same since. There was an emptiness in her world. A vacuum of nothingness.

Emily flopped her head down onto her hands and let the anger vibrate from the pit of her stomach until it flowed from her tightened throat in a feral growl. No longer empty but overflowing with fury. A fury she'd not experienced for so long. Not since the medication had flattened everything until she no longer lived, simply existed.

What the hell had happened? Where did it go wrong?

She thought she had it in hand. The whole situation. Convinced to stay away, she'd not driven past his house in more than a year, possibly longer. The days had all merged into a foggy passage of time she'd lost a grip on, no longer cared about while the medication lulled her, and her counsellor reassured her.

Wanda had persuaded her not to check on him. She'd said it would only make Emily sick again. Wanda, her counsellor. Her saviour.

Emily reached for the bottle of wine and took a good healthy swig before she slapped it back down on the floor again. She tipped her head back and let the mouthful of liquid wash the dryness in her throat away as she let out a little moan.

Wanda wasn't there any more to keep the demons away and now they came crowding back in, elbowing their way into her mind, like they did before Wanda, only louder and more voracious. As though the volume had been turned up.

The tears that threatened washed across her vision and made the over-bright lights in the ladies' room dance and sway.

It was a lifetime since she'd seen her beautiful black-haired, violet-eyed Welshman. She'd believed he'd be back when he was ready. She'd thought he'd return to her.

Wanda hadn't been privy to that thought. If she'd known, she'd have tried to persuade Emily otherwise, so Emily had kept it to herself. Nurtured it. Sure if she let him have his time, sow his wild oats, he'd realise how much he missed her and come back. He needed to grow up, be ready to settle down.

Well, he had grown up, he had settled down. Just not with her.

Emily rolled her head from side to side against the wall, the last of the pins grinding against her scalp.

'Too late. I left it too late.'

As pain consumed her, she brought her knees up to her chest and wrapped her arms around them as she rocked. Rocked to comfort herself. Rocked to lessen the ache burning in her chest as her heart threatened to explode.

She tucked her tear-drenched face into her knees and stilled.

In the silence, the voice she'd ignored for so long whispered its dark thoughts in her ear.

'Go away. Go away. You're not allowed here.' She scrunched her eyes closed and slapped her hands over her ears. 'You're banned. Wanda said I'm not to allow you in. Not to listen to you.'

But Wanda wasn't there to push it back and the voice didn't listen. It murmured sweet, sweet encouragement with sly insistence.

'Hello? Are you okay in there?'

From her sanctuary on the cool tiled floor of the toilet, Emily reared her head back and kicked the stall door closed with the flat brogues no one could see under her ballgown. Spitting, spewing fury burst from her lips as she stared at the closed door.

On the other side, the woman she barely knew from accounts, who'd dared to disturb her, whispered to someone else, 'Do you think she's all right?'

'Fuck off!'

Shocked silence followed a sharp intake of breath. 'I'm sorry.' The click of the woman's thin heels tip tapped on the tiled floor. 'I just...'

'I said. Fuck. Off!' The voice enunciated it clearly in case the woman was under any illusion that she required her assistance. The deep gravel of it grated through Emily's throat as it burst out, tearing her lips back from her teeth so the feral snarl flung white frothy spittle to spray over her naked knees.

A horrified gasp came from the woman on the other side of the cubicle, who fled, leaving the outer door to slam shut in her wake.

Satisfied, Emily listened for a moment for any further evidence of movement on the other side of the stall door, and then settled back against the toilet wall, the snarl of her lips curving into a sly smile. The voice had spoken. It was back.

It wasn't so bad. It was on her side. It knew where her heart lay.

Control slid with such ease from her. Comfortable and smooth.

She placed her palms on the cool, dirty tiles and pushed up from the floor, letting swathes of the soft black material of her ball gown swish back into place from where she'd scrunched it up in her fury and desperation, so it pooled around her ankles as she stood.

Emily cracked open the stall door to double check the ladies' room was empty before she made her way to the washbasin, reached for the lemongrass scented liquid soap and pressed two squirts into her hand. She rubbed, watching every move as she cleaned thoroughly in between her fingers like she'd been taught, letting the suds turn white before she rinsed them off with water hot enough to scald the flesh from her bones. But she never flinched, never retreated.

As she drew her gaze from her dripping hands to the mirror in front of her, plumes of steam fogged her image and made it waver in front of her. She stared into her own ice-blue eyes starkly emphasised against the black mascara and eyeliner smeared down cheeks white as chalk.

Recognition curved her lips.

'Oh, Emily. What are you going to do?'

2

SATURDAY 10 JULY 23:55 HRS

Jenna Morgan spread her bare arms wide across the back of the raffia furniture she'd taken delivery of earlier that day and tipped her face to look up at the stars canvassing the clear sky over her back garden.

The mere whisper of a breeze would be welcome, but despite the nightfall, temperatures soared, making for a sticky, over-heated atmosphere and thick air that clung to her skin with wet persistence.

The gentle buzz of alcohol melted her limbs and loosened her tongue as Domino, Fliss's Dalmatian, nudged his way onto the brand-new sofa cushion between herself and her sister.

'Soft sod.'

He circled around, then with a heartfelt groan as though he'd worked hard all day without a break as she had, the dog settled in a tight ball, his arse rammed up against Jenna's thigh with his head on Fliss's lap.

Instead of the twinge of annoyance she would have felt a year ago at him worming his way onto her brand-new furniture, a warm glow spread its golden wings to melt her heart. Jenna moved her arm, so her hand rested on Domino's black-spotted backside before she stroked the length of the raised scar that ran along his side. A scar he'd obtained the previous year when he'd taken on Fliss's kidnapper and come off worst in a fight with a large branch the attacker had wielded with force. He'd hit him hard enough so the dog had tumbled down a long, steep hillside in the Ironbridge gorge.

Jenna sank her fingers into his satin fur. 'I bloody love you.' The words slipped in a haze from her mouth.

Fliss's soft giggle told Jenna her sister had drunk enough too. Perhaps they should slip off to bed. If only she had the energy to move.

'Who are you talking to?'

Fliss's image wavered before Jenna's eyes. 'The daft Dalmatian. Who else?'

Fliss took a sip of her chilled Sauvignon Blanc and huffed out a breathy laugh. 'Me.' Her head gave a drunken roll on her shoulders. 'I know you do.'

Jenna laughed up at the stars, her world reeling in soft circles. It was time for bed. In a minute. 'I do.' She let her heavy head loll to one side so she could eye her sister. 'What did you think of the people you've interviewed so far?'

Fliss's smile stretched wide. 'I haven't interviewed them, it was just a quick chat on the phone with a few people.'

'People who you intend carrying out a job for you.'

'Dog walking.'

'It's a job.'

'It is.'

'And you interviewed people for the position.'

Laughter gurgled from her sister as she tipped her head back and shook her hair, so it spilled over the back of the furniture. 'Okay. You win. I spoke with three.' She shot Jenna a sly glance.

'Interviewed three. I wasn't keen on the first woman, Lesley. Nice enough but she seemed too much about the business and not enough about the animals. The other two were really nice. Harvey and Gill. Harvey's coming around to meet Domino on Monday evening. I checked your schedule to make sure you're available. I'd rather you were there.'

Jenna checked her sister for signs of self-doubt, but saw none, just a keenness to involve Jenna on the decision.

'It's a shame we need a dog walker at all, after the last one, but necessary.' She scraped her fingernails over the top of his spine and enjoyed the appreciative groan he sent up.

Fliss wriggled around and tucked her feet under her as she turned to face Jenna, wine glass cradled in one hand and the other stroking Domino. 'Even without the court case coming up, he needs additional exercise when we're both working.'

'I agree.'

'I've given Gill a couple of dates and she'll come back to me.'

'Good. Just let me know.'

Fliss murmured her assent as she took a drink of her wine and a comfortable silence held in the thick night air for a moment.

'It's been nice. Just the two of us.' Jenna raised her glass and took a sip of the wine, surprised to find she'd almost finished the glass. Another glass. 'God, I haven't had this much to drink in... an age.'

'Nor me. Thank God I'm not at work tomorrow. Twenty-five children would kill me.'

'Haha. Me too. I don't know how you do what you do.' Jenna could have nothing but admiration for her younger sister who worked as a teacher at Coalbrookdale and Ironbridge School.

'Same.' Fliss's smile stretched across her face. 'The things Mason tells me makes my blood curdle.'

Jenna didn't tend to divulge too much about the grim side of her job to her younger sister, instead preferring to focus on positive matters.

'Was he okay about tonight?' She referred to the fact that they were having an unusual girly night in without Fliss's boyfriend and Jenna's work partner, DC Mason Ellis.

'Yeah, no problem.' Fliss stretched her long legs out in front of her and let out a soft groan. 'He wanted to visit his brother anyway. Have some family time.' She rolled her head so she could look at Jenna. 'What about m'lord Adrian?'

Jenna grinned, a wide silly grin, as Fliss referred to Jenna's relatively new boyfriend, Chief Crown Prosecutor Adrian Hall who, a bit like Mason, spent more time at Jenna's house than his own these days. 'He's fine. Really busy. Plenty of work to catch up on his new case.'

'What about tomorrow?'

'He's coming over, but it's too hot to do anything.'

'What about the beach? Aberdovey.'

Wales and its rugged coastline were less than an hour and half's drive away.

'Too busy.'

'Llandudno?'

'Meh.'

It would be overwhelmingly hectic with such a lovely, long Victorian pier jutting out into the Irish Sea and the wide promenade which would be overrun with tourists. She wasn't in the mood for crowds, she saw enough of them at work. The unprecedented heat brought a deluge of criminals out of the woodwork. Flashers, domestic abuse, sexual predators.

'What about the west shore beach?'

With its sand dunes and privacy, Llandudno's west shore beach was much quieter.

'That would be good. Adrian and I can lie out in the sun and fry our skin for a few hours. Yeah, that might work.' Jenna drained her glass. 'What about you? Do you have plans with Mason?'

'He'll want to have monkey sex.'

Fliss gurgled out a wicked laugh at Jenna's flinch.

'For the love of Jesus, I've told you, I don't want to know anything about your sex life with Mason. I have to work with the man. I don't want that image in my head.'

'I was teasing.' Fliss's laughter floated on the warm night air, the scent of the jasmine Jenna had planted carried a headiness. 'We thought we might get up really early before the heat and take Domino over the Shropshire Hills. Back for brunch and then Mason said he could do with popping into the station to get some paperwork done.'

Jenna nodded, relieved she didn't have to listen to a blow-by-blow account of Fliss's sex life with a man she considered to be almost a brother.

With one last scrub at Domino's coat, Jenna pushed herself to her feet. Unsteady, she wobbled for a moment before she was able to put one foot in front of the other. 'I'm off. Are you coming?'

'I am.'

Fliss reached a hand up and Jenna closed her fingers around it and gave a hard yank. As Fliss lurched to her feet, Jenna steadied them both. 'Oh God. I'm going to regret this in the morning.'

'Me too.' Fliss swayed. 'At least you can have a lie-in. Mason said he'd be with me by 6 a.m.'

'Message him. Tell him to come later.'

Fliss scraped a hand through her hair as she closed her eyes. 'Nah, it'll be fine. We'll have a nice walk, won't we, Domino?'

In all fairness, the dog raised his head for a brief moment before he lowered his chin back down to his paws, but his eyes remained open.

'Come on, boy, time for bed.'

With a heartfelt groan, Domino slid from the soft cushion and ambled after Fliss as she wove her way up the garden to the house.

Relieved he didn't follow her, Jenna closed the patio doors and locked them behind everyone. She had no idea how Fliss coped with his hot body pressed against hers on the bed, pinning the bedclothes tight around her. During winter she could understand it, but never in the middle of a heatwave.

The cool shower did little to relieve her once she was dry and the heat hit her again. Too hot and mid-summer, it was barely dark enough to sleep anyway.

Jenna kicked the sheets back and sprawled naked on top of the bed, praying for a cool breeze to sneak through the open windows, thankful Domino had chosen to sleep on Fliss's bed with her.

The world gave a gentle rotation as she closed her eyes and hoped for a peaceful, dreamless sleep.

3

Imelda Cheetham-Epstein smiled at her new husband of three weeks as he scratched his head. Lines of concentration etched into his face, he picked up the sander so he could skim the dirty green flaked paint from the original oak door before they decided whether to leave it naked, just treating it with oil, or whether they needed to paint it. It all depended on the quality beneath once he stripped the paint off.

A smile split his face as he glanced up at her, placed the instrument down and reached out to take Joshua from her arms. At eleven months old, their little boy was a bundle of full on activity, which recently had tired her out quicker than expected.

She touched her hand to her distended stomach and smiled back at Zak. Unplanned, the second pregnancy had taken them both by surprise. They'd wanted more children but hadn't quite prepared themselves for another child hot on the heels of the first. She'd wanted to get married before they had Joshua, but she'd also not wanted to rush the preparations. By the time she'd planned their wedding, she was already pregnant with their second, and didn't see the point of bringing it forward. As neither one of them had been upset, it didn't matter. They loved each other.

Already twenty-eight weeks pregnant, the children would be extremely close in age by the time she gave birth. They'd be a handful, but it didn't bother her. She just needed a little extra sleep, which she'd already had that morning. Not that it had made any difference as the heat swiped away any freshness she'd felt when she first woke.

She lifted the thick swathe of hair from her neck and considered putting it up in a ponytail. 'I was going to make brunch. Are you ready?'

Zak kissed the top of Joshua's head and grinned as his son reached out with chubby fingers to tug at Zak's lips. He blew a raspberry while he nodded at her. 'I'm starving.'

He was always starving. A long skinny streak of a man, never still, he ate up his energy and sucked in calories to fuel himself.

'Full cooked?' It was a Sunday treat.

She wasn't sure she could manage sausage, bacon, eggs, baked beans and mushrooms, but she might throw a bacon butty together for herself and watch Zak inhale his food.

'That would be great.'

With a smile at her little boy, she reached her arms out to take Joshua back. 'Fifteen minutes, Zak. No longer. Fifteen minutes and I'll have a full English ready for you. Keep up your strength.' She broke into a grin as she balanced Joshua and stretched out, her fingers small against Zak's skin as she took a squeeze of his muscles and made him laugh. 'I'll see if he'll go down for a nap. He's been full of himself this morning. Perhaps we'll take him down to Dale End Park later this afternoon, let him run off some energy.' It would give Zak a break from DIY too.

Lined with ancient old trees with the River Severn idling its way through it at this time of year, Dale End Park, seated in the

Ironbridge Gorge, provided a wide expanse of shade and a vast enough area for a toddler to wear himself out. The little park would more than likely be full of other small children, but it didn't matter, there was plenty of wide-open space and the tree-lined football field would have very few people after practice finished around midday. She could only hope to catch the soft breezes that meandered through the valley in the wake of the river.

Imelda took hold of Joshua and adjusted him, so he sat on her hip. Not sure how much longer she would be able to lift him, she buried her face against thick hair, the same as his father's, as he wrapped his arms around her neck and cooed at her.

A flicker of worry ran over Zak's face as she looked up. 'Can you manage?' He placed a soft kiss on the end of her nose.

'Yes, of course.' She dismissed his concern while at the same time, her heart gave a little hitch. She was stronger than her new husband believed but his thoughtfulness warmed her heart.

Already on his feet at the age of eleven months, Joshua was still unsteady, and Imelda preferred to carry him down the two flights of stairs and then let him go at the bottom. At the stage where he 'toddled' at breakneck speed with no particular finesse or direction, he'd already given her several heart-stopping moments. Nappies had more than one use and the number of times he'd landed on his backside, Imelda could only be thankful for the amount of padding those nappies provided.

She held onto Joshua with one hand, balancing him on her hip as she gripped the banister with her other hand, cautious as she came down the flight of stairs to the first-floor landing as Zak turned on the sander and the shriek of it filled her ears.

With a quick glance upstairs, she winced at the whine of the electrical equipment and then turned towards Joshua's bedroom as her son's arms and legs flailed to show how full of energy he still was. Imelda sighed and hitched Joshua higher. There was no hope he'd take a snooze while activity and noise filled the house. He was too darned nosey. She'd do just as well to take him down with her and entertain him until Zak was ready to eat and they had some respite from the scream of the sander.

Imelda made her way down the stairs, her fluffy socks protecting the soles of her feet from the broken tiles on the hallway floor. That would be their next project. Hopefully done in time before their newest addition put in an appearance.

Imelda bumped open the door to the kitchen with her hip and let it swing shut behind them to close out the loud intrusion of the sander while she grabbed the remote to switch on the small T.V. The cheery beat of PAW patrol filled the room.

As Joshua kicked his legs in his enthusiasm to be set free, Imelda bent low and let him go. A wide smile spread over her face as he staggered like a drunkard over to the small box of wooden toys and snatched up his favourite train.

She pulled open the fridge door and stared at the contents, then reached inside to take out a packet of bacon, while Joshua chuntered in unintelligible delight to his toy.

She placed her hand on her stomach, pleasure spreading a warmth through her as the baby kicked.

There was no better way to spend her Sunday than at home with her boys.

4

There was no giveaway sign to indicate anyone was even at home. The curtains were open, but the windows appeared blank.

Emily shifted in her seat. Three hours was a hell of a long time, longer than she'd previously spent watching from the sanctuary of her little white Honda Jazz. Although the car windows were down, not even a whisper of a breeze could tease its way through to cool her overheated flesh. The heatwave was killing her. Killing everyone. It had flashed in with a suddenness that had rocked the country. The shift in the jet stream was held accountable. Global warming. Whatever the reason, it was like sinking into the pits of hell.

A trickle of sweat meandered its way down the length of her spine until she plucked her white cotton shirt from her skin. She regretted the decision to wear heavy jeans, but she'd wanted to show off the length of her legs, the curve of her hips. The white shirt was nipped in at the waist and emphasised the generous bosom she'd always been proud of, a bosom which had expanded in the last year or so.

Zak had liked her breasts. He'd always told her it was her best feature.

They were fuller now, more rounded. He couldn't be anything but impressed.

She stared up at the tall façade of the building, narrowing her eyes as she inspected each window, waiting for a trace of movement somewhere behind the panes of glass.

Zak was there. She knew he was home. There was his sleek, black Audi, street parked not far from the house. She'd have thought he'd have updated it by now. It was the same car he'd had when he first started his new job. That had to be almost two years ago.

Still, it was a nice car.

She dabbed her fingers at the thin line of sweat on her top lip and turned her head away from the car to study where he lived.

The three-storey double-frontage Victorian house with a central front door seemed narrow at the front and went deep, appearing to overhang the valley below. She'd never seen the rear of the premises but imagined a wooden balcony surrounded by an elegant balustrade with an unrestricted view of the valley that dropped into a steep slope of lush vegetation down to the River Severn.

A slow smile spread over her face. When she lived there, she would trail an abundance of brightly coloured flowers, so they bloused over the balcony in great waterfalls. Petunias in elegant skirts of purples and reds, or begonias in bright splashes of orange and yellow.

She pulled herself back from the drift of her imagination and with narrowed eyes scanned the house again.

Unsurprised by the lack of any movement on a Sunday morning, she shifted in her seat, sweat slicking her clothes to her, the shirt wet where it squeezed tight under her armpits. She swiped the back of her hand across her sticky cheek and dabbed at her forehead.

Her memory of long, lazy Sunday mornings with Zak sent a mellow warmth curling through her chest until the stab of dark envy chased it away.

It was no longer her and him in their cosy little flat.

He was there, in the big house with his new wife.

Emily's lips tightened over clenched teeth. A new wife. A wife he should never have married. He was supposed to be hers. She'd waited for him. He knew she'd waited and yet still he'd married someone else.

Heat circled deep in her belly as anger clutched at her throat.

To push back the anger, she sucked in a deep breath. As she'd been taught, she closed her mind off from the distasteful, the murky evil that clawed at her.

But the voice persevered in its subtle insistence.

She's there. With him.

It nudged into her consciousness.

He's yours. Not hers. It should be you. Not her. You can take him back.

Unable to ignore the voice, she chose instead to concentrate on the house. From the outside, it appeared he'd achieved so much more than she'd imagined possible. Since the last drive-by she'd made months before, he'd had the bricks sandblasted, taking off the thick coating of coal dust that had built up over the years as the trundle of coal carts wound their way through the Ironbridge gorge to the power station. Long since defunct, the machinations of the Industrial Revolution had nonetheless left their dirty footprints on the surrounding area.

She sighed out a long breath. Perhaps his home would suit her. Once he'd achieved all he needed to in order to make it liveable. She cast a look over the building again. It certainly looked hospitable. And big. Such a large property. She'd not realised before.

A smile curved her lips, and she crossed her arms over her chest, settling back to let her imagination take her on a long, meandering wander through their future life, once he'd shuffled his current wife along.

She was a mistake.

He'd know it soon enough.

As soon as he saw her again. He'd realise his mistake.

There was only one woman for him. One woman who had what it took to keep his attention.

Her breath caught in her throat as a shadow flitted past the frosted window of the front door. The slow pump of her heart turned to a race as she sprang upright to stare harder until her eyes dried and stung through lack of blinking.

Not allowing herself enough time to collect her thoughts, she reached out to flip the handle of the door and push it open. She stepped out of the car, keys in the tight grip of her fist with no consideration of the windows she'd left down. With a heavy throb in the base of her throat, spikes of anticipation crawled over her skin and sent another wave of heat to blast her skin and tingle the pulse points at the back of her knees.

Go and get him. The soft whisper of it echoed in her mind. *He's yours, not hers.*

She nodded to acknowledge the truth of it.

Go and get him. Take back what is rightfully yours.

The sheer thrill of seeing him again gave her the confidence to stride straight up to the little old pitch fencing gate that needed tending to and swing it open.

The moment he saw her, he'd know. She was sure of it.

Her white sneakers kept her footsteps silent as she strode the short length of the crazy paving path to the sage green painted front door and pressed the bell, its old-fashioned ring barely discernible above the screeching buzz of a power tool coming from inside the house. She'd not noticed the noise from her car, with music playing low on her iPod.

The watery shadow of someone approaching filled the small square of thick frosted window and shot her pulse into an erratic rhythm of nerves.

She reached up to run her fingers through the length of her straight, blonde hair.

What would she say?

Tell him everything. Tell him how you feel, how sorry you are, how much you love him. He'll understand. He'll know the truth of it the moment he sees you again. Why wouldn't he? The hoarse whisper instilled her with the conviction that wavered for a short moment.

The little woman who swung the door open made the words Emily had ready to pour forth stick in her throat as her jaw dropped to leave her open-mouthed and speechless.

Nothing like she'd expected. Petite, delicate. Much younger than Zak. Stunningly beautiful with big brown eyes brimming with happiness and a face flushed with pleasure.

That happiness should be yours, the voice sneered at her, its disgust a slithering darkness in her stomach. *She's snatched away your happiness. Your future. Are you going to allow it?*

The young woman raised her chin to look up at her, her perfectly plump lips tilted up at the edges in a friendly smile. 'Hello.'

In the silence, the woman's lips quivered uncertainly before the smile fell away.

'Can I help you?'

Emily battened down on the spike of fury that refused to be completely contained. It simmered away while she assessed her adversary, narrowing her eyes to take in the skinny, flat-chested woman whose head barely reached Emily's chin.

She stretched her lips in a wide smile, bright enough to chase away the shimmer of doubt that lurked for a brief flicker of time in the other woman's eyes. 'Is Zak home?'

'Zak...?' The woman's gaze skittered skyward to above where the noise came from before it settled back on her. 'He's busy. Can I help? I'm Imelda,' she grinned with overexaggerated delight, 'his wife.'

His new wife. The conceited bitch. How dare she flaunt her fortune in your face.

Emily tilted her head to one side, flickered her gaze down to take in the prissy gingham tea towel Imelda clutched against the distinct rounded bump of her belly.

Fire raced over Emily's skin to shoot up her neck and into her face in a blaze of fury.

His wife! the voice shrieked in her mind, setting her teeth on edge. *The little bitch is pregnant!*

'No!' The voice burst from her constricted throat in a threatening growl, deep and feral.

Sly and insidious, the voice grated in her ear. *That's how she got him. She tricked him. He'll know. The moment he sees you he'll know what a mistake he made. You just need him to see you. Make her get him.*

Emily breathed in through her nose and towered above the slighter woman. 'I said I want Zak!'

Imelda's long black lashes fluttered over deep brown eyes filled with shocked uncertainty as she took a step back. Her lips popped open as she reached out with one delicate hand for the door.

Emily clenched her teeth against the rise in fury as instinct kicked in and she snatched at the smaller woman's hand before

Imelda could swing the door closed against her. Grasped it in her much larger one, she gave her fingers a squeeze.

Got her. You've got her, now. The voice breathed its encouragement.

The jolt of pleasure warmed her insides at the fear churning through the other woman's expression.

She placed one foot inside the hallway and leaned in closer.

'I want Zak.' She couldn't make it clearer.

What does the woman expect? He belongs to you. Not Imelda. The soft purr filled her with conviction.

'Get him for me now.' She didn't need to raise her voice. It was deep, clear and there could be no misunderstanding.

Imelda twisted her hand around but failed to prise her slender wrist from Emily's hard grasp. She took another step back, and Emily followed her into the hallway as it widened out into a neat little square of cracked and broken red chequerboard Victorian tiles.

'Get out!' Imelda's eyes widened with panic. 'Get out of our house.' Imelda yanked at her wrist, but Emily held firm, determination and focus in her grip.

Recognition flashed over Imelda's features. 'I know who you are.'

The dark thrill of the other woman's fear kicked Emily's adrenaline up, sending her heart into a fast, uneven rhythm to overpower the small wash of drugs her body still retained.

'I know you.' Imelda jerked her head back, the edges of her faded smile turned downwards, she made a quick scan from head to foot. Annoyance replaced the fear in her gaze and instead of backing away, she took a step forward to bring their faces close together as she peered up into Emily's eyes. 'Zak told me all about you when we first met. *All* about you. And no, you can't see him. You need to leave. Right now, before I call the police.'

In the face of the other woman's anger, fury whipped up without warning and Emily let out the pained yowl of an injured animal as the sound of the electric tool vibrated through the house, filling her head with white noise. A noise she was all too familiar with.

Too late, Imelda realised her mistake in provoking Emily and the bravery washed away to be replaced with terror as she stepped further back into her hallway, her wrist still in the firm vice of Emily's fingers.

A red haze blanketed Emily's vision.

She tightened her fingers around her car keys, raised her hand and with one, hard jerk she had Imelda stumbling forward as she slashed at her face.

Dark satisfaction throbbed through her veins as the other woman's skin unzipped and scarlet bloomed to run from the thin gash on her cheek down the side of her neck. Her distressed cry was little more than a squeak as Imelda whipped her hand to her cheek, shock streaking over her face as she removed her blood-streaked fingers to stare at them.

Imelda teetered backwards, her petite body no real measure for the power of vibrating fury.

Filled with unsatisfied blood lust, Emily's fist connected with Imelda's face once more, vicious and focused, all semblance of sanity evaporating in the crimson cloud of rage.

She punched a third time and caught the woman on the end of her chin and grinned as Imelda went down.

Not an elegant crumple to her knees but a poleaxe.

The wet smack of Imelda's head as it made contact with the tiles would have made a lesser heart contract, but too intent, too focused on the woman who had stolen her soulmate, Emily never flinched.

Flat on the floor, Imelda's delicate body prone, the gentle bulge in her stomach drew Emily's gaze.

Incensed, rage boiled in a seething lava.

Get her, the voice roared in her head.

Unleashed, her temper erupted and she launched herself on top of Imelda, her knees either side of the woman's bloated belly.

She grabbed at the perfect chestnut locks and heaved the woman's head up until their noses almost touched, then slammed it down onto the hard surface.

Smack!

Smack!

The thud of it roiled around in Emily's stomach to give her nothing but satisfaction while the electric thrum from upstairs filled her mind to spur her on.

Silence dropped like a white blanket over the house as the whine and drone from the electric equipment overhead cut off to leave the distant throb of Jordan North's BBC 1 jingle drifting from upstairs.

Emily raised her head, breath soughing through her chest as she unravelled the thick hair from around her fingers. Her lips curled with distaste as she flicked off strands she'd ripped from Imelda's scalp.

Through eyes cleared of the raging hatred, she rested back on her heels, her backside on Imelda's skinny thighs.

Unsure, confusion stuttered through her at the scene.

Slicked with sweat, her blood-stained keys rattled in her sticky fingers as she raised her hands to her cheeks, her voice hushed and rusty.

'What have you done? Oh, Emily, what have you done?'

With no reply from the voice, she held her breath and waited. Where was it? Where was the support when she needed it most?

Her gaze focused on Imelda's face as the slow spread of blood pooled out from around the woman's head and drizzled from the gash on her cheek. Brown eyes wide, blank and staring up at the ceiling, frozen in death.

'Oh, you've killed her, Emily. What have you done now? You've killed her.'

She raised a trembling hand and covered her mouth, numb to everything as her world ground to a standstill to leave her in a vacuum of her own making.

She tilted her head to one side and held her breath.

The vague strumming of a child's song filtered through her consciousness to make the hairs on the back of her neck give a warning tingle as she became aware of another presence.

Heart pounding so loud, all other noise was blocked out, she turned her head in slow motion, her fingers gripping tight to the car keys, her one grasp on reality.

Her lips parted as the weight of her jaw pulled down and her mouth dropped open. Her breath stuttered out in faltering little puffs as her attention centred on the intent gaze pinning her in place.

As the plump-cheeked child stumbled forward with the awkward, drunken motion of someone who has just learnt to walk, Emily's breath came back in a rush of heart-rending love.

Dark curls tight to its head, violet eyes, so like its father's, were instantly recognisable.

Emily's heart soared as the child slipped its forefinger from between plump, wet lips and stared her straight in the eye. 'Mama?'

5

Damn, but it was hot.

Detective Sergeant Jenna Morgan dabbed a bead of sweat from her top lip and then flopped her forehead onto her arms, where they rested on her desk in Malinsgate police station.

Some cheeky sod had whipped her fan from her office for their own relief from the overwhelming heat. If only they had CCTV, she'd find out who the culprit was and whip their arse for them.

Overheated, she shuffled her backside in her chair.

She needed to buy herself some new black trousers. She'd yanked on her winter ones in the blur of her rush that morning. Far too warm for the current weather, but who the hell knew they were about to have a heatwave of epic proportions with the suddenness of a desert storm?

She blew out a breath designed to cool herself, but all it achieved was to make her fringe flutter above her damp forehead for a moment before it settled back to stick to her skin.

Plain-clothes she may be, but black trousers were the unofficial uniform for her and most of the other officers. She very rarely wore anything else. If her head hadn't hurt so much, she may well have made a different choice. One she'd not have regretted. A good-fitting pair of black trousers were smart, practical and, should the need arise, they never showed the blood or urine stains if she happened to get into a tussle with a suspect. Puke was a different matter, but who could live with the smell of that for more than five minutes in any case? In her position, she'd not been puked on for a number of years now, but the chances of it still made her think twice about her clothing choices. From a purely practical side, although she rarely got in a fight these days, when she did, she didn't want her knickers on display by wearing a skirt.

She rolled her forehead from side to side, the thin film of sweat rubbed off on her cooler forearm as she huffed out a breath.

The temperature had kicked up with unexpected suddenness, sending the whole country into a heatwave. And here she was, on her supposed day off, having to come in to cover for DS 'lazy arse' Stevens' shift in a compact office where the air con had given up the ghost and no one could fix it until Monday, at the earliest.

No surprise Stevens had called in sick, yet again, on his allocated Sunday. The man hadn't completed a full shift since he'd remarried earlier that year, evidently preferring a nine-to-five job.

The call at 6:05 that morning had done little to endear him to her. Her head, still fuzzy from the bottle of wine she'd consumed, stayed that way despite taking another cold shower and inhaling a single piece of toast before she dashed out of the door, travel mug full of coffee in hand.

She felt like shit, she'd probably feel like shit for the rest of the day, or at least until she finished at 6 p.m.

Jenna raised her head and pressed her fingertips into her eyelids.

She leaned to one side and peered through her open door into the main office. Quiet on a Sunday morning, barely even hushed voices as officers sat at their computers taking advantage of the time to process the paperwork that got side-lined during the week when they were busier.

From what Fliss had told her, she'd most likely see Mason later, and possibly Ryan catching up on paperwork, but currently none of the people on duty were in her team.

The last of the Saturday-night revellers had already been roused, interviewed or cautioned, processed and sent home. The most awkward was the old gentleman who'd recently lost his wife and thought that dropping his pants in public was quite acceptable. A telephone call to his daughter had set the cat amongst the pigeons. She was horrified. Threatened to put him in a home.

Not that a home would do the poor old guy any favours. He wasn't sick, just horribly lonely and very sad, not understanding what he was supposed to do now his wife of fifty-seven years was gone. His kingpin, his anchor.

Jenna tapped the screen of her iPhone and stared at the time: 11:38. At least she was on an early. She'd be off by 6 p.m. She'd possibly just go home and lie in the back garden with a cool glass of Pinot Grigio and a packet of Walker's crisps.

Recovery.

She'd let the early evening sun beat down on her while Adrian read his papers in preparation for a court case the following week. Birmingham-based, much of his time since they'd known each other had been taken up by a major case in London. Still on-going, it divided his time. Time with him she'd come to appreciate more and more. Time she should have spent with him today at the beach. It was a good job the man was understanding.

Something inside her warmed each time her sexy chief crown

prosecutor came to mind. And he was hers now. Not that she was possessive, but they'd established their relationship. They were exclusive.

They'd only known each other for nine months, but from the first moment they'd met, there'd been an instant bond. Not a simple attraction, but something much deeper, possibly connected with the situation. With her own sister's disappearance, Adrian had leant Jenna not only his support, his shoulder to cry on and his shared love of a good coffee, but also a solid, unwavering understanding of her deepest, darkest fears. Fears neither of them felt the need to discuss, but both of them were aware of.

She took comfort in the soft touch of his hand against the small of her back on those occasional moments when the dark wave of fear of what may have been, threatened.

For several precious moments, Jenna allowed her still hazy mind to drift.

It would have been lovely to watch the ripples of muscle move under the deep golden skin of his broad, shirtless back as they sat on beach towels in the sun today. Adrian had a gorgeous back. She sighed as the image of it flashed into her mind, and she almost reached out to stroke it as she did in the middle of the night.

With a little spark of irritation, Jenna pushed herself upright and picked at the sliver of nail she'd managed to catch on something.

Fliss had plans for her and Mason to take Domino out walking the Shropshire Hills for the morning with backpacks and a picnic. Too hot to go elsewhere, they'd be trekking through the shaded woodlands, enjoying the cooling breezes. Lovely plans.

Her own plans shot to shit by an inconsiderate colleague.

She glanced at the computer screen and tapped in the few last words on the email she'd been composing before she hit the send button. Satisfied she'd moved another piece of administration from her pile to someone else's, she picked up her coffee and took a swig at the last dregs in the bottom to finish it off just as Airwaves – the force radio – sparked to life.

She murmured in the back of her throat as she reached out. 'Please don't let it be anything time-consuming.' She'd enough of a backlog to get through without some petty fraudster interfering with her current workload.

'DS Morgan.' The whisky-soft Welsh tones of Morris King, the civilian telephone operator, melted her and if she could carve the contrasting image of his short, rotund baldness out of her head, she might just fall in love with his voice. Despite that, he still managed to bring a smile to her face as she answered.

'Go ahead, Morris.'

'We just had a 999 come in, Sarg. One Zak Cheetham-Epstein. There's a powerful name, don't you know? He claims to have found his wife dead in the front hallway of their home in Coalbrookdale. He could barely speak, Sarg. Sounded like he was in shock. Front door wide open, he claims. Mr Cheetham-Epstein says there's blood everywhere and he can't believe she's just slipped over and bashed her head. He's frantic, Sarg. He has no idea why the door was open.'

'Paramedics?'

'Just arriving.'

'Address?'

As he reeled it off, Jenna surged to her feet, already slipping her iPhone into the back pocket of her over-thick trousers and reaching for her small crossover handbag. She slung the strap over her head as she made for the door and glanced around the main office with a soft cluck of disappointment.

'I'm on my way, shouldn't be any more than fifteen minutes.'

'Uniform are on their way, Sarg. ETA approximately three

minutes, but this isn't a straightforward one, which is why I've tapped you. Inspector Davies is on his refs.'

'Not a problem, Morris.' Everyone was entitled to take a break. 'It was too quiet for my liking anyway.' The lie came easily to her lips. He didn't need to know how disgruntled she was with the other sergeant, Stevens, who'd bunked off just because it was a Sunday, and his new wife couldn't do without him. She could only hope DI Taylor would have a gentle word in his shell-like, because if it became her responsibility to sort it, gentle would possibly not be the way of things.

Jenna scanned the room. With none of her familiar team available to call upon, she sailed on through without picking anyone else up. She'd rather have Mason or Ryan with her, but they weren't on until later. If she grabbed someone from the other shift, she'd have to hustle things around so they could fit in with her or vice versa. Sometimes it wasn't worth the hassle.

She could deal with a sudden death on her own.

As a thought occurred to her, she clicked the radio back on. 'Morris, can you make sure you get a hold of SOCO.' More impor-tant than the dead woman they could do nothing for, it was essential to get a scene guard in place for preservation of forensic evidence. If it was an accident, all well and good. If it was murder and they'd failed in the first steps of preserving a scene, they were buggered.

'Already done, Sarg.' His melodic tones floated over Airwaves.

Of course, it was. Cool and efficient, Morris would have coped, doling out jobs in a controlled, efficient manner, no matter what the panic. His calm, composed nature a boon to the position he held. Not all operators were like that. Not all police officers were like her team.

She sucked air in through her teeth while she blocked the avenue of thought nudging at her. She had a good team. The best.

They'd be back on shift soon enough. She could redistribute the workload then.

In the meantime, she had a job to do and a little juggling with a case that could go either way. Accident. Murder. Her mind scanned through the possibilities of what she was likely to find when she arrived at the house.

Jenna's long legs ate up the distance through the dim electric-lit high-ceilinged corridors of Malinsgate police station. She opted to take the stairwell instead of the lift and made short work of trotting down, appreciating the dip in temperature through the hallways. She had no urge to go to the gym as others did but kept slim and gained her exercise through taking the stairs and walking a huge Dalmatian most days.

With Domino pushing into her thought process, she smiled as she bumped through the door and made her way to the front desk. She swiped up the keys to the brand-new police car and waggled them in the air at the civilian operator at the other end of the office. An edge of excitement spiked her pulse. One advantage of working Sunday, she got the choice of car and not the one that smelled of piss and puke this time.

With a quick stroke of a pen, she signed the car out and stepped outside Malinsgate Police Station.

Constructed in the 1980s, the ugly brick and flat faced glass building was in need of a thorough renovation, or possible demolition. She'd thought the air con in the rest of the station hadn't been working, but the truth of it was, it was a damned hot day, and anything would struggle to keep the temperatures down.

The heat of the day blasted through and made her regret even more the decision to wear her heavy trousers. She jogged over the bridge and made for the car, desperate to get inside so she could blast out some cool air.

The driver's seat was in the shade, if not she suspected she would have scorched her hands on the leather steering wheel. The fresh smell of new leather lifted her spirits as she slipped inside the car and strapped herself in. The job needed to be done, but it didn't mean you couldn't take your pleasure where you found it.

It took her a millisecond to find the push-button starter as she dropped the key fob into the central console. It took her a millisecond longer to realise the car she was about to drive was an automatic.

Secretly thrilled, she put it in drive and appreciated the smooth flow of it as she pulled out of the police station car park.

She headed towards the older side of Telford, navigating the quiet roads around the retail parks. Most people had already made their way to the garden centres and outdoor markets, avoiding the enclosed shops of Telford town centre on such a brilliantly perfect summer's day.

Jenna took one hand off the steering wheel and smoothed away the heavy vertical line that had started to take up residence between her eyebrows. She didn't put it down to age, but rather to nine months of continuous stress and the claustrophobic sensation of drowning under the weight of her own constricted chest when the image of PC Lee Gardner slipped uninvited into her mind.

If she closed her eyes for too long, splashes of crimson daubed the insides of her eyelids until they flew back open again in self-defence while she gasped in quick snatches of breath, each one lodging in her throat. It wasn't PTSD. There was no way she suffered from that. It was pure flashback, nothing else.

It didn't matter that she never wanted to see it again, but it was insistent, nudging at her subconscious each time she let down her guard.

Late nights and alcohol didn't help. She'd have to remember

that. Although, recalling the previous evening, it was sometimes the late nights and alcohol that got her through, allowing her to switch off and relax without judgement.

She blew out a breath. A whole bottle of wine was unusual for her. Too much alcohol and too little sleep blurred her sharp mind and allowed her defences to weaken.

Weakness wasn't something she'd have imagined in her psyche, but PTSD could affect anyone, she'd learnt. It didn't make her weak, just meant that she was subjected to moments of weakness.

The flashbacks she'd endured for the last four months. Visions of those final moments before PC Gardner had died. Flashbacks she pushed to one side so she could deal with the everyday. The job.

She made her way along the A442 Queensway towards Coalbrookdale, straight ahead at the roundabout with the mineshaft sculpture and took a left down Cherry Tree Hill, slowing to a virtual standstill as she took special care over the speedhumps that were far too big for any normal-sized car to get over without scraping the chassis.

The total silence in the car was unnecessary, she could have had any choice of music, but she appreciated it. It gave her time to think with clarity.

Without warning, a sharp pain shot from the centre of her ear downwards and she whipped her hand up to cup the right side of her neck.

If she had a chance to forget for a short while, it proved a vicious reminder of the incident. A burst eardrum from being too close to an exploding shotgun. The shotgun that blew her colleague's head off and splattered his brains all over her.

Lucky to be alive herself, she was left with an occasional sharp pain she was assured was psychosomatic rather than physical. Could have fooled her. Bloody pain wasn't her imagination. A red-hot poker up the arse of her consultant wouldn't be their imagination either.

His words hadn't been reassuring, they were a disinterested reaction from a man who possibly should have retired a millennium or so ago. Worse than his indifference to her situation was his insistence on continually rubbing the end of his bobbly, purpled nose while he seemingly bestowed her with his concentration.

Apparently, her hearing was one hundred per cent too. Nothing to worry about, except for the high-pitched whine piercing through the stillness of the night from time to time to throw her out of a peaceful sleep into sudden wakefulness.

Tinnitus, he said.

It'll go in time, he said.

Hadn't bloody gone fast enough.

With no particular urgency to reach her destination as uniform already had the situation in hand, Jenna stuck to just on the speed limit of 30 mph. She skimmed through the traffic lights, which were obliging enough to stay on green, and onwards along the narrowed road past the Coalbrookdale Inn with its abundance of flower baskets spilling their blooms in splashes of scarlet down the walls of the Grade II listed building. Built in the 1830s, its original purpose was to serve real ale to the ironworkers and subsequently to tourists who visited the Inn situated in the heart of the Ironbridge Gorge World Heritage Site, opposite the Museum of Iron.

She took a sharp left up the steep incline towards the Holy Trinity Church on her right and pulled over behind the queue of parked cars to let an oncoming Peugeot squeeze its way past on the narrow hill.

As she waited, she cast her gaze over the beauty of the church nicknamed 'the Jewel of the Dale' with its rare sixteenth-century Flemish glass window depicting the Last Supper.

She held her breath as the elderly driver almost scraped her wing mirror off, insistent on keeping away from the edge of the road in case it disappeared down the gorge. The Peugeot's mirror missed hers by a hair's breadth.

Jenna depressed the accelerator and took off before another decrepit driver decided to meet her halfway. It wasn't a hill to get stuck on, neither direction was good to reverse along.

As she climbed higher up the gorge, the houses became older and further apart, their brick walls coated with the coal dust from the Industrial Revolution. Coal had continued to be transported by train until relatively recently.

Approaching the address registered on her satnav, her heart gave an uncomfortable squeeze at the scene ahead of her.

She swallowed down on the ball of fear threatening to surface.

'Oh God.'

She'd been assured by the welfare counsellor that her PTSD was a side effect of experiencing a traumatic event. She'd assured the counsellor she didn't suffer from PTSD. Not if she wanted to return to active duty, she didn't. And active duty was her life. She didn't want to be stuck on desk duty, doing half the job she lived for. Not at the age of twenty-nine. She dealt with the brief moments of flashback.

She'd taken her eight allotted counselling sessions and reassured them she no longer needed them while she ignored the look on her counsellor's face as the man signed her off and confirmed she was healthy and fit for duty.

Jenna drew in deep breaths of cooled air through her nose, expanding her chest until it almost burst. She was fine. Fine as she'd ever been. She could handle it. She always handled it.

She glanced in the rear-view mirror as she edged along the road and idled the car so she could squeeze it into one of the rare spaces along the narrow lane where most of the Georgian or Victorian houses, due to their age, had no drive. They'd not needed drives before the invention of cars.

She caught herself chewing at her bottom lip and sighed.

When Mason was with her, she probably handled the little spikes in stress much better. So he never saw the blanket of fear draped over her for small snatches of time. He never witnessed the clamp of control she exerted every time her heart ratcheted up a beat. Something she knew had never happened until nine months ago, then one major event after the other had stretched her nerves to the limit.

Stretched but not broken.

She blew out a slow, smooth breath. No, she didn't need a counsellor any longer. She knew the techniques, understood how to keep everything under control. How to block, how to release.

Except on a bad day.

On those days, the little wisps of pain sneaked under the wire to torment her. Days like today when her resistance was low.

6

Jenna drew up behind the ambulance with its lights blazing and back doors wide open, sirens silent.

The heat of the day evaporated in an icy chill of premonition as she turned off the engine, unclipped her safety belt, opened the door and stepped out of the car. She turned, aimed the fob at the car and pressed the lock button.

Even the blazing sunshine couldn't chase away the cold unease that crept across the back of her neck in sharp little prickles.

She scraped her fingers through her thick, choppy hair to stop it sticking to her scalp as she crossed the narrow cobblestone street, focusing her attention on five onlookers from the quiet widespread neighbourhood. Concerned neighbours, or plain nosey, they'd have their use in the small community.

Raising her ID in the air, Jenna stepped up to them. 'Morning, I'm DS Jenna Morgan, everything okay here?'

At their wide-eyed looks, she threw them what she hoped was a reassuring smile, raising her eyebrows in something she knew resembled her mother the older she became.

'So, what have you heard?'

A desperate-eyed woman in her late thirties stepped forward. 'They said Imelda's had an accident. Fell and bashed her head.'

Jenna poked out her bottom lip as she nodded as though this was the first, she'd heard of the matter. Vagueness sometimes paid off, you got the feel for things. 'Anything else?'

'No, just to stay back.'

'Well, we would appreciate that, and obviously as soon as we know anything further, I'm sure we'll let you know.'

She circled her gaze around, a quick assessment of who the ladies were, aware that shortly she would most likely need to announce the demise of the poor woman to her neighbours. She'd gauge their reactions.

'Was it a fight?' With discontented lines pulling at her mouth, an older woman stepped forward, a spark of malicious interest lighting her eyes.

At this point, Jenna had no idea, nor had there been any hint of a domestic, so far. They were the questions that would need to be addressed.

She raised her eyebrows and didn't attempt to stop the woman in her onward rush to disseminate her knowledge.

'There's been a lot of noise coming from there recently.'

Irritation slid across the younger woman's face. 'No, Shelly, it won't have been a fight.' She tilted her head to one side in a quick challenge to the other woman and then turned to Jenna. 'They adore each other. I know Zak, he's lived here all his life.'

She jerked her chin towards the three-storey Victorian house that had the distinct look of a home someone had devoted time and loving attention to renovating. The painted windowsills without a speck of dust, the windows gleaming as though they'd recently been cleaned. The garden maintained a shabby, lived-in look. Perhaps they were working their way from inside to out.

The woman's voice drew Jenna back again. 'He's a lovely man, very gentle. His parents used to own the house, but they sold it to him a while ago so they could buy a smaller place with less work. He's in the middle of modernising it. Said they needed a little more space with the new baby coming along.' She turned her head to look at Shelly again. 'It will have been an accident. I'm sure Imelda will be fine.'

Aware of movement from the open doorway, Jenna mentally filed the information away as she cast the onlookers a quick, reassuring smile, not willing to impart the knowledge that Imelda had already departed this world. She needed to get inside and investigate, not stand around listening to gossip. Gossip had its place, though, and she always reserved the right to return to it.

She blew out a breath and then stepped through the old wooden gate as the small crowd talked in hushed voices behind her. They'd have more to talk about shortly when they discovered that Imelda was dead.

Jenna made her way towards the open front door of the tall Victorian house where the backs of the paramedics shielded the woman on the floor from inquisitive neighbours.

In her experience, most people watched, not necessarily out of a morbid sense of curiosity, but because they genuinely didn't know how to respond to a situation and simply wanted to help. And help they would if they could, but this was out of their hands.

Out of her hands, too, and in the hands of the double-crewed ambulance.

Jenna peered over the shoulder of the paramedic assistant who knelt on the floor at the woman's side. She frowned at the frenetic movement, her pulse kicking up a beat.

She squinted as she raked a quick gaze over the scene. It wasn't the incident she expected to be confronted with. Instead of slow and sympathetic, this was fast and frantic, indicating possible life.

Jenna blew out a surprised breath and bent over at the waist to get a better view. She rested her hands on her knees, but in the enclosed hallway she didn't have a clear view past the assistant's broad shoulders to double-check if the casualty was alive or not. From the activity, she'd roll with the assumption that she was alive.

'DS Jenna Morgan. Hi.'

'Hi.' With barely an acknowledgement that she existed, the paramedics continued to administer to the woman stretched out, feet closest to the door on the intricately patterned Victorian tiles.

Jenna had no expectation that they would take notice. Not until they were ready. Their priority was to tend to the wounded, save a life, not regale the police with information. That would come later.

She raised her head to glance beyond them at the desperate features of a tall, young man at the end of the hallway. Zak Cheetham-Epstein, she assumed. Husband of the injured woman and the person who'd called the incident in. She may have to listen to the recording later for verification, but right now, she assessed the man in front of her.

Strain lines feathered out from blue eyes darkened almost to navy while the peachy colour that should tinge his cheeks had leached out to leave him grey and pallid. The thick black flop of his hair over his furrowed forehead accentuated the paleness of his skin.

His broad shoulders curled forward in a self-conscious roll and his slender frame appeared to collapse in on itself. With his gaze fixed on his wife, Jenna knew he had no awareness of anyone or anything, but the agony he suffered, which pulsed out from him while he remained silent, his long, bony fingers clenching and unclenching. Shock hit people in different ways at different times, as she well understood from personal experience.

Jenna moved her gaze on, to take in everything so when she wrote her notes up later, she could recall the scene in the minutest detail.

Beside Zak stood one of her stalwart uniforms, almost bringing a smile of relief to her face, before she stopped it in time and nudged her chin up in silent acknowledgement as her gaze met the cool, calm and collected one of PC Ted Walker. The curl of warm gratitude circled in her stomach at the same time as the conflicting spark of defence pushed her shoulders back, so she stood erect.

He knew what she'd been through, just as the whole of the station did. But Ted Walker's experience was ingrained, and he took care to veil the sympathy, if any lurked in him.

A true professional, he'd seen so much in a long career that was just drawing through to its twilight years. Not that he allowed it to affect his work. If anything, she suspected they'd have to drag him kicking and screaming from the station when his time was done. If you cut him through the middle, he'd have the words 'police officer' written all the way through, like a stick of Blackpool rock.

As the paramedic shuffled around and opened up the view, Jenna took the opportunity to skim her gaze from the soles of the casualty's dainty little pink bunny rabbit socks all the way to the top of her bloodstained head, pausing momentarily to take in the gentle swell of her stomach to confirm that Imelda was indeed pregnant, as voiced by one of her neighbours. Gossip. It proved once again to have its use.

Jenna swallowed as she continued her check, culminating at

the puddle of blood the other paramedic had his knee in which spread out over the broken and cracked tiles.

In a vicious slap, shock struck her, and she sucked in a long breath through her teeth. Her muscles turned to liquid and her head reeled as she blinked away the flood of crimson, edged with darkness, that filled her vision.

A head trauma.

She closed her eyes, then flashed them open again as the image of PC Lee Gardner's head exploding in a shower of blood, bone and grey matter sneaked beneath her defences to squeeze a cruel fist around her insides.

She puffed out a heavy breath and stared at the slow filter of blood as the pool of it haloed out from the lifeless woman's head.

Weak-kneed, Jenna wilted against the hallway wall with the knowledge that even if she fainted, none of them would bat an eyelid. They'd carry on with their jobs in order of priority, so she'd better make it more of a genteel slide down the wall, rather than a face-plant-the-floor kind of faint.

If she had the energy to move, she'd take herself outside. Although that wasn't an option with the neighbours lined up out there. She didn't even want to imagine what they'd think of a police officer collapsing in front of them.

She hauled in a long, slow breath and drew on every ounce of inner strength she had. She was strong. She had this. The feeling would pass. It was purely a reminder of recent events, paired with lack of food and a dip in her blood sugar levels from drinking too much the night before. For the sake of self-preservation, she kept her back against the wall and slid further down until she rested on her haunches. It gave her the opportunity to put her head between her knees if she needed to, and without any of them taking much notice of what must be a very pasty, sweat-filmed face, they would assume she was getting down on a level with them. If it did come to the worst, she was closer to the floor, with less chance of her doing herself an injury if she keeled over.

She puffed out her cheeks and then released the breath she'd been holding. Bloody hell. She tipped her head back and blinked away the threatening blackness. She'd be damned if she gave in. The unexpected sight had whipped under her defences. But it was momentary. She had a handle on it.

As the activity around her intensified, Jenna blocked off everything other than the scene in front of her. She pushed aside the black clouds threatening her and squinted at the paramedic. His fast, efficient moves and intense concentration weren't those of someone verifying a death, but of someone fighting to preserve a life.

She cleared her throat, not to attract attention but more to release the paralysing hold shock had on her throat and encourage words from her mouth.

'The shout said she was dead.' Her voice croaked out in a gruff whisper so it didn't carry to the casualty's husband. Jenna appreciated the quick shake of the paramedic's head to confirm otherwise. She'd get nothing further from him, she wasn't his concern, the casualty was, but a quick sense of relief brought heat rushing back to her face and strength seeped back into her muscles.

The woman wasn't dead. Just injured. How badly, Jenna couldn't guess. She needed to wait for that information from the paramedics when they were ready.

She turned her head and met the gaze of the paramedic assistant as he handed over a needle and trocar to the paramedic.

'We need to get a line in fast. Al's going to give her tranexamic acid.'

She raised a brow to query, and he turned away to pick up

more equipment. This time, she recognised the syringes and bag of infusion fluid. 'What does that do?'

The assistant continued, keeping his voice low as he sorted through further equipment with neat precision. 'Tranexamic acid is used for rapid clotting of the blood. We need to slow it down, she's lost a lot.' He shrugged. 'Head trauma and GCS of eleven. We need it done before HEMS arrive.'

HEMS was the Helicopter Emergency Medical Services, which came equipped with a doctor, a nurse, very possibly more. The request for HEMS indicated the severity of the injury.

She glanced at the woman's feet. Not as severe as dead.

Jenna rolled her lips inward as she tried to imagine exactly where the helicopter could land in the steep hills of the Ironbridge gorge.

As if he could read her mind, the assistant raised his head, a crooked smile played across his lips. 'Coalbrookdale and Ironbridge School. We've used it before. They won't take long from there. Three minutes once they land. It gives Al time to prep so they can walk in and RSI her.'

Drawing a blank, Jenna frowned. 'RSI?'

'Rapid sequence induction.' He threw some of the equipment from the floor back into his bag and screwed up some of the debris Al had tossed down in his haste. 'They're going to have to put her in a coma before they transport her. That's a serious head injury. Possible skull fracture.'

Her own weakness forgotten in a blink, Jenna ran her gaze over the little woman flat out on the tiles, her attention zoomed in on the small bump. 'What about the baby?'

The assistant's mouth tightened, and he gave a slight shake of his head as he looked down at Imelda. 'Currently the baby seems okay. There's no sign of distress. Pulse and heart rate are fine. The oxygen levels from mum are good, but obviously if that fails...'

meaning if Imelda died, '... then a caesarean is an option as the foetus is viable at this age.' He glanced up and shot her a regretful smile. 'That means we need to get her stable enough to transport to hospital as soon as possible to get her on life support if required. HEMS will be here any moment, the doctor will make that call.'

At the loud thwack of helicopter rotors, Jenna raised her head and blew out a fast breath. It was a day of reminders. The last time she'd attended an incident which involved a helicopter, it was for a missing person and an injured dog. The missing person had turned out to be her sister and the injured dog had been Domino, Fliss's Dalmatian.

A lifetime ago it felt, but less than a year in reality and yet the thrum, thrum, thrum of whirling rotor blades flashed through her mind to transport her back. It didn't help that it was the same area as her sister had disappeared. Everything converged to send the reminder slicing through her.

Jerking her back to reality, the paramedic assistant's voice, filled with urgency, cut through her reverie. 'You've got three minutes to move before they burst in and trash your crime scene even more than we already have.'

With a static flash, her mind engaged, and Jenna whipped her gaze along the length of the little woman on the floor. The pool of blood, smeared and smudged from the movement of Al, the knees of his bottle green uniform soaked in it. The splash of it reached high up the pale cream painted wall, spuming out in a pattern that could have come from flicking a paintbrush. Only it wasn't paint. It was bright scarlet blood.

Jenna frowned as she leaned in closer, narrowing her eyes to follow the splatter pattern as she spoke to the assistant. 'I was told she'd taken a fall.'

'So were we. Bit of a confusing one. Initially we were informed the husband had told the operator his wife had slipped in the front hallway, bashed her head and was dead.'

'Yep.' She agreed so far.

'On that information, Al there checked her carotid artery and found she was still alive.'

'Good.'

'Yeah. Only...'

'Only, what?'

The assistant did a slow head turn until his cool blue gaze met hers and he lowered his voice. 'Have you seen her face?' He flashed the husband a quick glance before he lowered his head and moved his equipment bag to one side.

She'd not had a decent look at the casualty's face with Al's back partially blocking the view. She shook her head and then pushed to her feet so she could peer over the top of the paramedic.

Still unable to grab a decent view, she bent low, so she came nose to nose with the assistant. 'What am I missing?'

Lips barely moving, the assistant handed off another syringe to Al, who ignored them both as he administered to his patient. 'You don't normally get your face slashed open by falling backwards.' He raised his eyebrows before he ducked his head and continued to sort through his equipment. 'Or a bruised chin. Like someone maybe smashed their fist into it.'

Jenna straightened. With grim determination, she did a slow

turn and faced Zak Cheetham-Epstein across the hallway. The desperation lining his face did nothing to her emotions, but she sorted through the steps she now needed to take as the case took on a different route. Accidental fall was a whole lot different to full-frontal attack or domestic abuse. Whichever it turned out to be, Jenna had an investigation to conduct.

Face blank to cover any signs of suspicion, Jenna squeezed herself against the hallway wall to make her way past the casualty and both the ambulance crew. When she reached the end nearest the woman's head, she took the opportunity to get a better view.

This time, she managed to block any personal memories and feelings as ice washed over her heart to give her the clarity and direction she needed. The woman was injured. The paramedic may well save her life, but Jenna was about to represent her and gain justice. She belonged to Jenna now. She was one of her casualties.

Three steps further on and she turned her back on the stricken woman to place herself between her and Zak Cheetham-Epstein. Her prime suspect. She caught Ted Walker's calm gaze and hoped the seriousness transmitted from her to him in one long look. Time was of the essence before HEMS moved in and whipped the woman away. There was certain evidence they needed.

'Mr Cheetham-Epstein?' At his stunned nod, she recognised the shock setting in but continued. 'The helicopter has landed with a doctor on board to tend to your wife.' She reached out to touch his elbow, directing his attention away from what was going on behind her. 'Let's go through to your living room and give them the space they need to work.'

Glazed eyes moved slowly past her and back again to focus on her. 'But I need to be here, she might need me. Imelda...'

'We're about to be overrun with medics of one kind or

another, let's move out of their way and give your wife the best chance. They need to help her and we're going to get under their feet.'

His mouth tightened as he nodded, and she took the opportunity to skim a quick glance over him, her gaze taking in dust and blood-smeared hands and what appeared to be wood shavings scattered over his white T-shirt.

He turned to lead the short way down the hall to the room at the end while Jenna took the opportunity to make a quick assessment of his black trainers which left bloodstained smears across the hallway. Any further blood would be evident once they checked the trainers. It could wait until SOCO arrived. She couldn't assume at this stage he was guilty of anything. Many a police officer had leapt in with an assumption of guilt, the papers got hold of it and some innocent person became persecuted. All because the police rushed a matter. There was no rush. Evidence gathering was the bread and butter of their job.

Zak led her into the kitchen. She assumed he'd chosen it instead of the living room in order to keep one eye on the proceedings in the hall. That wouldn't be an option for him.

As she passed Ted Walker, she looked him dead in the eye and kept her voice low. 'Ted, can you get your bodycam up close and personal. As much footage as possible. I have a feeling we may need to use it. Get that blood-splatter pattern up the wall before someone's PPE'd backside smears it off.' She knew in the close confines of the hallway, the medics wouldn't be concerned with evidence. Their job was to save the life of the woman on the floor.

With nothing but a brief nod of acknowledgement, PC Walker touched the small, black, box-shaped device on his chest to show it was already activated, the little red flashing light indicated it was live. He stepped beyond her to get in close to the team working on Imelda.

Confident it would have been live when Ted arrived at the house, and they may have some relevant footage, Jenna left him to it and followed Zak through to the kitchen.

Jenna swung the door closed behind them to reduce the noise level and prevent distractions for Zak, aware she needed his full attention in those vital minutes straight after an incident, where his defences were compromised. The likelihood was that anything he said in that time would be the bald truth, or so obviously a lie borne of sheer terror that it would be transparent.

The flash of panic on his face as she shut out access to his wife stayed, his eyes rolling to reveal the white.

'Zak. Can I call you Zak?' she began.

He nodded. His hands linked together at his waist with knuckles turning white hinted at the anguish, but there was no room for sympathy for this man. One step at a time. There was nothing he could physically do to help his wife unless the man was a brain surgeon. If he had been, he would have taken charge of the situation.

'Zak, would you like a cup of tea?' The all-time solution for everything from exhaustion to shock, the mere suggestion of it an ice-breaker, the making of it a comfort and the drinking of it a natural sedative.

Zak shook his head and as his desperate gaze clashed with hers, he blew out a breath, unlinked his long, bony fingers and threw both hands on his head, scrubbing at his scalp. 'What happened? I don't understand what happened.' He strode away from her across the narrow kitchen which overlooked the back garden and valley below. He swung around and faced her.

She waited. Evidently Zak wasn't a talker, but he internalised. She needed him to share the frantic thoughts flashing over his features. 'Walk me through it. What happened this morning, Zak?'

He raked his fingers down his face, so his skin stretched, and she saw the whites of his eyes. 'Nothing out of the ordinary.' He dropped his hands from his face and placed them on his hips as he gathered himself, his mind obviously struggling to focus. He blew out a breath and, as he frowned, a deep crease appeared between his eyes to run vertically down his brow to the top of his nose. 'We're doing the place up. With the baby on the way, we need more space.'

Jenna said nothing but let the quiet man continue, taking note of the tremor in his fingers as he circled his hand in the air.

'We're limited. We can't go out any further, but we decided we could make more of the top storey, bashing through a wall and so on.' He bounced his head like a nodding dog as though it comforted him, raking through the mundane to steady himself. He plucked at his bottom lip with thumb and forefinger. 'I needed to sand the door down. The paint was cracked and peeling, so Imelda brought Joshua down for a snooze.'

Before she could ask who Joshua was, Zak's eyes flew wide with horror.

'Joshua!'

He made a dash for the door and Jenna stepped into his space to stop him, her hand held up to his chest. 'Joshua?'

Zak jerked to a stop before he collided with her hand. 'Our little boy. Joshua. Oh, my God, Joshie, he's only eleven months old.'

Shock rippled through her. There'd been no sign of a child. No indication.

She frowned, her mind whirring. The neighbour had said there was a baby on its way, but she'd not mentioned a child.

He darted his gaze around the kitchen as though the little boy would suddenly appear. 'Imelda brought him down so he could grab a nap. I forgot.' He almost ripped his hair from his scalp. 'How could I forget?'

Because the man's thoughts had been consumed by the glut of blood spreading from his wife's scalp. Shock did that. A temporary amnesia wasn't unknown. When the mind closed out every thought except the most important one. At that point, the most important thing was to get help for Imelda. Which he'd done.

Now the numbness had worn off, his mind was free to expand and think of other things. Like his son who was apparently napping somewhere.

With fast breaths escalating, Jenna knew it was a matter of seconds before the tall young man in front of her went into full panic mode, which would do none of them any good.

His voice rose an octave in full horror. 'How could I have forgotten him? Why didn't I think? I need to check him. Now.'

She whisked a glance down at his blood-streaked hands and considered the need to wrap them in plastic bags until SOCO arrived but thought better of it as the man's pale features drained even more. It could wait. There was blood everywhere, it didn't need to be exclusively sampled from his hands. He just needed not to touch anything until they had taken photographs.

To slow him down, Jenna engaged him again. 'You say your wife put him to bed?'

'Yeah. He's a handful at the moment. Just got his feet under him, racing all over the place like a drunken squirrel.'

At her slightly panicked stare, he expanded. 'He wobbles all over the place. Does crab like runs and then slaps down on the floor.'

'Right. But he's in bed now?'

He nodded with flustered enthusiasm and went to move past her once more. Again, Jenna stepped into his path. She couldn't have him racing all over the house in a blind panic looking for a child, buggering up her crime scene by treading his blood-stained trainers everywhere.

And it was a crime. Within fifteen minutes, it had gone from accident to possible assault. If Imelda didn't make it, it could be manslaughter or murder. No doubt about it in her mind. There'd been a crime committed.

A clever person would use any excuse to cover their tracks.

It would be interesting to get Jim Downey, the Chief Forensics Officer's view on that. She could imagine him clucking his tongue against the roof of his mouth while he scratched the top of his balding head as he assessed the carnage the medics left.

Any other situation, and he'd slice his own officers open with his sharp tongue for trashing a crime scene. This was a matter of necessity every officer and scenes of crime member understood and appreciated. Preservation of life. First and foremost. If the paramedics and doctors trashed the scene, there was nothing that could be done about it. The best any police officer could do was ensure it wasn't compromised any more than it needed to be. Like allowing a suspect to crawl all over the house with blood stained hands and feet.

'It's okay, Zak.' She needed to keep him calm, reassure him. 'These things happen. I'm sure he's safe.'

'Yes. I need to check on him. Please let me pass.'

'There's nothing to worry about, but we don't want you going past the paramedics while they're tending to your wife.'

Eyes glazed, he stared at her. 'Could you check? I need to know...' His voice cracked. He scraped his fingers down his cheeks, so his skin pulled down as his eyes filled with tears. 'Oh, God. I need to see him. How could I forget him? How?' The last word came out on an agonised howl that resonated in Jenna's heart.

It was only a matter of a few precious minutes since he'd found his wife and made the call. A few minutes longer since they'd all descended on him. She wasn't sure how Joshua could still be asleep, but there was always the possibility. She had no idea, no experience with babies. It wasn't her place to judge and a coolness flooded in so she could deal with the job at hand. Imelda was being taken care of so Jenna's prime priority was to check on the child.

'I can do that, but I need you to stay calm, Zak. Tell me where Joshua is sleeping, and I'll check on him right now.'

His hand fluttered skywards. 'Yes. Top of the stairs. First door on the left.'

A tall, lean man, even at her height, Jenna found herself having to look up at Zak. She held his gaze with hers and tried to convey the seriousness of the matter without sending him into a frenzy.

'Zak, I need you to stay right where you are.' Aware she had no backup other than Ted Walker, she needed to ensure Zak didn't move, didn't touch anything. Not until SOCO arrived. 'Zak.' His gaze locked with hers and understanding shimmered in his narrowed eyes. 'PC Walker is outside the door, if you need him, but I need you to stay right where you are while I check on Joshua. Understood?'

One short, sharp nod was all she needed as she took off out of the kitchen door.

She stepped into the hallway and pulled the door closed behind her.

The cacophony of sound melded into one mash-up at the arrival of HEMS as they surged into the front hall and threw kit down on the floor, all over the crime scene like flies on a piece of shit. It wasn't lack of respect, but a heightened awareness that this fragile life was under threat.

Al stood up and stepped back to let the doctor in, almost reversing into Jenna.

She backed up and then slipped around him. Jenna sent a quick glance over to PC Walker, back to her, concentrating on his own part of the job. She stepped in close and touched his elbow to gain his attention. 'Ted, apparently there's a toddler here. Eleven months old, upstairs asleep.'

Doubt shot over Ted's face. 'Asleep? With all of this going on. Bloody hell, Sarg, I would have thought you'd hear him screaming the walls down.'

Jenna tended to agree with him, but she knew little of children's sleep patterns. 'I'm going to run upstairs and check on him.' She cast a glance at the closed kitchen door. 'Watch Mr Cheetham-Epstein.'

He kept his voice low as he nodded his acknowledgement. 'I'll make sure he doesn't come out.'

Jenna sucked in a breath as she squeezed past the medics and took the narrow stairways to the next storey, sprinting two at a time, taking a quick glance at the time on her iPhone.

Damn, but time was racing away.

8

At the neat square landing on the first floor, Jenna considered her options as she stood in the middle of a wide expanse of hallway, four white-painted wooden doors, all closed against the threat of dust from the next storey up, an indication of a nice, tidy lifestyle. Something she'd long since abandoned hope of in her own personal life. It wasn't possible since Fliss and her raging Dalmatian had moved in. Not to mention Adrian and Mason, their boyfriends, edging their way into their lives and a house which when she first bought it had been more than adequate for her single status. Not so any more. But she wouldn't have it any other way. She'd learnt to live with the hustle and bustle, the lack of privacy, the race for her own kitchen.

She angled her head to one side to listen, the soft buzz of her tinnitus doing little other than providing a quiet white sound. Nothing. No sound of a little one. No crying, no happy sounds she imagined a toddler would make if they were awake but content. She could only hope he was fast asleep and had missed the entire episode, but a niggle of doubt circled. Wouldn't a child have been disturbed by all the noise, the activity?

She nudged open the first door on the left as per Zak's instructions and peeped inside to reveal a beautiful, light, fresh nursery in hues of mellow, reflective cream which prismed the sunlight over the room in soft haloes. They'd made it light and bright, a border around the middle with a display of sweet cartoon elephants in muted greens and blues, yellows and pinks. Something for all eventualities. She suspected they'd kept it neutral rather than an obvious boy/girl choice.

North-facing and several degrees cooler, Jenna stepped inside and closed the door behind her to take advantage of the opportunity to reduce her body temperature for a few precious moments while she checked on the toddler.

Her throat tightened as she flicked her gaze around. The silence a heavy blanket with no feeling of a presence within. Its emptiness echoed in the large, airy room. Jenna blew out a restricted breath as she stepped up to the high-sided cot and stared inside at the mattress, empty but for the thin, powder-blue cotton sheet and the little fluffy grey toy rabbit propped up in the top left corner.

She circled on the spot, while her pulse kicked up to send a rhythmic throb through her ears to block out the sounds of activity from below.

As she engaged Airwaves, grabbing Morris King with a deep sense of relief, she cruised her gaze around the room.

'Morris, patch me through to DI Taylor if he's there.'

'He's here, just popped in to tidy up some paperwork. Said he didn't want to be disturbed.'

'Disturb him for me.'

There was a brief pause before the radio clicked through.

'DI Taylor.' His clipped tones indicated that whatever reason she'd disturbed him for, it had better be good. 'Go ahead, Sergeant Morgan.'

Jenna marched across the room and reached out with her free hand to turn an ornate Victorian brass knob. She clamped down on the panic that threatened to strangle the words she needed to spit out as she raised the police radio to her lips. 'Sir.' She cleared her throat. 'Sir... A quick update for you.'

'Yes.'

She swung the door open to the vast wardrobe where a child could hide, except for the fact that she'd just turned a neat little brass key before she'd opened it. Locked from the outside, it would prove impossible for a child to close themselves in.

Regardless, she searched inside. Never assume.

'The sudden death in Coalbrookdale, sir, is not a sudden death.'

'That's good news.'

'Not really, sir. The woman is alive with trauma to the head. Lots of blood. HEMS have arrived and there's pandemonium at present. I'm not comfortable with the scene, sir.'

'Okay.'

Static crackled out across the silence and she appreciated that her inspector kept quiet while she filled him in with the situation. 'The paramedic says that for a woman who, by all intents, fell backwards, she has a gash on her face and a fat bruise forming on her chin... as though she's been hit.' She gave him a brief moment to absorb the information as she crouched down to scan inside the wardrobe, pushing aside the neat little row of clothes hanging there. She patted the wooden floor and reached to the back before she settled on her haunches, frustration stirring inside her.

As she straightened, she puffed out a breath. 'I've placed Zak Cheetham-Epstein, the husband, in the kitchen. Seems to be in genuine shock. I only have one back up, PC Ted Walker, who is currently scene guard in the hall. He has his bodycam on and recording what he can, but, as you will appreciate, the scene is chaotic.' Hell was a better description. 'He's also ensuring the husband remains separate and doesn't move from the kitchen, so forensics aren't compromised. I have no one in with the husband presently.' She pushed the door closed and turned the brass key to lock it again.

'Why not?' Surprise edged through his voice. 'What are you doing?'

Her gaze skimmed the room, onto the next potential hidey hole. She slipped open a door to the small cupboard under the changing table and ducked down to peer inside. Nothing.

'Searching, sir. My priority is more concerning. Their toddler, Joshua, sir. Mr Cheetham-Epstein was under the impression he'd been put down in his cot for a nap by his mum just before the incident took place.'

'But...?'

She closed the cupboard door and straightened as she scraped her hair back from her forehead with one hand. 'But I don't think he's here.'

The taste in her mouth turned sour as she scoured the room once more. Nowhere else for a small child to hide.

'I haven't had chance to check the rest of the house, but don't toddlers stay where you put them?'

At the soft snort on the other end of the line, Jenna considered she may have said the wrong thing.

'I'd like to think he's somewhere in the house, but the front door was wide open, apparently, when Zak discovered his wife flat out on the floor.' She spoke her thoughts out loud to gauge his reaction. 'Perhaps she hadn't put Joshua to bed. She may have changed her mind. Zak claims to have been upstairs. Maybe Joshua saw what happened, tried to rouse her, get her to respond.' She envisaged a toddler squatting beside his mum, chubby fingers poking at her cheek, and blinked the image away.

Facts. She dealt in facts.

Jenna circled around while she cast a quick glance at the wide windows and stepped over to test them.

Locked.

Relieved, she turned away. 'Maybe he went to find daddy.' Her mind trawled through the myriad of possibilities as she vocalised, trying to get inside an eleven-month-old's thoughts. Their abilities. She'd no idea the physical abilities of a child that age. What could they do? What were they capable of? She studied the high sides of the cot bed. Was he skilful enough to get out on his own? It seemed terribly high for a toddler to scale.

Her mind spun with possibilities now he wasn't where she'd expected him to be. Questions fired in her head. What vocabulary did they have? Would he cry, or go silent and hide?

Keep it simple, realistic. If he witnessed what happened, how would a child respond to his mummy being hurt? Where would Joshua go? What did he see?

What if Zak was lying?

She lowered her voice as she ran the possibility past her DI. 'Maybe Mummy and Daddy had a fight.' She circled around. 'Or Mummy fell, hit her head. Perhaps it was an accident.'

Taylor's soft tones came through the radio. 'SOCO will verify either way.'

Jenna turned her back on the window and squinted. 'Perhaps with the door open, Joshua wandered out, simply interested in the surrounding area that he's possibly restricted from seeing, or maybe he trotted away, worried, stressed, unable to understand what happened to Mummy. It's all happened in a short time-frame; he can't be far, sir. He's only eleven months old.'

'I have a grandson that age.'

She drew in a breath. 'I can't find him. He's not in the nursery, sir.'

The long silence told her everything. DI Taylor had a personal involvement. His grandson was the same age. Same sex. It made it personal, whether he wanted it to or not. They may be police officers, but they all had a heart and a weak spot, or possibly just empathy and understanding. An incident may happen to open their eyes to a victim's plight, give them more of an insight into their own emotions. It could make a better officer of them.

It had happened to Jenna. Life had never been the same since her sister had been kidnapped. It had taken another diversion again since she'd witnessed a colleague shot in front of her, half his grey matter sprayed over her.

DI Taylor's voice cut through the building tinnitus to drag her back. 'Jesus, kids. If they're not terrorising you, keeping you on your toes, giving you the run-around, then they're giving you a mild heart attack. Just when you think you have them pinned down, sussed out, they turn around and surprise you again. The fear never stops.'

As a grandparent, she suspected he felt the fear more than he had as a parent.

'Zak's fear appeared real, sir. He's beating himself up because he never thought straight away about his son. He was fully focused on Imelda. There's a lot of blood from the head injury.'

'That's not unusual. Probably in shock.'

'He feels he should have thought of Joshua sooner.'

'What do you feel?'

She cast her mind back. 'Either he's a bloody good actor, or his response was genuine. He's traumatised, both by his wife's 'accident' and because he forgot about his son momentarily.'

'He's going to be a whole lot more traumatised if you can't find his son.'

She drew in a long breath, the dread of informing Zak that his son was nowhere to be found tightened her jaw as she clenched down while Taylor's voice cut in.

'He could be anywhere. Under the stairs. Hiding because he's frightened. Asleep somewhere because he hasn't a clue what's going on. We've had it happen with us when grandma and I were on grandchild duty.'

She almost spluttered at the surprise personal insight but held onto the laughter before it came out. It was rare for DI Taylor to expose his private life in such detail.

'Little devil was under my desk, fast asleep with our Benji.'

She remembered Taylor's golden retriever. Huge, hairy and a great alternative for a child's cuddly toy. Soft and gentle, she could imagine the dog was the perfect childminder.

Jenna narrowed her eyes and surveyed the room while she was speaking with Taylor. There'd been no mention of a dog, or pet of any kind, but then Zak's shock had wiped his memory clean of his son for a few precious minutes.

She plucked her bottom lip between her thumb and forefinger. The place didn't have a dog. It was too sterile. No pet hairs. No indication. She cast her mind back, nothing in the kitchen to indicate animals, no water or food bowls.

She raised the radio to her mouth again to cut out any noise that filtered through from the hallway. 'DI Taylor, sir, I could do with some uniform backup. I can't imagine he's gone far, but the more eyes, the better.'

Knowing the man as she did, it wouldn't surprise her if he visited the scene himself. A strong police officer, a PC for years before he was promoted, he still held a belief in keeping his feet on solid ground and didn't hesitate to engage in front-line policing if he felt it was required. He'd roll his sleeves up, muck in. And had the respect of every officer on the force for that ability. He'd turn up on the pretext that he was overseeing, when in fact the man hankered after getting his teeth into a project. Whether he did with this one, she'd leave that decision to him.

'I'm certain we'll find Joshua in the house somewhere. If he wasn't in bed, if he was with his mum at the time, he's more than likely been frightened by whatever happened. Could be our only witness. I'd suggest we have backup on standby to start a search and possible house-to-house if I fail to find him here. Could do with an extra few pairs of eyes in the meanwhile.'

'It's all in hand, Sergeant Morgan. Morris had them all lined up on standby while he listened to the paramedic response.'

Relieved DI Taylor and Morris had that side of things in hand, Jenna paused with one hand on the brass doorknob as she cast one last look around the room. There was no point in retracing her steps. It was empty. There was nowhere else for the toddler to hide.

'Acknowledged.'

'The only thing we can't do is get the helicopter up in the air if you need a neighbourhood search, not until the Air Ambulance has cleared the area.'

She understood that too. The airspace around the gorge would be too constricted. They'd need one out, one in.

She turned the knob and swung the door open, almost swallowing her tongue as a huge figure stepped from the shadowed hallway into her space.

'Bloody hell, Mason, what the hell are you playing at?'

It took a mere split second for the surprise on his face to whip away and be replaced by his boyish smile. 'Hey, Sarg. Good to see you too.'

Her heart stumbled, and then raced on. 'Jesus Christ, I nearly shit myself.'

He gurgled out an unrepentant laugh. 'And here was me thinking you'd missed me.'

'Missed you?' She absolutely had. She just hadn't realised it until that moment. He was exactly the person she needed by her side, someone she could rely on. Someone who knew her mind as well as she did and would do exactly what she needed him to do.

She stepped into the hall and clicked the nursery door shut behind her, her heart still whipping up a storm. 'Jesus Christ,' she whispered under her breath this time as she poked DC Mason Ellis, her partner and her sister's boyfriend, in the chest with the hard tip of her index fingernail. 'What are you doing here?'

He moved back to allow her some room and him some relief from bruises her insistent prodding might inflict. 'I nipped into the station to do that paperwork I said I needed to shift, but they told me you'd been called out to an incident.' He rubbed his hand across his chest where she'd poked him. 'I think the official term is procrastination.' He jerked his chin in the direction of downstairs. 'It's chaos down there, Ted said I'd find you up here.' He cast a gaze around the neat, naked hallway and winked. 'Trying to get away from it all?'

She shook her head as his attention returned to her. 'They have a little boy, eleven-month-old. Apparently just started walking, still wobbly.' At his raised eyebrows, Jenna repeated what she'd been told. 'Like a drunken squirrel.'

A smile broke out on his face so deep brackets crinkled his cheeks.

'The husband, Zak, tells me he believes his wife, Imelda, had put him down to sleep before she went downstairs.'

'Right.' In anticipation of a problem, the grin dropped from his face.

Jenna thumbed in the direction of the door she'd closed behind her. 'That's the nursery. It's empty.'

Surprise flickered over his features, so she hit him with another piece of information. Didn't harm to have another opinion before her mind gathered speed and raced off in the wrong direction.

'Paramedic thinks there may be foul play. Imelda has a gash to her face.'

Mason's eyebrows lowered. 'Okay.'

'She fell backwards and smashed her head on the tiles.'

'Ah!'

'Yes. Ah.'

'Are we saying a little help may have preceded the fall?' Mason asked.

Jenna covered her face with her hands while she thought, pressing her fingertips into her screwed-up eyes. 'I really don't want to believe it of him.' She dropped her hands from her face. She stepped her way across the hall to the next door.

'He seems really nice. Genuine. Desperate.'

Mason's brow wrinkled. 'Desperation's a strange thing. Is he desperate with concern? Worry?'

With her back to the door, so she still faced him, she turned the door handle and knew she could rely on Mason's bright mind to work its way through the case along the same lines as her own thoughts.

He met her gaze, the tough policeman showing through. 'Is it borne of guilt?'

9

Sunshine poured through the vast windows overlooking the gorge and filled the beautiful bedroom with golden warmth without the stuffy heat. An inviting room with swathes of white linen, which Jenna assumed belonged to Zak and Imelda.

She raised her eyebrows at Mason. 'Hardly a practical choice with a child.'

'Not something you could have with a bloody Dalmatian.'

'Maybe babies are cleaner than dogs.' She couldn't imagine they were.

'Not as much fur and footprints. Easy to keep a place clean and tidy until the kid reaches full-on "all hell has broken loose" stage, which I suspect he's about to at that age if he's just started to walk.'

She dropped to her knees on the floor and flipped up the valance to search under the huge bed. With nothing under there, not even, it seemed any dust motes, Jenna tugged the valance back into place and came to her feet. A minimalist room with beautiful furniture and very few places for a toddler to hide, it took her a few more minutes to check inside the walk-through changing room lined with clothes hung in colour-coordinated perfection while Mason circled the main bedroom.

'Perhaps he has attempted to murder her.'

She spun around to look at Mason through narrowed eyes as he lifted the lid on a cream ottoman with antique gold appliqué along the edges and poked inside. 'Jesus, who could be so flawless?'

'Who would want to be?' Mason shrugged. 'I prefer something a little more lived in. Less... perfect. Shabby.'

Prepared to take offence, Jenna whipped the immaculately draped curtains back and took a peep behind them. 'Would you be implying my house is shabby?'

A little choked laughter burst out as Mason made his way to the bedroom door and held it open for her to precede him. 'I would never imply such a thing.'

She gave him a heartbeat of a moment to make his follow-up.

'Lived in would be more the term I would use.'

'It never used to be "lived in", not until you bloody lot descended on it.'

He nudged her with his elbow as she passed him. 'You'd not be without us though.'

She couldn't dispute it.

Sweat gathered in the hollow of her throat the moment he closed the door on the coolness of the bedroom. She centred herself back on the landing and opened the next door, the hope she had of finding the little boy there, crushed immediately.

Jenna looked at the wide expanse of a surprisingly bright and airy bathroom.

Huge roll-top cast-iron bath in bright white. An original, she'd guess, which appeared to have been recently re-enamelled.

'Nice bath.'

Her lips twitched. 'No matter how hot the water is, you'll still freeze your arse off on a cold day.' She knew from experience, and many years of living with her mum and sister in a dilapidated Victorian house her mum had never had enough money to do up. Cold and draughty hole that it was, they lived and loved there. There were few things she would have changed. Except the enamel bath. Unlike this one, their bath was never re-dipped and always had an ancient air of filthiness despite her mum scrubbing it to within an inch of its life. Which was precisely why there was no enamel left.

With dainty clawed feet and open sides, the bath perched neatly on a one-step dais and had nowhere for an infant to hide beneath, raised just a matter of four inches from the reclaimed Victorian black and white mosaic floor tiles. Jenna dropped to the floor and peered under just in case, unsure quite how small this eleven-month-old could be. A little disgusted with herself, she snorted as she came back to her feet and looked up at Mason.

'You'd have difficulty fitting a small kitten under there, never mind a child of any size.'

Not quite as neat and tidy, this room had a more lived in feel. With jade green towels to give the room warmth and a less clinical touch, a hand towel hung over a towel rail, with another draped over the side of the bath as though it had been discarded after a quick dry.

Jenna turned on the spot, with no need to walk deeper into the bathroom. Quite able to see the entire square room in one sweep.

The new white toilet and basin in front of the large, frosted window she assumed looked out over the road had nowhere for a child to hide. She resisted the temptation to open the window and check as she didn't want to rouse any further conjecture from the people in the street below.

Jenna moved the little white plastic step she imagined Joshua used to reach the sink where his PAW Patrol toothbrush lay abandoned next to a tube of toothpaste. Blue gel oozed out and clung to the side of the sink on its journey down to meet the white plastic lid that had skidded into the plughole. On the other side of the sink, two electric toothbrushes stood to attention with a Sensodyne pump dispenser placed in front.

Jenna opened the door to the little storage cupboard underneath the sink, just in case and tried to ignore the squeeze to her heart the sight of the little boy's existence brought. The small sign of messiness made him more real.

Zak and Imelda had obviously poured considerable love, effort and money into refurbishing the house with taste and thoughtfulness and the sterile perfection of it was just a little ruffled by the presence of their little boy trailing love and warmth through the room.

Mason leaned over next to her. 'It hardly gives off the vibes of a domestic-abuse situation.' She was inclined to agree. The whole atmosphere was one of mutual effort and decision-making. A team.

She pushed the door shut and stepped back into Mason who'd not bothered to move. He gave out a low grunt as her elbow connected with his ribs. 'You can never tell a book by its cover, Mason. You should know, not all domestics are low income.'

'Statistics say if they're female and come from a low-income family, they're three and a half times more likely to be abused.'

With a huge wet room she couldn't help but admire taking up the whole of one corner, Jenna swept her gaze all around. Again, nowhere to hide a child within the realms of the clear glassed space.

'Still, it's not exclusive.'

Mason grunted his agreement as he swung the door closed behind them.

Jenna took a brief glance at her iPhone for the umpteenth time: 12:20 p.m. She'd literally only been there fifty minutes from arrival to that moment, but time was ticking past and a child was still missing.

As she caught movement from below her, light relief tingled through her at the sight of her backup arriving.

She rested both hands on the stair banister and leaned over to smile at the woman making her way up from below. One of her favourite stalwarts – PC Donna McGuire. If she was on the job, there'd be no stone left unturned. She'd approach it with the calm, quiet confidence and experience both personality and maturity had developed.

Donna removed her hat and the blue-black swing of her short, sharp bob bounced light refractions from it as she dashed up the stairs. She raised her head and the liquid brown of her concerned gaze met Jenna's.

'Hey, Sarg. Missing child? I just heard.' She tilted her head and her hair swung in a curtain around her neck. 'No joy, yet?'

'No. But I haven't covered all the ground here.'

Jenna looked past Donna to the other officer beyond as she reached the top of the stairs. A light puff to her breathing and burnished flames over her rounded cheeks were a dead giveaway that the heat had already taken its toll on her. Still with her hat on, blonde hair pulled back in a tight bun with wisps escaping to stick to the fine sheen of sweat popping out on her temples and jawline, she raised her gaze to stare at Jenna.

Recognising her as one of the newer officers, one she'd struggled for a while to put a name to for some obscure reason but who'd recently become Donna's shadow. One she'd gained around the time PC Gardner had been shot. Which was probably why Jenna had memory loss with the woman's name.

The new officer hadn't made a bad move if she wanted to learn the job and still maintain a fresh outlook. There was no one better to teach her than Donna.

Jenna smiled at her to include her in their small group. 'You were quick.'

Donna took another step to pull up in front of her, leaving little room to manoeuvre at the top of the stairs, forcing Jenna to step back into the wide, sunlit space. 'Yeah, we'd already been dispatched by Morris. We were only down the road a way.' Her fast grin said it all. Everyone loved Morris. His attitude, his efficiency, his voice. Donna placed her hands on her hips and the smile slipped from her face as she nodded to the mess in the hallway below them. 'HEMS are here. We saw the helicopter up at Coalbrookdale school.'

'Yeah.' Jenna nodded. 'Serious head trauma. They're inducing a coma before they move her.'

'Bloody hell. It's a bloody mile and a half away, how do they get her down there?'

Jenna shook her head. That was one job she'd happily leave to the Air Ambulance crew.

The other woman huffed out a breath behind Donna and her name flashed into Jenna's mind like a revelation. PC Natalie Kempson. 'They're going to transport her by ambulance down the hill, then stick her in the helicopter. Nigel just told me.'

'Nigel?' Jenna asked.

'Yeah, he's my brother-in-law. Sort of.' She shrugged as though the matter was too complicated to explain.

On any other day, Jenna may have let Natalie run with it, but they were short of time. 'Good. Right, well, we have a missing toddler, that's all I know currently as I'd expected to find him in his cot. His dad assumed his mum had taken him for a nap. He's not where we expected to find him. We've checked the kitchen, the nursery.' She pointed at the closed doors in turn. 'The parent's bedroom and the bathroom. Which only leaves this one and upstairs. Donna, Natalie, if you want to take upstairs, Mason and I will finish off here. Let's get a clip on. It may not seem long, but he could have been missing some time now.'

Natalie nodded. 'Yes, Sarg.'

Both officers slid past Jenna and Mason, and as Natalie bolted up the next flight of stairs after Donna, Jenna called up after them, 'Be careful up there. Apparently, they were in the middle of DIY. There could be equipment all over.' She didn't doubt their intelligence, but a warning of what they might find was only fair.

Jenna rubbed the heel of her hand across her chest, a sense of foreboding lay thick across her with concern that Joshua was no longer in the house. Surely if he had been asleep, all the activity and noise would have disturbed him. Would he cry?

She'd deal with it step by step, but they needed to work fast to establish whether he was there or not, or whether they needed to pull in the whole team to start a neighbourhood search.

The sinking feeling that she was right didn't give her a sense of satisfaction. On the contrary, she'd have rather been proved wrong on this occasion.

The likelihood that Joshua was on the top storey and Zak had missed him on his way downstairs was highly unlikely.

Mason pushed open the door to the final room on that landing. 'Well, bloody hell, they are human after all.'

Jenna nudged him aside and stared at the room. A soft blue and white floral wallpaper which evidently had seen its best covered all the walls in what she imagined wasn't Zak and Imelda's taste from what she'd seen of the rest of the house. Too big. Too blousy. A huge carpet puzzle filled the centre of the room with only four pieces left to fill, scattered together at the edge of the room. Rainbow-coloured plastic storage boxes piled four high, three sets of them stacked against the right-hand wall.

Mason lifted the lid on the nearest one and took out a little blue wooden train. 'Nice train set in there.' He waggled the train at her. 'I love trains.'

Jenna raised an eyebrow. If they weren't in such a rush, she suspected Mason would have taken himself off to play with the set in a nice quiet corner. Boys and their toys. Did they ever grow out of them?

There was nothing else to see. Just more boxes. This time clear, white ones.

Jenna took the lid off the first. Baby's clothes. Small baby's clothes she suspected Joshua had outgrown and were stashed for the next child to use.

'Nothing in here.' The room was devoid of any storage space for them to check.

They backed out and Jenna clipped the door closed behind her. She looked up as Donna and Natalie trotted downstairs from the top storey of the house, both of them shaking their heads.

'No sign, Sarg. The top room is virtually empty. One enormous room. Stripped bare. No furniture, just newly prepped walls for painting and a door that looks as though it was being sanded. An en-suite – door missing – with a shower. One cupboard, ceiling to...' she indicated her waist-height, '... here. Below that is the boiler. Sealed in. Nowhere for even a small child to tuck into.' Donna puffed out her lips. 'Believe me, I made Natalie ram her head in there as far as she could.'

'Okay.' Jenna placed her hands on her hips. 'I haven't checked downstairs, yet. I expected to find Joshua in his nursery.' The fact she hadn't rolled a ball of concern in her stomach. 'The only room I've been in is the kitchen with Joshua's father.' She pursed her lips and shrugged. 'I never checked. I didn't feel the need.' She visualised the room. Big and airy. 'I doubt there was anywhere for him to hide, but we'll leave that until last.' She took her hands from her hips and clapped them together, blowing out a breath to cool herself. 'Let's get a move on. Don't get in the way of the medics. As we hit the bottom of the stairs, there's a room along the hallway, turn right at the bottom of the stairs.' Jenna put both hands together palm to palm and then arrowed her right hand to indicate the direction she needed Donna and Natalie to take. 'Mason, you take the downstairs bathroom.'

'Bloody hell.' His deep voice grumbled in her ear. 'How many bathrooms does one small family need?'

She opened her mouth and then clamped it shut again. He really didn't need a reply. 'I'll take the remaining room on the left, then all meet me there, so we don't get in anyone else's way.'

Jenna slipped down the stairs with the other three following close behind. She stepped inside the first door on her left. The living room she'd tried to direct Zak into earlier.

Children could be inventive, but there was literally nowhere for an eleven-month-old child to hide. Not that she knew much about toddlers. Was it likely he'd trotted out the front door? Been terrified enough to hide behind the settee?

She took a look. Nothing there. Disappointment surged at each failure to locate Joshua.

Jenna lifted a throw on the settee to peer underneath, but the furniture reached down to the floor.

She stretched out and gently slid open a cupboard door to peer inside. Nothing but neatly stacked children's games. She straightened and sucked air in through her teeth as she made her way over to the patio doors, which provided a breathtaking vista of the Ironbridge gorge, the River Severn obscured by the abundance of vegetation in full leaf. She touched the handles and tested them.

Locked.

With an element of relief, Jenna blew out a breath, making her fringe flutter over a brow streaked with sweat. At least Joshua wasn't hanging over the balcony above the sheer drop into the gorge. It wasn't exactly the most child-friendly area, but then again if the door was kept locked and Joshua was only allowed out there with his parents, it should be safe enough. The wrought-iron balustrades were high enough and the gap between the rails narrow. There were more perilous ones in the high-rise flats.

She took a step back out of the brilliant swathe of sunlight and heat pushing through the panes of glass. Her gaze bounced over the trio of photographs on the wall. Professional, clear. A beautiful young woman, Imelda, her lips curved in a wide smile as the toddler in her arms above the defined bump of baby tummy, stared directly at the camera with laughter filled eyes.

The second picture was of the three of them. Taken at the same time as Imelda and Joshua were dressed in the same outfits.

The third photograph, in between the other two, was of Joshua on his own, a broad baby grin on his face, a glisten of baby dribble on his bottom lip. Jenna stroked the frame with one finger and then lifted the frame from the wall. She slipped the picture out and placed the empty frame on the top of the small cupboard.

She assumed it was very recent.

She cast one last glimpse around the room before she slipped back into the chaos of the hallway.

The cacophony of urgent voices merged into one, but she blocked them out as she glanced at the closed kitchen door to check Zak hadn't emerged and then over to PC Walker, who gave a slow shake of his head to indicate that he'd kept an eye out and Zak was still inside the kitchen.

PC Walker squinted at her, his dark brows dipping with curiosity as he squeezed past the medics, a large-framed man tiptoeing through the seething mass of debris chucked on the floor as sterilised wrappers were ripped off equipment in the continued frenzy. He sidled up next to her. 'They'll be a while. They need to induce a coma so they can transport her to the QE or possibly Southmead.' His mouth pulled tight as he shook his head. 'It doesn't look hopeful, Sarg. There's huge blood loss.'

Even now, after seeing the gash on her face, Jenna acknowledged it could be anything from a simple slip on the floor whilst she was holding something in her hand, which hit her in the face as she went down. An item that had subsequently been kicked to one side in the effort to save the woman's life. Or it may be attempted murder, with a weapon wallowing around under the medics' boots.

The possibility they may not save her crossed her mind.

But Imelda Cheetham-Epstein was in very capable hands and if time was a factor, they physically could not have been quicker. A Sunday morning with the Air Ambulance crew immediately available. From all appearances, she'd hazard a guess they were about to move her as they slipped the stretcher underneath her slight body, the sounds of cooperation and teamwork controlled now they appeared to have stabilised her. All the elements gathered together to save this life.

That was for the medical crew to deal with.

Jenna concentrated on her part of the job. Finding a possible missing child. No panic yet, but as the minutes ticked by, she was aware of the need for speed and action. He wasn't upstairs, he wasn't in the living room and he certainly wasn't in the long, narrow hallway.

As she raised her head to peer beyond the paramedics, Donna and Natalie stepped out of the room they'd been sent to search, shaking their heads as they joined Mason. The grim set of his mouth plummeted any hope she may have had.

Before she turned to make her way to the kitchen to speak with Zak, she needed to deploy her two uniforms to search further afield.

Without a word, she handed the photograph to Mason. There was no need to say anything.

Her heart told her there would be no success.

What the hell had happened to Joshua Cheetham-Epstein? Where could he be?

10

Emily glanced across at the child she'd strapped into the front passenger seat of her little white Honda Jazz as she kept driving. Driving until the rhythmic motion of the journey rocked the toddler to sleep. Slumped forward with its cheek resting on its chubby little knees with nothing but a light breath blowing through lips soft with sleep.

'Well, fuck it. You've gone and done it now, Emily. How the hell do you get out of this?'

She pulled the car into a driveway and stared at the neat, new house with dove-grey venetian blinds still closed against the midday sun. She raised her hair from her neck and swiped away the sweat. At least it would be cool inside.

She sat back, popped her strap off but left the engine running so the air con continued to cool the interior of the small car while she tapped her fingers against the steering wheel.

It didn't really matter how cool the car was, sweat still beaded across her top lip and popped out on the back of her neck again. Panic more than heat had brought that on. She swiped it away with fingers that shook and made a half-turn to stare at the child, her heart squeezing in her chest as she rubbed her hands on her jeans.

Her stiffened lips barely moved. 'What am I going to do with you?'

She turned her gaze from the toddler and stared straight ahead through the windscreen at the house again.

Disapproval was all she'd be met with, but what choice did she have? She needed help. She closed her eyes and covered her face with her hands while she rested her elbows on the steering wheel. 'Fuck.'

She had no choice.

It wasn't your fault. With a slow move, she raised her head and spread her fingers wide to stare into the small mirror on the back of the sun visor she'd pulled down as she was driving.

The voice soothed. *How were you to know the little woman would turn all aggressive and attack you? You only defended yourself.*

She dropped her hands back down to grip the steering wheel.

You're not to blame.

'Who would believe that?'

No one. The sly voice gave a dig. *No one has ever believed you. Better to keep it to yourself. Better not tell anyone.*

Emily's stomach gave a rolling lurch as she glanced down at the centre console. 'Oh, God.'

Her fingers trembled as she reached out to pick up the two bunches of keys. One set smeared with Imelda's blood. The other she'd swiped from Zak's hallway table as she snatched up the child. She had no idea why, except maybe if she needed to return the toddler. Take him back to Zak. There had been no coherent reason at the time, except the sheer panic that she'd be discovered and the sound of footsteps making their way down from the stairs above.

She folded the two sets of keys into her hand, so they didn't rattle and wake the sleeping toddler.

Horror shot through in sharp waves while she stared at the dried blood across the back of her knuckles. The stray hair that definitely didn't belong to her.

She deserved it. You know she did. The dark insistence couldn't quite convince her as her stomach spasmed and threatened to spill its contents over her lap. She hadn't meant to.

She opened her fingers and allowed the keys to spill back from where she'd taken them. The sharp rattle of them made the youngster jerk in little spasms, although it continued to sleep.

Emily stabbed at the engine's off button, flipped open the door and stepped out to escape the condemnation of her own mind, which hunted her down in ruthless fashion.

Heat struck her as she gave the car door a soft nudge to keep the cool inside for the toddler while she decided what to do.

She glanced up and down the small cul-de-sac. Not one of the neighbours would take any notice of her, distracted by their own busy lives. Most of them would be in their back gardens with kids screaming in annoyance. Heat escalating bad tempers.

Emily circled around to conduct a quick reconnaissance.

Three doors down, his back to her, a man leaned in and stretched his arm across the roof of his car to swipe a soapy yellow sponge from front to back.

No one else visible, she dashed around the bonnet of the car and opened the passenger door. She scooped the two sets of keys from where she'd dropped them back into the console, rifled through the bloodied set until she found the front door key. She held it at the ready between the thumb and forefinger of her right hand before she ducked back into the car.

She peered through the car windows for a final check, unclipped the seat belt and scooped the sleeping child out, holding it close so only a muffled whimper sounded as she backed out of the car.

With the heel of her hand, she pushed the door closed and dashed to the house, past the neat rows of ornamental trees lining the short pathway to the door. She stabbed the key in the lock and barged her way in, her breath coming in panicked hitches.

Leaning her shoulder on the door, she blew out a breath.

'Did anyone see?' She rubbed her chin over the top of the child's head, the soft curls giving some comfort. 'No one saw.'

In the silent house, she pushed away from the door and headed for the stairs.

11

Zak spun around from where he looked out of the window, a dark flush stole over his face as he stared at Jenna across the wide expanse of the kitchen, his forehead wrinkled over dark brows, the beginning of panic edging in.

He held his hands wide. 'Where is he? Where's Joshua?'

With Mason behind her, Jenna stepped into the room and gave a long, calm study of the man in front of her to determine what part he may have played in the assault on his wife and disappearance of his son.

From his red-rimmed eyes and fresh smudge of tears down his cheeks, she could easily assume Zak was desperate for his wife and child to be fine.

Assumption would be exactly that.

There was many a felon turned out to be a great actor. Even more who were genuinely upset about what they had committed. It didn't mean to say they hadn't executed the crime. Just that they were devastated. Not necessarily for what they had done, but that they had been caught.

'Zak, I need you to be calm.'

Zak faltered, his shoulders jerked upright. 'What's happened? Where is Joshua?'

Jenna shook her head. The imparting of bad news could be done several ways. She regarded quick and straightforward the best in this case. 'Zak, Joshua wasn't where you told me he would be.'

Zak's lips moved silently, tears flooded his eyes as a look of disbelief streaked over his face.

She understood the fear, the devastation. 'I'm sorry.'

'Sorry?' His gaze shot up to hers. Not so upset she didn't catch his quick whip of anger. 'Where is Joshua? I want my son.' He puffed out a breath and then surged across the room towards her and she held out a hand in a stop motion.

'Zak, wait!'

He came to a standstill three paces in front of her, his eyes narrowed accusingly. 'You've been gone ages. We could have been looking for him.'

She felt, rather than saw, Mason step closer to her left side, his power a steady vibration of reassurance.

She gave a nod, slow, to keep an aura of calm. 'We have been looking for Joshua, Zak. We've conducted a thorough search of the house.' She half turned, enough to draw Mason into the conversation. 'This is DC Mason Ellis, and I have two further PCs here.'

Zak snorted, he drew back his lips to snarl at her. 'Four of you? What good is that?'

Jenna raised her eyebrows and saw the acknowledgement in his face that he'd overstepped the mark. Worried he may be, but it was no excuse to become aggressive. A big man, Zak could cause plenty of damage, if he was so inclined. She needed to keep him calm, onside, and proactive. Her priority was not him, but his son. 'Backup are on their way and will be here any minute, but as we weren't aware Joshua was missing until not long ago, there was no reason for further resources.' Before he could open his mouth with a retort, she cut him off, 'There is now, and they are in place, including the search and rescue dog which is en-route.'

Jenna reached out and took his elbow. She led him to one of the two long-legged bar stools tucked under the bench running the length of the left side of the kitchen.

'Zak, I need you to sit down.' She reached out with her left hand and drew a stool towards her, all the time keeping a gentle, restraining hand on his arm. 'Listen to me.' As he sat, his eyes came on a level with hers and she closed in. 'Zak, we need you to stay strong. Imelda needs you, Joshua needs you.' She removed her hand from his arm and slipped onto the other stool as she kept her gaze fixed on him. Instead of leaning back against the semi-circular back rest of the stool, Jenna leaned in towards Zak. 'I have two of my best officers looking for Joshua right now, with more on their way. We've scoured the house,' she indicated Mason who stood quiet in front of the door, his arms crossed over his chest. 'Every spot we could find that might be feasible, but if you know of any hiding places Joshua would use, tell me now.'

She knew it was a slim-to-no chance, but waited as he took a deep breath in and then shook his head.

'No. No. He didn't hide. Maybe he was too young for that, but I can't ever remember Joshua trying to hide.' He rocked back on the stool and made it creak. 'Why won't you let me look? I'm more likely to find him.' His voice had lost all aggression and turned instead to a plea.

'Zak, we're doing all we can at the moment. My officers have made a start in the side garden. Think of the house as a bullseye.' She touched her fingers together to form a circle. 'We'll work our way from inside to out in expanding circles until we find him.' She hoped. She leaned back on the stool and tilted her head to one side as her gaze locked with his and the anger seeped out of him. He slumped forward, and Jenna reached over to touch her fingers to the back of his hand. 'I can't allow you to join in the search, Zak. For one, any forensic evidence which has not already been destroyed while the medics were seeing to Imelda could be damaged by further movement out there.' She jerked her head in the direction of the hallway where, from the sound and movement as she'd entered the kitchen, they were in the midst of tending to Imelda.

Jenna squeezed her fingers on the back of his hand to gain his attention as it drifted to the hall. 'I need you to walk me through everything. Could you start from the beginning? We need to be clear. We need to understand.'

He jiggled broad shoulders. 'It was nothing. Nothing unusual for our Sunday morning.' He withdrew his hand from hers and twisted sideways on his stool to make it creak again. He squeezed his eyes closed and dug his fingertips deep into the skin of his creased forehead. 'Imelda was up early with Joshua. About 5:30 a.m. She took him downstairs to let me get some more sleep.' He looked up and gave her a sheepish shrug. 'Work's been crazy lately and what with the baby on the way...' His breath caught in his throat in a painful sob and he pressed his knuckles against his lips. 'What about the baby? Will the baby be okay?'

Jenna drew in a breath. How much could she tell him? At this stage, he needed the reassurance possibly without the intricate details. That wasn't her job to do. 'The paramedics told me the baby is absolutely fine at this stage. They've monitored it and found the heartbeat steady and oxygen levels stable. That's all I can tell you at the moment. As soon as they get Imelda to hospital, we'll get an update.'

He bowed his head, his shoulders slumped.

Jenna waited, patience always the best route. This was a man who, in the course of an hour, could very well have lost his wife, toddler and baby. Or murdered all three.

When he was ready, he blew out a breath. 'With the baby on the way, we wanted to get upstairs finished, but I've been working non-stop.' He stroked his fingers over his cheeks making the short, black stubble rasp with each move. 'I woke at around 8 a.m. Slipped upstairs and started sanding the door down. It's noisy and messy.' He opened his arms to indicate the dust sticking to his clothes.

'Did Imelda come upstairs?'

He nodded. 'Yeah. I reckon it was just after 10 a.m. I remember the news had been on the radio.' He ran his tongue over his teeth and then shrugged. 'Maybe a little later. I don't know. She had Joshua on her hip, and I was using the sander.'

'What did she say? Did anything annoy you?'

'No. I don't have much of a temper.' She'd heard it said before on many an occasion and had already witnessed Zak's quick whip of anger, which had soon dissipated. 'Not really. You know, sometimes we have a bit of a squabble. If I'm overtired or she's...' he shot Jenna an awkward glance, '... hormonal. But not today. We're not really arguers. We like a peaceful life.' He sniffed. 'We both have baggage, relationships in the past that were toxic. Too volatile.'

Interesting, but not necessarily relevant at this stage. It was worth following along the winding path at a later stage.

'Anyway, we're a good match. We like things nice and easy.'

Jenna pictured the scene upstairs and couldn't think of anything less easy than destroying your own house, pulling it apart and starting again from scratch. She'd far rather buy a brand-new house, carpet, curtain and furnish it and move in. It suited her. It suited her sister. No maintenance, low upkeep.

Each to their own, she supposed.

Zak swivelled the stool around and placed his hands palm down on the counter as though he was about to push up from his seat. 'My stomach was rumbling so loud, I told her I could hear it over the sound of the sander. We laughed.' He dropped his head, bringing his hands up to cup his face. His voice came out muffled from behind his spread fingers. 'We laughed.' When he raised his head, his eyes were tortured. 'She said she'd take Joshua down for a quick nap and then make brunch. I told her I just needed to finish off with the sander and I'd be down. I promised I'd follow. Fifteen minutes, she said. Fifteen minutes and I'll have a full English ready for you. Keep up your strength.' He paused, took a long haul of air in through his nose and then huffed it out from his mouth as he turned his head to look at the counter on the other side of the kitchen as though he'd noticed for the first time the packs of sausages, bacon, a half-used loaf of bread and an empty tin of baked beans beside a small pan.

Jenna waited in the silence and then prodded. 'And how long was it? How long before you went down?'

His eyes shifted from side to side as though he tried to remember, to pin it down to an exact time frame. 'Thirty. Thirty-five minutes maybe.'

Jenna nodded.

He smoothed his fingers over his skin, up towards his ears, which he cupped for a moment while he squeezed his eyes closed, screwing up his short, neat nose. 'She said fifteen, and I was thirty. If only I'd gone down when she said I should. The whole situation would be different.' His eyes sprang open as though he couldn't bear to see what was behind them and he bounced his fists down on the counter to make it shudder. 'I should have gone down when she told me to, but I wanted to finish it.' His gaze raced around, skimming to the door. 'It would never have happened if only I'd come down when I said I would.'

He drummed his fingers on the wooden countertop, the energy from them vibrating so hard the empty coffee cups Imelda had presumably readied, rattled in their saucers.

'Zak.'

Ignoring her, his breath came in fast gasps.

'Zak! Look at me.'

His gaze skittered to hers and then away.

'Zak. Look at me.'

As his attention drew back to her, she sighed. 'There's no use torturing yourself. This is the situation, and you can't change it. We can only go forward and do all we can to find out what happened to Imelda and find Joshua.'

Without making it obvious, she glanced at her iPhone for the time, imagining how long it would take for the doctor to prepare Imelda sufficiently to move her out of the hallway. Heartless it may be, but she needed to clear the area to get a clean sweep and find Joshua.

'Zak.' His gaze locked on hers as though her next words would put everything right. Heart softening, she knew exactly how it felt to lose someone. To not be in control. But she needed to concentrate, as she had when her own sister went missing, on the practicalities. The tactics that would find a missing person. 'Tell me, what was Joshua wearing? I need to let my search team know.' Men, in particular, didn't always have a clue what their child was wearing and as he'd been busy with the DIY with Imelda looking after their son he may not know, but she could do with verifying it.

'Ummm.' He raised his hand and plucked at his bottom lip with his thumb and forefinger. 'I think. Unless Imelda changed him, but I don't think so...'

Aware of time ticking by, Jenna still gave him the space he needed to think of details that could prove vital.

Zak raised his hand to his chest and patted it. 'A white T-shirt.' He flashed a quick smile full of sad regret that made her heart tumble as she checked out Zak's own dusty T-shirt. 'Like mine.' His breath hitched in and Jenna found it hard to swallow as tears welled in his eyes. 'And a pair of thin, cotton dungaree shorts.' He patted his knee-length navy shorts. 'Same...' His voice broke as his lips turned down and he placed his head in his hands.

She settled back in her stool to give him a moment.

He cleared his throat. 'Nothing on his feet. He hates anything on them. Loves to toddle around in bare feet, strips anything off that we put on him. He's been a nightmare lately. He's worn Imelda down to the bone while I've been at work. Never stays put. He's only just learnt to walk, so he combines that with a crab-like crawl and then staggers around until he falls on his bum again.' His voice caught in his throat and he paused before he could go on. 'Put him down and he's off like a rocket. And Imelda can't pick him up as much any more with the baby on its way.' He fisted his hand against his mouth and held still.

With a sigh, she turned her head as the kitchen door was inched open and DC Ryan Downey poked his head round.

Surprise and a little nudge of relief wrangled together as she stared at him while he pushed the door wide and stepped through.

Young, keen and enthusiastic, his energy bounded around the room, as would he, given half the chance. Never still, he filled his personal space to capacity as he stepped forward, ready for an introduction.

'Zak, this is DC Ryan Downey. Another member of my team.' Her voice was laced with pride as she introduced him. 'This is Zak Cheetham-Epstein.'

Ryan took a moment to shake the other man's hand. 'I've just spoken with PC McGuire. She's brought me up to speed.

I'm very sorry, sir.' Ryan dropped the other man's hand and took a step back. 'Sarg, Mr Cheetham-Epstein, I thought you'd want to know they're preparing to set off in the next few minutes with Mrs Cheetham-Epstein by ambulance down to Coalbrookdale and Ironbridge school to meet the Air Ambulance.'

Zak shot to his feet, fear slashed across his face. 'I need to see her, I should go.' He took a step and then twirled back around. 'I don't know what to do. What should I do? I can't leave Joshua.' He melted back onto the stool, his face a picture of misery and confusion.

'Imelda is in safe hands, Zak. There is nothing you can do for her. As soon as the doctors assess her, we'll get an update on her condition.' She circled a thought around in her head, it might be pre-empting, but she needed to know, just in case. 'Zak, do you know if there was anyone Imelda didn't get along with? Someone, maybe with a grudge?'

Confusion flitted over his face. 'I don't know a single person who doesn't love Imelda.' His brows lowered. 'Why...?'

'Dad...' Ryan's words stumbled out and Jenna appreciated his deliberate interruption to distract Zak from his train of thought. Now was not the time to explain that he was prime suspect if Imelda's fall proved not to be an accident. 'I mean Jim Downey, has started to set up SOCO, Sarg. He's been waiting outside while they tended to Mrs Cheetham-Epstein.'

'Thank you.' Jenna swiped a quick hand across her throat to wipe away the gathering sweat. 'DC Downey will also help with our enquiries.'

Aware of Ryan exuding an abundance of energy as he crossed over to the window overlooking the gorge, his sharp gaze took in their surroundings. Why wasn't he hot? Where she was slicked with a fine coating of sweat, the fresh scent of his deodorant and aftershave wafted through to follow him across the room. Did he never run out of energy?

Jenna turned her head to catch Mason's eye as he finished off the quiet conversation through Airwaves to pass on the details of Joshua's outfit to control as she knew he would. He shot her a quirk of a smile.

With his back to them, Ryan let out a low humming sound. 'Has anyone checked down here?' He pointed his finger, cruising it along the vast expanse of the gorge.

Zak surged to his feet to rush over to the wide bifolding patio doors, in a flash he reached his hand out for the door handle.

Jenna shot off her stool and with barely a split second to spare, she clamped her hand on Zak's as he went to open the door. 'Zak, don't touch it. DC Downey will check.' Aware that he'd immediately compromise any forensic evidence had the door handle been touched by someone else, Jenna gently drew Zak's hand away, puffing out a breath.

Distress flashed over his face as his panic surfaced. 'Joshua.'

'Give me a description if you will. Height, hair colour, eye colour.'

Confusion flitted through his eyes before his chin came up, his eyes cleared, and he breathed in deep. 'So high.' He indicated just above his knee height with his hand and she estimated around twenty-eight to thirty inches. Was that normal for his age? She'd no idea. He touched his own hair. 'Black hair. Ringlets, though.' It confirmed the ID of the child in the photograph. Zak's chest expanded and contracted as he dragged in deep breaths. 'He was due to have it cut, but he looked so damned cute, we couldn't bring ourselves to.'

'Eye colour?'

Zak raised his hand and tapped the corner of his eye with his forefinger. 'Blue, the same colour as mine.'

Unusual. More of a deep violet, than a bog-standard blue. Anything out of the ordinary that could be used to identify the toddler could serve them well as they took the search wider. Aware of time ticking past, Jenna held out her hand and Mason stepped forward, the photograph in his hand. 'Is this Joshua?'

Zak's breath hitched as he reached out to take the picture. 'Yes.'

'The most recent photo?'

Zak shrugged his shoulders. 'Probably not, we have hundreds of him on our phones, but that was only taken about ten days ago. I only hung them yesterday. His eyes flooded with tears as Jenna silently slipped the photograph from his limp fingers.

12

The kitchen door swung open and sound flooded the room. Zak turned his head with small jerky movements as the family liaison officer stepped through and pushed the door closed behind her to block out the white noise that was generated by a swarm of scenes of crime officers as the medics evacuated.

Expression awash with concern and sympathy, Harry Darling's sweet smile and cherubic face were the only things soft about her, unless you counted her name.

From past encounters, Jenna knew this woman had a heart of steel and a backbone of pure iron garnered through experience and necessity. In her job, she dealt with gruesome cases, getting involved at ground level with families who had suffered and often perpetrated the most horrific of crimes – child abuse, child abduction, sex trafficking, wife beating, husband beating.

She dealt with the ones that always got to you. With child abuse cases, where week after week Harry maintained close contact with the families, forming intimate bonds with the mothers, the fathers, the boyfriends. Having seen evidence of what the child had been through, knowing she was potentially befriending a murderer, an abuser, a sexual predator. And that was where the heart of steel, spine of iron came in.

For as long as Jenna had known Harry, an experienced officer, happily married with three children of her own, she'd never known her to become emotionally entangled in any of her cases. The woman exuded empathetic professionalism. She nurtured the families, the victims, the abusers, the murderers, the sexual predators. She gained their trust.

And she often garnered their confessions, too.

Jenna could not have wished for a better officer to take the first shift with Zak Cheetham-Epstein, with absolute confidence she could rely on an update from Harry later, which would be given in a succinct and precise manner, providing her with a thorough profile on the man in the room. Harry's opinion on that man and his involvement would be key. A clever woman. A qualified psychiatrist. Hugely respected in the profession. She was the best.

Jenna stepped towards her across the room to meet her halfway and, with her hand on Zak's elbow, she guided Zak forward so that she could introduce them.

'Zak. This is Harry Darling. Harry is our family liaison officer.' She deliberately used Harry's first name and not her rank of PC to settle them into an instant informality and friendliness as that was the relationship they needed to develop from an early stage. 'She'll be looking after you from now on.' She dropped her loose hold on his elbow as he stepped forward to offer his hand. 'She'll keep you informed and she'll answer any questions that you have.' Jenna offered Harry a warm smile. 'Harry, this is Zak Cheetham-Epstein.'

Jenna stepped back. It was up to Harry now. She needed to gain Zak's trust. While Jenna got on with her job. He would be dependent upon her for some time to come. And dependency often lead to confiding. Confiding was a short step into confession.

Harry stepped forward into his personal space. Her soft brown eyes turned to liquid as a sweet smile lifted her cheekbones into sympathetic perfection. 'Zak.' She took hold of Zak's proffered hand, enveloping his larger one in both of her small, neat ones in a show of unity and compassion. 'Let's sit down for a moment, and presuming DS Morgan has everything she needs from you for the time being...' she glanced at Jenna, who nodded, 'we can let her go and get on with her job.'

'I want to help. Why can't I look for Joshua?' His voice caught on his son's name.

Her hands still covering his, Harry led him back to the stools. 'The best way you can help is to sit with me and we'll run through what's happened. I know you've probably told Sergeant Morgan everything already, but I'd like to hear it again so we can get things sorted out.' She glanced up at Jenna and sent her a quick wink to let her know it was fine to go. 'We need to find somewhere safe for you to stay.'

'Safe?' Confusion flitted over his face. 'I'm in no danger, am I?'

Harry let go of his hand with one of hers and pulled the stool Jenna had just vacated clear away from the counter, inviting Zak to sit down. 'Let me explain the process.'

Jenna raised her chin and gave a quick jerk of her head towards the door, knowing both Mason and Ryan had caught the signal as they moved in tandem to join her.

Before they got there, the door to the hallway swung open again and DI Taylor strode into the room. Shoulders pushed back, thick neck bulging over the tight collar of his pristine ironed white shirt, emphasised by a severe short back and sides. Jenna had never seen him with so much as a single strand of hair resting on his collar.

A stalwart of policing. Jenna had nothing but respect for DI Taylor with his high standards and old-fashioned policing style, together with his absolute sense of loyalty to his officers. There wasn't a member of staff in the station who didn't respect him.

Jenna not only held respect for him, but also a deep affection borne of both working together and the considerable amount of support he'd shown her personally in the last year. There may be moments when he felt the need to rebuke, but more often than not, the man had her back.

Without a smile splitting his face, he somehow managed to make himself look friendly and warm. 'Mr Cheetham-Epstein.'

'Zak, please. Otherwise, it's a bit of a mouthful.' Zak gave a self-conscious dip of his head and revealed the shy side of his nature Jenna suspected was there. This wasn't a man who'd attempted to murder his wife and hidden his son. Her heart told her so, but it was her head that needed to take the lead. And she'd follow the process. But she'd grown used to trusting her own instinct too.

'Zak, then.' Without invitation, Taylor drew the stool towards him that Jenna had just vacated and plonked his hefty weight down onto it, making the fragile piece of furniture creak in protest. 'I'm DI Taylor from Malinsgate Police Station.' He cast his gaze around the room. 'I think we can let these officers get on their way now, so they can join the others looking for your son.' As Jenna, Mason and Ryan moved towards the hallway door, Taylor didn't pause. 'We're going to take you upstairs to your room, so you can change out of what you're wearing, then we'll gather some clothes and personal effects and take you to our safe house.'

Zak's reddened eyes turned desperate. 'I don't understand.'

'It's so we can conduct all the forensics we need to in your house without you moving around, possibly smudging any evidence that we may need. This will probably take a few days, so it's best if we move you out, make you comfortable elsewhere. Once we've gleaned all we can, we'll talk about who you can stay with. Do you have somewhere you can stay nearby once we're happy for you to move from the safe house?'

Zak ran a shaky hand through the long, dark flop of hair, scraping it back from his forehead. 'Yes. My parents.' His eyes went wide. 'I need to tell my mum, she'll be frantic.'

With her hand still on his, Harry nodded. 'We'll get to that shortly. Right now, we need to look after you, make sure you have everything you need, then we'll get all the information and contacts and ensure everyone is kept informed.'

As Jenna reached the door, all three Airwaves radios crackled to life.

'Air one to control, Air one. ETA two minutes.'

At the increased level of noise from above them, Jenna peered behind her through the vast window as the helicopter swooped in, skimming the walls of the gorge. It was their best chance of finding Joshua. She knew from past experience just how infallible the Air Unit could be. If there was a body transmitting heat, dead or alive, the crew of Air one would find it.

13

Jenna tiptoed her way past the SOCO officers, hoping like hell Jim Downey wouldn't call them out for not being properly hazmat suited and booted while they stepped all over his scene. It couldn't be helped. Accident morphed to possible crime scene had happened quickly and now they were on the inside trying to get out.

She glanced back at Mason and Ryan, tightening her mouth as she took in the plastic coverings they yanked onto their boots as they stepped out of the kitchen.

Mason jiggled his eyebrows at her as he hopped on one foot while he yanked the blue cover over his other foot.

Clever little buggers never offered her a pair.

It was only her who would get hell if Jim caught her.

With no sign of Jim, she ran the gauntlet and reached the end of the narrow hallway without being challenged. Determined to keep a lid on matters before the local neighbourhood was instilled with panic, Jenna stepped outside the front door and raised her hand to draw their attention as she walked towards the growing crowd.

She took her time to survey them and thought nobody other than Mason, who was directly behind her, would have caught the slight hitch in her stride as her gaze slammed into Kim Stafford, her nemesis.

Known to her since school, Kim had become the bane of her existence. The local reporter for *The Shropshire Star*, the man had managed to inveigle his way into West Mercia Police, picking up information he should never have had access to. That source of information was no longer of any help to Kim since PC Lee Gardner had been killed.

Since the demise of his foothold in the Force, Kim's intrusion had been considerably less, but he still managed to turn up at points in her working day when she could do without him. A painful reminder of where things had gone wrong.

Her heart gave a tight squeeze and she blinked away the image the sight of him conjured up. Her throat dried in an instant and in the heat of the day it was impossible to find more saliva.

Already hot in the midday sun, Kim sported dark sweat patches which spread from under his arms in a wide circle over his wrinkled, short-sleeved, pale blue shirt. His thin hair hung limp, spiking out over his ears as it clung to his neck.

'Slimy bastard.' Mason's breath puffed out above her ear. 'Do you want me to hit him for you, Sarg?'

Jenna ducked her head so the hint of her smile wouldn't show, appreciating Mason's injection of humour as a distraction technique. Whilst he made it sound like a joke, Jenna had no doubt that if she wanted Mason to take the slimeball out for her, he most probably would. And relish it at the same time. It wasn't something she was prepared to risk. Her best officer in a brawl with someone who wasn't worth the hassle. She had better things to think about than Kim at this moment and, realistically, reporter coverage would be to their advantage. Not that she'd ever known anything Kim had reported to assist the Force. She just may need him to spread the word. If there was one thing he was quite capable of, it was spreading the word, or smearing the shit. If she could just get him to stick to the former, he'd be useful. There was always a first time.

'No. We're going to need him. We need to get the word out.'

Ryan hovered at her shoulder. 'Looks like Facebook and Twitter have already done that for us, Sarg.'

'I assume that's how Kim heard, unless he's been monitoring the band waves.'

'I wouldn't put it past him.'

She turned her back on the crowd for a moment so no one could take advantage of reading her lips and kept her voice low as she addressed Ryan with a quick update. 'So far, we have every indication that this is a domestic dispute gone too far.'

'Zak seems like a really nice guy. Genuinely upset.'

Jenna pressed her lips together. 'I couldn't agree more. However,' she spread her hands, 'until we find evidence of someone else on the scene, we have nothing to go on but a badly injured woman and a missing child. Statistics show there's a high probability Zak was involved.'

Mason shouldered into the circle and dipped his head. 'What if the kid is already dead? If that was the catalyst for an argument between the two of them?'

Jenna nodded her agreement. 'All of these things we need to keep a lid on at present and hope to hell we're looking for a live child.' She took in a deep breath. 'Let's use the resources we have to hand and get on with it.'

She spun on her heel and made off along the short path to the garden gate.

As she approached the waiting crowd, Kim shuffled forward,

and Jenna scratched her head. She'd not let her intense dislike of the man interfere with the job.

She raised her chin, held up her badge and kept her tone low and neutral. 'I'm DS Jenna Morgan. Thank you for your patience.' She scanned her gaze around, aware as she did that often the perpetrator of a crime would be there in full view. They lurked within the crowd with voyeuristic interest to watch the progress of the case. Often volunteering to help, to distract, to lead the team in the wrong direction. Sometimes with the innate desire to be caught. The most prominent of those was the Soham murders, where two ten-year-old girls, Holly Wells and Jessica Chapman, were murdered by Ian Huntley. He then returned to the scene and claimed to have been the last person to see the girls alive. This was the truth, but not the innocent version he portrayed. Huntley had then conducted several television interviews which the police monitored and eventually his desire to remain a part of the crime was his downfall.

A valuable lesson had been learnt by every police force and each scene where the public had access was checked in case the perpetrator returned.

Confident that her team would conduct the same inspection, Jenna stood feet apart, shoulders back. 'As you've just seen, Imelda Cheetham-Epstein, having suffered a fall in which she has sustained head injuries, has been taken to hospital.' Before anyone could interrupt, Jenna continued, 'We are not in position at this time to update you on that situation.'

Her gaze flickered over the crowd to take in Kim, his eyes narrowed with concentration.

Tempted to blow out a cooling breath, Jenna focused on keeping her features neutral as the sun beat down on her head and sweat trickled down to pool at the base of her back. 'Unfortunately, it appears that Imelda's son, Joshua, is no longer in the house.'

A buzz of concerned murmurings circled around, and she gave them no more than a brief moment before she cut in, her gaze touching on each of the women she'd briefly spoken to when she arrived. Desperate concern wreathed every one of their faces. She held the gaze of the first woman she'd spoken to and addressed her directly. 'He may have got a fright when he saw his mummy fall and could be hiding. Little ones have been known to tuck themselves away into really tight spaces.' Jenna studied the member of public as she spoke, filing away their features for future reference, as she knew both Mason and Ryan, who stood either side of her, would do.

'We have checked the whole of the house, everywhere inside, and I have officers checking the garden at this time. We don't believe he could have got far. He's too young. Eleven months old. Zak, his father, says he was wearing a white T-shirt and cotton navy dungaree-style shorts. As far as he remembers, Joshua was barefoot, but his mum may have put socks or sandals on him when she brought him downstairs. I'm told by his dad that he's only recently started to walk and isn't yet steady, so he's unlikely to have gone far.' She raised the photograph of him high and offered it around for the group to see. 'He has lots of black, curly hair and distinctive blue eyes.' This time she did blow out a breath. 'Who here, already knows him?'

With a show of hands, the group of onlookers nodded with enthusiasm, and Jenna noted the quick reach for phones in their desperation to enlist others.

'In that case, could I ask that you spread out and start a search for him? If he knows you, he'll hopefully not be too distressed if one of you approach him.' She cruised her gaze around at their wide, concern-filled faces and nodded her encouragement while giving them words of warning. 'Please, if you come across him, let us know immediately. In this heat, it's essential we find Joshua quickly, so he doesn't dehydrate.' She could give them a lecture on the perils a lost child faced. Sunburn, sunstroke, but she sensed they were eager enough not to press those points too hard. She'd given them warning enough. She needed them keen and enthusiastic, not panic-stricken and running around like headless chickens, missing any clues.

Jenna placed her palms together and then pushed her hands out in a circle. 'If you can fan out from this point. We know we've checked or are checking this immediate vicinity, so it helps that you all start from this point. Work your way back towards your own houses. If you know him well, is it likely he'd have come to your house? Please check everywhere. Inside your houses, gardens, sheds and garages. Call out his name, but listen for a reply, a noise.' She paused to allow them to absorb the task. 'Any questions?'

Without hesitation, Kim Stafford stepped forward, the phone he'd just had to his ear now up in the air, very possibly recording. 'How was Imelda injured?'

Jenna turned her head to look directly at the older woman she'd spoken to when she'd arrived. Shelly's face wreathed with concern, Jenna assumed for Joshua, filled with a flush which ran up her neck and into her cheeks. Kim Stafford would get his information wherever he could find it and spit out the gossip and the lies, spinning them to his own advantage.

Jenna returned her attention to Kim and gave him her own spin. 'At this stage, we believe Imelda Cheetham-Epstein slipped in the front hall of her house, sustaining head injuries for which she has been airlifted to hospital.'

Before she could continue, Kim took another step forward to make himself a part of the crowd, a friend, the local journalist who would help them, be on their side. And they accepted him into their group, parting to allow him to become one of them in their worry and their desire to help. 'Sergeant Morgan, what about the baby?' He peered at his phone, she assumed to check his notes. 'I believe Imelda was pregnant.'

With the increasing sound of the thwack of the circling helicopter, Jenna raised her voice to be heard. She chose her words carefully. 'Yes, Mr Stafford, Imelda is pregnant. We will have an update later if you'd care to contact our press officer.'

'But—'

She cut him off without hesitation. Question time was to enable the neighbours to find the missing child, not for him to finesse his press article. 'If there are no further questions, we have a missing toddler to find. Let's get out there and search.'

The nods of enthusiasm leant a sense of relief. They'd provide their assistance, the best an officer could ask for. Neighbours and their determination to help were essential when it came to finding children. With any luck, they'd have him back and safe in the arms of his family before he even realised he was lost.

A hard fist twisted in her stomach as she failed to convince herself, but she resisted the temptation to rub her hand over it to smooth out the burn. She needed the community to have faith that they could find Joshua, even if she lacked the conviction she'd instilled in them, with the horrible suspicion that something much more sinister had taken place.

14

Emily stared at the contents of the almost empty fridge and angled her head as she placed three packs of Aptamil ready-to-feed follow-on milk inside. The jars of child food she'd already stashed in the cupboard were suitable for children between one and two. She had no idea how old this one was, but, at a guess, it was somewhere between those ages. Unsteady on its feet, it could nevertheless walk. No words apart from 'mama' had come from its mouth so far.

The cardboard wine carrier rattled as Emily lifted it onto the bench and slotted the six bottles of wine side by side on the bottom rack of the fridge.

As her mouth turned dry, Emily smoothed her fingers over her lips and reached inside the fridge again. The wine may not be cold, but it would be refreshing.

She elbowed the fridge door closed and turned to study the youngster. Dirty orange smeared over its face from the tomato-based baby food she'd served. Asleep when she'd left it in the house, just for a short while to dash to the supermarket. Just over half an hour was all she'd been gone.

'That was okay.' She smiled as she dipped her hand into the kitchen drawer and drew out a corkscrew. 'You didn't miss me, did you? You only woke up when I came back.' The cork popped as she drew it out of the bottle and then reached for a glass. The sweet glug, glug had her taste buds bursting as she poured herself a large measure.

Her fingers trembled as she raised the glass to her lips and took a long drink. Several swallows before she placed the glass on the bench and reached for the small plastic bag she'd bought from Tesco's, full of ready sliced fruit. She tipped it onto the new PAW Patrol plate she'd picked up from the end of aisle display and placed it in front of the child.

She snatched her hand away before she came into contact with the disgusting concoction daubing its hands.

She didn't need that filth on her.

Jenna raised the radio to her mouth as she strode away. 'Air one, this is DS Jenna Morgan. Can you tell me what you've got?' She peered down the gorge in the hope she could see what they could.

'With all the rain we've had in the past couple of weeks, there's a lot of steam rising and hot spots everywhere. We're picking up a lot of wildlife. Nothing more than that. Except, a long shot, we don't think so, but there's a hot spot underneath the balcony of the house. We can see the edge of a heat source. It's not fully visible, it's tucked under the balcony and it's not moving.' The helicopter moved off to swoop down into the gorge, taking the cooling downward draughts with them. 'Is it possible to get some foot soldiers out there, Sarg?'

Jenna flicked her gaze up to encounter Mason and Ryan's.

'What if Joshua's fallen over the balcony?' Ryan suggested.

Mason screwed his face up. 'What if he's been dropped over?' He shrugged as he voiced what Jenna had already considered. 'If Zak was responsible for Imelda's injuries and Joshua was missing, where else could he be if he's not in the house?'

Without hesitation, Jenna replied, 'Unit one, we're close enough to do this.' They didn't need to wait for anyone else. They'd simply pop down the hillside under the balcony and take a quick look. They may have to do a full sweep with uniforms later, but for now, it would have to suffice.

She strode along the edge of the garden to catch the two uniforms, PC Donna Maguire and PC Natalie Kempson, again. She'd started to view them as her personal angels. Sent to help at any given time as though they sensed her need.

'We need to search under the balcony of the house at the back. Air one has located a heat source. I'll take Mason and Ryan, if you can hold the fort here.' She handed the photograph to Donna who traced her quick gaze over it.

'Thanks.'

'Once you've finished here, continue to spread further afield.'

One dark eyebrow winged up as Donna nodded. 'Good luck, Sarg.'

Jenna turned her back and trotted to the side of the house as she listened to Airwaves, aware of Kim Stafford following them.

'Sarg, we'll give you some direction as you get nearer.'

She raised the radio to her mouth. 'Roger that.'

Swiping the film of sweat from her brow, Jenna stepped out of the shadows of the house into the bright sunlight and within a split second had the time to regret her choice of trousers once more.

That regret soon turned to relief as she cornered the house and stared down at the valley below and spared a brief moment to wish that she also had long sleeves. Thick vegetation of brambles and nettles rose up in front of them to make her question the speed of her offer to go down there.

Mason pulled to a stop, tilting his head in her direction. 'Right then, Sarg.' He sent her a quick wink. 'We're right behind you.'

His boyish grin did nothing to instil her with confidence. 'All the way.' He elbowed her in the ribs and almost earned himself a hard knee in the groin.

Instead, she turned her attention to the task ahead of them. 'Right, we're going straight there and straight back.' It was further than she'd realised. 'We don't have time to wait for specialists, if little Joshua is down there, we have to check now, we don't have any time to waste. Better call it in, Mason, and get some specialist help just in case.'

Dread rolled around in her stomach as Jenna breathed in the musty scent of mulched undergrowth and possibly the odd dead animal or two.

From all the experiences she'd had she already knew this was going to be a bad one. There was something about a job, an instinct on how it was going to run and from the word go, she'd been uneasy about this one.

The one thing she could be grateful for was her sensible, flat-heeled leather boots.

Jenna placed both hands on top of the low rail that edged the gorge and swung one leg over after the other. She caught a quick glimpse of Kim Stafford edging his way forward. She ignored him and waited as Ryan vaulted with ease over the fence, followed by Mason.

Jenna paused for a moment before she spoke. 'Right.' She glanced down through the thick vegetation of the hillside, mouth tightening as she shot Mason and Ryan a pained grimace. 'Take it easy. Watch your footing. We don't need any accidents. Let's not give Air Ambulance another reason to come out.'

Mason took a long stride and his foot shot out from under him in the thick, slippery undergrowth. 'Bollocks.' He jerked upright and his next step was more cautious as Ryan ducked his head to hide his grin.

Jenna turned sideways and considered the prospect of falling headlong down the gorge in amongst the thistles, the nettles, the brambles, and all the other shit that was down there. Possibly car tyres, a fridge and a kitchen sink.

Despite the solid boots, in her haste she slipped and tripped her way down four foot of hillside before she glanced back up again at the other two close behind her.

The heavy sound of the helicopter rotors way above them as it passed over again provided a downdraught against the heat which bounced back up at them in humid wafts from the wet, hot undergrowth transforming it into a tropical forest.

Unable to hear above her tinnitus competing for attention with the helicopter, Jenna rammed Airwaves hard against her good ear and plugged her other ear with her forefinger while she listened to what the pilot had to say. 'To your left, Sergeant, about another three feet lower than your current position, six foot along from your end of the balcony.'

Jenna swiped the back of her hand across her top lip, her heart racing in anticipation of what they might find. Not much further. She continued on a diagonal down the incline as Air One banked and disappeared to follow the flow of the river.

'Buggeration, but it's hot.'

She barely had the energy to shoot a swift smile at Mason, an arm's-length to her left above her. Grim faced, Ryan took another step to come close behind her, his breath puffing out.

She lifted her leg over a bush laden with underripe blackberries in bright greens and ruby reds and staggered as a bramble wrapped itself around her right leg. Its vicious thorns tore through the thick material of her trousers to rip at her tender skin. She hissed out as pain seared in a circle around the back of her calf.

Before she pitched forward, a firm hand wrapped under her

armpit and she found herself wrenched to a halt and jerked back into an upright position.

'I got you there, Sarg.' Mason's face came close to hers.

With a quick huff, she turned to look at him one step above her on the slope. 'Thanks.' She swiped at the sweat dripping from her chin as a flicker of concern crossed his face while he surveyed the surrounding area and she read his mind. 'I know, technically, we should probably wait for the experts to come in and do this. It's pretty damned dangerous, but if that's the little boy, we need to get a clip on. We don't have the time to wait.' She gave Mason's heavily muscled arm a quick squeeze as he stepped level with her while Ryan pulled up alongside, his pale skin brightly flushed.

She flashed them both a reassuring grin. 'If it's not Joshua, we'll go back up and call in some of the hill climbers and mountain rescue guys and let them deal with it. In the meantime, let's get moving.'

She turned her back, confident in the belief they would stay right on her heels.

16

Fern Shenton gave a long, slow stretch and pushed the blackness back as the tinny echo of a child's whimpers infiltrated the sluggish machinations of her brain.

She sipped in small snatches of breath while her heart raced. Her child. She needed to tend to her child.

A low, pained grunt surged from deep in the pit of her belly as she rolled onto her side and stared through the dim lighting of the empty bedroom while she pushed through the fog in her mind to find a small semblance of memory.

Nothing. There was nothing there. Her mind was blank. All memories wiped clean.

She propped herself up on her elbow and then swung her legs over the side of the bed to place her feet flat on the floor while the child's voice continued to echo. The soft mewls escalated to scratch at nerves raw and tender. She flopped her head into her hands, elbows on knees and blew out cooling breaths to stop the hormonal blast of heat from rushing up her neck into her cheeks.

It wasn't real. There was no child. There never had been. It was her imagination. Her deepest, most desperate desire.

It didn't make her heartbeat slow down, nor stop the sick lead weight of loss forming a ball in her chest.

She raised her head and pushed up from the bed, each step a painful squeeze on her delicate feet as she gingerly made her way across the landing into her bathroom.

Bloodshot eyes stared back at her. She'd been crying in her sleep again. Not that she had any memory of it. Just the evidence of the red-rimmed eyes. The stickiness in the corners.

Fern turned on the tap and let it run hot while she selected a sunshine-yellow flannel from a small stack on a little wire rack screwed to the wall.

As she soaked it while the sink filled, she stared through the steam at her reflection in the mirror. Quiet and accusing. Eyes blurred through alcohol and lack of sleep.

She shouldn't have had anything to drink on her medication. It was lethal. All the rules were there. Rules she'd broken.

Weary eyes met her through the mirror with little comprehension or communication. The previous day's make-up smudged to highlight the soft purple puffiness in the soft skin under her eyes.

The child's wails increased in volume, but she shut them out as she squirted three measured units of make-up remover onto her fingertips and then smoothed it over her parched skin. She closed her eyes and rubbed in soothing circular motions around her eyes and across her lips and attempted to block out the insistent cries. Cries that were only in her head.

With eyes closed, she dipped her fingers into the hot water, took hold of the flannel and wrung it out. Tighter and tighter, her fingers straining until there wasn't another drop of water left to squeeze. All the time, she breathed long, slow breaths through her nose while the child's voice rose in ever-ascending wails.

Fern flicked out the flannel and then scrubbed in soft circular motions the way the dermatologist had taught her. To stimulate the blood flow, remove dead skin cells and not stretch the skin, which was showing the first signs of ageing, she'd been informed.

With soft movements, she rubbed at her eyes. It wasn't what the dermatologist recommended, nor would she approve. She'd give Fern a lecture on the delicacy of the skin in that area, but Fern couldn't be bothered with that additional step today. It wouldn't make her eyes any less puffy or bruised-looking and those fine lines were not as fine as they used to be as she rapidly approached thirty-seven.

Three weeks' time and it would be her birthday. Another one she dreaded, as all hope of ever having a child slipped away. Especially as having one would involve actually being in a relationship. Or at least having unprotected sex – something she wasn't willing to risk with just anyone, even for the sake of a child.

She dropped the flannel into the water, ignoring the soft splash as droplets sprayed over the sink and her naked stomach. As it floated like a dead thing on top of the water, she stared at the smudges of black eyeliner and mascara and the streaks of vivid crimson lipstick she had no memory of applying that daubed the bright yellow flannel. She didn't own a red lipstick. She erred on the side of muted neutrals so as not to attract attention.

She tilted her head to one side. She had beautiful lips, softly curved with a generous Cupid's bow. She liked to think her lips were her best feature. Not the mud of her eyes, which had never decided between a dark brown or a clear green, but something slushy in between. Officially hazel on her passport, but that was too generous.

Porn star lips, she'd been told. She didn't need men to think that. She'd never wanted to be a porn star. She'd have settled for a wife and a mother, but it wasn't to be.

Her gaze slid back up to the mirror to inspect the fine lines that had started to feather outwards. Soon even her best feature would be beyond help.

She looked back down at the flannel and tilted her head to one side, confusion nudging at her.

Still, she never wore red. It wasn't her colour. She must have borrowed it. She narrowed her eyes as she searched her memory, but there was none. A complete blank.

With shaky fingers, she grasped the mirrored bathroom cabinet door and drew it open. Trepidation in every move, she stared at the contents. The box of medication stared back at her.

She drew the tip of her forefinger down the side of the box while her heartbeat quickened as the child's voice ramped up a notch. Undecided, she gazed for a moment longer before she slid the door closed again.

Her own dull eyes stared back at her before she turned and moved away. Away from the fear that lurked in her expression. Away from the acknowledgement that something wasn't right.

She stepped out into the short hallway of her nearly new house, set on a hillside overlooking vast numbers of houses rolling out over what used to be green fields. She'd thought she'd moved to the countryside on the outer edge of Telford, but within two short years every trace of countryside had been swallowed up by bricks and mortar.

Her mistake. She'd not been in a good place at the time of the move. Her decision had been about being bright and shiny again. Bright and shiny had tarnished in recent months.

Fern turned away from the narrow hall window and faced the closed, white-painted door. She reached out and put her hand around the doorknob and breathed in deep breaths. She shouldn't go in. It was no good for her. The child's wails were just an echo of time gone by. A deep desire she'd long missed the boat to achieve.

It wasn't real.

The child wasn't real.

If she just checked, she'd see there was no child.

Fern turned the brass knob and gave a firm push on the door.

The child's screams blasted her back a step and horror filled her chest as the breath she'd sucked in lodged there hard enough to choke her.

'Oh, dear God.'

She slapped her hands to her burning cheeks.

'Emily. Oh my god. Emily. What have you done?'

17

As she came closer, anticipation coursed through Jenna's veins, adrenaline pumping to form a rhythmic thud in her head. The excitement of finding Joshua.

She raced a few feet further down the hillside. Each footstep slipping in the thick mulchy vegetation. Her toes tangled in vines, which wrapped around her ankles and threatened to upend her.

At the sound of something large charging through the undergrowth towards her, Jenna's spine snapped rigid and she whipped her head around and staggered to a halt as out of nowhere, PC Blue, the Belgium Malinois search and rescue dog, shot from above her down the hillside to skim the space just in front of her. 'Shit.'

Sergeant Chris Bennett, his handler, stumbled to reach her side in a breathless burst. 'Sergeant Morgan. I heard you need help... Fuck!'

An enormous ball of fluff shot in front of him, skidding in between the two of them with Blue in hot pursuit. The dog rammed his head into the front of Chris's knees and took him clean out. Chris hit the ground and rolled in a fast whipping motion several feet down the hillside until he slithered to a halt.

A deep guttural grunt flew from Chris's mouth, along with a stream of obscenities even Jenna considered impressive. She thought she'd heard them all.

'Bloody hell.' Ryan drew up alongside her and puffed out a breath.

Flat on his back, wrapped in the undergrowth of brambles and nettles, Chris's voice echoed out over the valley. 'Blue, you bastard. Down!'

At the drop command, Blue stopped dead in his tracks and hit the ground.

Winded, Chris blew out puffs of breath as he flopped his arms out wide. 'Stay, you fucker!'

Filled with contrition, the dog never so much as twitched until Chris grunted out the command for him to return to his side. With his tail tucked between his legs, Blue made his way back to his handler, ears back, eyes filled with remorse.

'Do you think he needs help, Sarg?'

She glanced up at Mason, his features hovering between concern and amusement. She shook her head. 'I'll get it, Mason, don't you worry yourself.'

'Not worried, Sarg.'

Jenna picked her way down the hillside, a silent Ryan by her side as she lifted her legs high enough to escape entangling them in the vines, all sense of her own safety forgotten. As she reached Chris and leaned over to check him, the dog took one look at her and drew back his lips to expose long, sharp, white teeth. With a warning snarl not to approach his handler, Blue came to his feet, his head lowered, ears flat against his head while Jenna backed up a step into Ryan, adrenaline racing through her veins to send her heart into overdrive.

'Chris, are you okay, because if your dog bites me, you won't get any help from me.'

'Nor me.' Ryan backed up a step.

'No, I'm fucking not,' Chris grunted out again before he drew in a strained breath. 'Steady, lad.'

With some reluctance, the huge dog lowered himself to the ground to lie flat alongside his handler. His nose touched Chris's outstretched hand and the dog let out a long, pitiful whine, not taking his gaze off Jenna and Ryan until Mason came alongside and the dog raised his head at the newcomer, every muscle twitching on red alert.

Jenna's breath stuck in her throat for the sheer love the dog had of his handler. Certainly, he had the same attitude as most police officers. In the line of duty… and beyond.

While full of respect and admiration for the dog's attitude, Jenna still didn't fancy a bite from him. His breed was high up on the dangerous dogs' register. Mainly because of the size of his bite. It would only take one to cause some serious damage. Damage she wasn't willing to risk. She had a job to do. So did Chris, but if he was injured, they'd need to call in the Air Ambulance again.

She kept her voice quiet. 'What would you like me to do?' Aware Blue was about to take a piece out of her if she so much as touched his handler, Jenna stood frozen, Ryan at her back and Mason's close presence one step above her on the hillside.

'I've got your back, Sarg,' he muttered in her ear and Ryan snorted out a laugh.

The desire to punch either one of them rode high, but Jenna let it go. She'd get the opportunity to kill them some other time when things weren't quite as pressing.

Chris peered up at them from his recumbent position on the

ground and laughter rumbled from his chest. 'Good of you to put yourself in the front line, DC Ellis.'

It was a joke, as they all knew Mason would step in the line of fire for anyone, not least his sergeant.

Mason stepped to one side, with a healthy wariness of Blue, a grin splitting his face. 'Are you injured, Sergeant Bennett, or do you want a hand up? Because if you need help, I'll send the youngster down.'

Ryan snorted and muttered under his breath, 'Not unless the beast gets muzzled first. No chance.'

Chris raised his head in a cautious test and let out a soft groan. 'I'm okay. I'll hurt like buggery tomorrow, but I don't think there's anything broken.' He grunted as he propped himself up on one elbow. 'He fucking winded me.' He didn't appear to have any trouble expressing himself, so he must have got his wind back. With a heartfelt groan he pushed himself into a sitting position and brought his knees up to his chest. 'My arse hurts.'

Chris issued another command for Blue to relax and Jenna considered they were all lucky the man hadn't smashed his head on the ground and knocked himself unconscious.

Mason stepped past Jenna and leaned down to link his elbow through Chris's. He gave one smooth, controlled pull, and yanked Sergeant Bennett to his feet. As Chris came upright, Mason patted his back in a show of masculine camaraderie which earned him a low growl from the dog.

Jenna narrowed her eyes as she inspected the other sergeant. 'Are you okay? Are you hurt? Is anything broken?'

Chris made to step forward and came to a sudden halt, staring down at his feet, heavily entangled in thick undergrowth. As he kicked the vines off, his deep voice grumbled out his disgust. 'Nothing broken. My arse is going to be black and blue.' He raised his head and peered past her up the hillside 'Mostly, it's my pride that's taken a blow.' He narrowed his eyes against the glare of sun and wrinkles shot out in a starburst across his skin. 'Thanks to my fucking dog.'

Jenna turned her head to see what had caught Chris's attention and gazed up at the silent spectator, phone in hand. 'I hope that wassock hasn't grabbed a photo of me on my arse,' he nodded in Kim Stafford's direction. 'Otherwise I'll be front page of the bloody *Shropshire Star*.'

He cast a dark glare down at Blue, who flicked his ears back and ducked his head in a little display of contrition.

After a short pause, Chris turned his hand palm outwards and softened his voice. 'Come, lad.' In barely a heartbeat, Blue leapt to his feet to shove his nose into the proffered palm. 'Not your fault, lad, that the little fucker ran out in front of us.' Chris raised his head.

Jenna twitched her eyebrows as she met his gaze. 'What the hell was it? I wasn't close enough to see.'

'Unfortunately, that was your heat source.' His voice soured as he jerked his chin in the direction of the overhang. 'One of those massive cats, from what I could see. You know, the "ragdoll" kind that people have in their houses.' He huffed out a disgusted breath as he scratched Blue's ears, drawing the dog in with an affectionate hug so Blue leaned against his thigh. 'Size of a small bloody child. I think it was sunbathing under the eaves. That's your heartbeat. There's no child under there.' He flexed his shoulders and gave out a guttural grunt. 'We'll fucking double-check just in case.'

She'd never known Chris swear as much.

He glanced at the one remaining bramble embedded in his trouser leg and bent down from the waist. He gingerly took hold of the thick vine in between the thorns and wrenched it from around his ankles, ripping away until his leg was free, leaving small tears in the material. He shot his dog another disgusted look before he squinted his eyes to survey the surrounding area. With fists on hips, Chris circled around until his back was to her.

In the utter silence, Jenna sucked her breath in through her teeth as she caught sight of the back of Chris's muscle-thickened arms bulging out from below the short sleeves of his shirt. Blood oozed and dripped down the length of them where he'd slid through the blackberry bush, small tears had ripped through his white shirt, peppering it with streaks of blood.

Chris peered down at his arms, twisting around to get a better look and screwed up his nose as he swiped at the blood and scratches with his fingers. With an idle shrug, he rubbed his hands together, then brushed them down his trouser legs. 'Eh, it's nothing, I've had worse.' He centred his attention on Blue and scrubbed the top of the dog's head again in a reassurance that he was forgiven. 'Come on, lad. Let's get on with finding this kid.'

Behind Jenna, Mason's low voice murmured. 'I'll ask Air One to do another pass-over.'

In silence, she nodded her agreement as she watched Chris move off to check the area under the balcony.

'Air One, this is DC Ellis, that was a negative, repeat negative. The heat source appeared to be someone's cat.'

'This is Air One. That must have been one big cat.'

Jenna glanced up at the clear blue sky and the unforgiving sun and plucked her wet shirt from her body. 'We need more help. We're going to have to find this little boy soon. If he's out here he's going to get dehydrated very fast.'

Mason swiped the sweat from his forehead as he nodded. 'Yeah, it was. Resume survey, Air One. One last pass over.'

'Affirmative, DC Ellis.'

At his words, the helicopter swept up the valley towards them and made a pass over the top of them, sending a strong down-draught to cool the air temporarily. Jenna turned her face up to the sky and closed her eyes to appreciate the brief respite from the unforgiving heat as the sweat coating her hairline evaporated.

With a sigh, she opened her eyes and glanced down at her own trousers. Grateful now for the thickness of them against the thistles and nettles.

Jenna turned her head to check the area above her and squinted at Kim Stafford. Oh, yeah. Their images would be plas-tered all over the *Shropshire Star*, and they wouldn't be flattering.

She scouted higher up the hillside from where they'd come and spotted several more uniforms clambering over the fence to join them. Despite her relief at their presence, she wondered if it would be enough.

She raised her radio close to her mouth to be heard above the rotors of the helicopter. 'Anything further, Air One?'

'Sarg, we confirm we can see no other heat sources in that area at this time.'

Jenna knew this was because most of the animals in the area would have scattered far and wide at the sound and vibration of the helicopter.

'Do you need us to check anywhere else?'

Jenna squinted into the distance. There was nothing further they could do at this stage. They'd swept the area. 'Negative Air One. Return to base.'

'Affirmative.'

With a leaden heart, Jenna knew time was running out for the little boy. He'd been gone too long, and the heat of the day sapped the strength from a full-grown adult, never mind a child.

She had to hope he was somewhere safe, fast asleep, or a neighbour had taken him in without thought of letting someone know.

She swiped the drip of sweat from her chin. Please God, let the little boy be safe with someone. She squeezed her eyes closed. They needed to concentrate on the positive because the alternative was too horrible to contemplate.

18

Heart threatening to explode from her chest, Fern raced into the nursery and scooped the hysterical child out of the playpen and into her arms. She snuggled the hot writhing body against her bosom and closed her eyes as she took up the automatic rocking motion women do when they have a child in their arms.

'Oh, God. Emily. Emily. Where the hell are you?'

She spun around to face the open door she'd just come through, fully expecting to see her sister standing there.

The doorway was empty.

The hall was empty.

How could Emily have left her alone with a child? Her stupid, irresponsible sister. What the hell had she done?

As her heart slowed, taking comfort from her own soothing, rocking rhythm, the child's sobs fell into deep choking gasps as he held his breath, then let it burst out again.

Fern pressed her cheek against the little boy's headful of black curls and absorbed the sweet talcum powder scent while she made gentle humming sounds in the back of her throat. Brahms' lullaby softly floated through her mind and to give them both

comfort, she made up words to go with the tune. 'Close your eyes,
little boy. Close your eyes, go to sleep. Close them tight, little boy,
for the rest of the night. Close your eyes. Close your eyes, little
boy.'

As the child took the solace she offered, his little body relaxed
into a lead weight. The fear of setting the toddler off again had
Fern hitching him higher in her arms, all the time singing the
words, making them up as she went along. The heat of the child's
body transmitted through until Fern's skin vibrated with fire.

Arms numb, she made her way over to the window and
peered out at the Honda Jazz in the front driveway as a vague
recollection nudged at her consciousness.

She hitched the child up again as she turned from the
window and her breath caught in her throat.

'Emily.'

She'd not seen her in so long, she barely recognised her sister
as she leaned her shoulder with casual negligence against the
door frame. A glass of rosé wine in one hand, an e-cig in the
other. Her thin, crimson lips stretched in a tight smile splintering
deep brackets over her cheeks.

'Fern. It's been a while.'

Fern's sense of unease tightened her chest and sent heat
racing up her neck into her face. Always awkward and uncomfortable in the presence of her sister, she jiggled the child, whose
plaintive cries had subsided to delicate snuffles as he buried his
nose in Fern's neck. 'Not so long that you've managed to get pregnant, give birth and raise a child for several months.'

She skimmed her gaze over her sister. She may well have had
a child, she'd certainly piled on the weight. Fern tightened her
lips. Emily wasn't just overweight any more. She was fat. Flaccid
flesh spilled over the waistline of her overtight jeans in an unnatural bulge.

Emily's smile widened as she pushed away from the door and took the three steps into the room needed to bring her close to Fern. She raised her hand and smoothed her plump fingers through the child's black curls, then trailed the backs of them over his chubby, flushed cheek. 'It's not mine.'

Thinking she may have misheard, a disquiet settled on Fern. Dear god, what had Emily done? 'I gathered that. Who does he belong to?'

Emily gave a shrug and wandered across the small room to look out of the window. 'It doesn't matter. It's yours now.'

Fern jerked her head up and then held still as the child gave a threatening whimper. 'Mine? I can't have him, Emily. He's not yours to give and he's not mine to have. What the hell have you done?'

Emily swivelled from the window and shot Fern a bitter smile before she took a slug of her wine. Three long gulps which half emptied the glass. A sure sign she'd reverted to her old ways. 'Oh, give over, Fern. Stop being so judgemental. I'm only borrowing it. And why not? What harm can it do? You have the perfect set up here.' She waved her hand to encompass the room. 'A nursery, all ready to go.'

'A nursery you decorated and furnished, Emily, not me.' She'd not wanted it. It was a painful reminder of what she didn't have, couldn't have. She'd pulled the door closed on it when Emily left and had not been able to bear going inside since.

'But you've kept it. You still kept it the same.'

'I couldn't...' Not even to strip it out and redecorate. The pain too raw. Better to shut the reminder away and not allow the darkness of those thoughts to intrude. While Emily had been out of her life, she'd managed to do just that.

'I know. It was you who wanted the child, not me. I was glad when I miscarried. I didn't want it. It was your dream, not mine.'

'I would have helped, if you'd let me.' As usual, her sister ripped off the scab of the healing wound and left it to bleed openly again.

'It doesn't matter now.' Emily's thin lips twisted. 'The child's gone.'

Fern knew she shouldn't press the point, but Emily needed to be reminded. 'It was barely a child, Emily. You were only just four weeks pregnant when you lost the foetus.'

Emily's nostrils flared. 'You have no idea. That was my child I flushed away down the toilet. My little girl.'

'But you just said you didn't want it.'

Deep fury whipped across Emily's face as she took another long drink of wine. 'You confuse me. Don't confuse me.'

Reluctant to push any further on the subject, Fern softened her voice. 'We need to give him back to his mummy.'

Emily's gaze went flat, a sure sign of danger. 'Oh, I don't think mummy is in a fit state to care. She'd want you to have her, to take care of her little one. You're in a far better position to do that than she is.'

'You do know it's a boy, yeah?'

Emily's temper spiked again to danger levels. 'It's not a fucking boy. Why would I bring a fucking boy into the house? That's the last thing we need. We don't trust boys. If I thought it was a boy, I'd throw the fucking thing out of the window.'

Horror filled Fern's heart. It didn't matter what she told Emily, how she tried to convince her, there was no way she'd accept a little boy into the fold. Not after she'd lost the foetus she'd convinced herself had been a girl. And there was no way Fern could place the child in any kind of danger.

She studied her sister's florid face. If she could soothe Emily, lull her, then when she relaxed, Fern could decide on what to do, but for right now, the easiest solution was to go along with Emily.

Fern transferred her attention to the angelic face of the toddler. The last thing she needed on her conscience was for Emily to do something stupid. And Emily was capable.

She smiled, lowering her voice to a soft croon to soothe the child, to pacify Emily and to calm herself. 'What's her name?'

Even in her own mind, Fern would need to think of the child as a girl in case she slipped up in front of Emily.

As the silence lengthened, Fern raised her head to stare at Emily.

'Angel. She's called Angel.' With a careless shrug, Emily raised her glass and drained it before turning to make her way to the hallway. When she stepped out of the room, she half twisted around to look back at Fern. 'I imagine she's...' her lips curled with distaste, '... dirty.'

Fern slipped her hand under Angel's bottom. No wonder the toddler weighed so much, the heat and weight of the nappy was almost as heavy as the child. She raised her voice to call after her retreating sister. 'Did you bring any nappies?' Surely, she would have been given a changing bag, if someone had let her take their baby?

Emily's voice floated back as she descended the stairs. 'There are some in the wardrobe. Use them.'

Puzzled by the whole episode, but familiar with Emily's problems, Fern gave Angel a little jiggle on her hip and smoothed her hand over the child's hair. 'I need to put you back in your cot, sweetheart, just while I get things sorted. I'm a bit of a novice at this, but I'll do my best.'

Angel raised her head, indigo eyes no longer flooded with tears, but her bottom lip wobbled. 'Mama?'

Fern's heart soared as she cast a quick look at the open doorway before replying in a whisper, 'Yes, my darling. I'm your mama now.'

Satisfied Angel was content for a moment in her cot with her activity gym, Fern turned her back and opened the small white wardrobe doors. Emily wasn't about to return. She'd be downstairs in the kitchen sucking up the rosé. It was way too early in the day, but if it gave them some respite and thinking time, what did Fern care?

Fern reached into the bottom of the wardrobe, slid open the wide, integrated drawer and stared at the contents. Heat rushed to her face as she bent over from the waist. She straightened and took a long pull of breath to cool herself down and then kneeled on the floor, so her lungs were no longer squashed. She chewed on her lip as she picked out the largest nappy size and then removed baby wipes, tissues, a small bowl and some cotton wool. She placed them all on the colourful changing mat that resided on the top of a small cupboard. She trailed her fingers over the nappy as she contemplated the size of it. Surely, it was too small.

She threw a glance over her shoulder at the toddler and squinted at the boyish navy and white outfit. 'I think we have something a little nicer for you in here.'

She trailed her gaze along the rack of pinks, purples and whites. Each little dress neatly pressed and suspended from delicate hangers. Most of them far too small for her gorgeous toddler. She'd see what she could find that would suffice for now and then they could go shopping together.

A little thrill tingled over her skin. She would take Angel out. Emily was only borrowing the child, so Fern wouldn't buy too much for her, just the odd dress or two and a pretty sun hat.

With a satisfied smile, she reached in and took out the largest of all the dresses, white with pale lemon embroidered flowers. She gave the hanger a little shake, but there were no creases to remove from the pretty little dress. She slipped it off the hanger and draped it over her arm as she dipped into the wardrobe again and pulled out a pair of white ankle socks with a frill around the top. They would have to do for now. She'd get Angel changed, feed her and then take her out to the shops. Maybe. She'd see how things panned out with Emily.

With a quick glance at Angel, Fern slipped out of the bedroom and nipped along the short hallway to the bathroom. She kept her fingers under the tap until the water ran warm, then filled the little bowl and returned to the bedroom. A bright smile on her lips, she placed the bowl down carefully and whipped around, her arms outstretched towards the child. 'Angel, come to Mama.'

'Mama.' The child's lips turned down at the edges and her breath jumped in small snatches in her throat as though she was about to start snivelling again.

Desperate not to show the low roll of disappointment, Fern kept the smile on her face as she leaned over to pick Angel up. 'There, my lovely little Angel, don't worry. I'll be your mama for now. Just for a little while. Until Emily decides to take you away.' She laid Angel down on the changing mat, Brahms' lullaby turning over in her mind in a soothing rhythm. 'Lay you down, little girl, lay you down on the mat. Tickle toes, little girl, tickle toes while we change. Change you, change you, little girl.'

She took comfort from her own voice and the contented croon of the child as Angel kicked chubby legs in the air while Fern stripped off the heavy, urine-soaked nappy.

The lullaby stuck in her throat. The nappy dangled between her fingers while she stared for a long moment and then averted her eyes from the evidence of the child's genitalia. She didn't need to see it. It wasn't appropriate to look. If Emily said it was a girl, it had to be a girl. For the child's sake. For Emily's sake.

Determined not to let her desperate worry ruin the moment,

Fern rolled the warm, saturated nappy into a neat parcel and dropped it into the empty bin by the side of the changing bench.

Warm water ran through her fingers as she squeezed the wad of cotton wool and then wiped it over the child's lower parts with speed and efficiency and without taking her gaze from Angel's cherubic face.

'There. That's better.'

She patted her dry with the little white hand towel and then slipped the opened, disposable nappy under Angel's bottom. Barely big enough, the nappy just about wrapped around Angel's plump little body.

Irritation sparked as Fern checked the time on the little Winnie the Pooh wall clock. Sunday afternoon and the shops would soon be shut. She didn't have time to wander around and show off the new addition to her family. She'd have to make do with a quick trip to the twenty-four-hour Tesco for the nappies.

The pretty white cotton dress slipped down over Angel's body with ease, but it wouldn't fit for long and it was the only dress in that size. Nine to twelve months. She needed some twelve to eighteen months and beyond. In the bottom drawer, she had two sets of babygrows in a size that would fit. They would suffice until the next day.

Monday.

She swung Angel up into her arms and snuggled her against her chest.

Monday was an issue. She'd not got any childminding facilities in place. She couldn't just swan off to work and leave Angel unattended. Emily most likely would. She'd leave the child without a backward glance. She'd certainly be no help at all.

Fern peered down the stairwell as she reached the top of the stairs.

Emily was unreliable. She'd proved that in the past. She'd

proved it that very day when she'd left the little one unattended with the assumption that Fern would see to her when Fern had known nothing about her. When Fern had been fast asleep.

She may have to use her but only for short sprints of time when it was essential.

Fern made her way down the stairs with Angel on her hip and peeped into the kitchen. Relief coursed through her. Her sister had gone, but she had set up the highchair ready for Angel to sit in while she ate.

She was hungry herself. Reluctant to confront the whole empty blackness in her memory, Fern settled Angel into the chair, all the time crooning the tune to her in soft tones.

'I'll feed you, then we can order some clothes for you online. Next-day delivery. That's what we'll do. We don't need to go out. We'll stay here and spend time together.'

'Mama?'

'Yes, darling.' Pleasure warmed her stomach.

19

As every drop of moisture sucked from her, Jenna swiped her hand over her forehead and glanced once more up the hillside to see how far they had ventured.

Her heart sapped of any hope and energy in the blistering heat, she made the tough decision to call off the search in that area and allow the team a break for their own safety.

Reluctant as she was, she knew if she didn't look after the welfare of the people on the ground, her team would soon be depleted with exhaustion and dehydration and lose any edge they may have.

As they made their way up the hillside, her thigh muscles screamed in agony from keeping her balance on the incline. Her shoulders sagged in defeat as she took the last few steps up the hill with breath heaving as her lungs threatened to burst.

Jenna reached the fence line, relieved to accept Mason's strong arm for support as she stumbled, grasping on to him. The lead in her legs dragged them down as she struggled to lift one after the other over the top bar of the fence. Mason snaked his arm around her waist and tugged her over, setting her on her feet on the opposite side.

There were no jokes. There was no frivolity. Just a deep, abiding sense of sadness weighing down on her shoulders as Mason's concerned gaze met hers.

His low whisper hit her ears only, 'You all right, Jenna?'

At the sound of his unusual familiarity when they were on duty, she knew that her face portrayed the sense of defeat that pressed down on her.

Before she could answer, her breath sighed out at the sight of another wave of officers arriving. It did little to lighten her spirits as dread curled in her stomach. The expanding fear that it may be too late for Joshua almost crippled her.

She placed one foot in front of the other and made her way back to the Cheetham-Epstein house.

Jenna raised her head and tears welled in her throat, threatening to choke her at the sight of DI Taylor ahead of her. He stood under a vast white shelter that SOCO had evidently erected to provide shade for the teams, a crate of bottled water in his hands. He placed it on the ground and ripped open the plastic packaging, handing out the cool bottles to each of the officers as he surveyed them all, his keen gaze taking in each of them.

Jenna shook her head, with no words to offer, as he handed her a bottle, first taking a moment to unscrew the lid for her. She gulped the liquid down to wash away the tears that threatened. She took deep draughts of it until the whole bottle was empty, noting as she finished that Mason and Ryan were already on their second bottles. She accepted another without word from Taylor as he let her settle herself in the heavy silence of defeat.

Instead of drinking from the second bottle, she held it against her breastbone and rolled the coolness of it back and forth to give a much-needed relief to the burn in her skin.

She glanced around at the others, uniform wearers or not, they were all in short sleeves. At a guess, not one of them had taken the time, nor given the thought, to apply sunscreen, having not expected to spend the day out in the blazing hot sun.

It was her call to ensure they each took care of themselves, although Taylor was there and would step in if he believed she was too exhausted to look after herself and her team. He looked after her, she looked after them. That was the whole point of a hierarchy.

She circled around, checked her team.

Donna had her head tipped back, water streaming from her lips, off her chin and down the front of her uniform top. Tempted to do the same, or even dump the contents of the whole bottle over her head, Jenna raised it to her lips instead and this time took a slow sip.

They'd done enough for now. There was only so much they could do in the heat without a break, so far she could push them or herself. The second team were in place and probably better prepared. They'd have had a chance to apply sunscreen, they could take the bottles provided with them to hydrate while they searched.

The sun blazed down, not having a chance yet to lose any of its raging heat. It still had the capability to burn tender flesh.

DI Taylor waited a moment longer and then raised his chin to address them all, taking over Jenna's job. She must look worse than she thought. Evidently like hell. 'Okay, team, you've done your bit for today. You need to make your way back to the station, take your refs where you can if you're in the middle of your shift, then write up your notes. Go home if your shift is at an end. Any officer wishing to stay on will be paid overtime, but I need you refreshed first.'

As expected, most of the onlookers nodded their agreement.

It was a rare case for an officer not to continue their shift when a child was missing, but they all had personal lives, and they all had different priorities.

Jenna clutched her white shirt and held it away from the stickiness of her skin, while she breathed deep, sucking in precious lungsful of humid air. She rolled her body forward and arched her spine as she rested both hands on her knees while DI Taylor continued to brief the team.

'As you will have noticed, I've sent a second team down to relieve you. And there will be a third one in a few hours, should we need it.' Jenna raised her head as he paused. 'We have local volunteers who are hill climbers that have started at the bottom of the valley and are working their way upwards to meet in the middle. They are being coordinated by Sergeant Lopez. As many of you will know, he's an experienced officer in search and rescue. We have additional uniform officers who are conducting house-to-house and have been, without success, since the missing lad was called in by Sergeant Morgan earlier. Almost every neighbour in the area is out on foot or in their cars looking for this little boy.'

Taylor rolled his lips inwards. 'It is essential that we find him as soon as possible because every minute now is a minute closer to not to finding little Joshua alive. In this heat...' Taylor spread his hands, 'even as evening falls, the temperature isn't due to drop very much below twenty-five degrees. It is the hottest day of the year so far, reaching temperatures of thirty-four degrees, and that's in the shade, as I'm sure you are all aware.' He bent and picked another bottle from the dwindled crate, jiggled it in his hand. 'Help yourselves to more water. One of the local breweries has sent it for all the search team.' He twisted the lid off the bottle and took a quick swig.

'Further news is that I can confirm Zak Cheetham-Epstein is

in the safe house at Forty-Two, Falsworth Road, where Harry Darling will be with him until midnight tonight when she will be relieved until ten o'clock tomorrow morning. Having spoken to both Zak and Harry, I am at this moment in time not entirely satisfied that he is not involved in the disappearance of his own son. We have no evidence to suggest anyone other than Zak, Imelda and Joshua were in the house together before the incident. However, as time and circumstances change as we know from experience, this opinion may be turned on its head. We don't know for sure that Imelda was attacked. We have no forensics back to verify that, although she has suffered blows to the face. One is a gash to her cheek, which could have been caused by a sharp object. The other is a bruise to her chin.' With a grim tightening of his mouth, Taylor met each of their gazes and moved on. 'So far, there is no proof whatsoever that Zak Cheetham-Epstein is complicit in the disappearance of Joshua. Nor is there any to the contrary. He has been questioned, but at this stage there is no evidence to point either way.'

Jenna pushed herself upright and took another slug of water. She swallowed it and raised the bottle to catch DI Taylor's attention 'Sir, has there been any news of Imelda?'

Taylor nodded, swiped sweat from his chin and continued. 'I believe Imelda is currently undergoing surgery, having been put in an induced coma while they deal with the most serious injury which is a fractured skull.'

Jenna winced, looking around the team to gauge their responses, evidently, they all had the same sick feeling. 'What about the unborn baby?'

Taylor inclined his head again. 'For the time being, as the mother is stable, the medical team are monitoring the foetus. Unless there is good reason to, they will not take any further action, provided the baby receives adequate oxygen and does not become distressed. We won't know,' DI Taylor continued, 'for some considerable hours the outcome, but she is in a highly serious condition, I've been informed.'

Jenna closed her eyes while she listened, rubbed her fingertips across the thin line of her eyebrows and pulled her fingers away streaked in minuscule grits of salt where dehydration had set in.

'Zak is currently being comforted by his mother and father who have been allowed in the suite at the safe house. Tomorrow we will consider allowing Zak to go and join them in their family home should we be satisfied with his role in this affair while SOCO finish doing their bit in his house and the surrounding area.' DI Taylor gazed around the circle of officers. 'Any questions?'

Almost too exhausted to speak, Jenna looked around at the others to check if they had any queries.

As expected, Ryan's hand had already shot in the air. 'Sir.'

'Yes, DC Downey.' The twitch of Taylor's lips gave away the fact that he knew DC Downey as well as Jenna did and was well aware that he would come up with a question nobody else would voice but everyone wanted to know.

'Will Zak be allowed to join in the search for Joshua if we haven't found him by tomorrow?'

Taylor placed his fists on his hips and took a deep breath. 'That's something we'll have to wait and see, DC Downey. At the present time, he has a perfectly valid story. However, as far as we know at present, there were only three people in that house. One of them is currently seriously injured, the second one is missing. And therefore, we only have the word of the third one as to exactly what events went on within those four walls.' Taylor clucked his tongue against the roof of his mouth. 'Having said that, we also have no evidence to say it was anything but an accident until SOCO gather all of their information. As already mentioned, there was concern expressed by one of the paramedics that Imelda may have suffered blows to the face before her head hit the floor, not in keeping with the theory that she slipped and fell backwards. That would put Mr Cheetham-Epstein as our prime suspect. This is something we are awaiting confirmation of from the medical team. As we can all appreciate, their priority is to save Imelda's life and that certainly isn't a foregone conclusion at this time.' DI Taylor rubbed his hands together as he waited a heartbeat. 'Any further questions?'

Ryan's hand raised again. 'At what time will you call off the search, sir?'

DI Taylor sent Ryan a hard-eyed squint. 'Not until the boy's found, DC Downey, not until Joshua is returned to his family.'

Jenna pressed her fingertips into her closed eyes as the prospect of finding Joshua alive slipped away.

20

With legs as heavy as her heart, Jenna made her way back towards the police vehicle with Mason and Ryan in tow, their feet dragging as much as hers. Her stomach gave a low rumbled protest at the lack of food since her meagre breakfast earlier that morning.

'There's nothing more we can do at the moment.' Aware she was flagging, Jenna recognised she needed to charge her batteries.

'Excuse me. Miss. Miss!'

Jenna's feet faltered as the anxious, high-pitched voice scratched like fingernails on a blackboard. She made a quarter turn, just as Kim Stafford's head shot up from where he perched a few paces ahead on a garden wall in the shade, mug in one hand, iPad in another. His nostrils twitched as though he scented a story long before the news had broken.

'Hello.' The woman trotted on her toes in hurried footsteps from across the narrow road. 'Miss, I'm told you're in charge.'

'Sergeant. Detective Sergeant Morgan.'

Jenna thought the woman might not stop as she teetered close enough to touch. 'Well, miss,' Breathless, her voice squealed out. 'I'm Rose Anderson. I live at Cherry Tree House.'

Jenna almost replied, 'Of course you do.' But held onto her tongue.

'Nice to meet you, Rose.' Jenna smiled. 'What can I do for you?' She didn't recognise the woman from the neighbourhood crowd earlier and she'd definitely not have missed her. A strange little creature who wore a voluminous ankle-length dress in garish orange, purples and blues tied at the waist with a gold rope sash.

Rose Anderson's tiny pixie face screwed up in pain and distress. She squinted at Jenna through thick glasses, which made her eyes appear small and piggy. Devoid of make-up, except two bright circles of dusky pink on her cheeks, together with a vibrant stripe of fuchsia smeared over the thin line of her lips to give her the appearance of a strange china doll.

'I think it may be what I can do for you, miss.' She took a long pull of air in through narrow nostrils and stretched herself up to her height of no more than five foot two inches, full of self-importance. 'I think I have something you need to see.' She half-turned away and called out over her shoulder. 'I've just got back from the garden centre.'

Mason pulled up alongside Jenna as she crossed the road, striding out to keep up with the little woman's fast trot. 'Please don't tell me she wants us to see her clematis.'

Ryan caught up on the other side. 'I bloody hope not, I'm starving.'

Jenna kept her voice low. 'I hope to God she's going to tell us she took Joshua out with her and now he's asleep on her sofa.' It was a long shot, but she'd take it.

Rose stopped at her garden gate and swung it open, holding onto it to let them through. An unnatural spark of excitement filled her face as she whipped away and through her front door with the expectation they would follow her.

Jenna shot a quick glance over her shoulder at the journalist behind them. The desperate desire to follow them written all over his face as the rickety gate swung closed against his entry.

Jenna's lips twitched as she turned her back and strode after the little woman.

Built into the hillside, partially underground, the small, dark steel worker's cottage offered a well-deserved respite from the heat outside.

Jenna darted a quick scan around the snug room, straight off the front door. Populated with a threadbare sofa and cushions and at least eleven indolent cats draped over the furniture and a long wooden windowsill.

'Here.' Rose beckoned them over to a state-of-the-art laptop, in sharp contradiction to the rest of the house, placed on a small, battered coffee table. 'My son's a security guru. Insists I have CCTV.'

Interest sparked. Jenna had hoped to find a sleeping child in the small cottage, but this may prove to be the next best thing. Had Rose caught on camera the direction Joshua went as he toddled out of the front door?

Rose took a seat in front of the laptop. 'Fiona over the road told me about young Joshua. They're a lovely family.' She tucked a strand of grey hair behind her ear and tapped a button. 'I thought I would check my CCTV.'

Jenna held her breath as Rose tapped again and then swivelled the laptop round, keenness vibrating through her as she tapped her finger on the keyboard and pressed play.

As silence hung in the air, Jenna held her breath.

'Christ!' Mason leaned in as the word exploded from his mouth.

Ice formed in Jenna's veins as she squinted at the blurred image on the screen. 'What the hell?'

21

Jenna splashed icy water over her face and breathed deep, shock still reverberating through her body. She patted her face dry with three sheets of the thin paper towelling and straightened.

Well, who would ever have guessed?

Still ravenous, she considered her hunger could take a back seat until she was done. And she was almost done.

She yanked open the door and stepped into the long, wide hallway from the ladies' toilet in Malinsgate police station, turned right and headed for the incident room.

Crammed full of officers of every rank and discipline, their attention whipped around to her the moment she walked through the door to stand side by side with DI Taylor.

Without preamble, Jenna launched straight into her findings. 'Thank you to all of you here. I appreciate many of you have stayed well past the end of your shift.' She raised her hand to rub a finger over her eyebrow. 'Within the last thirty minutes, we have been provided with information vital to our investigation into the missing toddler, Joshua Cheetham-Epstein.'

She cast a quick glance around at the enthusiastic faces and gave a nod to Ryan, who adjusted the laptop and, with a quick tap, brought an image of an empty street up which transferred onto the white screen covering the whole of one wall of the incident room.

An empty street but for the rear wing of a car.

'Rose Anderson, neighbour opposite the Cheetham-Epstein house, arrived home from a garden centre visit with no knowledge of what had transpired this morning. As soon as she was told, Mrs Anderson checked her CCTV, which, as you can see, catches the edge of the Cheetham-Epstein property. She had hoped she might catch a view of Joshua.'

Ryan tapped another key and the video started. Six seconds in, a figure appeared. Ryan tapped again and the blurred image froze on screen.

'Mrs Anderson's CCTV caught this figure on screen. It's right on the edge of the shot and blurred. But...'

Ryan edged the image onwards several seconds to the next grainy shot as Jenna closed in to tap the white screen and make it wobble.

'That figure has a child in their arms.' A hum of interest buzzed around the room, a cacophony of white noise which throbbed in her head together with the high-pitched tinnitus.

As Ryan moved the video on, one frame at a time, Jenna brushed aside the pulsing vibration and pointed.

'At the very edge of the camera's vision, blurred it may be, but that appears to be Joshua Cheetham-Epstein in the arms of an unknown person.' She circled her hand around the image. 'As the child shields the vast amount of their face and body, we cannot immediately identify if this person is male or female. What we do know is that they abducted Joshua, put him in a white car and drove off.'

As the car drove away to leave the street empty, Ryan back-tracked until the image of the person showed again as it leaned into the passenger seat of the car at the very edge of the image.

'We have intelligence looking at this to try to enhance the images and identify this car.' She tapped on the screen. 'There's barely any of it visible, certainly no registration plate, just half of the front headlight and the wing. As the CCTV image is blurred at this distance, we can only identify that this is either a white, or a light-coloured car. Hopefully, we'll have more in the morning.' She pushed her bottom lip out as she tracked around the room. 'Obviously, we've now escalated this incident from an accidental fall with a missing child, to possible assault of Imelda Cheetham-Epstein and kidnap of her son, Joshua.'

22

SUNDAY 11 JULY, 22:15 HRS

Jenna turned off the water and stepped out of the shower, no more refreshed than when she stepped in as an instant slick of sweat formed on her skin. She rubbed it off again with her fluffy blue towel and applied deodorant under her arms, something she wouldn't normally use on her way to bed but with no respite from the stifling heat, she didn't need the dampness of her own sweat slicking the sheets by the time she woke in the morning.

Too hot even for the shower to steam up the mirror, Jenna was pulled towards it, tempted to check out the extra worry lines she must have developed that day. Eyes filled with sorrow stared back at her, while the lines bracketing her mouth had deepened with exhaustion, disappointment and fear. Disappointment that little Joshua was nowhere to be found and that time had ticked away. Precious time that made his rescue less viable with every minute. Fear for his safety.

Where the hell could he be? Who had taken him?

She picked up her pot of moisturiser and dipped her forefinger in, then smeared it over her face, hoping it didn't fry on her sun-reddened skin. Her face wasn't as bad as she'd thought it would be with the sun protection factor high in the overpriced moisturiser Fliss insisted she use. Jenna leaned in closer to inspect her skin. Perhaps her sister was right. Her nose was a shiny rose-tinted colour, but had she not used her moisturiser that morning, it would have been glowing crimson and peeling by now. She raised her sun burnt arms, still smarting from the torrent of cool water she had gushed on them in the shower and then reached inside the bathroom cabinet to take out a bottle of aloe vera gel. She smeared it over her skin and hoped it dried before it stuck to the sheets when she flopped face down on her bed.

She glanced at her iPhone. She'd not even had the chance to pick up messages and had no inclination to start as she checked the time. Those who counted, Fliss and Adrian, knew what she was doing and that she'd be uncontactable for personal reasons until Joshua was found.

Sorrow washed over her again. She needed to help find him, but a body and mind could only do so much without sleep. If she went to bed immediately, she'd get six hours and be back in the station at six o'clock the following morning. That should be enough. It would have to be because she wasn't giving up until they found him. The sorrow flowed into dread. Dead or alive.

Jenna yanked on the light cord in the bathroom and plunged the room into a dusky grey as she slipped out of the door, barely able to place one foot in front of the other as she crept across the landing with the hope that Domino, who'd already greeted her at the front door, would decide she wasn't worth getting up a second time for.

She nudged open her bedroom door and, with a jolt of surprise, Jenna's weariness dropped from her as a blast of icy air enveloped her in a cocoon of comfort and freshness.

Better still, the handsome face of Adrian Hall spread into a sympathetic smile, his beautiful topaz eyes filled with compassion as he lifted a plate on the palm of his left hand as an offering. 'I do believe you've not eaten, Sergeant.'

She flicked her gaze down at the contents of the plate. Simple and easy. Fulfilling. Tasty. Tempting.

He knew her weakness. Ciabatta, olives, sun-dried tomatoes, mozzarella and a whole row of spicy Italian meats laid on a bed of rocket. An effortlessness meal in itself, but lush and comforting when nothing else would do on a hot summer's night.

Wordless, she took the plate from him and sank onto the bed, tucking one leg under herself so she could swing the other from the side.

With a smile, he turned and picked up two small glasses of crisp, white wine and handed one to her. Enough to satisfy a small craving, not enough to affect the next day's work. She knew he would have thought it through and adored him for his thoughtfulness.

She breathed the cold air in through her nostrils and felt the exhaustion lift enough so she was able to pick up an olive and pop it in her mouth, something five minutes ago she would never have believed she was capable of. She'd been quite prepared to face-plant the pillow.

Without a word to her gorgeous chief crown prosecutor, Jenna took a huge bite of the ciabatta, little noises of pleasure coming from deep in her chest as she chewed and swallowed before she took a sip of the crisp white wine.

'How did your day go?' he asked.

Jenna took another taste of wine before she answered.

'Bad.' She screwed her face up 'Really bad.'

His expression filled with clear understanding. 'No word on the little boy?'

'None whatsoever. He's disappeared. Taken by someone. We

have no idea who. We just found out as we were supposed to come off shift, that's why I had to stay late. Sorry I didn't give you the heads up more than I did.' He gave a lopsided smile and shrugged his understanding while she rolled up a thin slice of prosciutto and popped it in her mouth. 'I've just spent the last bloody six hours chasing my tail and everyone else's.' She closed her mind to the clamour of thoughts, processes, leads she could still be chasing. She needed to refresh so when she returned to work, her mind was clear and focused instead of the mild fog that encased it. 'Every minute that passes is a minute closer to the fact that we may never find him.'

The cruelty of it was, they'd been there before. The last time, it was her sister missing. Jenna's heart involved. And yet, Fliss was an adult and she fought her own way home. This was a whole different matter.

In reality, an eleven-month-old child was not cut out to survive the heat and the terrain, even if his abductor let him go.

'We don't have a clue yet who the hell could have taken him. We've got intelligence trying to identify the car. Type, year, etc. We have everyone on it and I'll check on progress in the morning. I need to do another early.' She blew out a gusty breath. 'There's nothing more I can do tonight.'

Other than physically search for Joshua and she could no longer do that. Not on empty fuel tanks. She needed to recharge.

Eat, drink, sleep.

And possibly a distraction for a brief time. She was so willing to be distracted.

As cool air wafted across her overheated skin to send delighted shivers over her, she nodded at the huge air-conditioning unit in the corner of her room.

'Where did you get that?'

Adrian turned his head and looked at the piece of equipment

that blew out gentle gusts of icy air to cool the bedroom. 'I have a friend who's an engineer, an industrial engineer. He had two units left over from a job he'd been doing and let me have them for a snip.'

'How much do I owe you?'

The slow rise of his dark eyebrow made her understand she may just have teetered on the edge of insult when he answered. 'Nothing. Nothing at all. I never asked for payment, I don't expect it.'

Skin cool, but heart warmed if not a little confused by his generosity, Jenna took another bite of ciabatta and prosciutto, cramming a sliver of mozzarella into her mouth at the same time. She took a moment to think and chew.

'Well, I certainly do appreciate you thinking of me.'

Adrian smiled as he placed a hand on her thigh and circled his thumb in a soothing, circular motion. 'So does Fliss.'

Jenna angled her head to one side. 'Why would you give us both units?'

'Why wouldn't I?'

'Just...' He made her stutter. 'It's just I thought maybe you'd keep one for yourself, for your place.'

He kept his gaze steady on hers as he took a drink of his own wine. 'I spend more time here these days. I thought the units would be put to better use here.'

Aware they may be tiptoeing around the edge of a precipice and not willing to take that plunge yet, Jenna swallowed another bite of food. 'Yeah.' She nodded.

Her heart filled to overflowing with a feeling she wasn't yet ready to identify or confront as she came to the realisation that the man in front her somehow had become enmeshed deep into her life without either of them making any overt moves. A slow dance, with soft music, they'd waltzed their way into a relationship based on truth, honesty and a deep care for each other.

With slow, deliberate moves, Jenna brushed breadcrumbs from her fingers, set the plate on her bedside table, took the last sip of wine and placed the glass next to her plate. She turned to face him and shuffled closer to where he sat on the edge of her bed.

She raised her hand and stroked the thick, dark hair back from his forehead before she wrapped her arms around his neck. 'Thank you.' Her mouth touched his in a featherlike stroke before she drew back to check his reaction.

His straight lips curved up at the edges. 'The pleasure's all mine.'

'It could be mine, too.' She flicked one eyebrow skywards. 'You sure I can't pay you... in kind?'

His eyes darkened as she settled herself in his lap.

She allowed a slow smile to spread as she prepared to distract herself. After all, she was being forced to take six hours of downtime. What better way to recharge her batteries?

23

Anger bubbled and festered inside her, building momentum until it threatened to spill over in one searing, steaming cauldron full of rot as she glared at her reflection in the bathroom mirror. Skin pale and pallid with fiery red cheeks and a scattering of unattractive freckles smudged across her nose. Why couldn't she have the smooth perfection of Fern's flawless, tanned skin?

Emily picked up the bottle of wine and drank straight from it, gulping it down until it was drained. She placed it with over exaggerated care on the side of the bath and then turned away, back to the mirror.

Her brows lowered and petulant eyes glared back at her. It wasn't fair that Fern got everything. Good, firm skin, pretty face, an abundance of thick golden hair and a petite, slender figure. Unlike Emily's fat pink wobbliness.

Fucking bitch. She hated her.

She dropped her gaze and skimmed it downwards over her flaccid body with loose skin folds draping from her belly to touch her thighs. Disgust curled her lip while she stared with morbid fascination. She'd tried to lose weight. It didn't come off easily and, when it did, she'd been left with a pouch of empty skin dragging over the tops of her thighs she could do nothing with.

Fern didn't have that problem with her flat stomach and narrow hips.

Emily's thin hair straggled around her wide face. It didn't seem to matter how much she washed it, it still hung limp, lifeless and by the end of the day would be greasy again.

Hormones, the doctors told her. Each one of the male ones she'd ever seen. It was never possible to get hold of the lone female at the seven-doctor practice. Everyone wanted to see her.

She leaned into the mirror and squeezed at the little row of blackheads pebble-dashing the narrow ridge that ran horizontally over the top of her nose, and watched with satisfaction as white pus bloomed out of them onto the top of her fingernails.

What the hell did male doctors know about female hormones?

She rinsed her hands, dried them on the little yellow hand towel and slipped into her nightie before she padded across the landing into the pretty pastel room where she could sit in silence and peace.

She shot a quick look over at the peacefully sleeping child and slammed down on the revulsion that threatened as she slid her back down the wall to sit on the floor in the corner.

Her eyes fluttered closed.

Explosive cries rent the air and Emily curled into a tight ball, back against the wall, knees up to her chin as she rocked and rocked, the echo of her own tortured moans overwhelmed by the wail of the child.

She clamped her hands over her ears to block out the sound of the shrill shrieks, but nothing worked, even when she pushed the heels of her hands hard into her face until her jaw threatened to break.

The screeches intensified, increasing in volume, ramping up the pitch until the seething, roiling pressure of her mind threatened to explode.

She reared her head up, eyebrows low to darken her vision as she stared at the screaming child holding onto the cot rails with both hands. Her face suffused with dark, angry, mottled crimson. Desperate eyes bored into her as tears streamed down Angel's face and snot, thick and clear, ran from her nose, over twisted, distraught lips to dribble down her chin in a thin stream of silver.

Emily dropped her hands from her face while the cacophony of sound boomed around the room, ricocheting off the walls as her blood turned cold. The seething bubbling confusion came to an abrupt stop. Deadly nothingness seeped through her veins, encasing her heart in ice.

The backs of her knees smacked down on the floor, her legs stretched straight out in front of her. 'Little fucker.' She pressed her hands onto the top of her thighs and leaned forward. She drew her lips back from her teeth and snarled. 'Little fucker.' The strangled voice burst from her throat. Not hers. Never hers.

Emily tilted her head and reached out for the child from across the room, fingers stretching for her neck.

'What the hell do you think you're up to?'

At Fern's strident voice, Emily almost shot to her feet. Her legs spasmed and slammed back to the floor as she whipped her head around to stare, narrow-eyed, at her sister.

Fern shot through the doorway to snatch the child from its cot. Her eyes darkened as she spun on her heel to face Emily.

Ever the judgemental bitch.

The ice that had frozen her heart, never so much as cracked, but spread its insistent frozen fingers along her arteries, pushing through to her veins to freeze them too.

Emily curled her lip as she leaned her head back against the wall. The wall she'd never moved from as she'd sat in the corner of the room, well away from the toddler. The voice whispered in her ear, *She had never been in any danger of you touching her. Dirty little shit.*

She'd never go within a mile of her. Fern was welcome to the brat. She seemed so at home rocking the screaming, squirming child in her arms as though she was the best thing in the world.

She was never that. The only use she had was her connection to her father. Zak. The love of Emily's life.

She cruised her gaze over her sister's furious, accusing face. 'Fuck off, Fern, and take the grizzly little shit with you.'

Fern's eyes narrowed while she jiggled the child in her arms, sweat popping out on her forehead as the heat and the weight of the toddler had an instant effect on her. The skinny bitch. If she had more meat on her, perhaps she'd be capable of holding the brat.

Emily shot her head up as Fern ran her gaze over her. Her sister kept her voice low and soothing as she addressed her over the head of the sobbing infant. 'I think you need to leave. I think you need to go right now. And leave me to deal with Angel.' She cupped the child's head in her hand as she rocked her, the shiny spill of hair feathered out over her fingers and did nothing to endear the child to Emily. All she could see was snot smeared in silver streaks over the top of the arm of Fern's navy blue short-sleeved T-shirt.

'Angel, that's no fucking angel. You know that. Right?' She placed her hands on the floor, ready to push up to confront her sister. She needed to make her face the truth about the brat. Pleasure circled thick in her stomach at the leap of fear lighting her sister's eyes and Emily drew her lips tight across her teeth in a vicious snarl. 'She needs her scrawny neck wringing.' She spat out the loathing and the vitriol that festered inside her. 'Fucking child kept me awake all fucking night.'

Fern's eyes slowly widened, and the fear vanished in an instant as knowledge replaced it to burn there. She stared Emily down. 'You haven't been taking your medication, have you, Emily?'

Emily scrubbed the back of her hand against lips that had turned dry. 'I didn't need any fucking medication, there's nothing wrong with me.'

'Oh, but there is, Emily.' Her sister's voice turned sly and probing. 'We both know you need to stay on your meds.' Her body took on a natural rocking rhythm as the child stopped squalling as loudly and her knees, instead of pressing deep into Fern's flat, skinny belly, slid down to a more comfortable position, her feet dangling loose as her body relaxed.

Emily gazed at the pair of them, the hard ball of fury unravelling as the child's voice stopped dominating her thought processes and her mind re-engaged.

'You really have to get some control back.' Fern jiggled the child. 'Ssshhh, ssshh, it's okay, mama's here.' She never took her hard gaze from Emily, but she kept her voice soft as she continued to address her. 'You know what the counsellor advised. We were doing so well.'

There was no fucking 'we' about it. Fern wasn't the one with the counsellor. She wasn't the one taking drugs that made her feel as though the world revolved on a long, slow spinning wheel she could never quite get off. With sensations numbed so much that if she stuck her hand into a burning furnace, it would take her twenty minutes to realise what she'd done.

Dull. They'd made her dull as ditch water. So, she'd stopped taking the medication. Just like that! They said she shouldn't, she'd have withdrawals, but she hadn't. Not at all. Quite the contrary. Everything was so much clearer, brighter. Like an electrical current had passed through her body and brought it back to life. The edges of her vision glowed, shooting bright white light to accentuate every image.

Her legs gave a convulsive shudder. They were coming back to life too. After too long snoozing on the hard floor, her limbs jerked and twitched, life pulsing back into them. She'd take the pain if it meant she could live again.

If they knew, they'd never let her live her life. They'd force her to take her medication and she'd fade into nothingness again. She couldn't have that. Wouldn't allow it.

She glared at her sister, sucked in the fabulous sensations she'd lost for so long, wave after wave of them washing through her. Overwhelming her. Cleansing her of the numbness she'd lived with.

She curved her lips up into a smile. No more counsellor, no more meds. No more weight gain. They did that to her, too. Slapped on the kilograms. Well, no more. She was cured. Even if her controlling sister didn't understand.

Fucking wow!

'It was Zak's fault.' Her sister would understand this. Surely. She had to realise he'd triggered it. 'He should never have married that woman.'

With absolute conviction, she appealed to Fern, knowing she'd be on her side. She'd always been on her side, even when they fought. She'd always come round to Emily's way of thinking. She might give her hell, but she'd stand shoulder to shoulder with her against anyone else.

Except when they insisted on drugging her and making her see the world in a different light. When they'd made her live a half-life and told her it was okay to become fat. Fern hadn't stood by her then. She'd helped to incarcerate her by simply withdrawing her presence from any meeting Emily had attended. She'd made herself absent.

A myriad of emotions whirled around, throwing a blanket of anger and confusion over Emily to stifle her thought processes until she retreated back into the ugliness.

'You should never have gone to his house. What the hell were you thinking of?' Fern's mouth tightened with disapproval as she pressed the child's face into her neck and crooned, rocking her as though she was the most precious thing on earth.

More precious even than her own sister, the voice prodded.

Appalled at the lack of support, the lack of understanding, Emily's temper spiked again. 'I don't fucking care, it was his fault.'

'I don't think it was his fault.'

That voice of reason, the tone, the wheedling appeasement was starting to piss her off.

Emily's breath stuttered in her throat. How did she not understand? She was her sister, for God's sake.

Judgement hardening her expression, Fern reared her head back. 'I don't think you've taken your medication for a lot longer than just before you went to see Zak, Emily.'

The little hiccupping sobs faded as the toddler settled against Fern's flat chest.

Her sister's feet were planted wide as she snuggled her face soothingly into the child's curly, black hair.

Emily's fury petered out to leave a squirming mass of restless eels in her stomach ready to surge to the surface at any moment. Under control for now, but with the threat ever close, she watched as Angel snuffled into the soft skin of her sister's neck.

Lifting her hand, Fern stroked away the tears that streaked the child's face with sweet tenderness, but her narrowed-eye stare still pinned Emily. 'You need to start taking your medication again, Emily. I'll go get it myself.' Her pacifying tone spiked Emily's temper.

'I don't want my fucking medication. It wasn't doing any good.'

Her sister's pathetic, appealing voice ramped up her own annoyance.

'I think it does you good. I think you need to take it. How long has it been since you took your last dose?'

From under lowered brows, Emily glared at her sister. Fern couldn't make her take her medication. It's not as though she could force the tablets down her throat. 'I don't want them. You can't make me take them.' She tilted her head to one side in a challenge and grit her teeth until her jaw popped.

'Calm down, Emily.'

That voice. That fucking voice with her fucking control.

You no longer need control. You're good. Just great exactly how you are.

'Emily, everything's going to be fine.' Fern's weak smile made Emily want to punch her in the mouth, smoosh those thin, smiling lips until they lost all form.

The black eels squirmed in the pit of her belly, a dark threat desperate to emerge writhing and spewing while her sister looked on, ignorant of the danger.

'I'm just going to change Angel. And then we will get your medication.'

How much would it take for the woman to understand? 'I don't want my medication.' The voice emerged dark and feral, but, oblivious, Fern prattled on.

'I'll just do this. Angel has to come first.'

She lay the child down on the changing mat and reached for a new nappy, all the time keeping a gentle hand on the child as though she lacked the confidence to break contact with her.

Emily watched, temper still simmering. The brightness at the edge of her vision closed into a narrow tunnel while she kept a close eye on the proceedings.

If Fern let go and Angel turned, she'd roll onto the floor, her head would...

Emily's dark smile spread.

Like her mother. Dead in a pool of blood.

Emily narrowed her eyes while she watched her sister. Curious, she focused in on her as Fern turned her head, refusing to look as she swiped a wet wipe over the child's genital area, then grasped her feet and wiped her bottom. When she slid the fresh nappy underneath, it could have been with a sense of relief as her attention only returned as she pulled the nappy up between the child's legs and smoothed the sticky tape down over her tummy as Angel started to snivel again.

Fern's gaze met Emily's over the top of the toddler's head as she swung her back into her arms. Eyes calm once more, her sister smiled at her. This time genuine and warm as she came towards her. 'Angel's a good girl.' She came alongside her and leaned her back against the wall and, with slow, measured movements, slid down until her narrow bottom touched the floor next to Emily. She raised her knees and adjusted Angel, so she lay across her chest sideways.

Within that short space of time, Emily's heartbeat slowed, her pounding pulse stepped down and the fury filling her heart seeped away.

Emily stared at Angel. She wasn't so bad after all now that she'd stopped her squalling. In fact, she was rather beautiful with those special eyes just like Zak's.

Happy for her sister to take responsibility for her, Emily reached out a finger and stroked the soft skin of Angel's cheek, fascinated at the silken feel of it.

She did look like Zak, with her black hair and violet eyes. Eyes that were closed now as her perfect lips moved in a suckling motion. Lips that looked remarkably like hers. Her child. She'd brought it for Fern, but the child was hers.

Zak's child. Her child.

They needed to be together.

Fern's voice, moments ago grating and condescending, changed. Soothed while she concentrated on the child in her arms. She massaged gentle, circular movements over the child's tummy.

The soft lilt of her voice as she hummed along to Brahms' lullaby loosened Emily's muscles and her eyes drifted shut, her limbs melted while memories of the tune circled in her head.

'Close your eyes, little girl. Close your eyes, go to sleep. Close them tight, little girl, for the rest of the night. Close your eyes. Close your eyes, little girl.'

Aware of Fern making up the words as she went along, Emily absorbed the familiarity. Perhaps they'd heard them when they were younger. Perhaps their mother had sung to them.

Their mother. Wild. A party girl with so little care for the children she carried, she gave birth to, she reared. With nothing more than the basics and desperately lacking in any love.

Emily squeezed her eyes closed. No. She wasn't about to allow herself down that dark avenue of thought.

She blocked out her mother and let the melody wash over her, the gentle, soothing voice of her sister who'd provided her with that love, the love she so desperately needed. Sleep drifted closer, taking her under in a warm cocoon of comfort.

24

Fern cast a sideways glance at Emily, relaxed and pacified next to her, and realised that whatever else happened, her sister was never to be left alone with the child again.

She blew out a breath in the overheated room and adjusted Angel's position, so her heel no longer dug into the soft flesh covering her hipbone.

Content that she had the situation under control, Fern tipped her head back to rest it against the wall and allowed the soft drift of sleep to take her down.

When she stirred, Fern cracked open eyes thick and swollen with grit as a trickle of sweat traced down the length of her spine. She glanced up at the little nursery clock on the wall and with a jolt of surprise blinked at the time. Five past eight. How could she have slept so long?

Stiff with sitting on the hard floor, she groaned as she blinked the child on her lap into focus, a vague smile skimming over her lips at the sight of a contented little angel. Her angel.

She raised her hand and scrubbed the sleep from her eyes.

The weight of the child pressed down on her and relentless heat pulsed through the pair of them.

Aware they were alone, relief washed over her. Her sister had gone, sneaked off while Fern and Angel slept, oblivious of her exit.

She slipped her hand under the child to adjust the pressing weight of her on her sweltering body and froze as Angel's eyes fluttered open, and she let out a disturbed whimper.

Fern held her breath and smiled into the toddler's face, watching until Angel's eyelids fluttered shut.

Terrified to move, she waited until she could wait no longer, her skin slick with sweat. Angel's cheeks turned ruddy in the golden sunlight of the new day.

Fern watched the hand of the clock tick round, aware she needed to move limbs that had turned stiff with lack of movement.

Heart filled with tenderness, Fern inched the Angel's weight up until she lay across her chest. Evidently content, Angel's sweet bud of a mouth popped open, her wet lips shiny, she made soft sucking noises against Fern's chest, sending crest after crest of longing through her veins until her breasts ached to let the little one's mouth latch on to her.

Fern knew she had no choice but to move if she didn't want to set for all eternity. Decision made, she scooped her arm around the child's back and rolled to one side, keeping a firm hold of Angel while she let out small grunts as she came to her knees, hauling in deep breaths.

Angel's warm, sodden nappy gave a hint as to how long they'd both been asleep.

She came to her feet and staggered under the weight of Angel. She made a quick recovery and leaned over to place the whimpering child back into her cot as she prayed for a few precious moments so she could visit the toilet and brush her teeth and telephone work to let them know she was sick. She never called in sick. She was stable, reliable. She'd not had a sick day in a couple of years.

With a quick glance out of the window, Fern puffed out a sigh of relief at the absence of Emily's little white Honda Jazz in the driveway.

She placed her hand on Angel's tummy and rubbed in gentle circular motions in time with the slow, sluggishness of her own heartbeat, content and relaxed, until Angel closed her eyes again and drifted off. It really didn't matter that her nappy was soaked. Angel didn't seem to mind. She'd survive a little longer without it being changed. Just long enough for Fern to see to her own ablutions.

Fern whispered the door closed behind her and stepped the short distance into the bathroom, across the hall.

With eyes red and puffy, she stared back at herself through the mirror and considered her options. Her stomach let out a rude grumble, but food would have to wait, she'd feed them both together just as soon as she'd cleaned up. Personal hygiene came high on her agenda and right now she stank. The smell of her own dried-on sweat swirled, drifting under her nostrils until the scent of her body odour tightened her throat. Unlike the fresh smell of the child, she'd turned rancid.

Fern stripped off the nightdress she'd worn for far too long and let it drop to the floor. She slid the shower cubicle door wide and stepped under the torrent of water, breathing in through her nose. She tipped her head back and blew out as she wallowed in the cool gush of water sluicing over her body, rinsing away the staleness from too much sweating. She lathered up the fresh, lemon scented shampoo and dug her fingers deep into her scalp to clean nails she'd noticed were grubby and hair she'd somehow allowed to become greasy. She peered through eyes squeezed almost closed against the onslaught of water, grasped the old-fashioned bar of soap and scrubbed Imperial Leather all over her body until her skin glowed.

She swilled away the suds and sighed out her pleasure as the heat of her body flushed away down the drain with the dirty water.

Refreshed, she stepped from the shower and, instead of wrapping the thick yellow towel around herself, she gave her whole body a brisk scrub while she stood in front of the narrow open frosted window to catch a meagre waft of warm air as it sneaked in.

As she turned, Fern raised her hand and hesitated before she pulled the mirrored door open on the bathroom cabinet. She studied the box of drugs inside, a quiver of anxiety running through her. Reaching in, she tilted the box towards her to peer inside. She chewed her lip as she studied the contents. Almost full. She glanced at the issue date on the side of the box that had been there since her sister had disappeared from her life last time.

'Oh, Emily. What are we going to do with you?'

Fern wasn't her keeper, she couldn't force her to take her meds. It wasn't up to her, it was up to Emily to medicate.

'Emily, what have you done?'

With a sigh, Fern pushed the box back into the medicine cabinet. She clipped the door closed and stared at herself again in the mirror. Irritated, she grabbed her toothbrush and squirted toothpaste on it, noting Emily hadn't brought one with her so she possibly had no intention of staying.

Fear and relief warred with each other. She knew she shouldn't be relieved. She loved her sister. She would do anything for her. But life ran so much smoother when Emily wasn't there to stir the bubbling pot of jealousy and resentment.

Fern spat and rinsed, drying her toothbrush before she slotted it back into the holder. She reached for her hairbrush and ran it through the thick lushness of her sun-streaked golden hair just as Angel's voice piped from the bedroom across the hallway. Not a pained cry, but a chirrup, a happy call for attention rather than a cry for help.

Heart tripping with delight, Fern dashed naked across the hallway to Angel's room before the child's happy gurgles could turn to cries of distress.

She swooped Angel from the cot into her arms, heart bursting with joy as she snuggled her to her chest. Naked skin pressed against her little sweetheart.

Angel's mouth moved in a suckling motion and the hormones Fern had dismissed raged through her veins to heat her skin to boiling point again until sweat slicked over to make her skin slippery.

With the child's face close to her bare bosom, Fern mourned, her chest constricting with tears. She needed to feed Angel, but she had no milk inside her, nothing to offer her.

Overheated, Fern's breath came in short pants as she adjusted Angel against her, hitching her higher onto her shoulder and away from her aching, heavy breasts. She slipped her hand under Angel's bottom and the nappy that was heavy before, was drenched.

Humming in the base of her throat to soothe them both, Fern lay Angel across the changing mat and kept her hand on the child's stomach to stop her rolling onto the floor.

She reached for the neatly piled nappies next to the changing table and placed one next to Angel's bottom and then plucked two baby wipes from the wet wipe packet beside the nappies before she peeled off the saturated nappy and dropped the dead-weight of it into the bin at her feet. The strong stench of urine wafted up to assail her senses.

Averting her eyes, she swiped wet wipes over Angel's delicate area without taking a closer look, and then dotted on a little Sudacrem to keep her bottom from getting chafed.

She grasped Angel's ankles between the fingers of one hand and lifted her so her bottom came up from the changing mat while she slipped the fresh nappy under her. She smoothed the sticky tabs over the front of the nappy and tugged the little cotton dress down to cover it.

She cooed down at Angel, heart stuttering with joy as the child babbled back up at her.

The loud grumble of her stomach served to remind her that she hadn't yet eaten. Unlike her sister, who, it appeared, needed little or no sustenance. Especially when she was on withdrawal from drugs.

Fern desperately needed food, food to sustain her. She needed her energy now she had a dependent. She needed to keep fit and healthy. Healthy for the sake of her child.

She suspected Angel was ready for her feed too. Ravenous, in fact.

She swept her up into her arms, knees almost buckling beneath her at the unexpected weight. So much heavier than she should be at her age.

Fern stroked the back of her knuckles against Angel's cheeks and smiled down at her. 'We need to get some breakfast, my darling. I wonder what Mama has in the house for you.'

'Mama.' As the child cooed back at her, Fern smiled, delight rippling through her. 'I'm sure Mama has something, but first of all, I need to make myself decent.'

She tucked a small teddy bear against Angel's chest and made her way into her own bedroom. She placed her on the floor and yanked on her underwear followed by a pair of shorts and T-shirt.

She hefted Angel up, so she rested on her hip as she made her careful way down the stairs, no longer tempted to trot down, but to take her time, one hand firmly on the banister.

Downstairs, she slipped Angel into the high chair and moved across the kitchen to grab a slice of white bread out of its packaging, and with a sharp knife, she efficiently cut it into small fingers and placed them on the high-chair table, smiling as Angel grabbed a piece and crammed it into her mouth.

Her heart melted at Angel's delighted chuckles of pleasure as she kicked her chubby little legs.

Fern turned to open the cupboard. Baked beans on toast would do for her, but she reached inside to take out three jars of baby food.

'Everything's going to be okay, Angel.'

It was going to be just fine.

She had Angel and Emily was gone.

For now. And even if she returned, Fern didn't have the time to think about Emily, she had Angel now, and Angel needed all of her attention.

If only Emily hadn't left her in a right pickle. What the hell was she supposed to do? She could hardly go to work. She squeezed her fingers against her forehead.

Trust Emily.

She plopped one of the jars of baby food into a bowl of hot water and swiped up the phone as her gaze caught Angel's and she handed her another piece of bread to keep her quiet. 'Ssshh, Angel. Ssshh.'

On the third ring, when it was answered, she dulled her voice and made it nasal as she recognised the receptionist's voice at work. 'Hi, Maddie.' At the woman's quick response, Fern sniffed. 'Could you let them know I won't be in today. I'm sorry.' She sniffed again and let out a soft moan. 'I've picked up something. Probably from the other night. I may be off for a couple of days.'

25

MONDAY 12 JULY, 19:30 HRS

Certain people came into your life at a time when you needed them, Jenna firmly believed.

She assessed the man opposite her, perched on the edge of the settee with a Dalmatian on his lap, firmly wrapped in his long wiry arms.

Harvey Hopkins' smile could light up a room with a hundred people in. His contagious laughter rippled out as Domino took advantage and swiped a sly tongue over his face.

And before Jenna consciously made a decision about him, she'd already fallen head over heels in love.

Fliss shuffled forward onto the edge of her seat and squinted at Harvey. But Jenna could tell with a sister's instinct that Fliss was already as sold on him as she was.

His gentility and twitchy attitude endeared him to her.

Since the last dog minder turned out to be a drug pusher, they'd already ensured they'd carried out basic checks on Harvey Hopkins, confirming he had insurance in place. Professional, he'd had no qualms about providing copies of his insurance, together with three references who Jenna had spoken with personally. He came with a very high recommendation. Fliss's telephone interview with him had already been a success. And now his presence felt like a favourite old blanket that had been wrapped around them.

Taking their time in choosing a new dog walker, they'd rejected a number of them in desperation to find the right one to nurture Domino. Nurture certainly seemed to be an important word in Harvey's vocabulary as he gently eased himself from under the dog and lowered him to the floor so that he sat at his feet. A move Jenna could only admire as Mason seemed to be the only other person who could achieve that.

Doe-like, Domino's soft eyes gazed up at Harvey with desperate affection and Jenna knew that if this man was not the right one, there would be nobody else.

Despite their desire not to have a dog walker after their previous experience, both Fliss and Jenna had come to the conclusion that it was a necessity in their life after all.

With the court case against Frank Bartwell looming, both of them would be out of the house for long periods of time. Fliss as the main witness, and Jenna as the lead police officer in the prosecution of the man who kidnapped her sister and murdered his own wife and baby. It threatened to be long and gruelling and they were both ready to get it over with. Delay had been inevitable with Jenna as the main police witness having to take time off to recuperate after witnessing her colleague die in front of her.

The days would be long and Domino would have no guarantee that either Fliss or Jenna would have time to exercise him, or even feed him, as the court case would be held in Birmingham, an hour's drive each way at the best of times. At the worst, in peak travel time, it could take upwards of two hours.

As Mason was also involved in the trial and Adrian in London much of the time, they had no back-up.

They needed something more than just a dog walker. Someone with flexibility, but, most of all, they needed someone with empathy for a dog who had been maltreated in the past.

Jenna had a quiver of doubt that Domino would accept a strange man into his house after his experience with Frank Bartwell, but he displayed no such concern or animosity and simply launched himself at the delighted man the moment he'd walked through the front door as though he was a long-lost friend.

Within a heartbeat, Harvey had made himself at home.

'So, let me get this clear.' He squinted at the pad he'd brought and tapped his pen on it as he looked at the notes he'd taken. 'You'd like me to pop in daily, around lunchtime, to give him a two-hour walk for the next few weeks on a regular basis. After which you would like me to come three hours a day, split into two one-and-a-half-hour slots every day, starting in three weeks' time on the Monday, to walk Domino because both of you will be working out of Birmingham for possibly the following three months.'

With a quiet murmur of assent, Fliss inclined her head.

Jenna had told him nothing of the reason they would be in Birmingham and had no reason to assume he would know until it all hit the papers and her friendly neighbourhood journalist made sure their photographs were plastered all over the *Shropshire Star*. She couldn't even hope for a decent one of herself. Kim Stafford would make sure he found her worst side on the shittiest of days after hours in a courtroom.

Harvey smoothed back the hair at his temple and pursed his lips. 'Let's make that four hours a day to walk Domino and to child-sit him.'

A flicker of anxiety crossed Fliss's face, but she nodded as Harvey deftly outmanoeuvred her. His smile split his face, crinkling his cheeks from ear to ear, lighting up his eyes while he repositioned Domino so he could keep him in check.

Fliss glanced over at Jenna 'Would that be all right?'

Jenna shrugged her shoulders, it was Fliss's dog, her decision, although the fee would be split for both of them to pay.

'It's for an indeterminate length of time?' Harvey queried.

'Well, yes,' Fliss gushed on. 'Because, as I explained on the phone, the matter could take a week. It could be a year.'

In one swift move, the smile dropped from his face and Harvey's eyes filled with sadness, 'I'm so sorry for what happened to you.'

Fliss's eyes flew open and she dipped her head down to disguise the surprise and pain flickering over her as Jenna's heart jumped at his knowledge.

In the quiet, Harvey touched his fingers to his lips and looked at Fliss's bowed head. 'I'm sorry if that makes you uncomfortable. I thought I knew your name when I spoke with you on the phone. I didn't know why, but I recognised Domino straight away. From the newspapers last year.' He cast an anxious glance at Jenna who sighed out her relief. He was open, at least. He mouthed, 'I'm sorry,' and Jenna relaxed.

When Fliss raised her head again, her eyes were clear.

She took in a deep breath before she spoke, her voice determined and strong. 'Thank you, Harvey. It is not something I like to discuss in particular, but as it appears you already know my situation, or as far as whatever the newspapers have revealed, I will tell you it was a very painful time.' She flicked Jenna a sideways glance. 'Unfortunately, we have had matters prolonged due to other circumstances.'

Harvey's gaze swam with understanding. 'It sounds as though

you have been through a lifetime of experiences most people would never even dream could happen to them.' His voice stumbled to a halt, and as Jenna met his gaze, she knew with certainty that this man had suffered experiences of his own.

Distracted, Jenna watched as Domino settled on the floor at Harvey's feet with a quiet command from the man.

Harvey's face creased back up into a hesitant smile. 'It sounds like you're going to have a lot on your plate. For the next few weeks or months.' He repeated the words while he circled his gaze around the room. 'And I'm going to be your dog minder.'

It was a presumption he'd already made, one that Jenna wouldn't correct unless Fliss had any objections. Harvey cut in again.

'It seems a waste to walk for four hours every day. There's only a limited amount of time that Domino needs to be exercised, especially if this heat continues.' He raised his hand and wiped the back of it over his brow. 'Surely, three hours a day is more than enough? I can split it into two, so he has two hours in the morning. And then later in the day...' He tapped the pen on his pad again while he hummed in the back of his throat, tilting his head one way and then another. 'It will take some jiggling about, but once I get my diary sorted, I can come across and walk him late in the afternoon for an hour.'

He tucked his top lip in his teeth and chewed on it as he looked from one to the other of them. 'And, of course, if you want me for that fourth hour, perhaps I could stay here with him, keep him company. I could prepare a meal for you, five days a week.' Harvey glanced around again. 'I could do a little housework, it wouldn't be much in an hour, but five days a week, that hour a day would keep your house tidy. Otherwise you're going to spend your weekends catching up on that.'

Jenna hadn't given thought to housework as both sisters

tended to be relatively neat in the compact house that they lived in together. But with a dog and limited time, it would be sheer luxury to have some of the housework tended to.

Harvey leaned forward and slipped a small diary from his pocket, eliciting a smile from Jenna as she noted his lack of technology and dependence on good old-fashioned diaries and notebooks as he flicked through the first few pages. 'As I said, I'd have to jiggle things around a little as I do have other commitments.'

Jenna didn't doubt it, she imagined he was in high demand.

As she watched, she could have sworn he almost licked the end of his pen but pulled himself up short just in time.

'If I come eight to ten in the morning. Four to six in the afternoon.' He tapped the pen against his lips as he murmured to himself. 'Four hours a day, three hours walking and an hour housekeeping.' Harvey sniffed. Then removed a small stubby pencil from where he'd had it wedged behind his ear as he pushed the pen he'd held into the top pocket of his immaculately ironed shirt.

After a long moment, he pinned Fliss with a hawkish stare and waited for her answer as though the question had been posed.

Fliss shook her head, a smile curving her lips with delighted disbelief. 'That could be just exactly what all three of us need.' She glanced at Jenna and then over to Domino, who was flat out on his side at Harvey's feet. She let out a short bark of laughter and went to clap her hands, but as they closed together, she let them touch silently so Domino didn't leap back up and think that it was all a game. She grinned. 'Let sleeping dogs lie.'

In the last few months, the dog had definitely calmed down in his attitude, but his exuberance still occasionally got the better of him. Jenna considered Harvey may well be a great influence on him.

He tucked the pencil back behind his ear and rolled to his feet, holding his palm downwards as Domino scrambled up. 'Fabulous. That's what we shall do then.' His business like tone brooked no resistance and Jenna and Fliss both came to their feet at the same time. 'I'll get your contract in the post by tonight and then I suggest that I come around in two days' time and walk Domino just to make sure that we're all in harmony with each other.' His face crinkled into a smile as he raked his gaze over the dog in front of him.

Harmony, Jenna puffed her lips out. Harmony would be good. She hesitated to believe they could be so lucky.

As they approached the door, Harvey opened it to slip outside, but his hand briefly touched the top of Domino's head in a gentle swipe of affection.

'Just one thing.' Jenna halted him while she sent him a cheeky smile. 'Harvey, please tell me you don't do drugs.'

With a crack of laughter Harvey threw back his head. 'I can assure you, my lovely, not only do I not do drugs, I'm not even very good with paracetamol.'

As the door closed behind him, Fliss turned and leaned back against it, a pensive flicker crossing her brow with a moment of doubt.

Jenna met her gaze. 'Okay. Is everything all right? Are you happy with that?'

Fliss puffed out a breath and wiped the back of her hand across her brow, smoothing out the wrinkles. 'I'm not sure what happened then, but I think we may have been bamboozled into exactly what we want.' She broke out into a wild grin. 'I liked him. I really did.'

Jenna smiled back. She'd carry out some checks. Make sure this one wasn't a child trafficker or a flasher. She didn't even want a shoplifter.

26

'Put the child down, Emily.'

Surprised at her sister's return so soon, Fern's pulse hammered at the base of her throat, constricting the bubble of air that had lodged there as fear sent spikes of ice coursing through her veins.

She took a cautious step closer to her sister, hands held up in front of her. 'Emily.' She kept her voice soft, but the lowered tone remained firm and immovable. 'Put Angel down.'

Emily turned from where she'd been looking out of the open window. Her long, straggled hair slipped over one shoulder onto the child's screwed-up face and appeared to irritate her even more as Angel let out robust scream after scream. The child's dangling legs thrashed as she strained backwards to get away from Emily's tight grip.

'Emily.' With more urgency, Fern deepened her voice to make it heard above the wild wailing.

Unperturbed, a slow, sinister grin spread over her sister's face while her eyes remained a cold, hard glow as she exerted power over her sister. 'I won't harm Angel, you know. I'm not about to hurt Zak's child.' One eyebrow winged its way up her forehead as her lips twitched with cold humour enough to set Fern's teeth on edge. 'You do trust me, don't you?'

Not in a million years.

Speechless, Fern watched as Emily stepped closer to the open window. Her long, plump fingers turned white as she grasped the child to her bloated bosom in an attempt to stop Angel's desperate thrashing.

Bent backwards, Angel's howls escalated as Emily wrenched her away from the relative safety of her breasts and held her at arm's length towards the open window.

Emily tilted her head, her lips parted to reveal her perfect, white teeth. 'You do trust me, don't you?' she repeated, without a flicker of concern.

Panic sliced Fern's heart in two as tears tracked down her cheeks while Emily applied more pressure for her to bend to her will. 'Yes. Yes, Emily. I trust you. I really trust you.' Whatever it took, whatever she had to say, she would say it.

She gauged the distance between herself and her sister and knew she could never reach her in time if Emily decided to drop the child out of the window. It was one step for Emily and at least eight for Fern. She didn't stand a chance of getting there in time. The best she could do was to go along with the torturous game Emily wanted to play.

Angel's tiny face screwed up, turning puce in her hysteria as she dangled from Emily's hands. Arms and legs pumped in unison with a ferocity borne of panic. She couldn't know what her fate was to be but could only be aware of the whipping away of all security.

'Emily, put Angel down.'

'You don't trust me, do you?' She tilted her head to one side as her lips kicked up in a mocking smile, one Fern recognised as dangerous.

'It's not that. I know you wouldn't mean to, but you might slip.' If she could pacify her long enough to get her away from the window.

'I wouldn't slip. I never have before.'

Fern blinked away the image of the tabby kitten, leg broken, dangling from her sister's cruel fingers while words strangled in her throat. She knew she should say something, anything, to persuade Emily otherwise, but as she had then, she waited, breath backing up to burn her lungs as Angel's screams reached fever pitch.

The smile dropped from Emily's face and Fern stood frozen to the spot, not a whisper of a breath moving.

'Oh, for God's sake!' Emily shot her a disgusted sneer as she whipped the child back against her chest. She cradled her as though she was the most precious thing on earth and she'd never dream of hurting her. But Fern knew better. 'You're pathetic!' Emily spat vitriol from her lips, exposing her neat, white teeth.

It wasn't over yet as the squalling cries of panic reached breaking point.

Fern remained still, feet firmly planted on the floor, while she waited. The white-water rush filled her head as she swallowed the small amount of saliva that hadn't already dried up while she waited for her sister to make her next move.

'Oh, very well.' With a soft pout, Emily strode forward, shoved the child at Fern, who grabbed her with both hands, almost dropping her in her desperation.

Before she could respond, Emily was gone.

Fern flopped her head forward to bury her face in Angel's hair while she rocked the child, terror still sending shudders through her body.

'Shhh, Angel, shhh.'

To comfort them both, she jiggled Angel in her arms and walked over to switch on the music machine. The soft melodic notes floated above the crying wails of Angel as Fern rocked, rocked, rocked.

'Close your eyes, little girl. Close your eyes, go to sleep. Close them tight, little girl, for the rest of the night. Close your eyes. Close your eyes, little girl.'

27

Fern shot upright in bed, the thin sheet dropping from her sweat-slicked body. She hauled in gasp after gasp of breath, her mouth gaping wide open while she tried to control her racing heart.

'Angel, oh my God, Angel.'

With her pulse thundering in her ears, she tilted her head to listen, but in the silence, there was nothing but her own laboured breathing, the drum of her own heart.

No child crying.

No other sound in the house.

Nothing.

Just her tortured imagination that Emily had spurred with her infernal torment. The cat-and-mouse game of power.

She drew her legs up to her chest and wrapped her arms around them, dipping her head onto her knees while she fought to get her breathing under control.

'Emily.' Voice hoarse, she raised her head and looked towards the closed bedroom door, suspicion curling in tight bundles in her stomach. 'Emily. Dammit.'

There was no sound from the nursery. Nothing to make her think that her sister was back.

Except that small nugget of doubt. Doubt that fired her up enough to move. Fear of what her sister may do if she was left alone with Angel.

She plucked at the balled-up sheet and pushed it to the end of the bed as she swung her legs over the side and stood, her breath still rasping in her throat.

On naked, silent feet, she tiptoed to her bedroom door and reached out to twist the handle and crack it open.

Her breath still came in fast snatches while she hesitated.

Was she just being paranoid?

Maybe, but she needed to check Angel was safe.

She whispered open the door and sneaked onto the landing, avoiding the floorboard she knew would squeak when she stood on it. She touched the doorknob on the nursery door and waited again. She angled her head to listen, straining to hear any give-away sound in the silence.

Nothing.

With a cautious turn of the knob, Fern pushed the door wide.

Soft buttery light greeted her, glowing from the nightlight plugged in by the side of the cot. It cast pale golden stars across the ceiling, giving out enough light for Fern to be able to see there was nobody in the nursery but the little one.

Angel, who was fast asleep.

Fern sneaked over to the cot and leaned her forearms against the rail as she peered down at the sleeping child, contentment in every soft curve of her face. Skin a pale translucence, blue veins and smudges of purple under the eyes showed how deep in sleep Angel was.

As her heartbeat slowed and relief flowed over her to soothe her soul, Fern stood for a while longer, fascinated with the pure innocent beauty.

A smile played across her mouth.

Angel was fine. She was safe.

Emily was nowhere to be seen. No car in the drive. She'd not be able to get into the house anyway. Not since Fern had called the man and had the locks changed. It was simple paranoia, and fear.

Fern straightened and turned towards the nursery door. Breath catching in her throat as she caught the quick flit of a shadow crossing the dark landing.

Pulse escalating back to panic mode, Fern gave a brief glance over her shoulder to check on Angel. Still fast asleep, the child's light breathing never changed.

With soundless steps, Fern crept onto the landing and drew the nursery door closed behind her. She held onto the doorknob to stop the sharp click she knew it would give if she let go too quickly.

She clenched her teeth, her jaw flexing as she snapped on the landing night.

'Emily.' Her voice a hoarse whisper, she called out for her sister. 'Are you there?'

Nothing. No answer.

She kept her voice hushed as she stepped further along the landing, away from the nursery. 'Emily, if you're there, stop pratting about. You don't scare me, you know.'

She terrified her.

Greeted only by silence, Fern swung open the bathroom door to check inside. Her nerves jumped and anger swirled in the pit of her stomach in a mixture of doubt and turmoil.

If Emily was playing silly beggars, she was about to get her comeuppance. She'd grab her by the hair and bash her this time.

Finding the room empty, Fern blew out a sigh as she scrubbed her hands over her face and dug the tips of her fingers into her eyes to help them focus better. God, she was tired. She should be sleeping while Angel was, to conserve her energy for when the child wanted to play. Not spend precious time searching for her sister. A sister she wasn't about to bash because that wasn't what she did. She was the pacifist, the peacekeeper. The one who always calmed Emily down and brought her back into line. But Emily had never done anything like this before, never been so out of control. It had been bad enough when she stalked Zak and it had taken professional help to draw her back from the brink of a very dark precipice.

But this, this was worse.

All Fern could hope for was to keep Angel safe until she got Emily some help. In the meantime, she could only hope Emily didn't find her way into the house.

She backed out of the bathroom and tugged the door closed behind her.

Undecided, Fern took a moment before she opened the door to the fourth room.

In direct contrast to the mess that was Emily, her bedroom bloomed with pink rose print flowing over immaculately ironed bedding. Two beautiful throw cushions: one embroidered with an animation hare, the other with a hedgehog. Pale green daubed the perfect walls and the white ceiling was the centrepiece for a delicate crystal chandelier that dangled, catching bright sparks of light from the bulb.

Her sister evidently hadn't been there to disturb anything, although Fern often wondered how Emily kept it as neat as a pin when she was around.

Reluctant to step inside, Fern cast her gaze around one last time and then closed the door on the perfection of her sister's bedroom and tiptoed her way back to her own room on the opposite side of the landing.

Never as neat and tidy, she nevertheless found her solace there. Her throw cushions weren't embroidered, but faux fur that she could cuddle and take comfort from in the middle of the night. Fur which currently was far too warm to have on her bed and was residing in a heap at the side.

With a sigh, Fern straightened out her bedding and smoothed the still sweat-damp sheet while she allowed the relief of her sister's absence to calm her.

There was nobody there. Emily hadn't come home. It was just her imagination and expectation that her sister was always there when she least wanted or needed her. Always in the midst of trouble. She didn't find it, she created it. She built the smallest incident into a drama to cultivate panic and angst.

Fern slipped under the covers and tugged them up to her chin as she lay flat on her back and held her breath while she listened to her own heartbeat slow down to normal. Her eyes closed, she drifted back to sleep with the fresh waft of night air drifting through the window to cool her overheated skin.

Another few hours of sleep would be so welcome.

With trembling fingers, Fern reached out to pick up the small, blue toy elephant. Ears soft and floppy, the silken material cool next to her skin as she pressed it against her bosom.

Fear sent a rash of goosebumps chasing across her sweat-slicked skin as the light breeze danced through the open window of the nursery.

'Oh, Emily, Emily.'

'Of course, it's Emily, you fool.'

Fern whipped around, a pained gasp lodged in her throat as she stared at her sister. Confusion and horror battled for supremacy.

'Who else did you think it would be?' Her sister's red lips thinned and twisted with derision. 'No one's going to break in here. Who the hell else would want to?' She tipped back her head and, as the chubby folds on her neck stretched out, she chortled. The pure meanness of her laughter shot a warning chill through Fern's veins.

She cast a quick glance at Angel, fast asleep in the cot and swallowed her panic. If only she could keep her quiet, Emily wouldn't get irritated. If only Emily would stay quiet, Angel wouldn't wake and cry.

Fern turned back to her sister, determined to keep control. 'How did you get in?'

Emily raised one eyebrow as she drew her hand up in the air and dangled a key from her fingers, quirking her lips with derision. 'Oh, come on, Fern. Of course, I got in. Do you think you're ever going to stop me?' She gurgled out a delighted laugh. 'I'm not sure you intended to keep me out. You left the spare key where you have always left the spare key. I may never have used it before, but you've left it in the same place ever since you moved here, and I have always known where you kept it.' She snorted out her disgust as she tucked the key into her jeans' pocket. 'Such a creature of habit. So very foolish. Foolish and naive.' She spat the last word out, her eyes sparkling with wicked delight.

Compelled to defend herself, Fern raised her chin but kept her voice a soft growl. 'I'm not naive. Please don't say that.'

Fern's gaze flickered towards the cot and the sleeping child. Fear kept her from shouting at her sister, who it appeared had no such qualms, as she raised her voice, to draw a whimper from Angel.

'You are naive. Now what are you going to do? Pay another hundred and fifty quid to have your locks changed again?' She puffed out her breath and slammed both hands on her rounded hips. 'It won't stop me. You know, I'll still get in here.' She whipped her head around, scanning the bedroom. 'It's as much mine as it is yours.'

Fern stepped forward, one hand held out to stop her sister's anger from escalating. 'I never tried to stop...'

'Of course you tried to stop me. Why else would you have

your locks changed? You know, no amount of barriers will keep me out.' She paused, her breath heaved making her heavy bosom swell. Her voice when it came again was quieter, soothing. 'I'm not going to harm anybody, Fern. You know that, don't you?'

Fern gulped down the words that wanted to spew out. Of course, she'd cause harm. She'd done it before, she'd do it again. She'd harm the child. Her child. 'Emily,' she blew out a long breath, tried to reason with her sister. 'I think we need to speak to someone about this, get some help.'

In a swift move, Emily stepped in, her eyes narrowing, her lips pulled to a thin mean line. 'You tell anybody, *anybody*.' She closed the gap and grasped a tight hand around Fern's neck, red-painted nails digging in just enough for Fern to appreciate the threat.

'Emily, stop.' Her strangled voice burst from her throat. 'You don't need to do this.'

'Oh, I do need to do it. I think you need a lesson.'

'I don't need a lesson. I understand.' Every bit the pacifist, Fern raised her hands to rest them on Emily's, knowing her sister had the strength and capacity to strangle her if she wanted. Almost nose to nose, she met Emily's gaze. 'Shall we go downstairs?'

'No.' Emily's sour breath puffed out against her face.

Desperate not to risk a look at the sleeping child in case Emily noticed, she couldn't help the quick slide of her glance in Angel's direction before she whipped it back again.

Emily's face turned sly as her own gaze followed the direction of Fern's and then back again, her eyes narrowed. 'Oh, that child means more to you than I do, doesn't it?' Jealousy laced her voice. 'I see. I understand now.'

The hard dig of Emily's nails ratcheted up the panic, but Fern kept her face blank as she stared back at her sister. 'Of course, she doesn't. She's precious, of course, but only because you brought her. She was a gift from you. That's what makes her so special. Your special gift. To me.'

As Emily's face relaxed, Fern gave her fingers a gentle squeeze to encourage her to let go, holding onto her sister's hands as she lowered them away from her neck.

Emily's voice purred. 'She's only special because she's Zak's. The little girl we should have had together.' Emily narrowed her eyes, a tight smile spreading across her face. 'I could still have Zak. Did you hear the news?'

Fern stilled, terrified to acknowledge that she knew. Knew what Emily had done.

She'd beaten a woman almost to death and stolen her baby. Zak's baby. It was all over the news, how could she have missed it? Every half hour. Appeal after appeal to find little Joshua.

Rather than instil further rage in Emily just as she'd managed to calm her down, Fern gave a slight shake of her head, refusing to meet her sister's eyes. Frightened of what she might see reflected there. Terrified of what her sister may see in hers.

'Zak's wife had an accident, it appears. Their baby has gone missing.' The challenge from Emily was there for Fern to dispute.

Their baby boy. But Fern held back on saying it out loud. It would only infuriate her sister again. She needed to calm her. Get her in a good place so she could get help for her.

She linked her fingers through Emily's and made a deliberate effort to keep her attention away from the still sleeping child. 'Emily, let's go downstairs. We can have something to eat. When was the last time you ate?'

She scanned her sister's face. Her skin had turned dull and flaccid from lack of sleep. Obviously no longer taking care of herself properly, blackheads littered the top of her nose and in the crease on her chin. Lacklustre, her hair hung in limp strands down to her shoulders. In a matter of a few days, she'd turned from vibrant and vivacious to desperate and dangerous.

It wasn't just the lack of sleep that was responsible, but the fact that she'd stopped taking her medication. Withdrawal was bound to have an effect.

Fern stared into her sister's frantic eyes and sadness washed over her. It wasn't Emily's fault. She needed help. Help Fern doubted she was capable of providing. It was too late. They were too far down the road for that.

Fern reached out to touch Emily's cheek and hesitated as her sister flinched. 'It's okay, Emily. Everything's going to be okay, now. I'm going to take good care of you.'

Emily shook her head. 'You can't, Fern. You're not strong enough.'

Saddened by her sister's lack of faith, Fern cupped Emily's cheek with her hand. 'I'll find someone who can help. I promise.'

Emily turned her head, so Fern's hand slipped away from her cheek just as Angel let out a small cry and kicked the thin sheets off her legs. Still asleep, she snuffled, while both women held their breath.

The last thing Fern needed was for Angel to wake while Emily needed so much of her attention. Just a short while longer, Fern found herself praying as she made a deliberate turn away from Angel, taking Emily's elbow in her grasp.

'Let's go downstairs.'

Emily's shoulders drooped and the frenetic light extinguished from her eyes. 'Okay.'

Fern pulled the door closed behind them and tiptoed down the stairs. She glanced over her shoulder to make sure Emily followed her. She checked behind her every few steps, not putting it past Emily to push her down the stairs.

She reached the bottom and made her way along the short hallway to the kitchen.

Her gaze touched on the two empty bottles of Mateus Rosé, one of them on its side on her small, round kitchen table. Before she could stop herself, judgement spilled from her. 'Oh, Emily. You know you shouldn't drink when you're on medication.'

In a fast switch of temperament to leave Fern regretting her comment, Emily's lips pulled up in a feral growl. 'I'm not on fucking medication.' Eyes hard, she glared into Fern's face, towering over her. 'You know that stuff only fucks you up, don't you? Right?'

Fern's heart stuttered as Emily confirmed her dark suspicion. They were in serious, serious trouble. She needed to let somebody know. She needed to report it. But who to? Emily's counsellor was no longer around and nobody else had been put in charge of Emily since they'd declared her sister stable.

Stable.

How could Emily ever be classified as stable? The moment she missed her meds, her world started to shred into thin strands which unravelled slowly until her meds knit them back together again.

The fact that she'd gone cold turkey horrified Fern. That and the addition of alcohol. What chance did she stand of helping her sister get back on track?

Fern slipped onto one of the two small, hard, white-painted wooden stools as Emily reached into the fridge and extracted a fresh bottle of Mateus Rosé, efficiently popping out the cork as only someone who'd had ample practice could do. She reached for two large wine glasses and poured the pink wine into each of them. Slipping one across the table, she smiled at Fern as the chill of it bloomed the glass with condensation.

'Why don't you join me?'

Fern's mouth watered at the temptation of an ice-cold drink after such a scorcher of a day and she reached out to wrap her fingers around the stem of the wine glass, drawing it nearer to her. What harm could it do? If it pacified Emily knowing Fern joined her in a friendly glass of wine, perhaps then her sister would relax. Fern could maybe persuade her to take her meds, or if she would go to bed, Fern could make plans. Telephone around. Get them some help. She needed support as much as her sister did.

She'd be careful. Just sip a little. Drink it slowly. It wasn't a high alcohol content, more like drinking a light, refreshing fizzy drink.

Assuming it was the last bottle, she'd be doing Emily a favour by consuming it, just so her sister didn't feel obliged to finish off her third bottle. Low alcohol it may be but drinking three bottles of it was bound to have an effect.

She picked up the glass and took a slow sip, her mouth tightening at the taste of the sharp wine, but the cool wash of it down her parched throat coaxed an appreciative sigh from her. As her muscles relaxed, she wilted against the kitchen table, forearms resting to keep her propped up.

She smiled as she flicked Emily a glance from under dark eyelashes. In direct contrast to her relaxed muscles, her mind spun, racing through quick resolutions and scenarios. Of them all, the simplest was the best. Get rid of Emily. Get her out of her house. Get her out of her life. For good.

After all, Fern had Angel to care for. Angel was her priority.

She'd have to find a way to keep her sister parted from Angel before she caused her any harm. There had to be something. Someone. She needed to tell somebody. She'd told before, and that's when her sister had got all the help she needed, and she'd gone, leaving a great cavity of loneliness in her wake. As much as

Emily troubled and disturbed Fern, having her disappear completely from her world had been a shock at first but once Emily had been gone for a while, Fern started to really appreciate living a normal life without a sister to watch out for. To care for.

Life had been simple without Emily.

29

Emily tucked her legs up and wrapped her arms around them so she could rest her chin on her knees while she rocked back and forth. With her back to the corner, she roamed her gaze around Fern's bedroom until it fell on her sister's face.

In repose, Fern was prettier than ever. Her eyelids closed, long, dark eyelashes rested on the translucence of her skin above her high cheekbones. Any wrinkles she may have had been smoothed out with sleep. Her breath sighed in and out through her perfect, snub nose.

Dark irritation stabbed at Emily as she reached for the newly opened bottle of Mateus Rosé by her side. Not bothering with a glass, she tipped it up to gulp down several mouthfuls of the liquid while she kept her gaze fixed on Fern.

Fern.

She'd thought bringing that child, that brat, home would have delighted her sister. That she'd love her even more, want her to share in the delight of the child.

It hadn't worked the way she'd hoped, and Fern was so entangled with the brat, she'd virtually ignored Emily.

She straightened and pushed her spine deep into the corner to ease the ache in her shoulders through sitting hunched over for too long.

Her head thunked back against the wall as she took another slug of wine, letting it swirl around her tongue and mind. She placed the bottle back down by her side and raised her hand so she could gnaw at the delicate skin at the edge of her thumbnail. She pulled her hand back and studied her thumb where she'd stripped the skin from around the nail bed to leave the nail growing through pitted and distorted. A thin sliver of skin stuck out. She pressed her lips to her thumb and took the rag of skin between her teeth to peel it back until it broke off.

Fascinated, Emily chewed the minute piece of skin while she stared at the bloom of blood from the new wound she'd created. As a drop formed, she pressed her thumb to her lips and sucked. The metallic taste of her own blood filled her mouth as her less than focused gaze drifted back to her sister.

She dropped her hand to her side and her knuckles brushed against the cold, metallic handle of the kitchen knife. Unsure how it came to be there, she wrapped her fingers around it and brought it up to her face, her vision wavered as the alcohol took its effect. Her stomach lurched and the bitter taste of acid burned the back of her throat.

Emily slapped her free hand over her mouth as tears welled in her eyes to make her vision fog even more.

It's too hard, the hoarse voice whispered in her head. *You wanted Zak, but he wants his wife.*

Emily touched her fingers to the front page of *The Shropshire Star* with the half-page picture of Zak, Imelda and Joshua. A family portrait of three beautiful people as they laughed into the camera.

Her chest squeezed until she could no longer breathe.

'Zak.' Her voice slurred out the word. 'I love him.'

He doesn't love you, though.

She traced Zak's face with her fingertip. 'But I love him.'

The voice turned spiteful and mean. *Did you really think Zak would love you when you returned his child to him?*

Emily snivelled without replying. She didn't bother to cover her ears, she knew the voice would still get through.

You know she's going to tell on you, don't you? She can't hold on any longer.

She peered at her sister through the golden hues of the early-dawn light cutting in through the gap in the curtains to slash across the room.

The sly insistence of the voice threaded through her mind. *She's the one. She makes it so difficult. Everything was fine until she tried to take over. Fine until she insisted you get help. Look what happened last time. They drugged you and I went away.*

Emily blinked.

Perhaps she should put them both out of their misery. Just a quick stab to Fern's jugular and it would all be over. A slash from the inside of her wrist in a straight line to her elbow would ensure she'd bleed out quickly.

She swiped up the bottle and took another long swig before she cradled it to her chest.

Simple, the voice agreed.

Knife in hand, Emily pushed up from the floor and staggered towards Fern's bed, her slippered feet weaving across the thick carpet pile until she stumbled to a halt, towering above her sister.

She blinked her vision clear, only to have it fog over again. The knife in her raised hand blurred in the glint of the breaking dawn.

She closed her eyes and wavered as the black bloom of clouds descended, swarming behind her eyelids.

The shrill cry of a child shot her eyes wide open and rage whipped through to darken the edges of her vision.

The brat. Dark fury laced the gravelly voice.

Emily spun on her heel to face the bedroom door as the voice murmured its cruel encouragement.

It's the brat's fault. Not Fern's. Not Emily's.

The cries pierced through her head. It never stopped crying. It needed to stop.

'Why won't it stop?'

Alcohol saturation dropped from her like a silken cloak and she strode towards the bedroom door and the source of the ear-piercing screeches as clarity struck her. What was the point of having the child if she could no longer have the father?

The cries escalated and echoed around in her mind.

She gripped the bottle of wine in one hand, the knife in her other.

Filled with glee, the voice encouraged her. *You know what you have to do.*

Focused, Emily threw open the nursery door and glared at the toddler. She stepped inside and kicked the door shut behind her.

The bane of her life.

The brat.

30

As the shaft of dawn sunlight touched her face, Fern roused, and rolled over onto her side. She kicked aside the thin, cotton sheet to let the thick, heavy air at her naked skin. Not that it cooled her in any way. The temperature had soared the previous day and it already threatened to continue its upward spiral.

Angel's insistent cries nudged at Fern. With a grunt, she rolled out of bed and pushed aside the thick fog that blanketed her brain. She shouldn't moan. Angel was an excellent sleeper. She'd gone down at ten o'clock the previous night and it was now just past five in the morning. A good long stretch. The light mornings helped Fern to rouse quicker than normal.

It didn't make her feel any less exhausted. She'd never realised how tiring it was to look after a child on your own. If Emily had been of any use, it would have eased the burden, but she'd never done anything. Their whole lives, Emily had dumped and run. She'd never been able to rely on her.

Fern tugged her thin nightdress down, so it fell in soft drapes to her knees as she stumbled to the door. She pressed her hand against her forehead and took in long draughts of air to fill her lungs with enough oxygen to clear her head while she wrenched open her door and weaved her way across the landing.

She bumped open the door to the nursery.

Horror sent shockwaves pulsing through her to burn her already overheated skin so sweat popped out in beads, which slicked the thin nightdress to her within a heartbeat.

'Emily! What the hell do you think you're doing?'

Rather than whip around as Fern had expected her to, her sister took a casual, slow circle to face Fern. A long-bladed carving knife dangled by loose fingers at her side. The carving knife Fern had recently bought from TK Maxx. With a twelve-inch blade, the Sheffield steel was lethal.

'Fern.' The slow smile that spread over Emily's face never reached her stone-cold eyes as she raised the bottle of wine in her other hand and took a deep gulp.

Emily spliced Fern's heart in two as her sister cocked her head and raised the knife to point it with deadly carelessness straight at her.

'She won't shut up, Fern.' Voice slurred, the knife's point made an erratic circle in the air.

Fern took a cautious step forward, her voice caught in her sand-dry throat as she held both hands out towards her sister in supplication. 'Emily. Put the knife down, darling. There's a good girl. Put the knife down.'

Emily tilted her head on the other side, the vagueness of her stare portrayed her disinterest in Fern's words as Angel's cries pitched higher. 'But she won't fucking shut up, Fern. No matter what you do. She won't shut up.'

Her fingers spasmed around the hilt of the knife as she gripped it tighter until her knuckles turned white.

She arched it around and Fern's breath staggered in her chest as Emily turned and pointed the knife at Angel.

Two more steps brought Fern closer to her sister.

With her own head banging, Fern squinted through the pain and focused on Emily.

Could she make it? If Emily lunged at the child, could Fern get there in time?

'It's okay, my darling.' She kept her voice a soothing lull in the hope that Angel would take comfort in her tone and at least stop crying.

As the child met her stare across the room, Fern smiled. A little desperate, but a smile, nonetheless.

Angel's soft lips lifted at the corners, her wobbly smile full of desperation while tears trembled at the edge of her eyes.

Addressing her sister, but all the time keeping the soothing tone in her voice for Angel, Fern sidled closer and then closer still, her shuffling footsteps minimal to keep Emily from taking fright.

Fern raised a slow hand, palm upwards. 'Give me the knife, Emily. Everything's going to be fine.' She needed to keep the desperation and fear from her voice.

Emily's chin dropped while she took a long, slow study of the knife in her hand. She let the wine bottle drop so it hit the floor with a muffled thump and spilled pink liquid out in a silent flow. She opened her fingers, so the shaft of the knife balanced on her palm. She drew in a protracted, shuddering breath and then raised her bleak gaze to Fern's pleading one. 'It's all wrong. We made it all wrong, Fern.'

Fern rolled her lips inwards and took a deep breath. Trust her sister to make it about them, not solely her. Why did she have to drag her into her problems again? Time after time. She only ever came to her when she was in trouble. It wasn't fair.

She kept the resentment deep inside, reluctant to let Emily

see it shimmering through her eyes. 'That's okay, Emily. We can make it right again.'

Damn her. It wasn't *we*. There was no *we* about it.

Annoyance at her sister festered within, whirling around in a ball of heat in her stomach. She could kill her. If she was the one holding the knife, she probably would. Emily. A pain in the backside. The most demanding personality.

Acceptance of her own mistakes had never come easily to Emily. She refused to face them and placed the blame anywhere but at her own front doorstep.

Fern ground her teeth as she waited while her sister contemplated matters.

Emily's grip tightened and she circled the blade around in a lazy circle as though it was a sword she clutched. 'I watched you while you were sleeping, you know.'

Fern's blood ran cold through her veins, not enough to stop the sweat popping out all over her skin at her sister's words.

She stared at the glint of sunlight as it sparked from the knife in her sister's hand.

The mere thought of someone watching her at her most vulnerable. Asleep. Defenceless.

She drew in a deep breath through her nose, her nostrils flaring as she struggled to control the situation. She'd had it tough with Emily in the past, but never this dangerous. Never this complex.

A bitter smile crossed Emily's features as her fingers loosened again as though the knife was too heavy to hold. 'I thought to myself how much easier it would be if neither of us were here. How simple life would become without us.'

Again, the *us*. But Fern didn't want to be a part of the *us*. She yearned to be her own person, no longer connected to Emily. No longer responsible for her actions. No longer blamed for her deeds as she had been their entire lives. Emily always held her accountable.

Indignation stabbed little arrows into Fern's heart to harden it against her sister.

The knife in Emily's hand, no longer a threat, Fern stepped into her sister's space, her patience at an end. 'Give me the fucking knife, Emily.'

Emily's thick eyebrows shot up her forehead and a crooked smile crossed her face. 'Why, Fern. You must be pissed off. You never swear.' She snorted out a bitter laugh. 'Miss goody-two-shoes.'

The fury broke loose. After so long, so many years of putting up with her, the fine thread of Fern's empathy and patience unravelled fibre by fibre until the snap of it vibrated through her mind. She stormed at Emily, four long strides. Heat flooded her face until she thought her head would explode. 'Give me the fucking knife!' White saliva flew in droplets from her lips to splatter over Emily's chubby cheeks.

The initial pop followed by the cold slide of the knife into her flesh took her more than a full moment to register. Her head rolled forward until her chin almost touched her breastbone. Fern drew in one hard, gasping breath and held it there as she stared at the knife protruding from her belly, her own hand wrapped around the hilt.

Fern sank to her knees by the side of the cot and coughed out small, wheezy sobs. 'You've killed me.' She raised the lead weight of her head as black curtains flapped in the periphery of her vision. 'Emily. What have you done? You've killed me.' Through the tunnel of her vision, she caught the flitting movement of a shadow and turned her head. 'Emily. Help me.'

But Emily was gone.

31

Fern curled in on herself, the foetal position came naturally, her spine bowed downwards as she lowered her head towards her knees.

Each little sip of air burned her lungs as she reached out bloodstained fingers, stretching them towards the child.

Her Angel.

What would become of her little darling? Would Angel be safe now Emily was gone?

Tears sprang to her eyes and through the mist she stared at Angel.

With shaky fingers, she grasped at the rails of the cot to pull herself closer. Her fingernails scraped along the pale wood as the dark curtains fluttered to close down her vision, so she loosened her grip.

Devoid of energy as her mind turned numb, she let her hands fall away to flop palm upward at her side onto the pale cream carpet. Crimson streaked her skin, and for the first time in weeks, the heat that had pulsed through her body, slicking her skin with sweat, ebbed away to bring a welcome coolness that soon turned to an uncomfortable ice.

'It's okay, Angel.' Her voice croaked from her parched throat. 'Everything will be okay. Emily's gone. She can't hurt you now.'

Dazed, she rolled into a tight ball, her forehead touched the floor before she keeled over sideways. The burn in her side turned to a dull throb.

She drew her hand in to wrap it around the hilt of the knife. If she could pull it out, it might just help.

Fern's eyes slipped shut and the grasp she had on the knife loosened, while blood pumped a lazy pool to join the thinner, paler colour of wine and spread across the carpet.

There was nothing more she could do.

Emily had killed her.

32

Jenna tapped Harvey Hopkins' name into the computer and hovered her fingers over the keys. Somehow it didn't feel right. He'd seemed like a genuine man and if a minor misdemeanour came up on the system, she'd always be looking at him.

She stroked the keys and then backspaced to delete his name from the search engine just as her phone rang.

She swiped it up. 'DS Morgan.'

'Sarg.'

Jenna recognised Morris King's melodic voice immediately and, with a sigh of pleasure, sank her chin onto her hand as her insides melted in anticipation of his next words. 'Yes, Morris.'

At the stuttered pause, Jenna realised she'd unintentionally dipped her voice to intimate. She whipped her head up and slapped her hand down on the desk in front of her. Damn, but it had been another long night with barely a wink of sleep again. The welcome coolness of the air con had made her comfortable but the soft purr of it had filtered through her mind to compete with the squeal of tinnitus caused by her desperate sadness.

Her heart felt as though it had been wrenched apart by the

missing child and her inability to do anything to influence that situation except to keep looking. The clues were there. They just needed to piece them together.

She shot upright in her chair and kicked an element of authority into her voice, only grateful Mason and Ryan were in the main office and hadn't witnessed her slip. 'Go ahead, Morris.'

'Umm. Thank you. I think.' He pulled in a breath. 'I've a lady on the line, Sarg, a Mrs Hanson. I'd normally pass it onto uniform, but... there's something here, Sarg. I think you should listen to her.' If Morris had joined the police force, he'd have made an excellent detective, his powers of observation mixed nicely with instinct often flagged up situations most of their operators would never notice. He gave her no reason to doubt his hunch now.

'Okay, Morris. Thank you. Put her through.' She waited for the connecting click. 'Mrs Hanson?'

'Yes. Hello.'

Voice younger than she expected, Jenna pressed the phone closer to her ear as she leaned to her right so she could peer along the length of the main office and pinpoint her two sidekicks.

One hand deep in his trouser pocket, the other clutching a takeout cup of coffee, Ryan fidgeted as his skinny frame hovered over Mason's desk, avid concentration written all over his face. Sickened at the sight of the energy that pulsed off him at that time of the morning, Jenna let out a sigh.

By contrast, Mason was kicked back in his chair, his broad shoulders resting against the wall behind him. If the chair wasn't on wheels, he'd have had it on two feet, tipped back. Which was precisely why health and safety no longer allowed them to have four-legged chairs and they had five-footed wheelies instead. Not that it made them any safer when officers decided to have their occasional wheelie chair races across the threadbare carpet tiles.

'What can I do for you, Mrs Hanson?'

Nerves skittered through the young voice, so it rose and fell in soft squeaks. 'I've never done this before.'

Jenna came upright and reached for a pen in her desk drawer. 'Take your time, Mrs Hanson.'

'I don't normally tell on people. It's just, well, you know...' She blew out a gusty breath that vibrated in Jenna's ear, so she held the phone away.

'I'm sure you're not telling on anyone. Sometimes, you just need to check that things are right. What is it you don't feel is right, Mrs Hanson?'

'My neighbour, there's been a lot of unusual noise lately.'

'Okay.'

Jenna closed her eyes. Morris may be good, but if he'd given her a neighbourhood dispute to deal with, she might just flog him, especially now when they'd not made any progress tracking down Joshua with not a single lead to give them a direction to look.

She managed an interested murmur and waited, giving Morris the benefit of the doubt. If he said it was important, she'd run with it. The woman had all of two minutes before she handed her over to a uniform. It hardly required a detective to investigate a shouting match.

'Normally, she lives on her own. I've not noticed anyone else, but there's been so much shouting. In the middle of the night.'

Jenna slid her drawer closed. With her elbow on the desk, she rested her chin on her hand and let her spine slump as she reached for the mouse next to her computer, clicking it to kick the screen into action. She resisted the temptation to sigh. 'Mmm-hmm.'

'And then there's the child...'

Jenna hesitated, her hand hovered above the mouse. 'Child?'

'Yes. There's a child. Didn't I mention? Maybe I said it to the man I spoke to.' The nerves made her voice pitch higher. 'Crying so much. I keep hearing it. It's really...' She paused. '... pitiful.'

Jenna unrolled herself from the hunched-over position in front of her desk with a slow stretch of her spine until her shoulders cricked and she sat upright in her chair. 'Tell me about the child.'

'It's crying now, I don't know if you can hear it.' She went silent and the distant sound of a wailing child filtered through the phone, barely perceptible but supporting her point. 'It's been like that for the past hour. A whole hour.' Her voice cracked on a broken sob. 'My heart is pounding. I want to go in and check that everything's all right.'

'What makes you feel it shouldn't be all right, Mrs Hanson?' Children cried, didn't they?

'Lorna. Lorna Hanson. There was so much shouting. And then it went silent, except for the child crying.'

The flutter in Jenna's chest warned her that things weren't right. The woman's concern convinced her. Used to dealing with incidents where people's emotions ramped up to near hysteria, Jenna found herself largely unaffected, but something in this woman's tone caught at her. She placed her fingers at the base of her throat and absent-mindedly registered the escalation of her pulse rate. 'Is this unusual?' At the silence that greeted her, Jenna elaborated. 'Is it unusual for the child to cry for so long?'

The quick intake of breath on the other end of the phone had Jenna pressing it to her ear.

'Well, yes. It is unusual... I've never known a child to live there.'

Jenna shot to her feet as the adrenaline did its job. 'What do you mean?' A sharpness slid into her tone.

Lorna let out an impatient huff as though she couldn't believe Jenna could be so slow to catch on. 'When I said she lived alone, that's exactly what I meant. She doesn't have a child. I've never seen a child. Never heard a child before. I haven't seen this one. It was just there. Crying all the time.'

'Right. Lorna, when did you first become aware there was a child next door?' Jenna tilted her head and knew the moment Mason caught her gaze as he came to his feet and strode towards her across the main office with Ryan in hot pursuit.

'I don't know. I was away the weekend. Probably Monday night when I got home from work. It was only faint then. I thought Emily had the TV up too loud at first. I didn't really think much of it until the middle of the night, when the crying went on and on. And then last night it was silent. All night long, there was nothing and I thought maybe she'd had a visitor who'd left. But this morning. It's just crying and crying. The poor child.' The breath she drew in stuttered down the phone. 'I went round ten minutes ago, rang the doorbell, but there was no answer. Do you think she's okay?'

'Lorna, give me your address.' Jenna yanked open the top drawer of her desk and snatched the pen back out of the organiser. She tucked the phone under her chin and scribbled the address down as Lorna reeled it off. 'We're on our way. Give us fifteen minutes, Lorna.' She flung the pen across the desk and slapped the phone back down. She snatched up her handbag as she rounded the desk.

'Sarg?'

Heart now released from her restrictions, it pounded until her chest ached as she almost broke into a run. 'Child heard crying by the neighbour.' At Mason's raised eyebrow, she puffed out. 'No child known to live at that address.'

'Right.'

Ryan scuttled to catch up with her, pulling alongside. 'People visit with babies.'

'Neighbour doesn't believe she has anyone staying with her. Not seen anyone, just heard incessant crying.' Jenna slapped open the door into the long, narrow hallway with the heel of her hand and stomped through, giving in to the temptation to break into a trot. 'Lorna Hanson says she can remember the child being there from Monday. She said there was a lot of shouting early this morning.' It was still early. 'Then silence, except for the child crying.' She held open the door to the stairwell and turned to catch their gazes. 'It hasn't stopped crying for the past hour or so.'

She raced down the stairs, with Mason and Ryan right behind her, their footsteps echoing up the empty stairwell.

As she shot through the bottom doors, she reached out her hand and snatched at the set of keys Morris tossed at her and caught them mid-air, a grateful smile on her face. 'I owe you, Morris.' She certainly did as he'd made an effort to organise the keys and meet her at the front desk, taking the initiative and time away from the back office he normally worked in.

'I know you do.' The deep tones of his amusement followed her through the sliding automatic doors out into the blazing sunshine, where the heat whipped the moisture from her lungs to leave her gasping for breath after the relative cool of the station.

Not sufficient to slow her or her team down, they charged over the moat crossing and made for the nearest car. The new one.

Jenna allowed herself a quick grin. Morris King. Good lad.

'Do you think it's Joshua?' In a natural move of respect ingrained in him from his parents, Ryan grabbed the handle of the door and yanked it open for her to jump into the driver's seat. In his eagerness, he slammed it behind her with enough force to make the car rock. As he slid in the seat behind her, the car almost kangarooed at the weight of his enthusiasm.

'Let's not get ahead of ourselves, Ryan.' She tried to inject an element of restraint into her voice, but it cracked with excitement and eagerness on his name.

She whipped her strap around her and clipped it in as Mason slipped into the front passenger seat beside her, his own anticipation tightened his face as he clenched his jaw. She shoved the car into drive and took off through the car park, whipping out into the main stream of traffic in between two cars.

As she dipped her foot harder on the accelerator, excitement formed a hard knot in her chest. No matter the words she'd uttered to Ryan, hope flew high that this crying child was Joshua.

Please, God, let it be him.

As they pulled up outside Lorna Hanson's address, Jenna hit the off button and the engine cut. She smoothly moved the gear into park and leapt out of the car to dash along the narrow pavement to the address she'd been given.

'Sarg,' Excitement laced Ryan's voice. 'The car.' It was all he needed to say as she was already with him, but as he pulled alongside her, he lowered his voice. 'It's a white Honda Jazz.'

'No shit, Sherlock.' Mason's dulcet tones vibrated with the same excitement winding its way through Jenna as she approached the house.

Tall and willowy, the dark-haired young woman had her arms wrapped around her waist. Despite the weather, her shoulders rolled inwards in self-conscious agony. Fear filled watery blue eyes as she stepped over the small border into the next garden and pointed at the door. Her mouth moved, but no words came out, as though she wanted to keep her presence a secret.

Jenna couldn't blame her. So many disputes were started because neighbours were unable to keep from imposing their own morals, standards and thoughts on others. Reporting each other to the police often was the catalyst for disagreements to escalate into feuds.

In this case, the woman may well be correct.

Jenna's heart clutched as hope filled her chest. 'Lorna.'

The young woman nodded. 'It's still crying. I can hear it.'

Jenna tilted her head to one side, the distant strains of a child's wails drifted from the open upstairs windows of the small, modern house, it's exterior not dissimilar to the one Jenna owned.

Jenna nodded as she stabbed her forefinger on the doorbell of number sixty-eight and listened to the peal of it beyond the pristine, white door. She gave it less than a heartbeat before she reached out to try the handle. Locked.

'Do you have a key?' Neighbours often did.

'No. I'm sorry. I don't. We've never been that close. We're out at work all day. Barely see each other.'

The child's muted howls drifted on the heavy early-morning air.

'Any of the other neighbours likely to have one?'

Lorna shook her head. 'She keeps herself to herself. She'd put your bins out, lend you a cup of milk. The perfect neighbour. Until this.' Lorna chewed on her thumb as she stared at Jenna. 'I think it's maybe in the back bedroom. I can hear it better from my garden.'

Jenna bent at the hips, eye-level with the brass letter box and twisted sideways to catch Lorna's gaze. 'What did you say her name was?' She couldn't recall if a name had even been mentioned.

'Emily.' Lorna's rapid blinks accompanied her panicked gasps of breath.

Jenna poked the flap open on the letter box and placed her mouth as close as possible, projecting her voice into the hallway. 'Emily. Emily? Can you hear me? Emily, it's DS Jenna Morgan of

West Mercia Police. Can you come to the door?' She waited and
listened and only the distant strain of a child's distress filtered
through. 'Emily. Are you hurt? Are you able to come to the door?'

Nothing.

She stood upright and almost bumped into Mason as he
leaned over her shoulder.

She elbowed him back, twisting her head around so she could
look at him. 'I think we need to get in there. Quick. There's no
response, no answer.'

Concern flickered over his face as he nodded his agreement.
'Yeah. Perhaps she's had an accident.' He glanced at the closed
door and narrowed his eyes. 'Or left the baby alone?' It wasn't
unheard of.

'Can you break open the door?' Jenna asked.

At his soft snort, she turned all the way around to stare at him.
Willing to hit a charging rhino for her, it was the first time she'd
ever encountered Mason's resistance.

He raised his hand to cup one broad shoulder. 'There's no
way even I have the power to shoulder that door open. It's a five-
lock security door.'

Ryan's warm breath puffed out over the side of her neck, his
keenness brought him in close enough to touch her. 'Sarg, the
windows are open upstairs. We just need a ladder.'

She turned, her nose almost bumped his as he hovered next
to her, brimming with excitement, ready to make a move at her
command. She slid her hand up into the space between them and
raised her eyebrows to make him back off.

A swift blink was all the acknowledgement she received as he
took a stride back, evidently unperturbed by the lack of personal
space he'd granted her.

Jenna swivelled and took three strides forward along the path,
making him scuttle backwards to keep from her treading on him.

She spun on her heel, put her hands on her hips, tipped her head back and looked up at the first-storey window. She cruised her gaze over the fascia of the house. So similar to hers, possibly the same builder. No grips, no easy way up.

She could call for backup, but the child's screams squeezed at her heart and kicked her pulse into overdrive. Whatever the reason, the child needed help and they didn't have the time to wait for someone else to arrive. They needed to get in there without delay.

She turned to Lorna. 'Do you have a ladder?'

The woman's deeply furrowed brow cleared in a flash. 'I do! My husband just bought them a couple of weeks ago so he could clean the windows himself.' She cast a quick look at her house and lowered her voice. 'He's too mean to pay a window cleaner, but I reckon it'll take him three years before he reaps the benefit of buying the ladders.' She gave a sniff and then pointed in the direction of her rear garden gate. 'They're quite heavy.'

Mason stepped forward, the slow slide of his grin making the woman flutter. 'If you show me where they are, I'll get them.'

Jenna closed her eyes. Immune to it herself, it never failed to surprise her that Mason had no idea what his smile did to women.

Lorna raised her hand to her hair as her gaze skimmed over his thick, muscular arms and a low humming sound came from her throat. Not quite the shy, reticent woman Jenna had initially believed. Her only obvious reluctance was reporting her neighbour.

As they both strode off down Lorna's garden pathway, Jenna raised her chin to gaze up at the window, open to catch the lightest of breezes as the heat hung heavy.

Aware of the stickiness already setting in, Jenna plucked the thin T-shirt from her chest.

Not the biggest fan of heights, she flexed her shoulders and blew out a breath. It wasn't that high. It really wasn't that high. She could do it. It wasn't difficult.

'You want me to go up, Sarg? I can come down and open the front door,' Ryan offered.

The sobbing from upstairs stuttered and halted for a long moment and Jenna held her breath until the burn of it backed up in her lungs. 'Yeah.' As she stared up at the open window, she chewed her lips. 'Ryan, pull on a pair of gloves.'

As he snapped on a pair of cream nitrile gloves, she weighed up the pros and cons of telling him to slide on a pair of shoe protectors as he pulled a pair from his pocket.

She shook her head. 'Too risky on the ladders. Leave them for now.'

He stuffed them back in his pocket and squinted up at the window while they waited.

As Mason came from Lorna's house with his chest puffed out and shoulders back as he strained against the weight of the ladders, Jenna resisted the temptation to roll her eyes. Dear God. There were definite disadvantages to working with your sister's boyfriend. If Lorna raised her hand to stroke his arm, she'd not be amused.

At her deadpan look, Mason jiggled his shoulders with confused innocence and hefted the ladders upright to position them below the window. He gave a good hard rattle on them to make sure they were secure before he placed his foot on the bottom rung as the howl of the child started up again. He swept his hand through in an invitation. 'There you go, Ryan. All yours.' Dimples streaked across his face as he gave Ryan a wide grin. 'Quick as you like, pal.'

Without hesitation, Ryan raced up the ladder, agile as a monkey, while Jenna tilted her head back to watch him. As he reached the top, she pulled in a deep breath and held it as he curled his fingers around the window frame, leaned back into open space above them and pulled the window out towards himself and let it sweep by.

Relieved, her breath shot out of her as he leaned back in.

He peered inside and then shouted down. 'Empty bedroom.'

'Get inside, come down, open the door.'

With the child's insistent cries joining the buzz in her ears, Jenna snapped on her own gloves, aware of Mason doing the same, as they watched while Ryan swung his leg over the windowsill and hitched himself over to disappear inside.

'Oh!' Lorna puffed out a breathless word.

The thunder of Ryan's size twelves pounded down the stairs while Jenna slipped on a pair of shoe protectors and, a split second later, the front door was flung open.

Without pause, Jenna shot past him and headed up the stairs, two at a time, towards the sound of the child's worn-out cries with the knowledge her team would be right behind her. She slipped through onto the landing and followed the hoarse sobs of the child to a white-painted door.

Not hesitating, she barged through and staggered to a halt at the sight that confronted her.

34

Bright crimson pooled out in a wide circle on the cream carpet in the centre of the nursery. Not a perfect circle, but a jagged, uneven drag of blood splatter, indicating movement of the victim long after the wound had been inflicted. A shuffle, a crawl.

Without pause, Jenna strode across the room. Giving the body a wide birth, she sidestepped it and swept the hysterical child into her arms from where she stood clinging to the rails of the cot.

Jenna barked out commands as she went. 'Mason, check the body. Call an ambulance.' Her mind on full alert, she scanned the room as she instinctively hugged the howling child to her, cradling its burning-hot face into her neck, oblivious of the snot and tears it rubbed against her skin.

Mason dropped to his knees beside the body and reached out to place his fingers against the woman's neck. 'Alive. Weak pulse, Sarg.'

Jenna swung round to face the open doorway before Ryan could make his way through, aware they could all contaminate the crime scene. The less footfall in the room, the better. 'Ryan, stop where you are. Call for backup. Check the house, first upstairs and then down. Every cupboard and hiding spot. This woman's been attacked.' She glanced down at the victim, curled into the foetal position. 'The front door was locked. The perpetrator could still be inside. Search. Fast. Report back.'

'Sarg, I think the door is self-locking.'

As he turned, she halted him. 'All the same, Ryan, be careful. Keep alert.' She could do without another victim on her hands, which were already full of child.

With her palm against the back of the little girl's head, rocking came instinctively to soothe the beyond hysterical child. Exhausted, the toddler's body relaxed. A deadweight in her arms.

'Jesus.'

She turned back to stare down at Mason as he reached over into the cot and grabbed a thin blanket.

'Not that.' She barked. 'Evidence.'

He tossed it back inside and flung open the wardrobe door. He grabbed a folded sheet from a small, neat pile, balling it up as he whipped his head around to meet her eyes. 'The knife's still in.'

'Leave it there.' It could do more harm if he removed it than if he left it in for the paramedics to tend to. 'From the timeline Lorna gave us, this woman's been down for some time.'

Mason left the woman curled up in the recovery position and leaned over her. He wadded the sheet around the knife wound and pressed gently on either side with both hands 'Jesus,' he repeated. 'She's lost a shitload of blood.'

Jenna craned to take a closer look at the pallid woman on the floor. 'She's still alive?'

With his fingers on her carotid artery again, Mason nodded. 'Weak, but still kicking.'

Eyes screwed shut, the child snuffled into Jenna's neck, her whole body relaxing against her. Reluctant to move her, Jenna was conscious that the child had been crying non-stop for hours. Dehydration and heatstroke in those temperatures, two important elements that she couldn't ignore. She needed to get some fluids into the toddler before they had a problem.

With a gentle hitch, she adjusted the little one in her arms, so the child's bottom rested on Jenna's hip. She couldn't stop the little wave of disappointment as she tugged the pretty pink dress with its swirls of roses emblazoned across the hem. She'd thought she had him. Her heart had been set on finding Joshua. Instead, they'd walked in on a domestic, by the look of things, and the poor little girl had been traumatised, her mother stabbed in front of her.

Her gaze cruised across to the wardrobe filled with pretty dresses in whites and pinks. Jenna let out a sigh as she stood in the same place, reluctant to put her feet anywhere else. It was a crime scene. First and foremost, she'd rescued the child. Beyond that, every forensic detail needed to be preserved. She glanced down at her blue shoe protectors, relieved she'd taken a split second to pull them on.

Sirens sounded in the distance and Jenna gave a soft snort, snuffling her face into the child's thick, dark curls. The paramedics were about to bugger up the scene in any case to save the life of the woman curled up on the floor. Second one in less than a week. There wasn't a fat lot of good she could do to help that. Their priority was to save the woman. Emily, presumably.

On his knees at her feet, Mason whipped his head up, eyes filled with surprise. 'She spoke.'

'What?' Anticipation sped through her veins as Jenna stepped closer. Cradling the child, she leaned in 'What did she say?'

He ducked his head, so his ear came close to the woman's

mouth. 'Emily.' He reared his head back, confusion creasing his forehead.

'That's her name.'

'No!' He raised a hand to quieten her and Jenna clamped her mouth shut. 'Emily.' His dark brows slammed down as he tilted his head closer. Mason rolled back on his haunches to stare at Jenna, his intensity spiking her heart rate. 'This isn't Emily.' He blew out a slow breath. 'She says she's Fern and Emily killed her.'

35

Bright sunlight streamed in through the patio doors to flood the kitchen with a brilliant whiteness that made Jenna squint as she surveyed the room with its clinical white cupboards and surfaces. Immaculate but for the scatter of empty wine bottles across the small white table and the single wine glass by the side of the sink.

Curious, Jenna stepped closer to the sink and, with a quick glance over her shoulder, she manoeuvred the sleeping child to one side to free up a hand and dropped the nappy and wet wipes she'd swiped from the changing table in the nursery onto the bench. With her gloved hand, she opened the cupboard beneath the sink to peer inside.

SOCO would be there soon enough to join the double crew of paramedics who'd already made their way upstairs, leaving the blue lights flashing on the ambulance parked outside. A second one just pulling up behind.

But she wanted to know, now. To satisfy her own interest.

The small white bin inside the cupboard overflowed with more bottles. Mateus Rosé. In the region of five altogether. She didn't poke inside to count, just gave a guestimate from her vantage point before she slipped the door closed again.

She made her way back to the table. Seven bottles.

She blew out a breath. 'Christ, someone has a serious alcohol issue. Or they managed to get a job lot.'

She drew her head back from the child. Apart from being traumatised, the poor little thing hung exhausted on her shoulder, fast asleep. The weight of her cold, saturated nappy lay against Jenna's forearm and the strong smell of urine and poo seeped from the elasticated sides. The child may well be asleep, she'd cried herself out, but she still needed to be changed and fed.

Jenna swung open the fridge door and peered inside, surprised at the neat little line-up of four bottles of Aptamil milk.

'Please tell me you know what you're doing?'

Jenna whipped round, guilt at being caught firing up her languid heart rate.

'Jesus, Mason! Don't sneak up on me like that.'

His mouth twitched into a smile. 'I didn't sneak. You were preoccupied.'

She huffed out the breath that had backed up in her lungs. 'All the same, a little warning would have been nice.'

'There's nothing further I can do while the paramedics are up there, I'll only get in the way.' He rolled off his bloodstained gloves, turned them inside out, and then bagged them before he laid the bag on the kitchen counter. His smile stretched wider and he jerked his chin in the direction of the fridge. 'So, *do* you know what you're doing?'

'I haven't a clue. I can honestly say, I've never dealt with a child in my life.'

'Never?' Surprise etched across his face enough to make her consider what she'd said. She pursed her lips.

'No. Never. Fliss isn't that much younger than me and we don't have any cousins. Just us.'

'You never babysat?' Mason made his way across the kitchen and snapped on a fresh pair of nitrile gloves before he slipped open one drawer and then another. He flipped out a small, clean hand towel, which he flicked over his shoulder as he knee-bumped the drawer closed again and then picked up the nappy and wet wipes she'd left on the side.

'No. Fliss did. I was too busy kickboxing.'

He turned with a slow smile and held out his gloved hands. He flexed his fingers in an invitation for her to pass the child over. 'Of course you were.'

As Jenna placed the child in his arms, Mason hugged the little body into his wide chest in a natural move that sat easily with him. 'I babysit my nephews from time to time.'

Relieved of her weight, Jenna raised her hand and swiped away the sheen of sweat where the child's face had laid against the naked skin of her neck, heating them both to boiling point. She scrubbed her hands on her trouser legs. 'I've called social services. They'll be here shortly if you'd rather wait.'

'Nah, by the time they get here and sort their lazy arses out, it'll be another hour. We don't want her getting nappy rash.' He shrugged as he turned towards the kitchen table and pulled up short at the sight of the pile of bottles. 'Nice.'

Instead of attempting to move the bottles so he didn't contaminate evidence, he made for the small open-plan living room and dropped to his knees in front of the charcoal-grey settee. He leaned forward to place the child on her back, making shushing noises as she stirred. He whipped the towel from over his shoulder and smoothed it under her bottom.

Fascinated at this new side of Mason, Jenna watched from the kitchen as he held out his hand for her to pass over the clean nappy and wet wipes from where he'd dumped them on the sofa. He lowered his face to the nappy and sniffed, wrinkling his nose. 'I think we'll need more than a wet wipe, poor little soul. She's obviously had this on for some time.' He flicked a glance over his shoulder at Jenna. 'Any chance of a bowl of warm water, some cotton wool and some of that, you know, squirty stuff?'

'Washing-up liquid?'

At his look of horror, Jenna flashed him a smile as though she was joking, but, quite honestly, that's what she would have elected to use.

'Baby bath.' The dryness of his voice let her know he was on to her.

At the movement in the doorway, Jenna swung round.

Ryan linked his gloved fingers together. 'The second ambulance crew are here, and PC Ted Walker's arrived. He said he'll take over scene guard.'

'Excellent.' A quiet relief at the experienced officer's arrival ran through her. She could have her DC back now. 'Ryan, run upstairs and get some baby bath out of the cupboard.'

'Baby bath?'

She raised an eyebrow as though she'd never just shown her own ignorance. 'It's squirty stuff you put in the bath to clean babies' bums. And some cotton wool.' She'd glimpsed it in the wardrobe neatly lined up next to the baby wipes. It hadn't occurred to her she'd need them. 'Run.' She knew he would, and he'd be back downstairs in a flash.

Now her hands were free, she stripped off her own gloves to avoid cross-contamination, bagged them and placed them next to Mason's. She patted her back pocket and pulled out another pair of latex gloves. She preferred latex to the nitrile ones, so much softer and more flexible. She snapped them on, gazed around the small kitchen and reached for a cupboard beside the hob. Crockery. Dark blue with a cascading gold shimmer dissipating as the pattern fell to the centre of each piece. Opulent in comparison to the stark whiteness everywhere else. Dinner plates, side plates, bowls. She squinted at the contrast between the neatly lined up crockery compared to the abandoned bottles of wine scattered around.

She removed one deep cereal bowl, nudged the cupboard door with her hip and admired the soft-close. Perhaps she needed soft-close in her life when she replaced the kitchen in her house. The one Domino ate out of boredom when Fliss left him alone for too long.

She glanced at Mason, seemingly at ease as he murmured to the toddler, and then moved to the sink, turned on the tap and waited for the water to run warm while she stared out of the window at the flashing blue lights on the ambulances and the gathering crowds as another two police vehicles pulled up to the kerb. She'd leave it to them. They knew what their jobs were. Crowd control, preservation of scene.

And there he was. Her pain in the arse journalist, Kim Stafford. One of these days, that man just may have his uses, but today was not one of them.

She filled the bowl and turned with it in her hands just as Ryan zipped back into the kitchen and made his way through to Mason, who crouched over the little girl in the living room.

Mason reared his head back, shock making his spine snap ramrod straight and Jenna stumbled to a halt, spit drying in her throat. 'What? What's the matter?' Terror wedged the air in her throat as her mind refused to consider the horrors of what he may have found.

He did a slow head turn, confusion lighting his eyes. 'Fuck, Jenna. This is not a girl.'

Air whooshed out of her lungs. 'Pardon?'

The mere fact he'd used her forename instead of her rank to address her showed how shocked he was. 'What do you mean?' She took four steps through to the living room and stared down at the still sleeping child.

With the nappy wide open where Mason had discreetly curled the front down, doubling it over to tuck it under the child's bottom, effectively covering the poo, the little boy's genitals were on full display as he gave a lazy kick and opened stunning blue eyes.

'Fuck!' Jenna slammed one hand over her mouth as the water sloshed over the side of the bowl she held. Pure excitement zipped through her veins as she loomed over the top of Mason's shoulders to take a closer look. The black curls, the violet eyes that until now had been either squeezed closed in hysterical crying or asleep.

She raked her gaze further down.

The male genitalia.

'Fuck, indeed,' Mason agreed.

'It's a boy!' Ryan slammed the heel of his hand against his forehead. 'We've found him.'

She prided herself on her professionalism, always, but Jenna kept her hand over her mouth as an uncontrolled sob burst out and the hot prick of tears hit her eyes. 'Oh God. We've found him.' Her voice broke and she hitched in a breath. Knees weak, she sank down beside Mason. 'I thought when we attended... I'd hoped it was him and then it wasn't. Or we thought it wasn't.'

Ryan peered over the top of Mason's shoulder. 'Why would she dress him as a girl?'

Confusion chased around in her mind. They had all these threads and none of them knit together. 'To disguise him?' She looked over her shoulder at Ryan. 'Who went to the trouble of dressing him as a girl? Was it Emily? Or the victim upstairs? Fern. Who was hiding Joshua's identification from the other?'

'It sounds seriously fucked up.'

Jenna shrugged. 'If you'd stolen a child and you didn't want it recognised, the easiest way to avoid questions would be to change the sex of it.'

'Out in public maybe.' Mason lifted his head. 'But why in the house?'

'Maybe the Fern didn't want Emily to know,' Ryan offered.

'I don't know.' Jenna squinted as a memory nudged at her. 'Remember a few years ago, they found a couple who'd kidnapped a little girl? It took two years for the police, in Finland, I think, to find her as the kidnappers had disguised her as a boy.'

'Still strange.'

'We've had stranger. I'd like to know who our victim is though. Knowing she's called Fern just isn't good enough. We need more.'

'Maybe she's a lodger, a friend just staying for a few nights. Who knows until we get hold of Emily, or until Fern is in a fit state to talk.' She blew out a breath. 'Thank God we got here.'

Mason bowed his head to look at the child. 'Whatever, he bloody stinks.' His voice came out gruff and strangled and she suspected he was as moved as she was. He kept his head bowed as he grasped the child's ankles in one hand and raised his bottom from the rank nappy.

The hot scald of tears hit the back of her hand and she quickly scrubbed it across her cheeks as breath stuttered into her lungs. 'We've found him.' Her smile wobbled as she ran her fingertips under her eyes to swipe off any more tears threatening to fall, her heart exploding with joy.

She lowered her head and chanced a sideways glance at Ryan. For once still, he'd dug his hands deep into his pockets, his wide shoulders curling in. His jaw flexed and as his gaze flicked to hers, his eyes glistened.

'Fuck me, but we've found Joshua.' She let out a laugh as Mason dipped a wad of cotton wool into the bowl she still held, squeezed it and swiped it over the little boy's penis, lifting it with thumb and forefinger to cleanse underneath. Fascinated, Jenna never took her gaze from the child, watching each deft move Mason made. 'You're a natural.' He'd make a good father.

He grunted as he patted the toddler's bottom dry with the towel and then slipped a clean nappy under him. 'I'm good at dealing with shit.'

Ryan leaned over the top of them, resting his hand on Jenna's shoulder in the familiar way he'd adopted, as though she was his older sister, not his boss. Sometimes the lines became blurred in intense situations. His familiarity was inbuilt. He couldn't help himself. He showed her respect and deference to her rank, especially in front of others, but he was a tactile personality. He squeezed her shoulder, and she raised her hand to pat the back of his, nodding her head to acknowledge the sheer magic of the moment the three of them shared.

'Just wait until we get back to the station and I tell them what a *boss* at changing babies' nappies you are, Mason.'

The smile dropped from Mason's face and his brows lowered. 'Do that, young Downey, and I'll kick your arse from here to kingdom come.'

Ryan snorted, removing his hand as he straightened. 'What happens now, Sarg?' And just like that the familiarity slid off him with ease as he deferred to her rank once more.

'We need to be sure it's Joshua.'

'Oh, it's Joshua all right. Look at those eyes. Bloody gorgeous.' Mason blew a raspberry as he pulled the sweet dress down around Joshua's knees to cover the nappy. The child's chubby face relaxed and a cautious smile dimpled his cheeks. Mason's big hand squeezed the child's knee as he blew another raspberry, and the smile broke out in full as Joshua gurgled. 'It's a bloody travesty you've been dressed up as a little girl, son, but we'll soon have that remedied when we get you back to your dad.' Mason turned his puzzled gaze to Jenna. 'What the bloody blue blazes has gone on here?'

She shook her head as the energy fizzled back to her limbs. 'I don't know. I don't understand. But, Mason, we can't just hand him over and say, "Here's your little boy." You know we have to do this through official channels. We can't just roll out the red carpet and start flying the flags.'

As he opened his mouth to argue, she laid a gentle hand on his arm. 'I know we know it's him, but, as you say, "what the blue blazes has gone on?" This is the weirdest situation I've ever encountered. What if it's not Joshua?' She squeezed his arm before he could speak. 'The outside chance that we make a mistake. How devastating would that be for Zak if we say, "hey, we've found your son" and then we discover it isn't Joshua after all, and for some reason this child...' she waved her hand at him, watching him as his gaze followed her every move, '... has a mum who believes he should be a girl. That's not our realm. We have to hand it over.'

'We know it's him.' The desperation in his voice could persuade if she allowed it. 'It's his bloody description, Jenna, it's the child in the photograph.'

'Yep.' She pushed to her feet and glanced through the kitchen to the movement beyond the window, her gaze glanced off Kim Stafford as she considered how to get Joshua into the police car and away without him seeing. The last thing they needed was that information exploding all over the headlines before they had a chance to speak with Zak. With a roll of relief, her gaze moved onto the old blue Mazda just pulling up to the kerb as it squeezed in between the ambulance and police car. 'Looks like it's not an issue anyway, Mason. Social services are here.'

His indelicate snort said everything about what he thought of social services taking over. He wanted it. Wanted to take the child back to his father. To Zak.

Her chest squeezed tight. There was nothing more in the world she wanted but to reunite Joshua with his father. To put an end to at least part of his torture. But it wasn't the way of things.

Muscles cracked and groaned as she stretched her back straight, pushing her shoulders back and circling her neck before she made her way through to the kitchen. She opened the fridge and drew out one of the bottles of milk and swung the door to again.

She raised the bottle and tilted it in Mason's direction. 'What do I do with this?'

Joshua back in his arms, Mason made his way through to the kitchen. 'Drop it in a bowl of boiling water, heat it. Test the milk on the inside of your wrist so that it's just warm.'

The toddler hitched out an excited breath, lips smacking, and reached towards the bottle.

Panic spliced Jenna's heart at his apparent desperation. 'Can't I microwave it? Won't it be quicker?'

'Nope. It creates hotspots. Do it the old-fashioned way, Jenna.'

She flew across the kitchen, panic making her heart race as she grabbed the white retro kettle, snatched the lid off and filled it. 'Bloody hell, bloody hell, if you'd said earlier, I could have had the kettle boiled.' She slapped the kettle down and flicked the button. It was going to take an age to bloody well boil.

She peered out of the window at the woman from social services, still sitting in her car, a pile of paperwork wedged against her steering wheel as she appeared to study it.

Jenna turned her back on both the kettle and the window, puffing out a breath as she slouched against the counter.

Mason's lips twitched as the child bounced in his arms, excitement making him jiggle, his chubby naked feet kicked at Mason's stomach. 'Have a look in the cupboards, see if there's any Weetabix.'

Without argument, she swung open cupboard after cupboard, careful not to disturb anything. 'No Weetabix. The food in here isn't exactly child-friendly, which leads me to believe the woman upstairs was only visiting. Muesli?'

'Nuh-uh. Look in the breadbin.' He nodded to the white breadbin in the corner as he bounced the child on his hip.

Jenna tilted her head on one side. 'Who the hell are you and what have you done with my detective constable?' She could barely connect the man quite happy to deck another with the one just as at ease comforting a child.

Mason rumbled out his amusement as Jenna opened the lid on the breadbin and reached in for the paltry two slices of bread left inside. She pulled them out, one almost stale crust together with one slice of bread and pulled her lips back in disgust.

'Stick it in the toaster. If it's not mouldy, it'll be fine.'

She flashed Mason a quick look, lifted the bread to her nose and gave a quick sniff for any evidence of mould and then did as he said, aware of Ryan's close interest as he silently observed every last exchange and move.

Mason nodded at the fridge. 'See if there are any eggs.'

'Eggs? Can toddlers eat eggs?' How old did they have to be?

Mason's face wiped clean. He blinked. Opened his mouth. Blinked again. 'Of course, they bloody well can. What else do kids eat apart from Weetabix?'

'Well...' She opened the fridge and peered inside and then scooped up two eggs from the egg rack. 'I don't keep my eggs in the fridge. It's not good to. It does something to the albumen.' She swung the door to and appreciated the soft sigh of it as it self-closed. The sense of relief gave her a moment of self-indulgence, time to let her mind rest with trivialities. She turned and both men stared at her with the same puzzled looks on their faces. She shrugged, opened a drawer beneath the hob, took out a pan and placed the eggs inside. 'Apparently putting them in the fridge door isn't good for them as the temperature fluctuates too much.' She had no idea where she'd read that information, it may have been from one of Donna's *Good Housekeeping* magazines Jenna flicked through from time to time on her lunch break.

As the kettle clicked off, she picked it up, filled the pan, lit the gas under it and moved away to fill the dark blue bowl with the boiling water. She sank the bottle of milk into it to warm through. She turned and sent them both a bright smile. She had reason to smile. The sense of exhilaration turned her giddy. They'd just found their lost toddler. They'd found Joshua. If she could run around in circles punching the air, she would, instead she'd settle for a little banter.

'Also, they're porous, so anything you keep in the fridge that's smelly will soak through to the egg.'

Satisfied she'd wowed them with enough of her knowledge, Jenna slipped the delicate white highchair out from behind the open door of the kitchen and unfolded it. She patted the back of the seat. 'Would you like to put him in?'

Mason made his way over as Jenna lifted the bottle out of the hot water and gave it a shake before she removed the lid and tested the heat of the milk against the inside of her wrist. 'How do you know?'

'Did it burn?'

'No.'

'Was it cold?'

'No.'

'Was it warm?'

'Yes.'

'Then it's done. Give it to him.'

'Do I have to...?'

'No. He's a big boy, just give him the milk before he dehydrates, Jenna.'

She thrust the bottle towards Joshua. He snatched it from her hand and rammed the teat into his mouth so fast he squished his nose against it in his haste to drink.

Jenna's chest tightened at the desperation as he let out gentle squeaks of appreciation.

She narrowed her eyes as she contemplated the little boy. 'Don't you find it strange that there's a nursery, fully kitted out in a house that, according to the neighbour, had no baby until Joshua was brought here?'

'Don't you find the whole situation seriously fucked anyway?'

She blew out a breath of laughter at Mason. 'We need to find this Emily. Perhaps she's rented the house out to Fern. I don't know. It'll all come out in the wash.'

As the toaster popped, she grabbed the toast, slid it onto the blue plate she snatched out of the cupboard and handed it to Mason, before she swept the small pan off the hob and went to the sink. She blasted cold water into the pan as she spared a moment to look out of the window again. 'How long does it take to complete the paperwork? She doesn't even know what she's coming to yet.'

'Please tell me it's not Dot.' Mason grumbled from behind her.

Jenna snorted. 'It is.' It wasn't her real name, but Mason insisted on calling her it. For Ryan's benefit, she clarified. 'Dot the i's, cross the t's.'

She dipped her hand into the cold water and tested the temperature of the eggs. Warm.

She turned as Mason finished buttering the toast. He cut it into long fingers and placed it on the plastic tray in front of Joshua. 'Why can't it be Tammi? Tammi's bloody lovely with kids. At least she's got a heart. I'm not sure Dot does.'

The little boy grabbed a soldier in each hand and rammed one straight into his mouth while he squeezed the life out of the other in his excitement, kicking his feet against the plastic footrest of the highchair.

Jenna's breath stuttered with uncontrolled alarm. 'Don't let him choke. For the love of Jesus, please don't let him choke. Dot'll bloody kill us.'

'No worries. He won't choke.' Relaxed, Mason chuckled as though the prospect of a dying infant hadn't crossed his mind. 'He knows what he's doing. Don't you, chap?' He ruffled the long, black ringlets and shot the boy a wide grin. 'Aw, Joshua, you hungry, kiddo?'

Joshua gave an enthusiastic nod and rammed another soldier in his mouth, fisting another two in the other hand.

Jenna lopped the top off each of the eggs and placed one of them in an eggcup, one of two matching the blue service she could find in the cupboard.

As she placed it in front of Joshua, he lunged forward and stabbed the soldier into the egg, deep yellow yolk spilled over the side and dribbled across the plastic tray.

'He knows what he's doing with that.' Mason raised his chin and peered over the top of Jenna's head out of the window. 'Dot's on her way in.'

For a woman who had spent the best part of forty years looking after the walking wounded, the abused children, the beaten wives, Jenna had never been convinced that Dot even liked humans. Nothing about her screamed 'people person'. Deep lines of discontent etched the sides of her mouth and a long, thin line lay horizontally over her top lip, where it continually curled back with distaste. Dot was all about filling in the paperwork and nothing about the human aspect of her job. In the final year before her retirement, it appeared she'd given up altogether on the pretence.

A direct contrast to Harry, whose human element would never be undermined.

As Dot swept through the kitchen doorway, her sour glance took in the whole scene with one pre-judgemental scowl.

Jenna forced a smile and remembered to use her real name. 'Sylvia. Good to see you again. It's been a while. Not since...' She couldn't grasp the last time she'd worked alongside the other woman.

'Last year. Missing schoolboy. Found him setting light to the gym. Had to be put in special care due to his persistence in lighting fires. Little pyromaniac. Believe he's still not been cured of it. Set his dorm alight a couple of months ago, so the home had to evacuate. Charming young gentleman.' Every word spoken was deadpan. Flat. Emotionless.

Jenna let the silence hang in the air for a moment, unsure if the other woman had finished. 'That's the one.' She gave a slow nod, keeping her fixed grin in place.

Sylvia's nostrils flared as she took in Joshua cramming food into his mouth, his chubby little fist following so he almost swallowed it. 'What do we have here? I've been given very little information.' Disapproval dripped from her words. 'It would have been nice if they'd seen fit to give me more than a child needs to be taken into protective custody.'

She made it sound as though he was about to be imprisoned.

'Sorry about that, Sylvia. We weren't aware of the situation ourselves until a few moments ago. We believe this is Joshua Cheetham-Epstein. The little boy who went missing a couple of days ago?' Jenna's voice lifted on the end as though it was a question, but she just needed to know if Sylvia was up to speed on current affairs. 'It's been in all the papers.'

'Hmmm.' Sylvia inclined her head. 'That's a little girl.'

'Yes. Ummm. No. This is definitely a little boy wearing girl's clothing.' At the look of doubt Sylvia shot her, Jenna firmed up her tone. 'We can confirm this is a little boy. Mason just changed his nappy.'

Sylvia's eyebrows shot up to her hairline, horror flitting across her face. 'You changed him, before I got here?'

Mason drew in a long, gusty breath through his teeth, flexed his shoulders and cricked his neck as though he was about to take on a heavyweight boxer, a scrapper himself, he was more than willing to take her on as Ryan watched with interest. 'I'm adequately qualified to verify that he's very definitely male. We considered it wasn't necessary to wait for supervision under the circumstances, given Joshua was in considerable discomfort, wearing a wet, dirty nappy which we assumed had been on for some time.'

Jenna dipped her head to hide her smile, surprised that Mason hadn't told Sylvia the child's nappy had been full of shit.

'We've bagged the nappy for SOCO.' Ryan offered.

Sylvia's thin lips pursed with disapproval, wrinkles shooting out in a starburst to join the deep brackets at the edges of her mouth. 'Why is he wearing a dress?'

Jenna jumped in before Mason said something they might all regret; he'd shown enough restraint already, she didn't need a war zone. 'We have no idea. We've a stab victim upstairs, unidentified as yet, and can only assume either her, or Emily, the woman who owns the house, were trying to disguise the child's sex. For obvious reasons.' At Sylvia's steady look, Jenna added, 'Presumably because one – or both of them – kidnapped him.'

She glanced down at Joshua as the deep sounds of appreciation gurgled from him while the bright yellow yolk smeared up his face. A ghost of a smile curved Mason's lips while he watched the little boy.

Sylvia's sour smile did nothing to lighten her hard eyes. 'I'm not entirely sure that's the best meal choice for a child of his age.'

Before Jenna could use subtle intervention, Mason whipped his head around. 'I'm entirely positive that's the best meal choice for Joshua. The only thing we could add to it is a banana for dessert. Which he will have in just a moment.' He strode across the kitchen and snatched up a small bunch of bananas from a fruit bowl, his grasp on them tight enough to send his knuckles white. He snapped one off the bunch and peeled it, kicking the foot pedal on the bin down, he launched the skin into it with a touch more force than necessary. 'A balanced diet. Good nutrition.' He pointed at the white tray full of mushed-up food. 'Bread, part of a staple diet. Carbohydrates and fibre. Eggs, bloody marvellous source of protein.' He held up the banana. 'Potassium, f... f... fibre.'

Jenna almost snorted as he held onto that f-word as Ryan ducked his head, unable to hide his wide grin.

As he returned to the high chair, Mason's voice morphed as he spoke to Joshua in a low, teasing croon, something she'd never heard from Mason before, not even when she caught his soft murmurings in Fliss's ear, which she refused to think about.

In the awkward silence, Jenna kept her attention on the toddler, tempted to let out a childish laugh as the burst of excitement at finding him refused to fizzle out.

Sylvia clucked her tongue on the roof of her mouth and shuffled the papers in her hand, all bustle and business. 'Right then. As soon as he's ready, I'll take him to the hospital, have him checked over by a doctor, then onto the safe house, complete the paperwork, contact his...' she glanced at her notes, '... relevant parent.'

'Zak.' Eyes flat, Mason glanced up. 'Joshua's father is called Zak. Zak Cheetham-Epstein. His mother, Imelda, is currently in hospital with possible brain damage.' He vibrated with anger at the same time as he managed to break off a piece of banana making it look like it might just be her neck. 'That was also on the news. We won't know the results until they try to bring her out of the induced coma they put her in after she was attacked. She suffered considerable head injuries, possibly from one of the two women who have held Joshua – Imelda and Zak's *son* – incarcerated for the last few days.'

Sylvia narrowed her eyes and raised the hand that held the paperwork. 'So, I understand.'

Ryan let out a soft snort.

As Mason opened his mouth, Jenna stepped between them. 'Which safe house will you use?'

Without hesitation, Sylvia replied, 'Falsworth Road.' She knew her job inside out, but somewhere along the way, she'd lost her sense of compassion and human interaction. It was no longer a calling, had it ever been, but a nine-to-five job she carried out whilst treading water, waiting for retirement.

Mason ignored her and held out half the banana to Joshua. With laughter in his eyes, Joshua's cheeks rode up in plump happiness as he reached out, grasped the ripe banana and squished it between his fingers so it squelched out over the back of his hand and flobbed onto the tray. He lowered his head and sucked the banana from his skin making yummy, yummy noises as he smacked his lips.

Mason dropped down to his haunches, so his head was on a level with the white tray of the table and he peered up at the little boy. 'You were hungry, weren't you, mate?'

Joshua's legs kicked wildly up and down.

Jenna ran a tongue around her teeth as she considered her alternatives. She didn't want Joshua alone with the social worker for one minute longer than he had to be. Amazed at the transformation from the hysterical child to the smiling, happy toddler in front of them, they had no idea what trauma he'd been exposed to and the last thing he needed was Sylvia's cold aloofness. He needed warmth and understanding, someone who could keep him happy and entertained.

The doctor at the hospital would examine him for physical and sexual abuse, but there was no telling what the mental and emotional impact would bring at a later stage.

Mason blew a raspberry and jiggled his eyebrows, engaging the little boy.

Joshua's legs bounced erratically as he gurgled his approval and shoved the last piece of mangled banana in his mouth, opening wide for Mason to view his masticated food.

Without hesitation, Mason leaned in, a wide grin on his face as he peered into Joshua's mouth to elicit laughter from the little boy.

Damn, Mason might just kill Sylvia given the chance, but it was Jenna's best option. Before she could talk herself out of it, she addressed Sylvia.

'DC Mason Ellis will accompany you.'

Mason froze as Sylvia's brows shot up, but neither one of them would sway her in her decision.

Jenna smoothed the way. 'We need continuity of evidence, et cetera, et cetera.' She wiggled her fingers in a casual manner intended to show she understood that Sylvia knew the ins and outs of the job and the et cetera, et cetera was because Jenna didn't feel the need to elaborate on a subject matter Sylvia was well versed with. 'Also, we have no idea where this Emily has absconded to, so, for the safety of all concerned, you and little Joshua *will* be accompanied by my officer.'

Before either could make an objection, not least of all Mason, who definitely wouldn't want to be around Sylvia for long, Jenna turned to Ryan, who, for once in his life remained quiet, without question, evidently sensing the atmosphere.

Impressed with his development, Jenna afforded him a sly wink. 'DC Downey. You're with me.'

His perfect white teeth gleamed as his grin spread wide.

37

TUESDAY 13 JULY, 10:50 HRS

She may never be forgiven, but Mason had been the best option. The wintry gaze he'd turned on her would soon be softened when he spent more time with Joshua. She hoped.

Whatever, he'd forgive her.

Eventually.

She'd saved him a couple of hours of pure paperwork by going back to the station and completing it while she gave Sylvia and Mason enough time to visit the hospital with Joshua.

She kept a close eye on the progress of the hunt for Emily, but she'd needed to let go of that side of things for the time being. Her immediate priority was Joshua and Zak. DI Taylor had firm control of the search for Emily and identifying Fern.

Once Mason confirmed they were on their way to the safe house, she'd been able to make her move.

As she drew up outside Zak's parents' house, Jenna sent Ryan a quick glance. 'One step at a time, Ryan. We don't give him everything at once. We give him hope without desperation.'

'He'll be ecstatic to hear his son is okay.'

'He will. But we must be careful. Ryan, I'm 99 per cent sure that little boy is his, but we have to consider there's an outside chance he's not.'

'He's very distinctive-looking,' Ryan argued.

'Yes.' Jenna held a finger up, kicking strength into her voice. 'But what if we go in and tell Zak we've found his son and it turns out on the wide off chance not to be? We'd cause more devastation and heartache by giving him false hope. So, Ryan, it's softly softly. We can't go in gung-ho.' She turned her head and pointed out of the side window at the figure lurking along the street as though his instinct had already led him there.

Damn him.

'Kim Stafford,' She spat out his name.

'He was outside Emily's house when we were there.'

Jenna nodded. 'If he gets wind of this, it will be splashed all over the nationals in tasteless, over-sensationalised media panic. We don't know the full story yet. We have no idea where Emily is, and we haven't identified the victim. All we can do is go through our police procedures step by step, Ryan, without the media frenzy the likes of Kim Stafford promote.'

As Ryan unstrapped his seatbelt, Jenna reached out and touched his hand. 'Say nothing and don't respond to anything he says. Understand?'

Ryan grinned. 'Yes, Sarg. Don't let him see the whites of my eyes.'

Jenna smiled back at him and then opened the car door, letting the blast of heat whip away any benefit the air con had given. As she stepped out, Stafford was on her in an instant.

'Jenna.' She tilted her chin and stared down at him. Just shorter than her, when she drew herself up, she made a point of towering above his stooped stance. 'DS Morgan,' he corrected himself. 'What news do you have? Have there been any developments?'

She shot him a tight smile. If there had, she'd rather walk over him than give him any information. 'Nothing at this stage, Mr Stafford. Sorry, you'll have to contact our press officer if you want any information.' Short, sharp, professional.

She strode away without a backward glance, Ryan at her side.

The slight woman who answered the door had an abundance of black curls, just like her grandson's, but the eyes were a deep, dark brown filled with exhaustion that welled from her in a tangible cloud of sadness.

Jenna flashed her badge. 'DS Jenna Morgan, DC Ryan Downey. Mrs Cheetham-Epstein?'

'Just Epstein. Simi. Simi Epstein.'

'Simi. Is Zak home?'

'Yes.' She took a weary step back into the dark hallway and beckoned them forward. 'Come in. Do you have news?' As Jenna opened her mouth to reply, Simi pursed her lips and shook her head as though she didn't want to hear, just in case it was bad. 'It'll keep for Zak. He's in the living room.'

As Jenna had no intention of imparting information to Simi before she saw Zak in any case, she puffed a short sigh of relief. She followed the delicate woman into the cool of the Victorian, stone-built house, and without looking back, heard the door close on Kim Stafford as Ryan stepped up behind her like a faithful shadow.

A relief from the unforgiving sun, the darkness in the hallway almost robbed her of her sight after the brilliant light outside. Pale green light filtered through the high-ceilinged living room with its overstuffed chairs and sofas and wide breadth of windows looking out across a vast expanse of tree-lined garden.

North-facing, Jenna imagined the huge inglenook fireplace would be well used in the winter months, but she could only be grateful for the cool air that played across her skin, to wipe away the sweat she'd managed to work up before they were even halfway through the day.

Zak surged to his feet from the pale floral sofa, handsome face etched with lines of worry and hope. Bloodshot eyes met hers in a frantic appeal. 'Do you have any news?' The exact question his mother asked, but he wanted to know. Needed to know, although the desperation in his eyes begged for it not to be bad news.

Time and again, Jenna had been in this same situation, more often than not with bad news. It was the job, what she'd been trained to do. Training, though, didn't negate a certain compassion and sympathy, which some officers lacked. Since Fliss had disappeared, Jenna had learnt so much about herself and the personal experience had moved her to a whole different level of understanding when she dealt with delicate situations.

She narrowed the gap between them and took hold of one of Zak's large hands in both of hers. 'Zak. Shall we sit down?' She gave a gentle tug on his hand and sank down onto the sofa with him, their knees bumped as they settled. Without releasing his hand, Jenna ran her quick gaze over him. Worry and fear for both his wife and son had taken its toll and his unshaven face was slack with exhaustion. Although the line of enquiry had taken a sharp diversion down another route, Zak's innocence would remain in question until such a time as they proved he'd had no hand in his wife's attack.

Lips tight, Zak squeezed her hand and the kindest thing was to put him out of his misery, but Jenna held back, unwilling to see the pure excitement she knew would be there as soon as she mentioned Joshua's name. Excitement borne of hope. Hope she held precious in her hands.

She'd steady him first. Find out about his wife, because once she released the information about Joshua, she'd probably have no further sense from Zak.

'Do you have any news about Imelda?'

Zak's leg jigged up and down, vibrating through his hand into both of hers. Nerves destroyed his ability to stay still. 'We were there last night. Southmead.' His voice trembled as he waved his free hand in the air. 'They're going to try and bring her out of the coma this morning.' He glanced up at his mum, who hovered at the doorway, her fingers linked together at her waist, twisting in non-stop agitation. 'Her parents are staying in a hotel there, so I could come back and forth here. They'll ring us soon. We're just waiting to hear.'

'Waiting.' Simi stepped deeper into the room. 'Waiting all the time. Just for news. Anything. About Imelda, about Joshua...'

Jenna nodded her understanding as Ryan stepped closer to Simi. Not yet fully comfortable with imparting bad news, Ryan nevertheless had the natural inbuilt personality to offer sympathy without cutting him to the bone and ripping out his heart.

Jenna gave a gentle squeeze to Zak's hand and as his tortured gaze returned to her, she offered him that little snatch of hope. 'This morning we were called to a house in Lawley where there were reports of a child crying.'

Zak's fingers flexed in hers and his spine went rigid as he sat upright, wholly focused on her.

'When we arrived, we came across what we believed was a little girl.'

His forehead furrowed as his dark brows drew together, disappointment already turning his straight lips downward.

'However, when DC Ellis changed the child's nappy, we discovered it to be a little boy.'

Zak's eyes popped wide until Jenna could see the white all the way around the deep blue iris. He turned his hand over in hers and squeezed tight enough to take her breath away.

'Zak.' She kept her voice even. 'We have no idea why this

child was dressed as a little girl, other than to disguise him.' She paused as his grip slackened. 'We believe this *may* be Joshua. We *think* he's your son.' She felt the move as he considered leaping to his feet, but she held onto his hands. 'Zak!' His gaze shot and held onto hers. 'I need you to prepare for it not to be Joshua. Do you understand?'

He nodded, but the pure electric vibration shimmering through his body said he was prepared for no such thing. Jenna recognised the sheer desperate hope, had experienced it herself when news that Fliss had been found had reached her.

Decision made, she untangled her fingers from his, pulled out her iPhone and checked the time. It was time to put them all out of their misery.

'DC Downey and I will take you to the safe house, where we'll go and take a look at this little boy.'

'Safe house?' His panicked gaze dashed between his mum and Jenna.

'Yes. The same one you went to initially.' It had other names: the rape centre, the crisis centre. The same unit with a multitude of uses. It was West Mercia's designated safe house for anyone who needed counselling, protection, assistance.

'Right.'

They came to their feet together, him patting his pockets in frenzied confusion.

'I need my phone. I should take my phone in case the hospital call.' He turned his head. 'Mum...' Just as Simi swiped his phone off the coffee table and handed it to him.

Pale and fragile, she raised shaking fingers to her lips. 'Could I come too? Would it be okay?'

Jenna took her lead from Zak. It was, after all, his call. He may rather be on his own when he met the little boy, but Zak was already nodding before his mother had finished her question. 'Yes. I want Mum with me. We should let Dad know.'

'Your dad? Where is he?'

'He went into work. He... found all the sitting around tough. I think he just needed to... occupy his mind.'

Jenna nodded as her gaze caught Ryan's. Smooth as silk, he moved over to Simi. 'Would you like to come with me?'

Flustered, Simi raised her hand to her hair, and then gave a quick glance around the place. 'I need my glasses. My phone. Oh, I'm such a mess. I haven't...'

'Mum. Joshua's not going to care what his Nana looks like. He'll just be glad to see you.'

Eyes shiny with barely suppressed tears, Simi grabbed a glasses case from the sideboard and unhooked her phone from its charging cable, slipping both into the deep pockets of her tan trousers. 'I'm ready.'

For the first time, Zak's lips kicked up in a small smile. 'Perhaps lose the slippers, Mum.'

'Oh.' She slapped her hands against her ruddy cheeks, the quick rush of blood flushing them. 'Of course.'

She disappeared from the room and, when she returned, hair scraped back in a bun and feet firmly ensconced in a smart pair of leather brogues, she gave a nervous laugh.

'Now, I'm ready.' She stepped close to her son and ran one hand down his arm in a show of motherly affection as she brought her other hand from behind her back, a fluffy grey rabbit clutched in her fingers. 'Do you think he'd like Fluffy Butt?'

Zak choked and the sharp prick of tears hit the back of Jenna's eyes as he took the soft toy from his mother's hand and cradled it to his chest without speaking a word.

Eyes full of tears, Simi plastered on a smile and craned her head upwards to peer at Ryan. 'Shall we try again?'

'Certainly. This way.'

Jenna raised her hand to stop them for a brief moment. 'As a word of warning, Zak, Simi. There's a journalist outside, there will be more.' Like bees to a honeypot. 'I would ask that you don't engage with them at all. Not a word.'

With strained faces, they both nodded their agreement.

As Ryan took the lead, guiding Simi from the room, Jenna turned to Zak. 'I don't want to give you false hope. I do believe this is Joshua, but please be prepared for it not to be.'

Zak grimaced. 'That's not possible. I have to hope it is him. Hope is all I have left.'

With an understanding deeper than he could ever imagine, Jenna held out her hand for him to precede her. 'Let's do this, then.'

As they stepped outside the door, Kim Stafford rushed forward, iPhone in hand, presumably with the recorder on. 'Zak, Zak! Would you care to give a few words? Have there been any developments?'

Ryan spread his arms wide, turned his back on Stafford and used his body as a shield as Jenna guided Zak and Simi to the police vehicle. She opened the door for each of them and nudged them inside, noting the tight lines of their similar mouths as they avoided eye contact with Kim Stafford.

38

Jenna's nerves fluttered deep in her stomach as she drew the car up outside the safe house. Nerves in case it was Joshua, nerves in case it wasn't.

Zak had spent most of the journey in tense silence, his fingers tap, tap, tapping on his knees as he hugged the grey rabbit to his chest and sat bolt upright in the front seat of the police-issue vehicle. His mother in the back with Ryan, uttered not a word. As Jenna slid the car into park, she left the engine running to keep the air con on.

Zak turned his gaze on her. 'What was he doing in that house?'

She'd wondered how long it would take him to ask that question and she didn't have the answer. No one did at this juncture. 'We're not sure, Zak. First thing's first. Let's see this little boy. Identify him if we can.' As he reached to unlatch his seat belt, Jenna stretched out to touch the back of his hand. 'Zak. Whether this child is Joshua or not, you must understand that he has been through considerable trauma. I would ask you to show some restraint in your reaction. This needs to be a very positive encounter, no matter what.'

Zak's breath trembled as he drew it in while he gave a vigorous nod. 'Yep. Yep.'

Jenna raised her radio to her lips. 'Are you ready for us, Mason?'

Barely a split second passed when the radio crackled straight to life. 'Ready and waiting.' She tried to read Mason's tone, but there was nothing. Just flat-out business.

Jenna cut the engine and all four of them climbed from the vehicle together, slamming their doors in unison. The high-pitched beeping noise from the car stopped when she clunked the lock on the doors as they made their way along the side path to the front of the house. The soft whine in her head continued.

Mason stood with the door wide open as they approached. He raised his forefinger to his lips. 'He's asleep.'

Jenna's heart gave a stumble before it raced on again. Asleep was probably the best thing for the child after crying for so long. Even though the doctor would have made the experience as pain-less as possible, he'd still had to endure strangers handling him. At least if it wasn't Joshua, while he was asleep he'd be unaware of yet more strangers coming into his world.

Sylvia rose to her feet as they entered the downstairs room. Kitted out in bright primary colours, it served as both a nursery and playroom for those children who needed to visit or stay. Its design cultivated to distract and soothe. Although, in truth, given the trauma some of the children experienced, the task was impos-sible, and the long-term effects, the physical and mental scars they suffered couldn't be forgotten with a dash of paint and a burst of colour.

Jenna sent Sylvia a quick nod and appreciated the other

woman's cooperation as she stood by as witness, her participation not required at this point.

Asleep in the cot, the child lay under a thin patchwork sheet.

Tempted to approach, Jenna held off and let Zak move towards the cot on his own. His mother stood silent next to her, hugging the toy Zak passed over as he went, her nerves vibrating the air while she waited for her son's reaction.

Jenna's breath strangled in her throat as Zak peered over the cot at the youngster. He flung both hands up to his face as tears sprang to his eyes and leaked down his cheeks. 'Josh. Joshie,' His hoarse whisper barely made it from his lips.

If she'd had the strength to stop him picking up the sleeping infant, Jenna wouldn't have. It was Joshua and all the caution in the world couldn't keep a father apart from his son.

Zak leaned over and swooped the child up in a hug so tender it belied the man's desperation. With tears streaming down his face, he squeezed his eyes closed and ignored everyone else in the room as he rocked the still sleeping infant in his arms. The little boy's head tucked into his neck, the cotton sheet dangled from Joshua's body as Zak buried his face in his son's hair.

With a sob choking her, Jenna's heart couldn't take the tenderness of the scene. Bursting with joy and relief and every kind of elation imaginable, she turned her back to let Zak have his privacy with his child, only to have Simi throw herself in Jenna's arms.

It took a split second for Jenna's exploding heart to respond and she wrapped her arms around the smaller woman and let her sob into her shoulder, knowing it was the best thing she could do for her at that moment.

With tears blurring her vision, Jenna glanced over the top of Simi's head at Mason's broad grin, the same emotions she had

inside plastered all over his face. Relief. Elation. The deep satisfaction.

Ryan stood to one side, hands on hips, head bowed. Unused
to this kind of outpouring of emotion, his Adam's apple bobbed
in his skinny neck, but he still clung to a vestige of control.

Control Sylvia had an apparent abundance of as her sour
smile wrinkled her cheeks and she turned away to shuffle her
paperwork. Perhaps she went home at night with a sense of pride
in what had been achieved. A job well done. Another case
resolved. A tick in the box. But she'd long since stopped investing
her heart and soul, if ever she had, into the work.

Work Jenna could never imagine without the compassion and
empathy. Before Fliss had been kidnapped, she'd considered
herself a good police officer, honing her skills in the job,
displaying the right amount of understanding. Since then, she'd
discovered there was no shame in showing emotion. If she
wanted to cry, she'd damned well cry and sod the buggers who
laughed it off.

She rubbed her hand in soft circular motions over Simi's back
and spared Sylvia another glance as tears trickled down her own
cheeks. She'd far rather feel than return home after a day at work
with a dead heart.

Zak circled around with Joshua still fast asleep, cradled in his
arms, and beckoned to Simi. 'Mum.'

The woman flew from Jenna's arms to Zak's in a heartbeat and
made the fast prick of tears start again as she squished the little
grey rabbit between their bodies.

Jenna puffed out her cheeks as she swiped the back of her
hand over them.

'Cup of tea, I think.'

Grateful for Mason's suggestion, Jenna sent him a watery
smile.

They may have reunited a child with his father, but there was one hell of a lot of work to be done to find out why he'd been in that house in the first place.

Jenna moved through the room to the open-plan kitchen, followed closely by Ryan and Mason. She filled the kettle and snapped the switch on, then turned and leaned her back against the worktop, tears and emotion evaporating in the light of work they now had to do.

Mason rubbed his fingers over his chin and made the dark stubble rasp. 'A good result.'

'A great result.'

Jenna glanced over at the huddle of three in the living room. 'You found some clothes for him.'

Mason's lips curved upwards. 'Couldn't have the poor bugger going into the hospital in a dress.' He lowered his voice. 'I made Sylvia stop at Next. Took me all of three minutes to grab something. She wasn't bloody happy, I can tell you. Apparently, it wasn't in the fucking handbook, stopping off to shop for the poor little sod. Anyway, I convinced her by saying I needed the forensics on the clothes as soon as possible.'

'Where are they?'

'Still in the bloody car. Bagged and tagged. I'll hand them over to SOCO at my earliest.'

Jenna's lips twitched as she sent a furtive glance at the little boy decked out in a white short-sleeved T-shirt with navy blue and fawn stripes and a little pair of dungaree shorts in mid denim blue. There were no shoes, just a dainty pair of navy-blue socks.

Mason had just surged up the charts in her estimation.

Ryan bounced on his toes. 'What happens now?'

'We'll let the DI know, get Harry out here to wrap things up with Zak.'

'She's already on her way. I spoke with Taylor earlier once

Joshua fell asleep. What a nice temperament the little bugger has. He was bloody exhausted and still he never kicked off. Just fell asleep while I was holding him.' Mason's gaze slipped over to Sylvia as she packed her paperwork into her briefcase, he kept his voice low. 'It seemed Sylvia and I didn't have much to talk about, so I updated the DI from our side and he told me they still haven't tracked Emily down.' He leaned forward and reached over Jenna's head to take mismatched mugs from an open shelf. He placed them on the bench and raised his voice, a curl of a smile in place. 'Coffee, Sylvia?'

A mild look of horror slid over the woman's face before it cleared to blank again as she realised he may possibly be teasing. 'As I said earlier, I don't drink coffee, DC Ellis. Normally green tea. So much better for the skin.'

Jenna swallowed the response she would have loved to have given about the woman's parched, dry skin. Sylvia's bitterness was none of her business, but in the absence of substance abuse, coffee, cigarettes and alcohol, the woman only had her disappointment in life to blame for the deep lines etched in ever-increasing brackets over her skin. 'I don't think we have green tea in here.'

Mason obligingly opened a cupboard and swept his fingers across the array of herbal and fruit teas and Jenna sent him a grateful smile. 'Fruit tea, or camomile?'

Sylvia made a point of glancing at her analogue wristwatch. 'No, thank you. I'll be off now.' Her lips crinkled inwards. 'I should have finished fifteen minutes ago.'

Never a clock-watcher herself, Jenna stayed until the job was done to the best of her ability and at a point at which she could hand over to the next shift, or when Taylor booted her out of the door as he'd done recently when she'd hovered on the edge of complete exhaustion.

Unlike Sylvia. This woman was about to simply walk away.

'When can we expect your report?' Jenna prompted.

'Report?' Sylvia blinked. 'It'll take me a few days.'

'We could do with it as a matter of urgency.'

Sylvia swiped up her briefcase and smoothed her impeccable steel grey hair with the back of one hand. 'I'll see what I can do. I'm off now.'

Without a backward glance at father, son or grandmother, Sylvia strode to the front door and let herself out.

'Shit.' Mason drew in a long breath.

'What the hell did you say to her, Mason?'

'Fuck all.' He kept his voice low, so it didn't carry to the others. 'She's a fucking automaton. Not a single fucking emotion to be had. I wish to God they'd sent Tammi out.' He sent a quick glance over to Zak, Simi and Joshua. 'She never so much as offered to touch Joshua. Cold fish.' His voice urgent, he shook his head. 'Poor little man had to be examined by a doctor, and Sylvia didn't flicker. Bloody good job we had a fabulous doctor on board because, Christ only knows why, but Sylvia just stood back and let her do what she wanted to Joshua. Never asked a single fucking question. Never queried anything.'

Jenna unscrewed the lid on the coffee jar and spooned out instant coffee into five mugs. 'I assume you did.'

'Too fucking true.'

The woman had obviously got to Mason; if he couldn't hit it, he was going to swear profusely about it.

As she poured water into the mugs, Mason leaned around her and pulled a milk carton from out of the fridge. He slopped milk into two mugs, swiped one up and offered it to Ryan.

'Sugar?' Ryan's eyebrows jiggled and Mason passed the mug back as Jenna opened the cutlery drawer, took out a spoon and reached for the bag of white, granulated sugar. She dumped two spoonful's in and, just as she was about to plunge the spoon into the mug, Ryan leaned in close. 'One more, Sarg, if you don't mind.'

She plopped another spoonful in. 'Do you want me to stir it to the left or the right?'

With a cheeky grin, he snagged the mug from the bench. He took the spoon from her and stirred it himself, turning as DI Taylor walked in through the front door and straight into the kitchen.

The man's astute gaze ran around the room, taking in every last detail as he made his way towards them. He held out his hand, wiggled his fingers and whipped the coffee from Ryan's clutches before the officer had time to raise it to his own mouth. 'Thanks, lad. Perfect timing.' He took a quick slurp of the coffee, his short nose wrinkling with distaste. 'A little sweet for me, young Ryan, just so you know for the future. No more than a spoonful of sugar, I'm sweet enough as it is.'

Speechless, Ryan's mouth dropped open. A little in awe of Taylor, Ryan rarely had direct personal contact with him, apart from his enthusiastic questioning whenever they ran a case.

Jenna suppressed her grin, put another three sugars in the remaining mug with milk, gave it a quick stir and handed it to Ryan.

'Better rustle up another one.' Taylor nodded to the kettle. 'Harry's on her way in.'

'Excellent.' It meant with the team all in place, they could do a debrief in-situ before returning to the station.

Mason reached over the top of Jenna's head and slid another two mugs from the shelf above her as she grabbed the coffee jar again.

'Harry drinks water.' Jenna flicked Ryan a quick glance. Observant as he was, she didn't dispute his claim and reached up for a glass. She let the tap run for a moment and filled the glass, placing it on the bench next to the coffee mugs. Turning, she squinted at the family, still cocooned in each other's arms, the soft rabbit snuggled in tight, so it squished against Joshua's plump cheek.

Chest tight, Jenna turned away conscious that she didn't want to intrude on such an intimate moment.

As Harry swept through the door, Jenna held out the glass of water and had it plucked from her hand in an instant.

'Cheers.' With little finesse, Harry glugged the water down, tipping her head back until she'd drained the glass. 'Fucking hell, but it's hot. The devil is definitely in his playing ground today.' As DI Taylor had, Harry cruised her gaze over the scene in the living room, only she took her time, her narrowed eyes taking in every detail of the reunited family. 'Good news, then.'

Jenna nodded. 'Brilliant news.'

'I had thought otherwise when I saw Sylvia hoofing it to her car, face like a slapped arse.'

Ryan almost snorted his sweet coffee out of his nose and Mason obligingly gave him a few hard slaps on the back.

Taylor, having spent his working life with police humour, merely raised a brow and took another sip of his own drink. 'I've never known Sylvia be otherwise and I've known her for a long time. It's a sad day when a woman with Sylvia's knowledge and experience is so unwilling to impart any of it, not to mention the woman's absolute lack of any emotion other than annoyance, when she doesn't get off shift in time.' Taylor turned his head to take in the family. 'Pity Tammi hadn't been assigned. No matter, we won't be needing Sylvia now.' He turned to Jenna. 'I don't suppose she was obliging enough to let you know when we'd receive her report.'

Jenna flashed him a tight grin. 'I can't see that it will be imminent.'

'Fucking cold-hearted...' Jenna shot Mason a look and stopped him mid-flow.

'Okay.' Taylor took another look at the family group. With a healthy swig of his coffee, he drained the mug and snapped it down on the bench. 'Right. Let's get some answers.' He clapped his hands together once and nodded at Jenna. 'Sergeant, you take the lead.' As they made a move towards the living room, Taylor held up a hand to stop them. 'Do we really need the entire crew?'

Mason dipped his hands deep into his pockets and shrugged. 'Continuity, boss, I need to be here to fill in the gaps regarding Joshua's journey through hospital.'

Taylor turned his gaze on Ryan. 'Now you've had your coffee, son. What's your reason for being here?'

Ryan's desperate gaze darted back and forth between Jenna, Mason and Taylor, then a boyish grin sparked out as he jiggled his bony shoulders self-consciously, swiped up the two remaining coffees and raised them as he nodded towards Zak and Simi. 'Experience, sir. I need the experience handling this kind of case. Not had one like this before, so it's really interesting and I'll be completing the paperwork for the Sarg to approve.'

Impressed with the lad's creativity, Jenna pursed her lips and waited for Taylor to call him on it.

'Better get your notepad and pen out then, son. There's a hell of a lot of paperwork to be completed for this case.' Taylor shot Jenna a dry twitch of his lips. 'I won't be paying overtime on it, so anything above and beyond will be unpaid, DC Downey, and in your own time.'

'Sir.'

'If you bloody well salute, I swear I'll deck you,' Mason

murmured as he snatched up his own mug of black coffee and turned away.

Jenna picked up her mug and headed towards Zak and his mother, still clinging onto the sleeping child. 'Zak.' Eyes bubbled with pleasure as he met her gaze. 'We need to talk. If you and Simi would like to take a seat.' She never suggested putting Joshua down, didn't see the point. He could hug him until the end of time, but it still wouldn't take away the trauma they'd all been through. Trauma they had yet to discover as far as Joshua was concerned and may never, if the truth of what happened in Emily's house wasn't uncovered.

As they all took their seats, Ryan placed the mugs of coffee on the small wooden table and Harry took the closest seat to Zak. The first time Jenna had ever seen the other woman tear up, Harry placed her fingers over her lips and shook her head. 'What a beautiful, beautiful little boy. I can't tell you how delighted I am for you.' An obvious bond having been established with his father, she reached out to stroke Joshua's cheek.

With a grateful smile, Zak adjusted his son, so he lay sideways across his lap, leaned over to grab the coffee and sipped at it while he raised his gaze to meet Jenna's.

'Right. Well.' Jenna's heart still refused to settle to a normal rhythm, but she continued, knowing she gave little away of her emotions now she'd had time to park them. 'Let me take everyone through the situation so far, so that we're all apprised of the facts and the relative questions.'

'This morning at 06:55 hours, we received a phone call from a lady who claimed her neighbour had a child who had been crying continually for some time.' In order to avoid putting Zak and his mother under any further stress, Jenna didn't divulge just how long Joshua had been crying for. 'The woman's concern was that, as far as she knew, there was no child at that address. It was only after she heard shouting, then silence, other than the child crying, that she called us.'

Zak never took his gaze from her as he trailed the back of his knuckles across Joshua's cheek, time and time again, as the little one slept on, evidently feeling the security of his father's hold on him.

'When we arrived at the address in Lawley, we discovered an injured young woman, Fern, whose full identity has not yet been confirmed, but who we believe may have possibly been a friend or relation of the woman whose house it was.'

Zak's eyes went wide, and his mother let out a whimper as she covered her mouth with one hand. Possibly too much information, but they were bound to hear it sooner or later.

'On entry to an upstairs nursery, we discovered a child, who we now know is Joshua. Initially we believed he was a little girl as he was wearing a dress, we can only assume to disguise him. Disappointingly at that stage, we believed there was no connection to Joshua's disappearance and that we'd walked into the fallout of a domestic dispute.'

Jenna took a sip of her hot coffee. 'It was only when DC Ellis offered to change the child's soiled nappy that we discovered it was in fact a little boy. The similarity was too close to dismiss. Joshua has very distinctive hair and eye colouring, which obviously saved us some considerable time. DC Ellis and I pretty much knew immediately that we had Joshua, but obviously we needed you to verify that.' She couldn't help the wide smile that spread across her face as the warmth enveloped her heart at the sight of father and son reunited.

Zak cupped the little boy's cheek in his hand and lowered his head to place a gentle kiss on the end of his son's nose. 'Thank God. Thank God we have him back.'

Jenna nodded. She needed to keep them on track and time

was still an issue. 'In the interim, while we arranged to visit you, DC Ellis and Sylvia Cross from social services...' she glanced at Zak, but he showed no recognition of Sylvia's name, 'took Joshua to the hospital.' She paused to let him absorb that fact for a moment and waited for the question, which came relatively quickly.

'Why? He's not injured.' Panic flashed over Zak's face.

'No. But he could well have been. It's standard practice, for Joshua's own protection, to ensure that nothing... physical had occurred whilst he was out of your protection.'

Zak's lips tightened as understanding came to him. 'And was he? Abused?'

Simi's hand fluttered to her throat.

'No.' Mason raised his head, his gaze firmly fixed on Zak. Now wasn't the time for subtlety. The man needed to know what had happened to his son. 'The examination revealed no evidence of sexual or physical abuse. Joshua has no bruises, nothing to indicate he's suffered anything physical.'

Zak visibly melted as his eyes closed for a long moment. When he opened them again, winter passed through them. 'But he has suffered abuse. In another form, mental and emotional. He possibly witnessed his mum being attacked and then was kidnapped. He was found crying. He's witnessed someone being stabbed.' Frantic, he turned to Harry. 'Will he be affected by this? Will he remember?'

Harry reached out a hand and patted the back of Zak's. 'Research shows that most children have no cognitive memories until they're beyond the age of two. From now on, it will be about how you handle the situation and whether your stress and emotions rub off on Joshua.' She squeezed his hand as he nodded, desperate for the reassurance she offered him. 'We'll make sure we have counselling in place for you to deal with this.

You and your family have already been through so much, Zak, and you still have a long way to go, but we'll make sure everything is in place to help you all move forward, that you have the support you need.'

With his breath coming in deep pulls, Zak looked around at all of them. 'Mum and I will see to that. When Imelda comes home, we're going to make sure it'll be okay.' His eyes filled with tears and he blinked, while his mum let out a small, distressed sob that jerked at Jenna's heart.

She dry-swallowed as Zak's pain stripped the spit from her mouth. 'Good.'

The sharp peal of Zak's phone had Jenna jumping, her heart rate, already too high, skipped and stuttered before it settled into its overly fast rhythm as he fumbled, trying to keep hold of the infant while he grappled his phone. 'Yes!'

Simi leaned in and scooped the child from Zak's arms as he stood up. At the change in hold, Joshua whimpered but snuffled into her neck, the familiar scent of her evidently soothing him as he fell back to sleep in her arms. Exhaustion getting the better of him.

Zak moved away, skimming his fingers through his thick, dark hair. 'Yes. Yes. I understand.'

Tempted to follow him, Jenna came to her feet and hovered behind him while he stood with his back to them all.

'When? Yes, I'll be there as soon as possible. Thank you.' His voice choked on his final words petering out to a tearful whisper. 'Thank you so much.'

His shoulders shook as he ended the call and slipped the phone into his pocket. He raised his hands to cover his face, his breath coming in harsh gasps in the silence of the room.

They gave him time, and when he was ready, he dropped his hands to his sides and swivelled to face them, his gaze taking them all in and then landing on his mother. 'They've brought Imelda out of the coma.' His chest expanded as he hauled in a long breath. 'I need to go and see her. They're carrying out tests right now, but said by the time I get there, they'll have more information.' His lips quivered as he pressed them together. Eyes filled with sadness turned to Harry. 'I don't want to leave Joshua with anyone. I can't let him out of my sight.'

Jenna knew exactly how he felt, she'd not wanted to leave Fliss's side once she'd found her again. Nothing would have persuaded her to leave Fliss in someone else's care. Except maybe...

Harry's smile came fast and natural. 'You don't need to leave him. It isn't an issue.' She flipped her phone from her back pocket and glanced at the screen. 'We'll all go. You, your mum if she wants to.' Simi gave a wild nod. 'Joshua and myself.' Harry turned to Jenna. 'He's had the all-clear from the medics, so he's good to go from that point of view. DI Taylor, if I accompany them, do you have any issues?'

Taylor poked his tongue on the inside of his cheek, making it puff out as he gave it some thought. 'Other than the fact that there is someone out there on the loose. We don't know if they're responsible for attacking Imelda and kidnapping Joshua but we do know they are dangerous. We have a victim in hospital who can attest to that.'

'Hospital? Who's in hospital?' Zak's eyebrows twitched downwards as he turned to Harry and then Jenna. She knew she'd mentioned the injured victim, but stress affected people in different ways and he'd evidently not taken in the information she'd relayed. It hadn't processed because he'd been focused on his son, but they were used to having to repeat things. She'd go through it again.

'In the house we found Joshua in, there was also a victim of a stabbing. The victim is currently undergoing surgery at The Princess Royal Hospital to remove a knife from her stomach.'

An inkling of recognition washed over his narrowed gaze. 'So, who stabbed her? I assume you have them in custody.'

Jenna was already shaking her head before he'd finished asking the question. 'Not yet. We have an all ports call out on her, but, as it stands, we don't have any leads as to where she may have gone.'

'Who is she? Just, who the hell is she? Is this the woman who stole my son, or did the stab victim?' Now the initial shock had worn off, it appeared Zak's brain was starting to fire on all cylinders again and anger began to filter through.

Jenna shook her head. 'We don't know what happened or who stole Joshua. All we know is we have a stab victim who claims Emily attempted to kill her.'

'Emily?' Zak's frown deepened.

'According to the Council records, an Emily Shenton is registered as living at the address where we found Joshua.'

Colour leached from Zak's face to leave it pallid and sweaty as he staggered back a step, his mouth gaping open. He sucked in breath after breath, but his knees gave way, and he sank onto the small sofa. His hand went to his heart and he patted his chest as he gasped.

'Oh my God, Emily.'

With a zap of electricity fizzing through her veins, Jenna flew to Zak's side, sinking down onto her knees at his feet. She pushed her face close to his. 'Zak, you know this woman? You know Emily Shenton?'

He nodded, his mouth opened and closed for a moment, then he cleared his throat. 'You asked me if I knew anyone who held a grudge against Imelda and not once did I imagine the grudge was against me, not my wife.' He lowered his head and banged the heel of his hand against his forehead. 'Why didn't I think? Everyone loves Imelda. She doesn't have any enemies. Why would she?'

Jenna leaned in. The frost in his eyes as he raised his head gave Jenna a moment to consider that the gentle man they all thought him to be might not run all the way through and that the spine of steel he'd so far exhibited might also run to a tougher core. 'Tell me how you know her.' She squinted up at him.

He gave Simi a quick sideways glance. 'Mum knows. Emily and I were... together.' He puffed out a breath and sat back, running his hand through his hair. 'I thought... It never occurred to me that she'd have anything to do with this. I thought she'd moved on, got a new life. I've not heard from her for so long.' He leaned forward and rested his forearms on his knees. 'Emily and I worked together at Wright, Thomas & Hooper, an accountancy practice.' He met Jenna's eyes. 'She still works there, as far as I know.' He chewed his bottom lip. 'When we first started seeing each other, we had so much in common. We worked together, had the same circle of friends.' He sighed as though he couldn't drag in enough air. 'She was full on, you know. She took the initiative. Moved the relationship on, probably faster than I wanted at the time, but I was okay with it... to start with.' He tossed a glance at his mother. 'Mum wasn't keen.'

Simi's mouth tightened and her eyebrows twitched up.

'Before I knew it, she'd moved into my apartment. Her stuff...' Zak shook his head. 'And then she started talking about getting married. We'd been together less than four months and I knew I didn't want to marry her. She was fun, you know. Vivacious. The life and soul.' He blew out a gusty sigh and shook his head. 'At first, things seemed fine, if a little intense.' He glanced over at his mum again. 'Then she accused me of seeing other women. Women in the office. Women we both knew.'

'Were you?' Jenna asked.

'No. I'm not like that. If I don't want to be with someone, I'll let them know and move on. What's the point of testing the waters elsewhere? I've been brought up better than that. If you don't want to be with them, you don't. And I didn't, so I told her.' He sucked his breath in through his teeth.

Jenna sat back on her haunches. 'And then what happened?'

He rolled his lips inwards and nodded. 'Hysterics. Crying, begging. Constant phone calls. Texts. It was awful. She threatened to take her own life. She threatened to take mine. Going to work became a nightmare. She wouldn't leave me alone. I couldn't leave my desk and she was on me.'

'Did you report it to anyone?'

'Yes. But it was awkward. You know.' He flicked a hand to indicate himself. 'A big guy like me being stalked by a woman. The MD thought it was funny, told me to grow a pair.' Zak's lips thinned.

Double standards worked both ways, Jenna was all too aware. Progress had been made within West Mercia to take complaints of this nature seriously but by and large, companies and the wider world still lagged behind in their thought processes. Jenna had witnessed plenty of instances of men being harassed, stalked, abused by women. It wasn't something she would ever dismiss if a man came to her with such a problem.

'What about HR?'

Deadpan, he turned his gaze on her. 'She was HR. The manager.'

'Jesus.'

'Yeah. I had no alternative. I found another job and left the company. Gave them a month's notice. A month of hell. She broke into my apartment...'

'Broke in? Did you report it?'

Zak scraped his hair back from his forehead. 'No. She still had a key. She wouldn't give it back. I spoke with the MD of the company and we agreed I could take the holiday owing to me and just leave. There was no way I could concentrate on my work with her there. He didn't seem to think it was anything out of the ordinary. He said he spoke with her and she seemed calm and rational. Nothing like I'd described to him. She'd worked there longer than me, never been a problem. Quiet. Kept to herself on the whole, but really good fun at social events. Not that many friends but quite often HR don't, because of the nature of their jobs.'

Zak shrugged. 'I moved out of my apartment. At the time, my parents were looking to downsize, the house had become too much for them to handle especially with so much gardening to be done. The house has been in our family for three generations, four now.' He glanced at his son. 'I didn't want to see it go to someone else. So, I sold my apartment, moved in with Mum and Dad while they found themselves something smaller and we did a deal.' He sent his mum a grateful smile. 'I had to inform the company of my forwarding address, which concerned me at the time, but Emily went quiet and I thought that was it. I believed she'd moved on. That was almost two years ago now. I've not heard from her since. It never occurred. I met Imelda pretty quickly after that. We found out she was pregnant within a couple of months.' He shrugged, from the lack of defensiveness in his voice, he was more than happy with the situation. 'When she became pregnant the second time, we got married.' A smile kicked up the edges of his mouth. 'When you know it's right...' His lips straightened to a flat line. 'I haven't given Emily a thought ever since. Why would I?' He ran his gaze over each person in the room, begging for help. For understanding.

They all understood.

Zak shook his head. 'What the hell triggered this? I knew she wasn't stable, bit of a head case, but this. This is on another level. Why would she attack Imelda? Kidnap Joshua?'

Jenna had no solution to the question.

What had triggered Emily? After so long, why would she suddenly react again?

She patted Zak's knee. 'We have a search out for Emily.'

His gaze bored into hers. 'So, she's still out there? On the loose?' Panic cracked his voice.

Jenna shook her head. 'She wasn't at the house when we arrived. She'd gone.'

'And who was the stab victim?'

'We don't know. Scenes of crime are on it right now, but it appears there's no evidence of identification in the house for either woman.'

He sat up straight. 'I can give you a description.'

'That would be useful. I'm sure SOCO will find something, a photograph, but so far, we've got nothing.' Jenna pushed to her feet at the same time as Zak. 'I don't suppose you have any photographs?'

His lips twisted. 'I may have.' He raised his hand and scratched at his head. 'I'm not sure. I'll have to have a look. I possibly deleted them all when I had my new phone. There would be no reason to keep them.' He pulled his phone from his back pocket and glanced at the screen. 'I need to go. I should gather some stuff for Joshua. We could be some time.'

Mason picked up a plastic carrier bag and opened it wide so the contents could be seen. 'Nappies, wipes, food, milk. One change of clothes. Will that keep him for now, save you going back home?'

Surprise flashed over Zak's face, but he sent Mason a grateful smile. 'That should do it. I'm sure we can always grab more if we need it from the shops over there. There're bound to be some close by the hospital.'

'I have a child seat in my car.' With an embarrassed bob of his head, Mason winced. 'It was in Emily's house. We used it to take Joshua to the hospital. It's brand new.'

Zak squinted, and then shrugged. 'It makes no difference to me. If it's new, we'll use it for now and then get rid of it. We need to get off. I want to see Imelda.' Zak offered his hand to Jenna. 'Thanks for your help, DS Morgan.' His dry hand encompassed hers.

'Let me know how you get on.'

'I will.' He dropped his hand from hers and nodded at the rest of the team.

Harry smiled. 'No worries, we'll be in constant contact.'

As they headed for the door, Jenna flipped her phone open and typed in the name of the accountants, DI Taylor by her side.

'Whereabouts are they?' DI Taylor scratched his chin and reached for his radio.

'Little Dawley. We'll go.'

Taylor shook his head. 'Salter and Wainwright can go. They're chomping at the bit right now. Nothing but dead ends so far, they'll be pleased to get out of the station for a while.'

She wasn't so sure, the cool of the air con at the station was enough of a temptation to keep them inside even if it rattled and groaned and wasn't as effective as it could be, but she'd go with Taylor's decision as he nodded at her.

'You get yourself back to the station, get everything written up.'

She finished off the last of her coffee and picked up her phone and radio from the coffee table as she listened with half an ear.

Taylor directed a stony look at Ryan. 'You make sure you keep that promise and, in the meantime, you stay here until your shift ends. You should be able to get some notes in while you wait. Not a lot for you to do but drink more over-sweetened coffee.' He cruised a gaze over Ryan. 'No wonder you can't stay still for more than a second. I thought it was excess energy. Now I see it's a sugar rush.'

Ryan flushed to the tips of his ears as words stumbled out of his mouth. 'Does anyone need to stay here, sir? It's not like I'm protecting anyone. They won't be coming back, will they?'

Taylor scratched the side of his nose. 'They will be coming back, DC Downey. Until we find Emily Shenton, Zak and Joshua are at risk. Very possibly Simi and her husband too. So, they will all need to stay here for the foreseeable future while Emily is at large. She's already proved that she's a danger.'

Jenna raised her radio to her mouth. 'I'll get someone to pick up Mr Cheetham from his place of work. Perhaps he can pack a couple of cases for Simi, Zak and Joshua before he meets them back here.' The least amount of coming and going, the better, just in case Emily Shenton was bright enough to follow.

She'd proved clever enough to evade the police so far.

40

Emily blinked open gritty eyelids and stared at the square, white ceiling tiles above her that swirled in a fuzzy haze as she tried to focus. Pain pulsed in ever-widening ripples from her centre to the very tips of her fingers and toes.

Lungs burning, she breathed in little sips of air and closed her eyes again while the encroaching darkness threatened and churned. She was never going to drink again.

Her left arm refused to raise until she used her right one to guide it upwards. Cool air pumped across her overheated skin, but beads of sweat still popped out, the thick smell of alcohol and toxins seeping from her pores, so her nose wrinkled with disgust at her own stench. She needed a shower. She needed water. She needed food. Her stomach heaved, rebelling at the mere thought. Steeped in acid, it clenched in protest at the abuse she'd heaped on it.

The vague memory of her loose grasp on the third bottle of wine surfaced. Self-disgust curdled her stomach while flashes of dark memories assailed her senses.

'Oh, God.'

Her tongue adhered itself to the roof of her mouth so she could barely draw in a breath through a throat that throbbed as though she'd been stabbed...

Stabbed.

The memory surfaced. She'd stabbed Fern.

You killed your own sister. The dark amusement in the voice stirred her.

She pulled in a deep breath and then coughed it out again as pain seared through her chest.

You stabbed Fern and now she's dead.

She took her time, memory circling like black crows gathering in the dusk.

The crisp white sheets crackled as she rolled onto her side, grunting out her agony. She reached for the glass of water from the bedside cabinet and propped herself up on one elbow while she gulped it down. Her throat parched like a desert after all the alcohol she'd consumed. The coolness of it should have been refreshing. Instead, it merely made her crave more. She reached out for the jug of water and every muscle screamed at her. She flopped back on the pillow, the white, starched cotton cool on her cheek as she allowed herself to drift.

She'd stabbed Fern.

With a sense of relief rather than regret, Emily allowed herself a slow smile. Pious cow that she was. She'd deserved everything she got. At least Emily no longer had to listen to her preach her miss goody-two-shoes perfection.

In the silence, she strained to hear.

Nothing, except the sly voice. *Fern's gone. Emily's free. Free as a bird. You can fly now, you have nothing to stop you.*

She closed her eyes and let the darkness pull her down.

41

Jenna pushed her fingertips into her closed eyelids and pressed until bright sparks dappled the blackness.

Disappointed Adrian had been waylaid in London, she had to acknowledge she probably didn't have the strength to speak with him if he had made it home. It would have been nice just to curl up next to him though. One short, to-the-point text was all she'd managed in response. She was proud enough she'd used three emojis and a kiss.

'Long day?'

She raised her head and smiled at Fliss as her younger sister handed her an ice-cold glass of white wine and shuffled her backside on the raffia settee next to her, allowing enough room for Domino to climb up beside them. Instead of taking up the space left for him, he settled his backside and then stretched out across both of them as though it was important for him to connect them all.

As the heat of the snuggled up pair pulsed through, Jenna took a sip of her wine and hummed her appreciation as it slid down her parched throat. She tipped her head back to rest it on the sofa. 'Horrendously long. In some ways satisfying, in others not.' Too exhausted to run into complicated explanations, she bullet-pointed it for Fliss. 'We found Joshua.'

'Fantastic.'

'Yeah. It was... satisfying.' Understatement of the year, but if she went into detail, she might just blart all over again and she was already worn down. 'We reunited him with his dad.'

Fliss patted her own chest as she blinked a hint of tears away. 'That's amazing. What a relief.'

'Yeah. More than I can tell you. The mother, Imelda, is out of her coma.'

'Wow!' Fliss jiggled herself upright and pushed Domino off her lap so he lay on the sofa instead of her. 'Another relief. How is she?'

Jenna shrugged. 'They'll be carrying out tests over the next few days to see how much she's been affected by the head trauma.'

'That's positive. What about the baby?'

'As far as we've been told, all the obs on baby are good. They don't think it's come to any harm.'

'Amazing.'

'I know, isn't nature so wonderful that a mother's body can protect her own child? Even in the face of such trauma. Unfortunately, initial signs indicate that Imelda may not be able to walk. Or talk.'

'Oh, no. How desperately sad.' Fliss raised her arm as Domino squirmed his way back across her lap.

'Mmm, it could improve, according to the Glasgow Coma Scale.' Jenna hitched her shoulders. She had no in depth knowledge of the scale, she only knew that they hoped for improvement.

'And have you caught anyone?'

Important enough question and the one that troubled Jenna the most. 'Not yet. It's been a long day. We've been carrying out all the relevant enquiries, but we still have so much to do.' She swiped a hand over her weary eyes. She'd wanted to keep it short and sweet, but the case was too complex for that. 'SOCO are in the house where we found Joshua, but they can't find anything. They've taken prints, but they can't be matched to anything on the system.' As Fliss squinted at her, Jenna expanded. 'It means the person living there hasn't committed a crime in the past, so their prints aren't on file.'

'Ah, of course.'

'We've identified the car type and are trolling through the registered owners in Telford to check if we can find a match. It's just legwork now.' She met her sister's gaze. 'Do you mind if we talk about something else. I'm knackered.' Mentally, physically, emotionally.

Fliss threw the veil of sadness off and painted on a bright, false smile. 'You want food?'

Jenna rolled her head sideways to look at her sister and grunted. Her ankles and feet throbbed with the heat and every ounce of energy had drained from her. 'I can't be arsed to move, Fliss.'

'We have pizza.'

Jenna huffed out a laugh. 'Fucking marvellous, you miracle. If I can manage to raise my arm, I'm sure to love it.'

'Christ, Domino, it's too hot to snuggle.' Fliss slipped her arms under Domino's deep chest and lifted him clear so his feet stood on the floor. She pushed herself up and headed towards the kitchen. 'We're slumming it. I'm not sitting at the table tonight. I had a long day too.'

Domino hung his head for a moment, then sighed before he ambled after Fliss, ever on the lookout for food.

Jenna raised her glass, took another sip of wine and closed her eyes as the savoury smell of pizza wafted through the open doors from the kitchen. She damned well loved her sister.

She just knew.

She always knew exactly what it was Jenna needed.

42

Dim lighting filled the room with a soft glow.

Emily's tongue remained welded to the roof of her mouth despite the amount of water she'd slugged down every few minutes during the night. She'd lost count of how much she'd had, filling her glass from the jug on the side, finding no relief as her dry, split tongue remained swollen.

She reached out for yet another glass of water and gulped it down, and her bladder responded with a sharp spasm to remind her she hadn't been to the toilet all night. She searched her memory for the last time she'd visited the bathroom, but it remained a fog.

She shuffled up onto her elbows and then swung her legs over the side of the bed, kicking aside the single, starched white sheet as her head reeled and her vision wavered. Her naked feet touched the ice cool of the tiled floor and she sucked in a breath at the deliciousness of it on her overheated flesh.

The lead weight of her entire body dragged at her, so she had no choice but to sit while the wild spinning in her brain settled to slow revolutions.

She took her time, gazed around her and then reached for the drawer in the bedside locker. She slid it open to find nothing apart from the bunch of keys she'd kept on her for days. Since she'd been to Zak's house. She closed her fist around them to stop them from rattling as she slid them from the drawer and then checked in the cupboard below. Nothing.

Emily rubbed her fingertips over her dry lips as she considered the set of keys in her hand. Four keys. Front door, back door, no idea what the third was, but the fourth was the key to a car. An Audi.

She raised her head and drew in a deep breath, coughing it out again as she ran her gaze around the room with its dim lighting, barely enough to see by. It served her purpose. She preferred the dark.

As she slipped to her feet, she wavered for a moment before she stumbled towards the brighter light of a bathroom. She paused, pulled open another cupboard door and peered inside before she took out a small holdall, then moved onto the next cupboard. A handbag and a plastic carrier bag containing what could be toiletries and pyjamas.

Emily sneaked into the bathroom and slid the lock across the door before she rooted through the bags while she sat on the toilet and peed, the warm gush of it alleviating the pain in her full bladder. She sighed out her relief, closing her eyes against the bright white light of the bathroom.

When she opened them again, she held up the handbag. She tucked her hand inside and drew out a purse. She flicked through the contents, snatched out the cash and shuffled through it. Forty-five pounds. It would do. It would get her a taxi.

Hand on the grab rail, Emily hauled herself up from the toilet and stared at the dark yellow urine as she flushed it away, the overpowering scent of ammonia wrinkling her nose. Too much alcohol. Dehydration.

If Fern was there, she'd be giving her shit by now. But Fern was gone. She was no longer answerable to her. It was for the best. Pious bitch.

Fingers shaking, Emily dragged clothes out of the plastic carrier bag and held them up before she flung them to one side, annoyance curdling in her stomach, the sharp acid punch of it spiking her temper.

'Fuck it.'

No way could she fit into them, they were way too small. Skinny cow with clothes no use to a normal person.

She shoved her hand into the holdall and pursed her lips. No underwear, but she dragged out a pair of pyjamas. Grey stretchy bottoms, which she yanked over her legs. The material strained over her thighs and the elastic stretched as wide as it would go to get it halfway up her belly, leaving a roll of fat to spill over the waistline.

Frustrated, she grabbed the thin, matching top and inched it over her bosom, tugging it down until it barely met the waistline of the bottoms.

Heat rushed up her neck into her face as she ground her teeth, biting down on the urge to scream at the top of her voice as she met her gaze in the mirror under the unforgiving white light.

See, you don't need Fern. You can do it yourself, the reassuring rumble whispered in her ear.

Dark purple streaked in heavy bruises under her eyes and her once bright skin dulled, angry red spots peppering over the top of her nose and across her forehead. She'd been like this once before, but it was a vague memory. Distant and foggy.

She sucked in a breath through flared nostrils and whistled it out through gritted teeth. 'Fuck.'

Insistent, the dark voice whispered in her ear while butterflies carried out their wild dance in her stomach to make it jitter and jump.

She stared at the discarded bags littering the floor at her still naked feet.

'Well, that was a fuckfest. No fucking good to anyone.'

She pulled the light cord and plunged the room into darkness as she sneaked from the bathroom, heading down the long corridor and out of the door.

Surprise streaked over the taxi driver's face as Emily wrenched open the door and slipped inside. She bounced onto the back seat with guttural grunts as she pulled the seat belt around her while the pyjama top rode up to let her belly slither out while the taxi driver watched her in the mirror. If she had the energy, she'd tell him to where to go. But she needed him.

She bit out the address before the last vestige of strength seeped from her body. Her head flopped back on the seat and she closed her eyes, allowing the soft bloom of clouds to take her under...

'We're here, mate. You want to wake up?'

Emily cracked open her eyes, the temptation to tell him to fuck off on the tip of her tongue again before the memory of where she was nudged into her consciousness. 'How much do I owe you?' Her voice didn't sound right to her own ears. Rough and raspy, it growled out of her throat.

He turned in his seat. 'Eleven pound eighty, mate.' His judgemental gaze flickered over her as she unfolded the money she'd held scrunched in her hand and passed him fifteen pounds. 'Keep the change.'

She pushed the door wide, whipping in a sharp gasp of breath as she straightened.

The taxi driver wound his window down. 'Are you going to be all right, mate?'

The voice inside screamed for her to scream at him, but instead she sent him a tight smile. 'Just lost my baby, *mate,* but I'll be okay.'

The driver's face went blank before he turned away, awkwardness in every angle of his shoulders.

As he drove off, Emily stepped through the gap in the hedgerow and made her way further up the street to the address she really needed, her bare feet tender on the cracked and broken footpath.

Zak's house stood tall and imposing, light reflecting from the upstairs windows as the sunrise bathed the landscape in golden hues and bounced back from the darkened glass.

Emily pulled back as her gaze caught the distinctive uniform of a police community support officer, the vibrant yellow of their high-visibility jacket jarred her senses.

Clothes already too tight for her seemed to squeeze even more as the humid start to the day heated up.

Emily sank down and curled into a tight ball in the floppy overhang of the hedgerow. Brambles and nettles pricked at her skin as she concentrated on the figure outside Zak's house. Heavy eyelids slipped closed and she tucked her head down, resting her forehead on her knees. Her usually bright mind stumbled and shut down.

43

Jenna swiped her coffee from her desk and headed for the incident room with the hope that matters had moved on overnight and they'd have more answers than they had the previous day.

Frustration bloomed at the slowness of the information filtering through. She wanted it now. Bam, bam, bam. But that wasn't the way the system worked.

They should be celebrating the discovery of young Joshua and the recovery, albeit minimal, of his mother, Imelda. Instead, everyone was on tenterhooks, searching for a ghost of a woman who barely existed.

The dull murmur of early-morning voices enveloped her, blocking out the high-pitched hiss in her ears as she stepped inside the incident room.

Salter and Wainwright were the first to fall under her scrutiny as she waited for the team to assemble. The pair were polar opposites and completely inseparable. They'd worked together for the past twenty-three years and rubbed along nicely, neither one of them aspiring to promotion, happy to do 'real policing', as they saw it. Grafters. Stuck in a time warp both were content with, they put in good old-fashioned policing, doggedly working through each case. Every time a new computer system was introduced, they'd attend the course, grumble about how much more time they spent doing paperwork since computers had been introduced to cut down on paperwork. Then they'd return to their age-old methods of getting out of the station and talking to real humans with real lives who knew the gossip. Between them, their detection rate was one of the highest in the force.

Jenna had confidence the pair of them would have information from their visit to Emily's workplace they'd made the previous afternoon.

Pleased to see Donna and Natalie together at Donna's computer, Jenna sidled over and nudged her backside onto the edge of the desk. 'I thought you were on a late today.'

Donna glanced up and shot her a bright smile. 'Not on your life, I'm not missing out on this. The most interesting thing since... well, since Fliss went missing.' She grinned again. 'Never had a case like this one. So complex, I want to help fit all the pieces of the puzzle together.'

Jenna smiled back. She'd quite liked the lack of high-profile cases. Just for a time.

DI Taylor scratched his head as he ambled in, his crisp white shirt tucked into his neat-as-a-pin trousers with their perfect, straight crease down the front. No evidence of sweat under his armpits, his pristine wife simply wouldn't allow it. His black clip-on tie snapped neatly on his over-tight collar so his neck bulged over in a little roll of skin. His gaze skimmed the room and settled on Jenna as he inclined his head.

Flustered, Ryan rushed into the room, eyes filled with panic as he skidded to a halt in front of Taylor. He veered off and shot to the back of the room to hand over one of the takeout coffee cups to an indolent Mason, who leaned against the windowsill, taking in the little fresh air that the safety catch would allow through. The rattle and hum of the ancient air-con system struggled to access the incident room, one of the hottest in the building. Ironic, as it was the most frequently used and more likely to be filled to capacity, as it was now.

Harry wandered in, eyes puffy from lack of sleep. She hadn't needed to come back on an early, but she'd want to stick with her assigned family as much as possible. She gave a wide yawn as she found the last empty chair and slumped into it.

Satisfied all her team were there, Jenna drained her cup, dropped it in the recycling bin, pushed away from the desk and made her way to the front of the room to join DI Taylor.

As silence fell, she took in the additional members, not necessarily regulars but there were none she didn't recognise from recent cases. Several uniforms, press info lady, the new intel analyst, smart, attractive, long legs, short skirt. She wore what she wanted. Sexual harassment didn't feature on her agenda. One death stare from her and she could slay a man from twenty paces.

'Good morning,' Jenna began.

The grumbled responses brought a crooked smile to her face. It wasn't that early. The sun had been up for around four hours. She'd been out with a prancing Dalmatian at five o'clock, the cooler air at that time of the morning a refreshing change. She could breathe. The pleasure of walking through knee-high grass and watching Domino dance across a field full of early-morning rabbits that he really wasn't interested in except for a gentle lope after them before he returned to her side.

By the time she returned home later, it would be too hot again to walk a dog, and yet he still needed the exercise. She could take him down to the River Severn at Ironbridge and let him swim in the shallows. The water levels had dropped so far that the current was more of a meander than a mad rush. Fliss would probably come with her. It was rare their days finished together and having Harvey call in when they both had a full day might prove useful. They'd yet to trial it properly. Today was the first day he'd visit, but they'd all agreed that if it was too hot, he shouldn't take Domino out. Although the woodlands would be ideal, Jenna had her reservations. She'd always have her reservations about those woodlands. Possibly any woodland ever again since that's where Domino had been attacked before Fliss was kidnapped.

'Okay.' Back to business. 'We have a dangerous woman still at large. Let's do a quick round-up and get back out there looking for Emily Shenton.' Jenna turned her head. 'Salter, Wainwright. What have you got from your visit to Emily's employer yesterday?'

Wainwright leaned back in his chair, his cool casualness a reassurance. 'Aye, we met with the MD of the company, Phil Lowestoft.'

'Bit of a wanker,' Salter inserted.

'Bit of a wanker,' Wainwright agreed. 'Believed that sexual harassment is a one-way street. Only men sexually harass. All women are innocent.'

Jenna rubbed her forehead. As a police officer, she knew with conviction that men were abused, stalked and beaten, not on such a high scale as women, but far more often than the general public believed. Twenty per cent of women and four per cent of men suffered some kind of sexual abuse from the age of sixteen. Men were less likely to report such abuse as they found it an embarrassment. Professionals, in particular, were reluctant to report it.

Jenna had heard rumours of a solicitor who'd recently been beaten up by his police officer girlfriend and declined to inform the police to save face, in his opinion. Her opinion was any police officer physically or mentally abusing a partner wasn't fit for the job and she'd keep a close eye on that officer from now on. Until then, she'd take it as a rumour as she had no information from the horse's mouth as such.

Personally, Jenna would never tolerate abuse on any level, physical, emotional, obvious or insidious. She'd recognise it immediately and put a stop to that shit straight away. She was lucky with her current love interest. Not only was Adrian lacking in any prerequisite to be abusive, but it appeared he was a nurturer. She also went with the theory that absence made the heart grow fonder as so much of his time was spent in London on hot cases.

At the questioning stares from her team, Jenna jerked herself back to the present. 'Did he have anything to say about his kidnapping, stabbing member of staff who happens to be female?'

Wainwright inclined his head. 'He did. He was shocked. Deeply shocked. According to him, Emily is quiet, keeps to herself, is impeccable at her job. He knew about the problem with Zak. Thought Zak was a pussy. Nearly fell through the fucking floor when we put it to him that his sweet Emily may possibly have beaten a woman into a coma, kidnapped a child and stabbed an unidentified woman in the stomach.'

Salter sent a bitter smile her way. 'He may possibly have pissed himself when we stressed that had he acted sooner, these events may never have happened.'

Wainwright's dry tones interjected. 'Aye, and then he shit himself when we reserved the right to come back to him for further questioning. He was on to his solicitor before we left the building. Bloody wanker.'

'Wanker!' Salter repeated, just to keep up his side of the double act.

'Did he give any relevant information? Address? ID?' Jenna pressed.

'He confirmed the home address as the one Joshua was found at.'

Jenna nodded. 'Was there any ID on file?'

'No. She was HR. There was nothing on her personal file, not even a birth certificate or driving licence.'

'Fuck!' Mason murmured from the back of the room.

'Yeah!' Salter nodded his agreement.

Jenna raised a hand. 'No one checks up on HR?'

'It appears not. Not in this case. MD claimed she was so anal, she carried out every single job to perfection. Which was one of the reasons he was so reluctant to take action when Zak accused her of stalking him. He said he'd spent years trying to get a decent HR who would stay. He reeled when he took her file out and saw how little it contained. No mention of her being a stalker. Obviously.'

'Obviously.'

'Salter made him aware that the responsibility of an employer is to ensure employees have had "right to work" checks carried out, Sarg. Just slipped it in there to give him the willies. Which evidently those checks weren't done on Emily, or if they were originally, she'd removed them from her file.'

'Interesting. How about next of kin on her file?'

'None. No one on her Death in Service statement. She'd never spoken of any relatives, although I'm not sure Lowestoft would have bothered enquiring. He said she took some time off after Zak left. Came back to work as though nothing had ever happened, maybe a little more laid back and he believed nothing ever had happened. He certainly closed his eyes to it.'

'Okay. Thank you. Obviously, SOCO are in the house as we

speak and, again, they're having difficulty finding any ID. When she bolted, she could have grabbed her handbag, there was no evidence of one in the house. Would she have a passport? Driving licence? Do you keep all of those things on you all the time?' Jenna knew she certainly never did. Maybe her driving licence, but not always.

The intel analyst raised her index finger and Jenna's attention centred on her immediately as she looked over the top of her designer black-rimmed glasses. There was something about the woman's cool, composed attitude that just commanded attention. 'I checked the electoral register and council tax. The house is only in her name, electoral register confirms Emily Fern Shenton resides at that address. I've requested a copy of her driving licence, together with the photo ID. That was last night.' She shot Jenna a tight smile. 'I don't expect they'd have picked that up until 9 a.m., so should we say mid-afternoon before we receive a reply to our *urgent* request?' One perfect, straight eyebrow winged up. 'I'll get it to you the moment it becomes available.'

'Perfect.' As Jenna started to turn away, the slight rise of the intel analyst's chin let her know she'd not finished.

'In the absence of any evidence so far, and bearing in mind she has a driving licence, I checked if she has a car registered in her name. It's a white Honda Jazz, registration number HB20 PRD.'

Jenna gave her a nod and turned to take in the uniforms. 'Could I have volunteers to check the streets outside her house? I don't believe anyone has picked up on the vehicle yet. SOCO will be working their way inside out.'

Two of the officers raised their hands and she sent them a grateful look, noting the intel analyst writing down their names against the job. If they slipped up, Jenna wasn't going to have to follow up. Her intel officer had it all in hand. A secret admiration for the woman curled in Jenna's stomach. Her efficiency had definitely started to pay dividends.

Jenna opened her mouth to speak just as Morris King poked his head around the doorway. 'Sarg. You got a minute?'

She raised a finger to hold him there for one moment while she finished her train of thought out loud. 'Harry Darling called through earlier to let us know that as Zak feared, there were no photographs of Emily on his new phone and he hadn't saved any of them from the old phone.' Why would he? It made sense.

Jenna turned her attention back to Morris. Puzzled at the quiet interruption, she sidled over to the door, DI Taylor following her, and let the quiet buzz of voices in the room escalate while she turned her attention to Morris. 'Hi, what's up?'

Morris's thick black eyebrows twitched downwards. 'I had a couple of things to distribute, so I thought I'd drop by personally on my way.' He sniffed, his gaze intent on her. 'I just took a call from The Princess Royal Hospital. That stab victim from yesterday...' He poked out his bottom lip as he paused. 'Turns out she's disappeared.'

'Disappeared?' Jenna's voice pitched up an octave.

Shit.

'Yeah. Seems they went to check her obs and she'd gone. They thought at first she'd just popped to the loo or something, but when they returned an hour later, she still hadn't returned.'

Shit. Double shit.

Jenna tilted her head to one side. 'I don't understand. We had someone there, didn't we?'

'Yeah, but our victim had been moved to a general ward, so the officer was outside the entrance. Never saw anyone come in or out during the night. Claims to have gone to grab a coffee and visit the toilet earlier. Says he never thought to check the bay as all the curtains were round each bed and he didn't want to disturb the other patients. As the victim had been heavily sedated from her operation, he said it never occurred to him that she wasn't there. He had no reason to believe she'd have the interest or energy to abscond.'

DI Taylor leaned over her shoulder. 'Apart from the very real possibility that she'd kidnapped Joshua Cheetham-Epstein and knew she was in hot water. I'll have a word with him. Who was it?'

'PC Rankin, sir.'

Taylor drew in a long breath through his nostrils. 'That's not like him. Phil Rankin is normally very astute. Bugger. We'd better get some uniforms deployed to look for her. Full description, what she was last seen wearing, when she was last seen. What state she was in.' Taylor's harnessed fury vibrated through the thick shoulder he leaned against her, the clean scent of his cotton shirt wafted over her in a cloud of heat.

'Thank you, Morris.' Jenna swung around to face the room.

'One more thing.' She spun on her heel back to Morris. 'Apparently, they checked the bathrooms in case she'd collapsed, and they found a discarded gown, a handbag and contents scattered on the floor and a rucksack. It appears she may have stolen them from other patients. PC Rankin's looking into that right now.'

'Thank you.'

Morris pulled the door closed and both Jenna and Taylor faced their audience, who fell silent.

'Right. We need to get onto this. This is urgent. We've just received information that our stab victim of yesterday has disappeared from the hospital. I need the hospital CCTV checking. See what she wore, when she left. Where did she go? Was she picked up? Did she hop on a bus? Did she get in a taxi? We need to trace this woman. We still have no verification of her ID, so we don't know who the bloody hell she is or where she lives.'

Ryan raised his hand.

DI Taylor never even bothered to sigh. 'Yes, DC Downey.'

'How long ago did she disappear? How much of a jump has she got on us?'

Taylor rolled his lips inwards, irritation sparking. 'We haven't pinned that information down yet, but I'll be dealing with it shortly.' He whistled air out through his teeth before he addressed the new intel analyst. 'Any new information you gather, bring it straight to me or DS Morgan.' At the flick of her eyebrow, he indulged in a quick smile of appreciation. 'I know. You're on it.' He checked to make sure he still had their attention and gave one short, sharp clap. 'Right, we need to get a trot on. DS Morgan, who is currently watching over the safe house?'

'PCSO Dalton, sir. Harry and I are about to go and relieve him.'

Harry raised her hand. 'Zak requested we allow him to his house to pick up changes of clothes for Joshua and himself. By the time we got back from Southmead last night, it was too late and apparently his dad hadn't exactly excelled in the area of providing for his grandson.' Her lips twisted in sour amusement. 'DC Ellis had provided a set of clothes and plenty of nappies, but Joshua needs a lot more and his own toys and such to keep him entertained. I offered to go out and buy replacements, but Zak said he wanted Joshua to have his own stuff, make him feel less anxious about all the changes. It's bad enough not having his mum about and being in a strange house, without having to do without his own clothes, with his own scent on them and possibly his mum's, for comfort.'

Taylor inclined his head. 'I can understand that. Very well. DS

Morgan, DC Ellis, DC Downey. You can all go. Ellis and Downey, you stay with the child at the safe house.'

'Sir, I don't think Zak will want to leave Joshua. He's hugely protective of him and very anxious not to have him out of his sight.'

'Quite frankly, Harry, I don't give a damn. That child is under police protection, which overrides, in this case, any rights his father has. Joshua stays at the safe house under the protection of DCs Ellis and Downey. DS Morgan and you will accompany Mr Cheetham-Epstein to his house, where you will not stay for coffee, but whisk in, gather up all essential items and return to the protection of the safe house in quick-smart time. I have confidence that you'll handle it with diplomacy and tact, as you always do, together with a great deal of speed.'

Harry nodded, the calmness in her gaze showing she took no insult at the direct instructions. It was her job. He was the boss. Nothing he said was unreasonable, nor something she could disagree with.

Jenna made her way back to Donna's desk, where she'd left her handbag. She swiped it up and caught Mason's and Ryan's gazes as she made her way to the front of the room again, confident she could leave the rest of the team under Taylor's remaining instructions. Someone may just suffer the fury of his wrath.

44

Emily cracked open her eyelids as the sun beat down on her. It had risen so high while she'd dozed. Dozed possibly wasn't the right word. She'd fallen into a heavy sleep, her backside wedged deep into the hedgerow. A quiet neighbourhood it may be but she couldn't believe no one had spotted her.

She rolled over onto her knees and pushed her way to her feet as she grunted in agony. Her whole body throbbed under the stretched cotton pyjamas, sweat seeping through to saturate under her armpits and in between the crotch where she'd been curled into a tight ball. So stiff she could barely straighten. Her knees protested, crackling their objection. She pushed her shoulders back and regretted it immediately as the pull on her stomach shot burning stakes through her body, setting her blood on fire.

'Fuck.'

She peered along the road to where the PCSO clambered into a car, head down in the footwell as though he was looking for something.

Emily took her opportunity and hobbled across the road, every move shot pain through her. She kept low and made her way up the garden path to the front door, unable to risk the side gate, which was nearer to the PCSO's car.

Her breath came in panicked snatches as she rammed the key in the lock, missed and then pushed it in with trembling fingers, supporting one hand with the other. She huffed out a quick sigh of relief that she'd selected the right key. There was only a choice of four and one of them was the key to the Audi.

With a rapid glance over her shoulder, she slipped through the doorway, just as the vibrant yellow jacket backed its way out of the car.

Brown blood splatter smeared up the wall and across the Victorian tiles of a passageway littered with small, white markers. Emily narrowed her eyes, her lips tightened as she skimmed the tips of her fingers over the dried-on blood. Strange how it had reached so much higher than she'd remembered.

She drew her hand away and stared at her fingertips. Tiny brown flakes scattered across her skin and dropped to the floor. She tilted her head to one side, idle curiosity giving way to a stirring anger as she brushed them off and watched them drop to the floor where she'd left Imelda.

'I hope you die.'

The darkness swirled inside her stomach, giving a boost to her energy as she picked her way along the hall, the cool of it a relief from the heat of the day outside.

Pain throbbed through her head as she squinted at the vastness of the cupboards lining the kitchen. She threw open the first floor-to-ceiling one and stared at the racks inside, jealousy poking a sharp nail into her. It was all too much, this display of wealth and opulence.

Her jaw clenched. 'A lot of good your wealth and opulence did you. You self-satisfied cow bag.'

Neat rows of tinned food, soup, tomatoes, puree, all lined up on the top shelf with their labels facing forward. She was lucky if she managed to identify the crap she had in her cupboard. She mainly lived on takeout's and ready meals from Tesco.

The second shelf was stacked neatly with baby food. 'That won't be around much longer.' Tempted to sweep the whole lot into the bin, she raised her arm and grunted out as the stretch wrenched at her strained muscles. 'Ah, shit.'

Instead, she reached into the basket below, with the family-sized packets of crisps neatly wedged one behind the other. She ripped open the Kettle's sea salt crisps and crammed a handful in her mouth, breathing in through her nose as her stomach clenched to remind her she'd not eaten for an age. Possibly days. Her mind drew a blank as she stuffed in more, the salt satisfying the craving her body evidently had to replace the minerals she'd leached out in sweat and dehydration from the alcohol.

She circled around, leaving the cupboard wide open behind her while she pushed more crisps in, chomping down on them open-mouthed so crumbs spittled from her lips to flurry across the floor.

She narrowed her eyes as she headed towards the perfectly neat, filled wine rack, each of the red-wine bottles label up, not one of them she'd recognise or afford. She could only stretch to a cheap rosé when it was on offer.

None of them with a screw lid.

She took hold of the neck of one bottle and half pulled it from the rack. Châteauneuf du Pape. She yanked it the rest of the way out and placed it on the thick oakwood kitchen counter in front of her.

As she opened one drawer after the other, she poked her bottom lip out, irritation curdling in her stomach. 'Where the hell do you keep your corkscrew?'

Without stopping, she threw the next one and then the next one open until she came closer to the gas hob.

Sunlight blasted into the next drawer as she flung it open, and it bounced on its hinges.

Emily paused. She tilted her head, her gaze transfixed by the refraction of light skimming off the six-set of sharp stainless-steel knives graduating from small paring knife all the way through to a long-bladed carving knife.

The spit dried in her mouth, all thoughts of finding a corkscrew evaporated like the wisps of a cloud on a hot day.

She turned her head and gazed at the vista beyond the window across the Ironbridge gorge, then up at the cloudless sky, washed-out denim-blue as though the sun had scorched the colour from it.

Her fingers itched to pick up the knife. The long, wickedly curved, carving knife. If Fern was there, she'd whine in her ear, tell her not to touch it.

But Fern isn't here, the reassuring voice murmured.

Emily's lips curved in a self-satisfied smile.

You killed her. The pathetic soul. She can't command you any more. You can do what you want.

She curled her fingers around the sleek, black handle and pulled the knife from the drawer.

Fascinated by the glint of sunlight bouncing from it, Emily slid one tentative finger along the flat of the blade from hilt to tip, letting out an almost silent hiss as the edge sliced a paper-thin cut into the tip of an already broken nail.

She stared at her forefinger and waited for a bloom of blood. As none came, she inspected her finger closely. It was only the nail she'd caught.

While she paused, exhaustion seeped back into her body and

Emily turned from the kitchen counter, wine long forgotten as the knife she gripped in her hand became more important.

Too heavy, she flopped her hand to her side, her feet dragged as she shuffled back out of the kitchen and looked up the long flight of stairs to the sunlight streaming onto the landing above.

She trembled as she sank down on the third step from the bottom, her heart hammering in her chest, excitement and trepidation entangling to ball in her stomach and making it burn.

All she needed to do was wait for Zak to come home. She could explain everything.

He used to love you. He'll understand. He'll love you again. Husky encouragement drifted through her mind as she rested her hand with the knife on the step above, her gaze fixed to the blade.

She didn't want the toddler. The brat. She'd given Angel to Fern, but Fern was gone. There was no further use for the child. Zak wouldn't want it. Not another woman's child when he was with Emily.

On her hands and knees, Emily dragged herself up each stair, knife clutched in her fist, her breath soughed in a stabbing burn. As she reached the first landing, her muscles turned to water and she slithered down. Her cheek grazed against the rough, woollen carpet. She scraped snapped and broken nails over the dense fibres, her gaze fixed while she studied the rhythmic motion.

Each grunt of pain echoed from a distance. Knife still gripped in the fingers of one hand, she used the wall as balance to push herself to her feet. The white door ahead of her stood open to expose the bathroom beyond. Sweat slicked down the length of her spine, gathering at the small of her back in an uncomfortable puddle. If she could reach the shower, surely she would feel better. She wracked her memory for the last time she'd showered, the stale scent of her own body odour filled her nostrils.

Every muscle screamed as she leaned into the shower cubicle

and turned the retro cream, porcelain lever. It wasn't the genuine article. She curled her lip. Just a cheap copy of the effect she supposed he'd wanted to create.

As the steam rose, she placed the precious knife on the side of the sink and peeled the tight, sticky cotton from her flesh. She ground her teeth at the simple effort of lifting her leg to step out of the bottoms, quiet whimpers escaping her lips.

She squeezed through the narrow opening into the cubicle and turned her face upwards into the streaming flow of water hot enough to flay the skin from her body. Too hot for the weather, the torture of it a blessing. She blinked through the steady downpour and reached out for one of the four bottles of shampoo in the shower rack, then whipped back her arm as the stretch of it shot daggers through her body. Her breath caught in her throat and she sieved air in through her teeth while she waited for the burn to subside.

With more care, she made a slow stretch with her other hand, picked up the macadamia nut shampoo and sniffed. It belonged to her. The bitch. The woman who'd stolen her man. She placed it back and wrapped her fingers around another bottle, admiring the male scent of it before she upended the bottle and dumped a load of shampoo into the palm of her hand.

Slow and cautious, she raised her arm and smoothed the shampoo onto her head, stepping out of the torrent of water to let it pound over her shoulders and down her back so she could froth up. She dug her fingers into her scalp, her broken nails grating deep, disgusted with the thick slide of grease coating her hair. She stepped back and let the heat of the water sluice away the grime before she squeezed a second helping of shampoo into her hand and started again.

Each breath an effort, Emily leaned against the icy white and blue tiles of the cubicle, almost slithering to her knees before she caught herself and grabbed the bottle of conditioner. As she smoothed it on, her eyes slipped shut and exhaustion swirled around her, the darkness closing in to engulf her. Before she was overwhelmed, she ran one hand through her rinsed hair a final time and then closed off the water.

She staggered out of the shower and stared around until her gaze fell on the pale-mint towels neatly folded over a rack. She reached for one, but as the light floral scent of it touched her nose, she dropped it on the floor and took hold of the other one, further up on the rack.

The musky remembered aroma of Zak soothed her senses as she wrapped the towel around her. She curled her fingers around the hilt of the knife and indulged herself in the hypnotic pull of the shiny blade before she padded off, barefoot, to find the bedroom.

As she opened the wardrobe, Emily stared at the vast array of beautiful clothes, hanging in colour-coordinated perfection. She reached inside and took out a short sleeved blouse in a pretty pale pink and held it against her body before the fury gripped her and she stabbed the tip of the knife into it and slashed a tear all the way to the hem and then flung it to one side.

'Skinny bitch. I wish you were dead.' She'd never have worn the other woman's clothes, even if they had fit.

Fury biting at her, she slammed the wardrobe door and opened a second one.

Predominantly grey and black, Zak's clothing had less hanging space and more shelves. Emily reached in and snagged a plain black T-shirt and a pair of pale grey shorts. She had no underwear and the skinny bitch's wouldn't fit. Not in a million years. She hated skinny women. It was always the skinny ones who caused her problems. Fern. Imelda.

She buried her face in Zak's clothing and drew in the aroma.

Exhausted, she tugged the T-shirt over her head and let it fall into place. It stretched over her bosom, but his chest and shoulders were wide enough so the fit wasn't over-tight. At least it didn't strangle her like the last set of clothing.

The pale-yellow flowered pattern on the duvet cover bloused cool and inviting as Emily's eyelids weighed heavy. With a slow stretch, she put one knee on the bed, followed by the other and lowered herself gingerly onto her side, pulling a full soft pillow under her head. Her fingers tightened around the shaft of the knife as she brought her hand level with her face.

As her eyes drifted closed, the reassuring scent of Zak rose from the pillow to cocoon her.

45

The frosty silence in the car thickened the atmosphere as Jenna stared out of the back-seat window behind Harry as the other woman drove. She ground her teeth as she pressed down on an imaginary accelerator to make the car go faster. A poor back-seat driver, Jenna couldn't wait to arrive at their destination.

Persuading Zak to leave his son had taken an inordinately long time. Wasted time. They needed to get there and back, as per DI Taylor's instruction.

He'd wasted even more time, declining to wear a stab vest as it was too hot, he was claustrophobic, he was pissed off. She'd had to insist on it to the point of refusing his request to go home. Once that point was established and Zak, Jenna and Harry had stab vests in place under their T-shirts they were set to go. They might die from heat exhaustion, but at least they were protected if the suspect came at them with a knife. All provided she didn't slash their throats or their arms, or face. Or any other place the stab vest didn't cover.

Jenna scrubbed her fingers through her thick hair as she gazed out of the side window. She bloody hated the back seat.

Zak had pushed his as far back as possible, so she'd scooted over behind the driver, but each bump and grind into the pitted tarmac of the road had her stomach pitching. It may be a new car, but the visibility from the back seat was limited and the scenery whizzed by through the side window and had her stomach giving a sickly lurch.

Grateful as they drew up outside the house, Jenna reached forward with a firm hand on Zak's shoulder. He could sulk all he liked, but she wasn't about to let him out of her sight or protection.

'Harry?'

'Yeah. Street's clear. We've a PCSO there. Don't know him. Do you?'

'Yeah. That's Tony. Nice guy. They must have swapped shifts.'

Jenna twisted to look out of the back window and then turned round to face the front again. 'Zak, I'll have a quick word with Tony, then I'll come and get you.'

'I can—'

'No!' Voice firm, she met his gaze as he turned to her. 'I appreciate you can, Zak, but we're under instructions here, so I would request you don't.'

His eyes darkened with moodiness, his mouth tightened, and she met the challenge with one of her own. They'd already tried the soothing approach, but Zak needed to be on a leash, not mollycoddled, or he could put himself, and effectively them, in danger.

'Give me a few minutes.'

She caught the quick twitch of Harry's eyebrows and knew he'd be in safe hands with her. She'd stand no nonsense for the sake of a little lost pride and bullishness. She'd kick his arse to keep him safe if she needed.

Jenna slammed the door behind her, shaking off the small

peal of irritation. Not even annoyance. She understood his anxiety, his desire to get on, protect. But it wasn't his job. That was down to her and her team.

'Hey, Tony.'

'Sarg.'

The gleam of sweat beaded out over his top lip.

'You should get yourself in the shade, the sun's fierce.'

'Yeah, I know. It's full pelt on the front of the house though and nowhere to hide without losing the full view.'

'Anyone in or out this morning?'

'Nah. Not a soul. It's been very quiet.'

'Not SOCO?'

'No. They've recorded everything, collected all the physical evidence and said they might return later. They've left the place in quadrants and asked that the scene remain preserved in case they need to revisit it.'

Jenna inclined her head. 'Okay, we're going to be as quick as we can, because our suspect is still at large.'

Tony puffed out his ruddy cheeks as he shook his head. 'Disappeared completely. She must be holed up somewhere, Sarg.'

Jenna rested her hands on her hips and squinted as the sun beat down. 'Got to be. We have everyone on it. She can't be far.' She surveyed the surrounding area and brought her gaze back to the PCSO. 'Go down into Ironbridge, grab yourself something to drink, something to eat. Some shade for half an hour. It's too bloody hot to be out in this. I'll have a look at what we can do to provide some shade when I get a minute. Get that bloody tent up we had the other day. Don't know why they took it away, but I'll check.'

Tony's eyes filled with concern. 'You sure you don't want me to hang around?'

'No, we're good. I've got Harry Darling with me.'

Tony snorted. 'You wouldn't want to mess with her.'

Jenna let out a laugh. 'I don't.' She gave him a moment. 'Go on. Half an hour, forty minutes tops.'

Relief circled through his eyes as he turned and slipped into his car. He'd roll it down the steep embankment to the Co-op at the bottom of the hill. Air conditioned, he'd probably spend the best part of the forty minutes with his head in cooling units gulping down icy water.

With her own throat already parched, Jenna made her way back to the car as Harry switched off the engine Jenna presumed she'd kept running to keep the air con circulating.

Jenna pulled the front passenger door open and cast another glance around, completely aware of the vulnerability of their situation. As far as she could see there was no one in the vicinity.

She took hold of Zak's elbow as he stepped from the car and marched him to the front door, glancing over her shoulder as his fingers fumbled with his keys.

'Take your time.' She hoped her voice soothed as her gaze caught Harry's. The other woman shrugged and made her way across the road and up the front garden path. For a hot summer's day, not a soul was around. The majority of them at work or school, leaving the mums and toddlers, who had probably all gone down to Coalbrookdale to sun themselves along the banks of the River Severn and indulge in leisurely picnics while the kids ran around in circles in the shade of the ancient trees.

Zak pushed open the door and indicated for Jenna to step inside ahead of him, not, she suspected, out of a sense of self-preservation but more an in-grown old-fashioned courtesy.

She hesitated. 'No alarm?'

Zak shook his head. 'Your scenes of crime guys rang last night, they had an issue setting it when they left. I was on my way to the hospital, so I told them to leave it until I returned.'

Jenna stared at him. So, he left it to now to inform her?

He didn't seem to think it was an issue.

She stepped inside and took in the complete annihilation of his hallway by SOCO. Small flags and demarcations littered the floor and walls with the dirty brown smudges of dried blood smeared up them. She made a mental note to check when they would return to clear the area in readiness for Zak and his family coming back.

Jenna turned her back on the scene and stood between Zak and the length of the hallway as she indicated for him to precede them up the stairs. As he went, she caught Harry's gaze. 'I'll check things out down here while he gathers his stuff.'

'Okay.' Harry trotted up the stairs behind him, keeping close on his heels.

Jenna turned and stepped her way through the mess as she headed off into the large lounge. In the absolute silence, she scanned the serenity of the room, in complete contrast to the scene in the hallway. She wandered over to the rear windows which reached out into the dappled, tree-populated gorge, the lush greenness of it stretched for miles beyond her eye-line.

Perfect peace engulfed her, and she never had to question why anyone would buy a property in such a place. The harmony of it wrapped a blanket of comfort around her.

Coolness in the shaded room pushed back the heat of the day and allowed the zing in her ears to subside. A mild buzz vibrated, giving her a massive relief from the whole frenetic movement of the past few days.

She raised her hand to place it on the window but withdrew it before it connected. From the white dust, they'd already taken fingerprints, but just in case they decided to tackle it again, she wouldn't want to complicate the situation by introducing her own DNA.

With one last look over the panorama, Jenna turned her back and wandered through to the hallway, her keen gaze touched everywhere as she made her way through to the kitchen.

The instant she pushed open the door, her blood ran cold.

'Fuck.'

Not even SOCO would make such a mess.

She dashed her gaze around the room to take in each drawer almost off their hinges, every cupboard wide-open, the scatter of crisps over the otherwise immaculate tiles. Tiles she remembered being completely clear the last time she'd been there a mere couple of days ago. Cupboards that had been neatly closed.

Jenna stepped deeper into the room to peer at the contents of each cupboard and drawer, her mind focused on the bizarreness of it, her feet crunched over the crumbs littering the floor.

She stopped as she came alongside the bottle of Châteauneuf du Pape. It definitely hadn't been there before. There was no reason for it to have been placed on the kitchen surface now. Not unless someone was about to drink it.

She stepped closer to the vast windows providing the perfect view and held her breath until it burned while she stared into the open drawer containing sharp knives. Each one laid neatly next to the other, even spaces between them, stepping up in size from left to right, with a gap where one last knife should be.

Jenna puffed out the breath that burnt her lungs and back-tracked to the dishwasher. She cracked the door open and cast a quick glance over her shoulder before she peered inside. Clean. Empty. No missing knife. Nothing. She pushed it closed and came up onto her toes to walk across the expanse of the kitchen as she raised Airwaves to her mouth and kept her voice low.

'DI Taylor.'

'Sergeant Morgan.'

She drew in a long breath through her nose, her sharp gaze

flitting around the room to take in every anomaly. 'Sir, I believe I may have a situation.'

'Go ahead.'

'I believe someone has breached our security at some point.'

'In what way, Jenna?'

Her pulse skittered to a halt in her throat and then tumbled onwards.

'Someone's been in. Done a search. Not SOCO. Untidy.' She assessed the room. 'Panicked.'

'Are they still on the premises?'

Jenna raised her chin and listened for sounds from above. The silence resonated in her buzzing ears. Unnatural silence.

'Possibly.' She started for the door, conscious every word spoken the minute she stepped into the hallway could be heard.

'Sergeant Morgan, get yourself out of the building and wait for backup. It's on its way. ETA seven minutes.'

'Sir. I would. Only Zak and Harry are already upstairs.'

'Shit.'

'Aye, sir. It's silent up there.' She hung back, desperate to race up the stairs, but aware she needed to keep communications open. 'They should be gathering Joshua's belongings, but I can't hear a thing. I'll leave Airwaves open, but I need radio silence while I check.'

'Sergeant. Take no risks.'

'Acknowledged.'

On light feet, Jenna stepped through into the hallway and placed her foot on the first step. She took a deep breath and toed her way up the stairs, tilting her head to catch the slightest sound, aware that the complete silence was more ominous than the hustle and bustle she'd expect of someone gathering items in a hurry.

As she reached the landing, she pressed herself against the

wall and held still, straining to hear anything. But there was not a single sound, just the heavy pulse of an eerie silence.

She touched her fingertip to the bathroom door and gave a gentle push. She narrowed her eyes as the untidy pile of clothes on the floor grabbed her attention. They'd not been there before. She knew that for a fact. She glanced around the otherwise empty room before she moved past the doorway and further along the landing.

'You brought another fucking woman into our house?'

The sour vitriol in the woman's whispered tones froze her to the spot and she leaned her hand against the wall to keep her balance. The bright flash of gunshot filled her vision as she squeezed her eyes closed.

Jenna shoved her own memories aside and held her breath. She took a step forward until Harry's left shoulder came into view.

'Emily.'

'Don't you fucking 'Emily' me. We've been through this before.'

Jenna crept another step closer to the open doorway of Zak's bedroom.

'No.' His voice held a thread of steel. No shake to it. No hesitation. 'Emily, put the knife down.'

The chill in her veins turned to ice as Jenna gave a quick glance down at her radio to make sure it was open. The reassurance of the red flashing light eased her mind.

As she nudged into the room, Harry moved to one side, out of Zak's large shadow, to expose the woman beyond.

A woman Jenna instantly recognised. Could never forget. This wasn't Emily. This was the woman she'd watched bleeding out on the floor of Emily's house the day before. This was Fern.

Jenna raised her fingers to her lips as her mind struggled to comprehend what her eyes told her, but with no time to dwell on it, she pushed it to one side to deal with later.

Between her and the woman were Zak and Harry. Both at risk from the twelve-inch blade the woman dangled with casual disregard from thick, swollen fingers.

Her gaze clashed with Jenna's and she sucked in a whistling breath. 'Now, who the fuck is this one?' She raised the knife to waist-height.

Her mind waded through the confusion as Jenna narrowed her eyes at the woman in front of her. Not Emily. She claimed Emily had killed her. So, who? Emily *Fern* Shenton.

As Jenna's mind cleared, comprehension hit her in a wave of disbelief. She took a step deeper into the room. 'Fern?'

Harry stiffened and Jenna stepped up behind her so she could peer over Harry's shoulder.

With no reaction to the name, the woman continued to stare at her, her expression fixed and blank.

'Fern?' Jenna repeated, to be rewarded by a flash of irritation.

'Fern's dead. I killed her. She was a fucking paranoid bitch.'

'No. You never killed her. You injured her.'

'She's dead.'

Jenna ran her gaze over the woman as she took another step closer to move alongside Harry. 'She's very much alive.'

Emily's eyes darkened. 'She's fucking dead. I should know. I shoved the knife deep into her stomach myself.' She touched her fingers to her own stomach, pain flitting across her face.

'You only injured her, Emily. You never killed her.'

Emily's breath wheezed in and out, a thin layer of sweat broke out over her waxen skin as Jenna took another step forward, her stab vest no reassurance in the face of the long, sharp blade.

'Fern is fine. Do you think I can speak with her?'

The slow turn of Zak's head as she came alongside him

almost had her snorting out her breath as horror filled his face at the sudden revelation.

'Fern? Can I speak with you?' Jenna pressed.

The blade wavered in Emily's loose grip and a pained gasp ripped from her lips.

'Fern, are you there?'

'God.' The barely whispered words came from Harry as her own comprehension slipped into place.

Emily's shoulders rolled in and her expression collapsed as she appeared to shrink in front of them.

Jenna tipped her head to one side and sent the other woman a gentle smile. 'Hello, Fern. How are you doing?'

Emily gave a shake of her head, evil spiking through her eyes before a softness took over and a gentle, almost childlike, voice came from Emily's mouth. 'She stabbed me.'

'I know.'

'She couldn't help herself.'

Instead of the confusion rippling through her, Jenna plastered sympathy on her face. 'I'm sure she couldn't.'

She raised her hand and grasped Zak's elbow, squeezing her fingers hard against his bone to transmit the urgency of her silent request as she gave a tug to make him move backwards.

Suspicion wreathed over the woman's face as she watched him make a move away from her and her gaze darted to Jenna's hand. 'Don't touch him.' Her lips pulled back from her teeth as the guttural snarl came from deep down.

Without taking her gaze from Emily, Jenna removed her hand from his arm and let it drop to her side as she raised her left hand in a gentle persuasiveness. 'It's okay. I'm not doing any harm, Emily. I'm just talking to Fern.'

'Fern wants you to fuck off.' Spittle gathered over Emily's lips in a white froth as her gaze turned manic and her hold on the knife tightened as she extended her arm and flicked the blade upwards.

Jenna ignored Zak's sharp intake of breath, her entire focus on the woman with the twelve-inch blade. She'd used one before, she was more than capable of using one again. Tempted to touch her stab vest, Jenna's fingers twitched, but she kept her hands still, her gaze steady on Emily. 'I think Fern can speak for herself, Emily.' She kept her voice low but insistent while she delved inside to find the other woman.

Emily's shoulders twitched as she placed her hand on the swell of her belly. Her eyelids fluttered over a gaze filled with inner turmoil.

'Fern. Put the knife down.'

Her head wobbled in small jerks, her voice, when it came, was young and miserable. 'Help her. Help Emily.'

The breath burned in Jenna's chest as she held it in while Emily drew her arm in and swapped the knife from one hand to the other, turning the blade inwards to offer the hilt to Jenna. Wretched desperation wallowed in the gaze she kept on Jenna.

'I'll help her, Fern. Just hand over the knife and I'll help.'

The hair plastered to the back of her neck with sweat gave an uncomfortable tickle as Jenna took one cautious step forward and extended her arm, her fingers reaching for the black handle of the knife. Committed, she took another step closer.

With a flash, Fern disappeared, and Emily's expression turned from pitiful to vicious in less than a blink.

With a sudden insight of Emily's intentions, Jenna's heart hammered as she lunged forward, her fingers grabbed for the knife at the same time Emily tightened her grip. Emily's knuckles turned white, as she plunged the knife into the depths of her own belly, all the way to the hilt. Her eyes stared into Jenna's as the vitriol seeped away and a pathetic sadness took its place.

Emily's lips cracked open. 'It's done.' Scarlet against her white skin, blood trickled from the corner of her mouth as her lips curved up into a pathetic smile and her gaze roamed over to Zak. 'I'm sorry. Emily never meant any harm. She just loved you so much.'

As Emily dropped to her knees, Jenna grabbed her by the shoulders, grunting as she took the full weight of a twenty-stone woman to stop her toppling onto her front and pushing the knife further in. If it was even possible for the knife to go further in. 'Shit!'

Ears ringing with the sound of sirens and her own tinnitus, Jenna flipped Emily onto her back, her breath singing through her teeth as the woman went all the way down.

'Fucking hell.' Harry's face, bleached white with shock, appeared at Emily's head as she stripped a pillowcase from a pillow and leaned over the body sprawled on the floor. She flung the pillowcase at Jenna and grabbed for another pillow, stripping that one too.

Jenna balled up the pillowcase and pressed the flesh where the hilt of the knife stood proud as blood spurted out in small fountains.

She kept the pressure on and jerked her head round. Zak stood frozen, his glazed stare rooted to the knife. 'Zak, go down-stairs and open the front door. Let police and paramedics in. Direct them straight here.' Much as she appreciated they weren't all made of the same stuff and not everyone could deal with a well of blood from a knife wound, she needed him, which meant he needed to shake himself out of the hypnotic state he'd slipped into. 'Zak!'

His head reared back, and the glaze slipped from his eyes to leave horror in its place.

'Go downstairs and let everyone in. Quick!'

The doorbell pealed and, as though the shackles had dropped from his wrists and ankles, Zak was free. He spun round and sprinted for the stairs.

Jenna turned back round as Harry's fingers pressed down from the other side of the knife and linked with hers.

'Shit, I hope they're quick. I don't even know if this is the right thing to do. Do we leave the knife in, or take it out?'

Jenna shook her head. 'Leave it in. Definitely. We can do more damage if it's pierced a vital organ and we remove it.' She stared at the froth coming through the bright red blood. There was no doubt Emily had pierced a vital organ this time. Most probably a lung, from the evidence bubbling from her mouth. Not as much blood as from around the knife. Jenna pressed down on the soaked pillowcase.

At the sound of voices, Jenna and Harry looked up as a paramedic stood above them. He dropped the medical equipment bags and snapped nitrile gloves on his hands.

She'd not even had time to yank on a pair of nitrile gloves, it had never been a thought. 'Dammit.' She looked up at Harry opposite her. 'If she's a drug addict, we're stuffed.'

Harry's lips twisted in a bitter grimace. She cruised her gaze over Emily's arms. 'No track marks.' Her skin smooth and plump, devoid of all colour, not even the blue of her veins as they retracted into her body.

The paramedic hunkered down next to Jenna, his bottle-green personal protection overall gave a slight rustle as he leaned over Emily and drew in a breath before he addressed them. 'Can you hold still just a minute longer?' Placid eyes checked on them both as he reached into his bag and a second paramedic came through the open doorway. 'Okay, let Lisa slide into place and then you both let go and stand back.'

Jenna blew out the air that had backed up in her lungs, aware from the ache in her chest she'd been holding on to it for longer than natural.

From the look of Harry, she had been too.

As they stepped back to let the paramedics do their job, Jenna raised her hands, ready to rub them against her face, before she froze and stared at the blood smeared over them. She took a deep breath and then dropped them to her side. 'I'll need to take a statement from you.' She shot Harry a quick look as the other woman nodded her agreement. Jenna held out her hands. 'We need to get cleaned up and back to the safe house with Zak.' She circled her gaze around the room and found him hovering just inside the doorway. 'I need a statement from you too. Better to do it sooner rather than later.' Aware his safety was still her concern, even though the threat was disabled, Jenna jerked her head. 'Zak, would you come closer.

Harry glanced down at Emily. 'I can't believe she stabbed herself. Jesus.' She rubbed her nose against the back of her wrist. 'That's some scary shit.' She gave a rapid blink as her eyes filled with tears.

The ice that had formed around Jenna's heart in order for her to carry out the job cracked. Not for Emily, but for Harry, who she'd never seen tear up before this case.

Their gazes held and understanding flowed between them.

'What in the blue blazes happened, Sergeant Morgan?' Face a rusty red, DI Taylor blustered into the room, heavy breath puffing out as he leaned his shoulder against the door jamb. He whipped a folded white handkerchief from his pocket, flicked it open and swiped it over his sweaty forehead, his hand swishing it around to the back of his neck.

Where to start? Jenna glanced at Harry before she delayed for time. 'You got here quickly, sir.'

'I was on my way the moment I heard security had been

breached. There will be an enquiry into that. Right now, though, I want to know how the hell she got into the house. Why wasn't the alarm set?'

Jenna shrugged. 'It wasn't set when we walked in. Zak said SOCO had an issue with it when they left yesterday. He was on his way to the hospital to visit his wife. He told them to leave it until we got here, and he'd sort it.'

'Then what?'

Harry let out a delicate cough to attract his attention. 'We came up to the bedroom, sir, while DS Morgan checked out downstairs. Emily was there.' She pointed. 'Behind the bed, fucking big knife in hand.'

Eyes hard as steel, Taylor glared around. 'And where was the subject at that point?'

Currently between the two of them, Zak raised his chin, his lips a thin line. 'Right behind Harry.' He pushed his hair back from his forehead with his fingers, the shock giving them a fine tremble. 'I'm sorry. It was my fault. I should have backed the hell out of there, but I was furious that Emily was there, I had no idea she had a knife in her hand at that time and I bumped Harry further into the room.' He touched Harry's elbow in apology and spoke directly to her. 'I wanted to reach out and strangle Emily. I might well have done.' He turned his face back to Taylor. 'It was only Harry grabbing my arm that stopped me as Emily circled around the bottom of the bed to come closer.'

His teeth chattered together as the shock set in and he raised his clawed hands. 'I never gave it a thought. I wanted to just grab her and throw her out of my house. I wanted to shake her until her teeth rattled and ask her why. Why would you attack my wife? Why would you take my little boy away? And then I saw the fucking knife. It's our knife.' He tapped his chest with his fingertips. 'From our kitchen. Who the fuck was she going to stab?' He squeezed his eyes closed. 'It was my fault, Inspector.' His voice shook, 'If I'd been more aware.' His eyes popped open and he gave a grim smile. 'I'm not a trained police officer and my actions put your officer in danger.'

DI Taylor raised his thick eyebrows and looked at Zak, Harry and Jenna. His gaze skimmed over each of them as he took in their stab vests. His chest expanded as he filled it with air. 'Good to see you took the appropriate measures, DS Morgan, DC Darling. Make sure you note your protective equipment and that of the subject in your notes when you write them up.' He sucked his top lip in to scrape his bottom teeth over it. 'How is the suspect?'

Jenna dragged oxygen in through her nose as crimson filled her vision, pressing down on memories too fresh to dismiss nudged aside by the present. 'In a right bloody mess. Stabbed herself in the upper stomach, I think she punctured her lung. I'm no expert, but she had frothy blood spilling out of her mouth. The paramedics are obviously doing their best.'

Taylor nodded. 'Air ambulance are en route.'

Jenna paced away and stared out at a vista you couldn't wish for. 'Bloody hell.' She watched the approach of the red air ambulance dipping through the gorge in a line headed straight for the bedroom window. 'The neighbours must think they're in the twilight zone.'

She spun on her heel to stare at Zak, Taylor and Harry, wondering if Zak would ever want to live there again. It wasn't her business, that was up to them to decide with the help of counsellors. Whatever the future brought to this family was nothing to do with her, but she knew without doubt she'd stay in contact, the bond too strong to walk away from.

She curled her fingers into her palm, the dried blood crinkling over her skin.

As though he'd read her thoughts, Taylor pinned her with a look. 'Get your hands washed. You have blood all over them.'

On the defensive, she held her hands high. 'We didn't have time to pull on PPE.'

'You didn't have time to blink, Sergeant.' His mild tones soothed. 'Well done. Now, clean yourself up.'

'What about SOCO?'

'SOCO have plenty of evidence they can collect from your shirt, Sergeant, but preservation of life comes first. Always. Now clean that blood from your skin in case there is any contagion within it. Both of you.' He included Harry. 'I assume all your hepatitis vaccines et cetera are up to date?' At their nods, he tossed out a smile. 'Clean up, strip off, go home. This day has been long enough for all of us. I expect your notes available tomorrow.'

Harry's eyes widened. 'But, Zak...'

'Zak will be safe with me until another member of your team is available. I'll take him back to his son. The threat is over, DC Darling.'

Jenna took in a deep breath. 'And Emily?'

He cast the woman on the floor a lingering look. 'We'll have someone on guard duty, no worries. Go home. Both of you. Go home.'

46

Jenna tipped her head back to stare up at the clear, star-sprinkled sky.

Her fingers closed around Adrian's as she dragged in the first fresh taste of air for six weeks as the heatwave broke.

'God, this is good.'

'It is.' The soft rumble of his voice could do nothing but serve to soothe.

She raised her head and took a sip of ice-cold Prosecco.

A long day, deserving of not a celebration but a consolation.

Despite Taylor's instructions, Jenna had returned to the station, changed her clothes and carried on. For her own sanity, she needed to write up her notes, almost as an exorcism. She had other matters to check on, leads to follow, answers to get.

Fliss squatted next to her chair and drank from her own slender glass of Prosecco as she placed a hand on her knee. 'Have you heard anything more?'

Jenna wriggled until she was upright. 'Imelda is conscious, although she has shown no signs yet of being able to walk. Physiotherapy will help, but it will be an upward struggle. She's young, healthy and the child is still viable.'

'Viable?' Adrian squeezed her fingers. 'Does that mean undamaged?'

'Not necessarily. It's alive and that's all we can hope for until it's born. They made the decision to allow the pregnancy to continue without inducing labour or carrying out a caesarean. They'll have to monitor her closely, but all indications are that the baby will be okay.'

Fliss pushed to her feet as Domino padded over to rest his head against Jenna's thigh as though he sensed the depth of her sadness for the Cheetham-Epstein family. They were safe from any further attacks, but they had a long road of recovery ahead of them. A lovely family, with no reason for bad to happen to them. That was the kind of fucked-up world they lived in.

Jenna ran her hand over the satin-coated head of the Dalmatian and smiled as Mason whipped a slice of steak, a sausage and a breast of chicken off the barbecue, dumped it on a plate and handed it to Fliss.

Her sister spooned a pile of salad onto the plate, threw a thick slab of garlic bread alongside and placed it on the table in front of Jenna.

The special treatment didn't go unnoticed, nor unappreciated. The norm would be for them all to help themselves, but she wasn't sure if her legs were any more than overcooked spaghetti.

'What about the woman? Emily... or Fern?' Fliss accepted another plate, this one piled high and passed it to Adrian, giving an affectionate tap to Domino's nose as he rested his chin on the round garden table in a sly move to bring himself closer to the food.

Jenna stabbed a piece of cucumber and held it on her fork.

'Emily Fern Shenton.' Anger was the last of her feelings for the woman. Confusion, pity, sadness. 'A diagnosed schizophrenic.'

Mason hovered over the top of her with the bottle of Prosecco, expression full of concern as he topped her glass up. As it fizzed to the rim, he sent her a smile. 'Diagnosed and left unsupervised. Poor bloody woman, you must have pity in your heart for her. Even if you managed to give me a bloody heart attack again.' Mason handed Adrian a bottle of Dogfish Head Ale with a casualness that warmed Jenna's heart. The boys had bonded well in the last few months. It was a good feeling to know there was harmony.

Fliss's frown shot a long vertical crease between her eyebrows. 'How could that happen? How could someone be abandoned like that?'

Mason scooped up his beer and plonked his backside in a deckchair as the sun shot its last golden and amber rays across the clear navy sky littered with the flutter of pipistrelle bats. 'A counsellor whose pregnancy, she believed, would affect the rationality of her patient and therefore declined to continue to see her. Couldn't blame the counsellor, it's the system that's shite.'

Fliss joined them and sank into the remaining chair, with far more elegance than Mason had displayed. 'Surely, she was assigned to someone else?'

Jenna sliced off a strip of steak and nodded. 'She was in the process of being passed over. Because of her history, they were uncomfortable assigning a male to her case. They believed because she was steady on her medication, she'd be okay for a few weeks without a counsellor. What they didn't account for was that her abandonment issues might kick in.'

She pierced the steak with her fork and held it for a moment.

'And they did. Apparently, the moment she self-withdrew from a hefty meds programme without informing them, not only did she suffer major withdrawal but also reverted the complexity of her psychosis. Enhanced, it ran unchecked.'

She opened her lips and pushed the tender piece of steak into her mouth, groaning at the rich flavour.

'Poor lady,' Fliss offered.

'Absolutely.'

'Will they hold an enquiry?'

'Without a doubt. But how many people with mental health issues fall through an overstretched net?'

As Domino abandoned her for the more likely treat from Mason, Jenna took another taste of her Prosecco, appreciation sending a soft groan through her lips.

'It was one of the saddest moments I've witnessed. To stab yourself in the belief that it would exorcise another being living inside of you. She had no idea she was plunging the knife into her own body. It was Fern she believed she was killing. Fern was the calm, sweet voice of reason by all accounts. When Emily was medicated, Fern was strong. She had control. Emily respected her. In her mind, she was the younger sister.'

'According to her counsellor, Wanda Stilgoe, who we managed to get a hold of today, once Fern lost that grip, Emily turned on her, the evil voice inside of her took over. All her problems, all her shortfalls, became Fern's fault. A person to blame because she had never been to blame. Wanda told me nothing Emily had ever done had been her fault. It was the way she was brought up, the way she was treated by her mother, the fact that her father left them when she was still young, and her mother had a string of boyfriends. All of whom she was expected to call daddy.'

Jenna put her glass down and cut into her chicken as the tension seeped from her muscles. She gathered chicken and salad on her fork, and pushed it into her mouth, sending Mason a quick wink. 'Delicious.'

He shot her a smile back as he chewed on his own mouthful of food and then picked up his glass to salute her.

Fliss's forehead wrinkled. 'Did the counsellor believe Emily wasn't to blame? Had she encouraged Emily's belief?'

Jenna huffed. 'She still doesn't believe Emily is to blame. She had a psychotic episode which wasn't, in the counsellor's opinion, her fault. She believes once she's back on medication, she'll become stable again.'

'And how is Emily now?'

Mason slipped a slice of sausage into Domino's mouth and gave the top of his head a quick scrub. 'She's still in intensive care. They operated.' He inclined his head to Jenna. 'As Jenna suspected from all the bubbly blood...'

Fliss turned pale and snapped her knife and fork down on the table as Domino deserted his food source in preference for Fliss the moment he sensed her discomfort.

Oblivious, Mason carried on. 'The knife had gone straight through her left lung.' He touched his stomach and then swivelled his hand upwards to indicate the direction of the blade. 'She's just lucky. With the direction she plunged the knife in, she almost stabbed herself in the heart.'

'I suspect that was her intention.'

Mason nodded. 'She'll be intensive care until she no longer needs help to breathe.'

'And then you arrest her?'

'Yes. She has to be detained. She's a danger. To herself and to others. The likelihood is she'll be sectioned under the mental health act.'

'She's in the best place now.'

'It could be weeks or months before she's ready. It depends how badly she injured herself.'

'But she'll survive?'

'Oh, yes.'

Adrian set his fork down on his plate as he picked up his beer. 'You're going to be busy for the next few months with the prosecution against Emily and Frank Bartwell's case. Both major.'

Jenna nodded, well aware of the pressure she'd be under. She'd take it as it came.

Mason raised his head and talked around the mouthful of food. 'Wasn't it today Harvey was meant to start? Nobody's mentioned him.' He sent Domino a hard-eyed look, but the dog never met his stare, preferring instead to keep a close eye on Fliss's steak.

Fliss's face broke out in a smile with the change of subject and she picked up her cutlery again and started to eat. 'There were more important things to talk about.' But the smile stayed in place. 'Harvey took Domino out for a couple of hours as a trial and sent photos and videos of their walk together. It appears they got along very well, and Harvey will be back the day after tomorrow. Then he starts regularly from next Monday.'

Adrian placed a hand on Jenna's knee. 'Didn't you say you have tomorrow off?'

'I do.' She puffed out a breath and smiled. 'I think I need it.'

'I've managed to free up my day too, if you want to take that trip out to Llandudno, perhaps we could treat Domino to a day at the beach.'

She didn't hesitate but leaned over and placed a quick kiss on his cheek. 'That would be good. Really good.

ACKNOWLEDGMENTS

Thanks go to Simi Epstein who paid a considerable amount to The Hope House charity to win the opportunity of having her son's name used in The Ex. Zak Cheetham-Epstein, many happy returns for your 18th birthday on the 17th May 2021.

Thank you too to the lovely Harvey Hopkins who won the opportunity of a mention in my books. This is not the last we will see of him...

As usual my research far outstretches the actual amount I write into the story and often sends me down a rabbit hole of intrigue which may very well trigger the next story.

My thanks go to Al Wright for his paramedic advice and his dad, Peter Wright, for police matters.

Thank you to my husband, Andy Parkes, who I frequently nudge in the middle of the night as a thought occurs to me and I need to run the scene through and pick his brains for all things police procedural.

Despite all the advice, any errors are my own, possibly because I simply didn't listen...

Malinsgate Police Station is real and a place I have frequented often. I have, however, taken some liberties in the descriptions (though not too far off piste) for the benefit of my fictional characters and storylines. I hope I will be forgiven.

To my gorgeous girls, Laura and Meghan, both of whom cheer me on with every book.

Last, but never least, my heartfelt thanks go to my sister, Margaret, who has never flagged in her faith in my abilities. For all the reading and re-reading she does of my manuscripts and for her honesty, I will be forever grateful.

MORE FROM DIANE SAXON

We hope you enjoyed reading *The Ex*. If you did, please leave a review.

If you'd like to gift a copy, this book is also available as an ebook, digital audio download and audiobook CD.

Sign up to Diane Saxon's mailing list for news, competitions and updates on future books.

http://bit.ly/DianeSaxonNewsletter

Discover more crime novels from Diane Saxon.

ABOUT THE AUTHOR

Diane Saxon previously wrote romantic fiction for the US market but has now turned to writing psychological crime. *Find Her Alive* was her first novel in this genre and introduced series character DS Jenna Morgan. Diane is married to a retired policeman and lives in Shropshire.

Visit Diane's website: http://dianesaxon.com/

Follow Diane on social media:

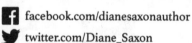 facebook.com/dianesaxonauthor

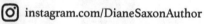 twitter.com/Diane_Saxon

instagram.com/DianeSaxonAuthor

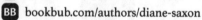 bookbub.com/authors/diane-saxon

ABOUT BOLDWOOD BOOKS

Boldwood Books is a fiction publishing company seeking out the best stories from around the world.

Find out more at www.boldwoodbooks.com

Sign up to the Book and Tonic newsletter for news, offers and competitions from Boldwood Books!

http://www.bit.ly/bookandtonic

We'd love to hear from you, follow us on social media:

facebook.com/BookandTonic

twitter.com/BoldwoodBooks

instagram.com/BookandTonic

Lightning Source UK Ltd.
Milton Keynes UK
UKHW040723200221
379060UK00001B/35

9 781800 488564